TO THE
EASTERN
SEAS

JULIAN STOCKWIN

TO THE EASTERN SEAS

HODDER &
STOUGHTON

First published in Great Britain in 2019 by Hodder & Stoughton
An Hachette UK company

1

Copyright © Julian Stockwin 2019

Maps drawn by Rodney Paull

A CIP catalogue record for this title is available from the British Library

Hardback ISBN 978 1 473 69868 0
Trade Paperback ISBN 978 1 473 69869 7
eBook ISBN 978 1 473 69870 3

Typeset in Garamond MT by
Palimpsest Book Production Ltd, Falkirk, Stirlingshire

Printed and bound in Great Britain by Clays Ltd, Elcograf S.p.A.

Hodder & Stoughton policy is to use papers that are natural, renewable
and recyclable products and made from wood grown in sustainable forests.
The logging and manufacturing processes are expected to conform to
the environmental regulations of the country of origin.

Hodder & Stoughton Ltd
Carmelite House
50 Victoria Embankment
London EC4Y 0DZ

www.hodder.co.uk

For Monique
and all her doughty crew in Tasmania

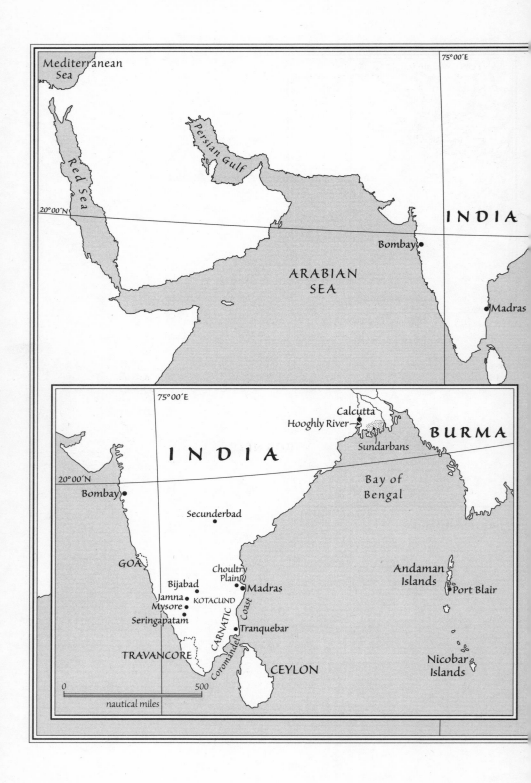

Mediterranean
Sea

Red Sea

Persian Gulf

20°00′N

75°00′E

INDIA

Bombay•

ARABIAN
SEA

Madras•

75°00′E

Calcutta
Hooghly River—
Sundarbans

BURMA

INDIA

20°00′N

Bay of
Bengal

Bombay•

Secunderbad•

GOA

Choultry
Plain
Bijabad•
Jamna• KOTACUND
Mysore•
Seringapatam•

Andaman
Islands

•Port Blair

•Madras

Tranquebar

CARNATIC

Coromandel Coast

TRAVANCORE

CEYLON

Nicobar
Islands

0   500

nautical miles

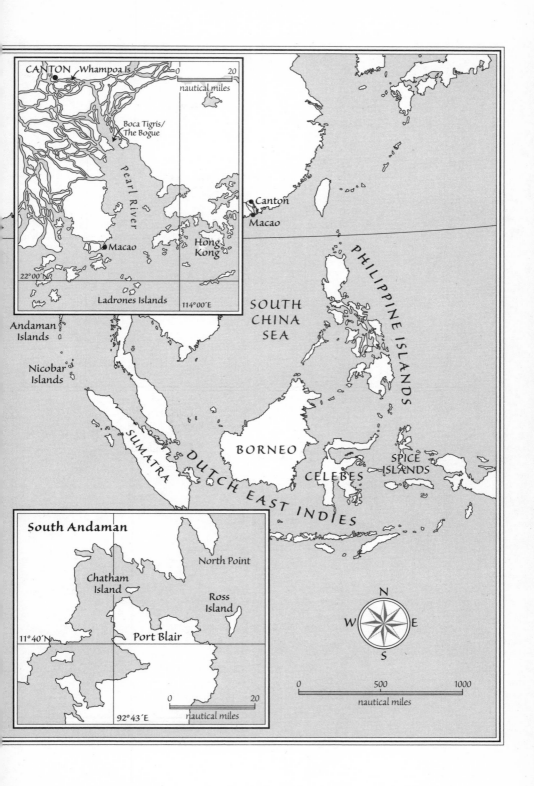

CANTON • ✕ Whampoa Is

0   20

nautical miles

Boca Tigris/
The Bogue

Pearl River

• Canton

Macao

Hong
Kong

• Macao

22°00′N

114°00′E

Ladrones Islands

Andaman
Islands

SOUTH
CHINA
SEA

Nicobar
Islands

PHILIPPINE ISLANDS

SUMATRA

DUTCH EAST INDIES

BORNEO

SPICE
ISLANDS

CELEBES

South Andaman

North Point

Chatham
Island

Ross
Island

11°40′N

Port Blair

92°43′E

0   20

nautical miles

N
W   E
S

0   500   1000

nautical miles

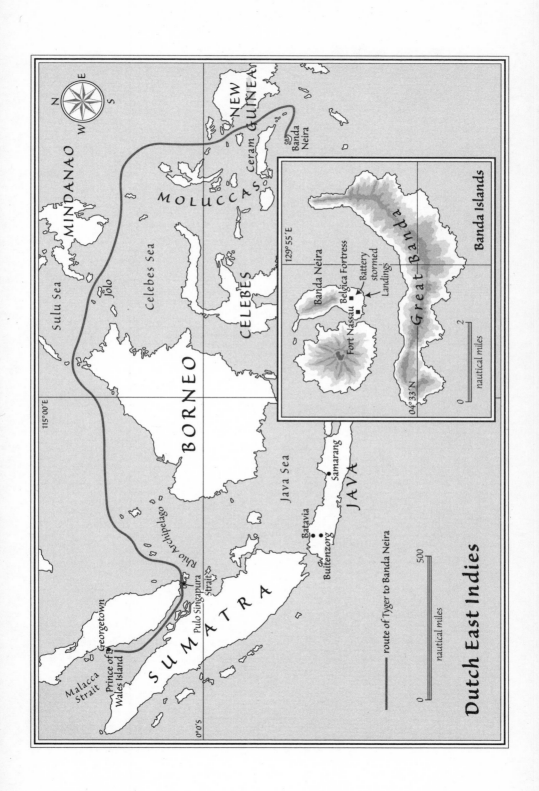

Dutch East Indies

N
E
S
W

MINDANAO

NEW GUINEA

Sulu Sea

Celebes Sea

MOLUCCAS

Ceram

Banda Neira

Jolo

CELEBES

BORNEO

Rhio Archipelago

Singapura Strait

Pulo Singapura

Java Sea

Samarang

Batavia

Buitenzorg

JAVA

SUMATRA

Malacca Strait

Georgetown

Prince of Wales Island

115°00'E

0°0'S

—— route of Tyger to Banda Neira

nautical miles

0   500

Banda Islands

Banda Neira

Belgica Fortress

Battery stormed

Landings

Fort Nassau

Great Banda

129°55'E

04°33'N

nautical miles

0   2

Dramatis Personae

indicates fictitious character

*Sir Thomas Kydd, captain of HMS *Tyger*, a.k.a. Tom Cutlass

Tyger, ship's company

*Bowden	second lieutenant
*Bray	first lieutenant
*Brice	third lieutenant
*Clinton	captain, Royal Marines
*Dillon	Kydd's confidential secretary
*Doud	petty officer
*Farrant	replacement first lieutenant
*Halgren	Kydd's coxswain
*Harman	*Tyger*'s purser
*Herne	boatswain
*Joyce	sailing master
*Maynard	master's mate
*Pinto	quartermaster's mate
*Poulden	petty officer
*Rowan	midshipman

*Stirk	gunner's mate
*Tysoe	Kydd's manservant

Others

Auchmuty	lieutenant general, commanded army in the taking of Java
Avery	captain of *Thalia* frigate
*Bailey	ensign of 9th Madras Native Infantry
Barlow, Sir George	governor of Madras
Barlow, Eliza	daughter of the governor of Madras
* Bouarjee, Sui Rana	*dubash* to Kydd in Madras
Broughton	initially commodore of Java expedition
Capper	adjutant general of Madras Army
Chia Ch'ing	reigning Ching dynasty emperor
Cochrane	10th Earl of Dundonald, controversial but successful frigate captain
Cox *Russell*	captain of Drury's previous flagship
Collingwood	succeeded Nelson to command the Mediterranean Fleet
Daendels	governor general of the Dutch East Indies, replaced by French nominee Janssens
*Dalawa of Kotacund	vizier and adviser to the ruler, Rajah Narendra
*Danby	retired lieutenant of Plymouth
Drury Pellew	rear admiral, second-in-command to
Duke of York	commander-in-chief of the army
Foote	captain of frigate *Piedmontaise* under Kydd
Gillespie	colonel, tasked with tracking down and capturing Janssens

Raffles	Thomas Stamford assistant colonial secretary to the Presidency of Prince of Wales Island
Rigby	captain of frigate *Dedaigneuse*
*Rix	'Cluffer'; long-term expatriate resident of Madras
Roberts	president of East India Company select committee
*Rouvier	captain of privateer *Vengeur*
*Russell	captain brig-sloop *Eaglet*
Smythe	lieutenant general second-in-command under Macdowall
*Snell	colonel of the 33rd Regiment of Foot
*Steinbergs	German cousins of Caroline Lowther
Stewart, Robert	Viscount Castlereagh secretary of state for war
Stopford	rear admiral, commander-in-chief Cape of Good Hope Station
Suffren	French naval commander in the Indian Ocean during the American war
Surcouf	French privateer
*Wickes	lieutenant colonel of the 32nd Regiment of Foot

Chapter 1

Plymouth Hoe, England

There was nothing to be seen but a dismal miasma of grey fret, a drifting curtain of mizzle over the listless water. It hid everything to seaward, but the crowd on the high vantage point were not deterred from their vigil. They were not going to miss the occasion – rumour had it that in these dispiriting times there'd been a great clash of fleets somewhere far out there. Why else would the flagship, now expected hourly, be said by the dockyard to be standing in for this great naval port?

Another wash of cold light rain settled on the sodden spectators, who doggedly continued their watch. It eased off and visibility slowly extended out. Suddenly there was a cry: out of the grey murk firmed the unmistakable outline of a man-o'-war.

'Clear a path, you villains!' an elderly gentleman with the distinct air of a mariner spluttered, wiping the lens of a large old-fashioned sea telescope and bringing it up to train on the vision.

Respectfully, the press of onlookers pulled back to give him a clear view.

'What is it, L'tenant Danby?'

'As I needs time t' sight their colours!' he replied gruffly.

'Well?'

'A frigate, is all.'

'Which one?'

'How do I know?' Danby said irritably, finding it difficult to hold the big glass steady. Then he lowered it and paused before declaring, 'An' if I'm not wrong, you're clapping peepers on none other than the flying *Tyger* 32, Cap'n Kydd!'

There was a ripple of comment.

'Not a flagship, then?'

'No, you loon – she's an escortin' frigate. Your flagship's still out there on her way in.'

All eyes were on the warship as she worked into the Sound in the fitful light airs. Unaccountably, she did not shape course around Drake Island for the last run into the Hamoaze and the dockyard. Instead, as one, her three topgallant sheets were thrown off letting the sails flog about disconsolately.

'My word, an' they're a sorry crew,' murmured someone in the crowd.

Danby had his glass back up. 'Not at all, m' friend. That there means they're signalling distress as to they's had a sad loss o' life.'

The crowd grew silent, watching as the frigate rounded to, took in sail and anchored before them in the Sound.

'Bless me an' I don't like what I see,' the old lieutenant muttered. 'It's no grand victory she's telling us of, that's for certain, lads.'

It was nearly an hour before *Ville de Paris* hove into view, the great bulk of the 110-gun flagship emerging out of the featureless grey drizzle before she, too, came to anchor out in the Sound.

Danby had his glass up again. 'Be damned to it – she's lost her flag!'

'Wha—?'

'Not her ensign,' Danby said impatiently, 'Her admiral's flag. What the devil . . .?'

Her sail was brought in, and one by one from forward her yards slowly canted over to one side on one mast, then to the other on the next.

'A-cock-bill,' he said in a low voice. 'It . . . It can only be . . .'

'Tell us!'

Danby lowered his telescope and addressed them gravely. 'I'm truly sorry to inform you that there's been a dreadful battle o' some sort, in which we're seeing just them as survived. It's saying as how the commander-in-chief himself must have been mortally struck down in the action, just as the great Lord Nelson was. Friends, ye should prepare yourselves for some grievous news.'

Chapter 2

Lieutenant Brice, *Tyger*'s third lieutenant, returned on board promptly after delivering Kydd's report to the shore. Soon after, the bleak sound of a minute gun thudded from the Citadel and its flag descended to half-mast.

'No one to hail 'em or tell 'em anything!' snarled Bray, the first lieutenant, eyeing the swarm of small craft putting off from the waterfront. Like all aboard *Tyger*, he wore a black armband in shared grief.

The boats arrived and began circling, shouted questions from them going unanswered by the frigate's crew.

'Er, one to board, sir?' asked the second lieutenant, Bowden, indicating a passenger craft heading determinedly towards the side-steps.

'Of course not, damn it,' Bray barked.

'Sir, I believe it's the captain's wife,' he said quietly, eyeing the slight figure standing alone in the stern-sheets.

Bray hesitated. 'Ah. I'll speak with her, then.'

He went to the side and motioned the boat in. Persephone, Lady Kydd, looked up at the sea-worn frigate, her eyes searching, her hand clamped tightly to a stay.

She went up the side like the admiral's daughter she was. Bray took off his hat and stood uncomfortably.

'Where's the captain, Mr Bray?' she demanded, looking about in anguish, her face white and strained.

'Ma'am, I has my orders an' none to land or come aboard, I'm sorry t' say.'

'I'm going to him!' she blurted, and hurried over to the main hatch.

'My lady—'

But Bray was too late, and she thrust past two sailors. Flying down the ladder-way, she hurried aft to the great cabin and threw open the door.

Kydd looked up from his desk in surprise, then rose in delight. 'Persephone, my dearest!'

She burst into tears, hurrying to his arms, burying her face in his shoulder and weeping uncontrollably.

'What's this, my darling? It's not been so long that—'

'Thomas! Oh, Thomas, my love,' she sobbed. 'I was so frightened!'

'How's this?' Kydd said softly, holding her tightly, kissing her hair. 'You'll upset the men, they see you like this.'

She choked back the sobs and said unsteadily, 'I heard about the great battle only this morning while at market here – they'd just seen you make port. And . . . and I looked, and there you were, and they were right. *Tyger* lets fly her t'gallant sheets and *Ville* puts her yards to mourning. There's minute guns at the Citadel and – and—' She broke off to look up, searching his eyes. 'My dearest – what terrible fight have we lost?'

Kydd gently held her at arm's length. 'There's been no battle, Seph. All this – it's our grieving for the admiral, Lord Collingwood, now gone from us.'

'But—'

'Not in action but worn out by duty, the noble fellow. Did you know he's been at his post since taking command from the dying Nelson at Trafalgar, never once returning to England? When he finally lays down his arms to take his rest with his family he dies at sea, only three days out from Minorca on his way home.'

'Mr Bray's orders . . .?'

'None to land? That the government might make announcement of the grave news in their own time, my love.'

'So how long . . .?' she asked, a small smile breaking through the tears.

'We lie in the Sound for two days more. Gives them time to set in train as grand a funeral as they may contrive. There's talk they mean to lay him next to Nelson in St Paul's. We'll stay by him while he lies in state and then I'll pay my sincerest respects at the service.'

Kydd's servant appeared bearing a restorative.

'Thank you, Tysoe. Has the captain been diligent with his morning constitutional, pray?'

'Just so, your ladyship,' he replied, blank-faced.

'That is well.'

The man left quietly, and they kissed passionately.

'I'm such a silly,' Persephone said softly, breaking away. 'But when you didn't return from London after your last visit to Lloyd's I did worry so. And then I heard you'd been sent away, and you didn't see me before you left.'

'Oh, yes. A pier-head jump, as it were. I was going to write, Seph, but—'

'Never mind, dearest.' She laid a finger on his mouth. 'You're here and that's what counts.'

'Well, now is not the time for rejoicing, my love, but I can tell you that your land is secured.'

Kydd was now able to buy a nearby farmer's land that

they'd learned was to be sold to a mining venture. There would be no clay pits above Knowle Manor trickling their vile effluent down from the moor on to them.

'Oh, you are a clever man!' she said, clapping her hands in delight. 'You go to wage marine insurance with the best of them and win!'

Kydd coloured, the emotion of near bankruptcy and ruin from his ventures at Lloyd's still with him. 'Well, such was a sight too much hard work, I can tell you, Seph.'

She knew nothing of what had really happened, and he had his story ready. 'It's just that I was lucky with a prize, is all. You'll read about it in the newspaper, I'd think.'

His wise friend Nicholas Renzi, now Lord Farndon, had been correct, and even after rights of various eighths and sixteenths had been allocated, his share had well taken care of his debt, with enough left over for the land purchase. 'They'll make over much of its value in the rag, I've no doubt,' he added, carefully offhand, 'but after the partialling there's not so much more, I'm afraid.'

It certainly wasn't the case that they were suddenly wildly rich. At least *Tyger*'s company had done well and there would be a glorious roystering, once leave was granted.

'I don't care where it comes from, my darling – you've got us the land. And do you know what I'm going to do with it?'

'What's that, Seph?'

She smiled winningly. 'Start a riding stable of my own, for the daughters of gentlefolk.'

7

Chapter 3

Blackwall Yard, River Thames

It was a brave sight. The monstrous bulk of the ship on its ways ready for launch was festooned with enormous flags and pennants in honour of the occasion – the committing of an East India Company trading vessel to the waves.

This was a substantial-sized ship, intended for the China trade in voyages of up to six months at a time with a freighting of unimaginable wealth in her bowels. Built like a man-o'-war on the outside these were impressive creatures, and the crowd attending the launch paid due respect to her and the distinguished guests on the ornamented stage-work near her rearing bow.

Chairman of the Honourable East India Company Charles Grant could be seen in the front row and beside him sat Robert Stewart, the Viscount Castlereagh and secretary of state for war, but it was the Duke of York whose splendour gave the scene its moment.

'Should you wish a more sedate refreshment afterwards,

old fellow, I dare say East India House will be open to us,' murmured Grant, his long face set in disapproval.

Two bands below were now raucously out of beat one with each other. Castlereagh said nothing, his composed features in contrast with the fuss and uproar below them.

'Always quantities of the mobility abroad at these launch occasions,' said Grant, through his kerchief. 'It is a trial, but I hold myself philosophical in this providing due entertainment to the common public.'

On signal the Duke of York moved to the front of the stage and the bedlam calmed.

His words were brief and military, punctuated with good-natured shouts.

Fortune was duly enjoined for the good ship *Earl of Malmesbury* and all who sailed in her as she went about her business on great waters, adding both to the wealth of the nation and those who had caused her to be set a-swim.

Traditional observances having been made, the great moment arrived. With a deafening screeching and thunderous rattle of drag-irons, the thousand-ton vessel slid down the way and into her native element where she slowed in a decorous wallowing to await her tow to the fitting-out wharf.

'Well, Charles, you mentioned refreshment . . .?'

The calm and opulence of the dining saloon was at a startling distance from the genial squalor of Bellamy's, that which passed for supping at the House of Commons, and Castlereagh always appreciated his visits. It would have to be paid for, of course, the price being to give ear to whatever was exercising the overlord of the most powerful and influential source of revenue in the land.

Over the admirable serving of turbot, Grant opened, 'A fine thing, I believe, our launching.'

'Quite,' Castlereagh answered cautiously.

'And we've lost two of her sisters to the French so far this season,' Grant continued. This would be a fearful blow to the Company and Castlereagh gave a guarded expression of sympathy.

'Indian Ocean and Bay o' Bengal.'

'Not in convoy?'

'Does it signify?' Grant said huffily. 'What we need is a damn sight more King's ships as can put themselves about. Things are quiet in Europe, Boney getting what he wants, so there must be some ships o' force to spare.'

'The Bombay Marine?' This was essentially a private navy run by the East India Company.

'A green-water force only and, pray, why should we pay for protection against the King's enemies when others do not?'

'You have a not inconsiderable force stationed there now, commanded by the best we can find for you.' Castleleagh was referring to the East India Squadron based at Madras and the ships-of-the-line and frigates under the flag of the carefully picked Pellew, respected commander of the famed *Indefatigable* of a previous era.

Grant raised an eyebrow. 'Who is himself the loudest of all in demanding an accession to force.'

Castlereagh was well aware of this: he'd passed Pellew's latest plea to the first lord of the Admiralty, who had promptly returned it with the best of reasons why it was not possible. What Grant did not know was that the government was considering a daring but very risky stroke: an actual landing on the continent itself. This was not to be in Spain, where Wellesley remained helplessly immured behind the defences of Lisbon, but directly into the heart of Napoleon's Europe – a strike against Antwerp, the pistol pointed at the heart of London. It was all in aid of the newly raised Fifth Coalition and took precedence over any other, but he couldn't reveal this to Grant.

'You have my most considerable sympathy, Charles, but there's been lately much call on our resources and—'

'I've eighty-seven votes in the Commons who say you'll find a way,' Grant said smoothly.

'One such does cross my mind,' Castlereagh came back, without missing a beat.

'Oh?'

'While I haven't at hand the weight of metal you're proposing, I've something even better. A proven thief-taker of privateers and such scum, whose exploits are much in the public eye. Should he and his dauntless frigate be let loose in your part of the world, I dare to say his effectiveness and reputation will terrify same, multiplying the deterrence extremely.'

'Hmm. Together with a clutch of lesser others, possibly. Who do you have in mind?'

'How does none other than Lord Cochrane and his famed *Imperieuse* sound?'

'Rosas and the Spanish coast? That's more the medicine.'

'He's yours, then. He'll be receiving Admiralty orders within the week.'

Castlereagh stifled a smile of satisfaction at his plan. The troublesome frigate captain whose ranting in Parliament was so upsetting the nation would be given employment he couldn't refuse – in the richest grounds in the world and at a gratifying distance from the centre of things.

Chapter 4

The Admiralty, London

'Oh, do come in,' said Mulgrave, first lord of the Admiralty, rising to greet his visitor. 'I shan't offer you sherry at this hour but a refreshment?'

Disdainfully, Cochrane strolled over to the window and, pursing his lips, stared out over Horse Guards Parade where a troop of redcoats was raising dust in a complex series of manoeuvres. 'No, thank you. I can only imagine you've interrupted my important public life to offer me some species of command at an eminence. Am I not right?' He looked sideways, his expression antagonising with its patronising air.

Mulgrave held himself in, then replied, 'You are, sir. As being the most suited to the peculiar circumstances of the situation.'

Cochrane turned to him, clearly pleased. 'Basque Roads writ large.' He laughed.

'I beg your pardon?'

'Why, all the world knows of your Antwerp invasion. You are now going to offer me untrammelled command of the first wave of assaulting – the explosion vessels and mortar ships that will clear the Scheldt of hostiles before ever the soldiers get their feet wet.'

Mulgrave swallowed awkwardly. This was not going to be easy. 'Ah, yes. Not in so many words. Planning is still under revision. We rather thought that a more immediate post would satisfy, one with considerable long-term advantages, not the least of them being a most gratifying degree of prize to be had.'

Cochrane drew back. 'What post?'

'Senior frigate commander on station.'

'Under?'

'Admiral Pellew, a frigate captain like yourself.'

'Ha! You're saying, then, the East India Squadron! Do you take me for a fool? Banishment to past the Cape where I'd be lost to my people? No talk of fat prizes – which I very much doubt in these starvation times – will induce me to abandon their cause! No, sir, I will not accept.'

A dangerous glint appeared in Mulgrave's eyes. 'My lord. You are aware that continued refusal to take post, even by the most lauded of commanders, usually finds their lordships unable to offer any further employment. Should you—'

'You threaten me with that? The public would never stand to see one of their number, a hero of the sea, lie idle for want of backbone at the Admiralty. No, sir, your proposition I reject utterly. Good day to you!'

Mulgrave followed him out with his eyes and, after the slightest of pauses, rang his desk bell. His secretary appeared with commendable promptness.

'Kydd and *Tyger*. Where are they both at this moment?' he demanded crisply.

Chapter 5

The funeral had been dignified, redolent of the strongest feelings of noble sacrifice and duty done. In keeping with the deceased's modesty his tomb bore only the legend 'Cuthbert, Lord Collingwood. Died 7th March 1810 Aged 61' and was indeed placed next to that of his friend Horatio Nelson.

Kydd felt the passing of an age. These were his heroes, who had held the helm of high command steady through the worst that Bonaparte could bring against England until Trafalgar had locked him in his continental prison. Only the granite-faced Earl St Vincent remained of these men of courage and individuality. They deserved to be remembered.

He was in company with two first lords, thirty admirals and countless captains. He stood talking with them afterwards for over an hour, even winning a distant acknowledgement from Cochrane who, it seemed, had attended for the same reason as they all. Kydd's friend Renzi had been devastated to be unable to attend due to pressing matters on his estate but had insisted Kydd and Persephone stay at his London residence.

The wan sunlight outside somehow emphasised a new, greyer world of war and endless striving.

Persephone met him with their carriage, touched also by the mood.

They sat in silent contemplation as they returned to the town house.

'Sometimes I believe this war will continue for ever,' Kydd murmured, his whisky untasted. 'It's been, what, seventeen years now, and where have we reached? Boney supreme on land, we rule the seas and it's a right stalemate.'

'There've been some famous victories, my love,' Persephone soothed, sensing his depression. 'Even if they've all been at sea.'

'For what? We're like two bare-knuckle bruisers who've knocked each other about until we're too done in to go on.'

Something had touched him and she was not sure what it was.

He went on, 'But we dare not throw in the towel, not with Bonaparte owning near the whole of the civilised world. If peace were declared this very day, trade everywhere starts again tomorrow. And what is its character? Where today we have the planet our marketplace, tomorrow we compete against one who can throw open the entire continent for import, industry and then export. Our small islands could never stand.' Moodily he took up his whisky. 'To tell you true, Seph, to think we'd then be rated a far outsider among nations doesn't bear thinking on.'

'You're cast down by laying Lord Collingwood to rest,' she said.

'Old Cuddy? About the last of the heroes I grew up with and admired. The world's a sadder place — a lonelier place without him, sweetheart. Who do we look to as will teach us the meaning of duty? Where are the heroes of the day, that we're in sore need of 'em?'

A soft smile appeared. 'Some would say I'm looking at one, right here before me.'

Kydd turned to her, his expression fond. 'I'm not really, dear love. It's you that I take into battle, you that I want — need — to come back to.'

'And others would say that you've done your part,' she said steadily, 'from the first days of the French wars right to now. Without stopping. And it could be time to lay down your weapons and claim reward — in the arms of your loved ones,' she ended, rather less steadily.

He closed his eyes, reaching for her hand. 'That would be Heaven itself, sweetling.'

She half tensed, knowing in her heart what was coming next.

His eyes opened again and in them was a faraway look that did not include her. 'Seph, it's the navy alone as keeps these islands shielded and preserved and it needs me. I can't let 'em down like that.'

'There's so many young men coming along who—'

'They haven't the experience in a navy stretched thin like it is and besides . . .'

'Besides?'

'My dearest, have you ever thought where I'd be if the navy hadn't come to claim me for its own that night in the Horse and Groom? I was contented to be a common wigmaker and then my life was all upset. And I tasted what the sea was — is — and it agreed with me. I'm now a knight, known to the King and his tribe, and all because, for some

16

reason, I'm one with the sea. It's saying I owe it all to the navy and I'm not about to turn my back on 'em now.'

'I dare to say I have a debt to the navy as well as you.'

'What's that, Seph?'

'It was the navy that made you, shaped you into the most desirable and handsome catch a woman can possibly ask for.'

'Why, thank you, m'lady,' Kydd stuttered, in masculine embarrassment.

Persephone paused for a long moment, then said in a barely controlled voice, 'Wherever your navy sends you on the seven seas, you go with my love and longing, in the trust that you're where you belong. I promise you shall never find me jealous.'

The note was brief and to the point. 'I should attend on the first lord at my convenience, Seph,' Kydd told her. 'That means directly. I've a feeling the navy is about to trifle in my destiny again.'

He was back promptly. 'Well, and I'm right in the particulars.' He took his wife's hands and looked into her eyes, 'It's the Indies.'

She waited for him to go on.

'The East Indies, sweet love, which is to mean the opposite to the West Indies, comprehending India and all its seas.'

She fell back in dismay. 'So far away, darling,' she said faintly. 'And strange and . . . and unhealthy.'

'It may be, but it's where the biggest fortunes of all are to be made. Think on it, Seph – I may return a nabob with an elephant and troop of servants to carry my pearls. Or—'

'Don't jest, Thomas. This is a serious matter.'

'Yes, my love. But who knows what India has for me? All I've heard is that most of those coming home after a spell there are rich as Croesus and call no man master. Why not me?'

'And just as many have left their bones. Dear Thomas, do take care. The navy has no use for dead men.' Her eyes filled.

'I've a notion there's a purpose behind my going. I don't know what it is, but it's something to do with what I was saying before.'

'You owing a debt to the navy?'

'I do, but it's not that. No, it's more concerning our two nations being at stalemate. Here in Europe there's nothing will happen, but out there it could. We took most of India from the French in the last century, who knows if there's more for the taking?'

'I've not heard talk of any rich lands there as are waiting for a flag,' she replied tartly.

'Nor me, my love. That is not to say there aren't any, o' course.'

'How long?' she asked, in a small voice.

'I suppose you should not expect me back for at least a couple of years, Seph, if not more. The Admiralty doesn't relish the expense of sending a ship halfway around the world for it then to turn about and come back.'

Kydd's throat tightened. This talk of years apart was hard to say, and he could see the effect of his words on her. 'All the more time to pile up our spoils, sweetheart,' he tried, with forced gaiety.

She turned away and sobbed, once.

Chapter 6

Aboard HMS Tyger

'Mr Bray, turn up the hands, if you will. I've some news for them.'

Kydd was not known as a loose tongue and the lower deck cleared rapidly to hear him. Crowding the after end and settling in the rigging to get a better hearing, they waited patiently. Behind him were the officers whom he'd taken delight in not enlightening – they were just as much in the dark as the seamen.

'Ship's company mustered for ye, sir,' rumbled Bray.

'Thank you.'

Kydd stepped forward to face his men. 'Tygers. Tomorrow we sail.'

There was an immediate ripple of interest, and disbelief. The ship was neither stored nor with her full stow of powder and shot. What did it mean?

'For Portsmouth.' Incomprehension showed on their faces. Why lay aft his men to tell them of a routine shift of naval ports?

'To fit foreign.' This was met with a massed sigh of under-standing, quickly suppressed.

'We are part of a reinforcement sent to join Admiral Pellew – in the East Indies.'

Excited babble broke out and Kydd let it spend itself before nodding to the master-at-arms, who roared for silence in confected outrage.

'I don't need to tell you that things have quietened in this part of the world, including Spain, and we are being sent to support Admiral Pellew guarding our most valuable trade route – that to India and China.'

Every man had heard of the fabulous treasures crossing the ocean in those stately Indiamen, on their way to enrich both shareholders and those with some snug placing in the grand East India Company. Tales were told of the huge riches that had been made in India, those returning with vast wealth the envy of all.

'This is to say that we shall be on station, not passing through on a cruise and as such might expect to remain for some years.' A hush fell.

'There may be among you those who do not desire to go foreign for this length of time for one reason or another. I'm going to make these men an offer. Should they find one of the same rate among the ships in the fleet at Portsmouth willing to exchange into *Tyger* then so be it.'

Kydd turned to his first lieutenant. 'Mr Bray. Ship is under sailing orders. Carry on, please.'

That evening *Tyger* was curiously deserted: officers had hastened ashore with much to tell their folk, only Brice, whose family was in the north, remaining. A skeleton crew of 'non-native' seamen left aboard settled down agreeably as even their captain had been seen to step off indecently quickly.

* * *

20

They weighed for Portsmouth the next morning with no stragglers reported, but Kydd knew it was there, on the last eve before sailing foreign, that laggards might contemplate, through the bottom of a bottle, with consternation, years of service in exotic parts. But there'd be no trouble in finding those around the fleet more than willing to exchange into a frigate of the renown of *Tyger*, wherever she was bound.

As they shaped course around the Mewstone, he reflected that Persephone was somewhere under their lee travelling in the Portsmouth mail – they'd agreed to meet in the George – but *Tyger*, with a fair westerly, would be making better time.

Tyger took up her berth in the inner dockyard and began preparing.

The process was thorough for there were no royal dock-yards in India and any defects would reduce their effective time on station. If not attended to at the outset of the commission they could not be remedied later. Every effort had to be made to bring the frigate up to the highest pitch of efficiency and repair in all her parts.

They were headed to a tropic station and slops had to be laid in which reflected that: lightweight cottons in place of stout serge, material for sennit hats, linen duck for trousers. Officers would take care to equip themselves with their own appropriate wardrobe.

There would be sultry nights in the mess-deck and *Tyger*, being a frigate, had no open air via gun-ports. Kydd set the carpenter and sailmaker to devising wind-sails, devices to set above the hatches to scoop down passing sea-breezes.

Awnings were made up to spread over the quarterdeck. Extra supplies of pitch ordered in would counter the losses when a fierce sun bubbled the caulked seams between the deck planking. The list of preparations was endless, and there were always experienced old hands who could be relied on to suggest yet more.

As the date of sailing approached there was a handful who were unwilling to embark on a voyage of such dimensions, seamen with settled family, those who had heard of the heat, diseases and heathen races and wanted no part of it. Most, however, exulted in the belief that a known prize-taker like Kydd would lead them to plunder undreamed of.

As preparations went forward, it became evident that *Tyger* was going to act the store-ship for her voyage out. Precious spars of Baltic pine, unobtainable out east, were laid on deck and tightly lashed. Fresh-forged anchors of assorted sizes were wedged in every conceivable place while long bolts of canvas made progress in 'tween decks a trial. Later there would be yet more stores and, finally, quantities of the latest newspapers as well as the vital lading of specie – hard coin to pay whole garrisons and offset the bills of exchange that victuallers and others were issuing on various government authorities.

Individuals made their own arrangements for an absence of years, taking on board games of chance, a cabin rack of reading matter, tomes of study, artists' materials. Wiser heads got together to pool their treasures of distraction while others adopted the view that the usual amusements would suffice, it only amounting to the same sea-time but being spent in foreign parts.

The gunroom took on a homely look, a polished commensal cask of wine snugly in place hoisted at the deckhead, a well-polished bread-barge with accompanying cruets of the quality to be expected in such a noble frigate. Pictures of England, both bucolic and sentimental, landscapes and seaside confections, looked down on them and, in those far-off places, would take on an almost holy radiance.

It was hard on Persephone. She was torn between fussing over Kydd's comforts and furnishings and the knowledge that this was most assuredly a man's world, the peculiar demesne of he who was at the same time her lover and the stern lord of this sea world. She fell back on the only person who could truly advise her – Tysoe, Kydd's manservant and valet.

Having served Kydd in the swelter of a Caribbean summer Tysoe knew what to expect and laid out the essentials to her – a large quantity of linen shirts, stockings of the sheerest silk, a cocked hat of the lightest felt. Other necessities of a tropic climate – a mosquito net, bed linen, a patent wine cooler – would be better purchased on arrival, cheaper and more suited than anything England could produce. There would be more and Tysoe delicately accepted a purse against their acquiring in India, then awkwardly allowed that for his master an item or two of a personal nature would be acceptable.

An ivory-backed hairbrush, a crystal water jug, and then a small picture, painted by her in the favoured end-of-century mode of the two of them in a formal pose outside Knowle Manor. The inference was not lost on Kydd – she was recording their union in the traditional way that would be passed along through the generations. The Kydd line starting its stately progress down the centuries would be traceable from there, in due course to be joined by other works that would include progeny in line of succession. It was touching and awe-inspiring, speaking as it did not only of her love but her faith and trust in their future.

Kydd himself had his own secret dreams. His recent brush with financial disaster had shown him how close the boundary was between gracious living and harsh penury. In the process it had also thrown into clear perspective just what position he had acquired by the purchase of Knowle Manor and its lands.

He'd justly been proud of his possession, the only Kydd in the family to become a squire and a member of the landed gentry – but he'd since gone far in society and knew exactly what it meant. Knowle Manor made him a worthy but minor country personage, with an income in the lower hundreds and, but for his sea renown, a lowly figure.

He'd seen for himself, though, what a real sea hero could achieve: Admiral Boscawen in a previous war had been honoured by his country for his victories in these same East Indies, acquiring the Hatchlands Park estate not far from where Kydd had grown up. That was what it was to be a man of prominence, to have an estate, a home of above a hundred rooms, to be steward over as many servants and workers, build follies, extensions, gardens.

It was not unknown for victorious admirals to be granted a barony, to have a title to hand down the generations. Kydd knew that, while it was unlikely for him, it was not impossible and perhaps this move to that part of the world could lead to a glorious destiny, honours and riches.

Or a fever bed and squalid death.

Be damned to it – he would give it his all, whatever the dangers and menace of the future. Was this not for both of them?

Chapter 7

The day of departure near, the pace quickened. Two more frigates were to accompany *Tyger*, with five store-ships and three brig-sloops. The East Indiaman convoy had preceded them with its own escort so Kydd made the decision for the three frigates to sail ahead together and let the slower store-ships follow, escorted by the brig-sloops.

To his exasperation, he found that his little band of frigates had to be dignified with the title of squadron – the East India Joiner Squadron. With this came the need to provide proper directions in the event they fell in with the enemy and even sailing instructions to define such matters as the rendez-vous after tempest and storm, specific signals for alterations in the order of battle, sailing and so forth.

They would sail under the red ensign of detached Admiralty service by the quickest available route, which was not neces-sarily the shortest. In this instance it would mean standing south to catch the trade winds from the north-east in a swift diagonal across the Atlantic, through the doldrums and making landfall on the coast of Brazil. From there they would be in a sovereign position to pick up the corresponding trade winds from the south-west in a bold curve across the south Atlantic to touch at the Cape before rounding Africa to meet the Indian Ocean.

By that time the south-west monsoon would be in full flow, urging them up past the tip of India to the Coromandel Coast and Madras, where they would make their number to Admiral Pellew at his headquarters, joining his East Indies fleet.

It would be months at sea before this happened; all the time they would be on their own and any stores, personal or ship, that had been overlooked would be impossible to make good. The greatest pressure would be on the purser, the careful, shrewish Harman, who must ensure the men were fed and clothed in all weathers, expendables such as candles, coal and train oil never exhausted and, most importantly, that there was enough tobacco and grog to last the entire voyage.

His was the risk – if he failed, his bond with the Admiralty would be forfeit. If he laid in stores never used, it would be to his own cost. It was the business price he must pay.

Last-minute stores came aboard. Excitement grew among the squeakers who would return to their native shore as young men with a hundred yarns to tell of a land of allure and enticement that their stay-at-home folk could only dream about.

And then the Blue Peter was hoisted, a warning to all that this was the last day when *Tyger* was land-bound, when communication with the shore was still open and fond messages could be passed. When the signal was taken in and the anchor weighed, only letters months old could convey news and feelings, hopes and fears.

Ashore, life would continue with the daily round, as it always did, few understanding that the good ship *Tyger*, putting out into the vast outer seas, was now her own world, far more real to the souls aboard her than the recent memories of land, which must now be treasured but allowed to slip into the past.

Boats began to circle *Tyger*, women in them waving and weeping by turns, the last hoys and wherries coming alongside with packages, insensible seamen and officials, all sending the officer-of-the-day to distraction.

Kydd said his goodbyes to Persephone in private in the George. There were no words that could meet the occasion and they simply clung to each other for long minutes until he said huskily, 'It's time, my love.'

In response she held him fiercely before releasing him, her arms dropping away in a poignant realisation.

They walked together to the Sally Port where his barge waited.

A chaste kiss, the sparkle of tears and he boarded, the boat's lively movements giving notice that he had abandoned the dead earth for the vigour and power of the sea – and an unforeseeable future.

With crisp orders from Halgren, his boat's crew stroked evenly for *Tyger*, one of several warships at anchor in Spithead, outward bound.

Kydd twisted round twice, each time seeing Persephone's diminishing figure give a wave and, once, blow a kiss. His eyes stinging, he concentrated on *Tyger*, the one who from now on would command his affections, probably for years.

Bray had taken the deck, roaring and pacing like a caged lion, and saw him aboard with relief. Kydd left him to it, deliberately not noticing the untidy heaps of stores and gear scattered about.

He went to his cabin. Dillon was there, furiously scribbling, but looked up when Kydd entered. 'Dispatches for the station. I've signed them in, sir. These are dockyard vouchers, must have a signature before we sail, and these are—'

'Thank you, Edward,' Kydd said heavily. 'I know my duty.'

A little later he came on deck as the capstan was manned and the fo'c'sle crew gathered. He surreptitiously looked round: the little figure was still there by the Sally Port. A lump came to his throat and he turned away quickly, then guiltily glanced back.

'*Thalia* conforming, sir,' Brice told him. This was one of his frigates, a handsome sixth rate and apparently ready for sea.

'And *Hebe*?' The other was an elderly twelve-pounder with a new captain.

'Seems to be having some sort of bother forrard,' Brice said neutrally. 'Sail bent on, though.'

Tyger's number, however, was at the dockyard signal tower, with the instruction to proceed. If *Hebe* was not ready, she would face a stiff stern chase later to catch up. 'We weigh anchor at eight bells,' Kydd snapped. 'She knows that.'

At the beginning of the first dog-watch, they'd sail into the evening with sunset on the starboard bow. He'd done it so many times but only once before with such an immense voyage ahead.

He looked ashore again, the figure now growing indistinct in the fading light. He gulped, fighting off a wave of desolation. An insane thought rushed into his mind – he was captain and nothing could stop him suddenly ordering away his barge and flying to her side, gathering her up, kissing her – and telling Bray to take *Tyger* away to those eastern seas. It would be the end of his career but . . .

'Sir – stations for unmooring?' asked Brice, as seven bells sounded from forward.

'Yes, and ask Mr Bray to report if you will.'

His first lieutenant marched aft and barked that in all respects *Tyger* was ready for sea.

'Very well. Hoist preparative, unmoor.'

It was acknowledged in *Thalia* but *Hebe*'s answer was kept at the dip.

Kydd bit his lip. If the squadron delayed sailing, the port admiral would want to know why and he would be blamed. *Hebe*'s captain – Moorsom – was new to the ship but was well experienced and should have cleared any pother far in advance of sailing.

He had to make up his mind.

Precisely at eight bells he ordered the signal for the execute, and *Tyger* began winning her anchor. There were men about the fore-part of *Hebe* but that meant little. *Thalia* on the other hand had her anchor a-weigh and began to take the wind even before *Tyger*, but wisely flatted her headsails to keep her way off until *Tyger*'s anchor cleared water and she cast to larboard in the gentle westerly.

With another glance at *Hebe*, Kydd saw her cable still down and something approaching confusion on her deck. Later there would be an accounting with her captain, he promised himself savagely. 'Brace in, course south b' west, Mr Bowden,' he ordered.

Tyger took up for her run south, a sunset forming on the starboard bow as expected, and as the watch took over, beginning the age-old routine of securing for sea, he glanced astern. *Thalia* had tucked herself in comfortably behind *Tyger* and the two swashed out into the open sea.

'Reduce to tops'ls,' he growled at Bowden. They were in no real hurry. He'd let the errant *Hebe* catch them before dark and hear the excuses in the morning.

With a sudden pang of feeling he wheeled round but it was too late. In the gathering dusk and widening distance, the Sally Port was near indistinguishable, let alone any solitary figure.

At this moment Persephone would be looking out to sea at the dark silhouette of the ships, a picture of grace and beauty, beating out into the sunset. They would be hull down in about half an hour and in less than two their royals and topgallants would dip below the horizon, and then it would be as if they'd never existed.

Chapter 8

Several months later

Almost as if it were a theatre stage, with the curtains swept aside to reveal the scene setting, the compelling sight of the continent of India made its appearance as the monsoonal downpour eased: a dreamy blue-grey far-off shore, innocent of the hand of man but charged with an allure conjured from half-remembered childhood tales of Sinbad and the fabled Moghul emperors.

In minutes the deck filled with curious sailors, now toughened and browned by their time at sea, agog to clap eyes on the mythical East.

They were still a good way off from Madras, though, their voyage end.

Kydd kept his offing as they were urged on by the driving south-west monsoon winds until they reached the appropriate latitude, at which point the helm went over for the final approach.

It had been a fairly uneventful passage, as Kydd had decreed there was to be no touching port at either the Brazils or the

Cape. Every unknown sail sighted was allowed to proceed on its occasions untroubled by any attentions from the flying frigates. A direct run to the East Indies Station was required, due to the pressing demand for their presence. This had had the effect of keeping the ships healthy and preventing desertions. After provisioning on arrival, they would be rapidly effective in whatever tasks awaited them.

There'd been a spectacular but harmless electrical storm in the foetid passage of Africa's north-west coast. They'd gazed in wonder at two waterspouts as they neared the Cape, and while rounding Agulhas they'd fallen in with a pod of whales. Further on there was the unnerving experience of cleaving through an untold number of deadly sea-snakes making blindly but purposefully for a distant shore, their sinuous black and yellow bodies close to the surface in a steadily weaving mass, stretching as far as the eye could see.

There were several enforced stops, and anchoring in the lee of a small island, watering parties ashore, enabled Kydd to take measure of his two captains.

Thalia's was a Captain Fanshaw Avery, a young man lucky enough to catch Collingwood's eye at the right time and now on the quarterdeck of his own rather elderly 32-gun sixth rate. Forthright but willing to please, he appealed to Kydd with his ferocious dedication to Bonaparte's downfall.

Moorsom was of another sort. Made post unexpectedly late in his career, he had nevertheless been entrusted with *Hebe*, another 32 but pierced for eighteen-pounders, her force not so inferior to *Tyger*. He was, however, cautious and slow, giving the impression of fearfulness that any stroke of his too daring might result in mortifying embarrassment. With solely big-ship origins, Kydd wondered how he'd been able to land such a command – interest at the highest? He'd protested that the confusion on deck at their sailing was due to his unfamiliarity with his new vessel, but Kydd suspected he'd been unprepared for the much more lively level of activity in a frigate over a ship-of-the-line.

And now their destination lay close ahead.

Kydd had brought along his little band at a respectable pace and had no reason to expect anything but a warm welcome from the commander-in-chief East Indies Station, the legendary Admiral Sir Edward Pellew.

It had been a spirited topic of discussion at their last dinner before arriving – what kind of admiral would be the gifted frigate captain of the age just past? Would he be merciless in his expectations of a frigate of today, one so lately in the public eye? Or would he retreat into jealousy, feeling under threat by a rival to his laurels?

Speculation mounted also as to their prospects on station. No one in the gunroom could offer previous service in India and it was a matter of conjecture as to how a King's ship would fare in what amounted to an immense private fiefdom. With its monopoly, the Honourable East India Company forbade any sail in trade to pass east of the Cape.

What was known was that India was a land of fabulous treasures and it would be strange indeed if, in the fullness of time, they did not find themselves carrying some of it back to England.

Joyce, *Tyger*'s sailing master, stumped importantly up to Kydd. 'Madras Roads,' he said, as if about to impart a confidence. His sturdy wooden leg, shaped and fitted by *Tyger*'s carpenter from the fore-topsail yard of a French conquest, had the lustrous gleam of vigorously applied beeswax. 'As there's no harbour in Madras,' he continued, 'the rutter has it we anchors off, clear o' the line o' surf, which is monstrous heavy. All has t' go ashore in native boats, like, being as ship's boats are not handy enough to make it in.'

'So be it then, Mr Joyce,' Kydd told him. That was his reading, too, from a turgid account of travel in these parts he'd picked up in Portsmouth. But a major seaport with a naval presence and no wharves and piers, reliant only on boat boys?

In the event the anchoring was simple enough, the bulk of two ships-of-the-line clear guidance to where the navy moored. Neither vessel had an admiral's pennant a-fly, so there was no salute to prepare. The three frigates followed suit to the others nearby and went to two anchors at a seemly distance from the sail-of-the-line.

The shoreline was a continuous stretch of pale beach, above it the stout walls and overtopping grand buildings within what Kydd guessed must be Fort St George. Its huge Union flag at a central staff streamed out imperiously. Was this where Pellew had his headquarters, that he should report?

It looked so different from when he had touched at India as a young seaman in *Artemis* frigate – but they'd gone direct to Calcutta and he'd had no liberty ashore. He vividly recalled the heat and stink of the long upriver journey.

But he didn't have long to ponder the past. A naval cutter appeared alongside and an officer hailed up to come aboard. He turned out to be a lieutenant sent by one of the battle-ships to pilot the newcomer ashore to the Admiral's House, where Pellew resided when in Madras.

In a practised gesture, he had one of the circling boats come alongside. 'A masula boat,' he explained. 'Only way to get to shore.'

It was a lengthy, flat-bottomed craft manned by twelve whipcord-thin oarsmen wearing nothing but loincloths and threadbare turbans. The steersman standing in the stern holding his oar looked up questioningly. A price was soon struck and the passengers embarked.

Kydd found himself perched on a bamboo pole laid across in place of a thwart and contemplating the peculiar construction of the craft. Flush-straked, with the seams that were sewn together with what he could swear was coconut husk fibre.

'Don't worry, sir – they're every one born on the Coromandel Coast and know what they're about.'

Under twelve oars the boat surged shorewards, effortlessly riding the massive swells now shortening and rising for their charge inshore.

Two catamarans fell in close astern. At Kydd's quizzical look, the lieutenant said drily, 'If we overset in the surf and these fellows save us, it'll be to their considerable profit.'

Kydd smiled weakly, clutching his bamboo-pole seat as they squared away for the final rush.

With carefully selected timing the steersman lined up the boat and, atop a suddenly mounting monstrous wave, hurtled on to the beach. In a wild hissing and shuddering the craft came to a stop well clear of the receding water.

They hastily got over the side and up the beach before the next rolling surf swashed in.

'You see? A perfect landing – what we call high and dry.' Kydd hadn't more than a drop or two of water on him to show for it.

Once on the beach, further transportation was summoned in the form of a kind of covered box-like litter carried by four bearers. They set off along the foreshore and Kydd looked out at the busy prospect. As they reached deeper into the town, he was bombarded with impressions of exotic humanity crowding around roadside stalls mingling with animals – cows and monkeys, dogs and birds – and, here and there, a naked, bedaubed man sitting on his haunches in the dust.

On the air Kydd detected an exciting reek of spices that was unmistakably Indian, as different as could possibly be from the stench of horse-droppings in London.

The Admiral's House was a grand edifice with an elegant porticoed entrance pillared to support a cool veranda, which continued around the building. Kydd descended and was greeted by a flag-lieutenant who escorted him inside past tall turbaned servants, whose flashing dark eyes gravely followed him.

He stiffened into a formal walk. This was the most important time of the commission, when he would discover whether he would get along with the commander-in-chief, himself a fabled frigate captain, made baronet for his triumphs.

Kydd knew little of Pellew's current command, other than he'd been appointed rear admiral before Trafalgar for this station and had been here since, but his previous victories and successes were part of the folklore of the navy, enough to leave him most respectful.

'Captain Sir Thomas Kydd, new arrived in *Tyger* 32, sir.'

There was a muffled rumble from inside the room and the lieutenant waited patiently.

This was followed by a grunt and Kydd was shown in.

Admiral Sir Edward Pellew looked up from his papers. The moment hung. Then he rose wheezily and, with a gruff 'Good to see you, sir. Take a seat an' tell me about your passage,' he came around to greet him.

Kydd replied evenly, 'Why, sir, quiet and uneventful is all.'

'The best kind.' It seemed this passed inspection for Pellew took another chair and regarded him keenly. 'So, only the three o' you?'

His homely Devon-accented words brought a stab of feeling to Kydd, who replied, 'A joiner squadron of frigates, sir. We thought to press on ahead of the others, who follow.'

'And these are . . .?'

'Store-ships, sloops, unrated vessels, sir. I have a list—'

'Quite. I'll have you in no doubt, Kydd, that your presence is much to be welcomed.' The admiral was not in strict uniform: his white cotton waistcoat fitted loosely for the climate while Kydd was beginning to perspire heavily under his stout English coat.

Seeing this Pellew, with a dry smile, told him to lay it aside. 'Not unless we're at a public spectacle, I'm persuaded.'

'Thank you, sir,' Kydd said gratefully. Soft creaking above them resolved into a long slat woven with watered reeds being slowly swept backwards and forwards by cords led outside the room. It provided a welcome cool.

'Now you may have heard this to be a flabby and tranquil backwater, Kydd. Nothing could be more wrong.' Pellew's geniality faded and something of the grim warrior showed.

'While all attention is on Boney and Europe, we've troubles here that rob me of sleep at night and have me petitioning m' lordships week by week to give me additional force. You'll learn more of it in due course, but you have my word on't that you'll not have an easy time.'

'Sir.'

He paused, his head oddly to one side. 'You've done well for yourself, Kydd, have you not?'

'I've been lucky in the particulars, sir.'

'Just so. The *Naval Chronicle* puts it down to good old-fashioned seamanship and always crowding on sail for the enemy where you could.'

Kydd saw where this might lead and kept his silence.

'As reminds me of myself at your age.'

'Sir.'

'Strange sail in the forenoon, hands to quarters and Mongseer's colours doused by the dog-watches. That's what it was to be alive with the deck of a crack frigate under m' feet. Ha!'

'You've much to be proud of, Sir Edward.'

'As may be, but things have changed for me, Kydd. I haven't a taut ship to command, I sit in an office and sign fool papers all day. And yet I'm expected to preserve the John Company trade against all perils and menaces that chance by.'

'A hard thing,' murmured Kydd.

'And all the time I'm getting as grey as a badger and running to belly. But all that's saying is that the war is mine t' lose, b' George.'

Why was Pellew being so open with him and on such a short acquaintance? Uneasily, Kydd tried to make sense of it. Was Pellew, the man of action of a past age, reaching out to one who would understand – would have empathy for what it was to be shackled so, to spend his days in guessing enemy intentions, then be responsible for making frightful decisions on behalf of those actually doing the fighting?

Far from being jealous, was the man seeking one of his own kind to understand and conceivably share his burdens? But how far this would be extended into an interest under which Kydd could flourish and rise in his profession, as was the time-worn practice in the navy, remained to be seen.

'Aye, sir,' Kydd said, with as much warmth as he could muster. 'That has to be admitted, but I'm sanguine no better flies a flag in these waters.'

The eyes regarded him coolly, then Pellew's manner eased. 'We'll get to the hard talking later. Tell me, Kydd, are y' spliced yet?'

38

'I am, sir, this year past. I'm now most fortunate to call home Combe Tavy, down from the moors.'

'Devon?' said Pellew, chuckling. 'Your domestic choosing does ye credit, sir.' He paused, beaming indulgently, then said, with a sigh, 'And now you must make do with India. You have my leave to take some days in acquiring a residence and, o' course, sleep out of your ship. Do let me know when you're settled. Er, I understand a garden-house this side of Black Town answers with most.'

'Thank you, sir,' Kydd answered formally, standing to take his leave. 'You'll have *Tyger*'s readiness for sea as soon as possible.'

'And I shall be seeing you again shortly, Kydd,' Pellew said.

Chapter 9

Returning to *Tyger*, Kydd knew what he'd see when he got on board – the officers nonchalantly pacing the deck, seamen finding work to do at the after end of the ship within hearing of the quarterdeck and still others in the mizzen rigging stretching perilously above.

'Mr Bray.'

Work ceased, all eyes on Kydd.

'Stand down sea watches, secure for harbour. Larboard watch to liberty at noon.' The rest of his words were lost in excited babble, but it didn't matter – Kydd was announcing leave ashore and that was all that counted.

He turned and went down to his cabin.

To his surprise, a figure was sitting in his armchair, gazing out of the stern windows at the spreading spectacle of the anchorage. Hearing Kydd enter he rose and bowed. 'Hornsby Rix – those who know me call me Cluffer.'

Kydd was impressed that he had been able to persuade both Tysoe and Dillon to allow him access to the most important person on the ship. Both hovered anxiously until Kydd sent them away while he dealt with the interloper. 'Might

I enquire what you're doing in my cabin, Mr Rix?' he said tightly. The man was dressed oddly, for while undoubtedly English, he wore a loose tunic and ornate curved shoes. His appearance was not improved by a profusion of whiskers and long beard.

'Oh, as I've a favour in my gift to grant you, sir, should you see fit to accept.'

'Explain yourself, sir!'

'Captain, I know a little of you even at this far remove and I dare to guess that, as we say in these parts, you're here as a griffin to shake the pagoda tree.'

'You make little sense, Mr Rix.'

'Meaning that as a well-placed but fresh-arrived newcomer to India you will want to ensure that your return to your native shore will be attended in some way with a portion of riches, as who's to say.'

'I come here to do my duty and no more, Mr Rix,' Kydd said stiffly. 'Turn to your John Company man, if you want a seeker after profits.' He was not about to share any personal hopes of a fortune with this man.

'Then at the least I can offer you my favours in that regard.'

'I'm a busy man, sir. Please be brief.' The heat in his cabin was close to stifling and he eased his collar to allow something of the sea-breeze through the windows to cool him.

'Very well. You are here to be part of the East India Squadron and therefore set fair to spend some time in Madras. As a not inconsiderable asset to the polite society of Madras, you will be setting up your residence wherein your entertaining will be conducted. Have you considered how you might do this in a wholly strange and not altogether friendly land?'

Kydd hesitated. 'You spoke of favours.' Despite the man's outlandish airs, he felt inclined to allow him a minute or two further.

41

'I did, Captain. As a denizen of Madras, I'm in a position to see you into a most desirable lodging and suitably equipped with staff to wait upon you in a manner others might see as essential for one under the public gaze.'

'And in return for this favour?'

'Merely that you count me as a friend. That and to provide me with all the newspapers you've carried out of the old country, whatever their condition, as long as they are the latest of their species.'

No doubt he was a player of sorts in the Madras Exchange, or whatever passed for one, and by careful study of the last-known market conditions could make his dispositions accordingly. 'And that is all?' Kydd asked innocently.

'A friend,' Rix repeated. 'You will need one. And if we are so then we shall together indulge in the sport of visiting, which being the chief occupation of your compatriots. I've a notion you're an interesting man as will serve to keep them tolerably entertained.'

Kydd gave a wry smile. As gatekeeper to a fresh face of note, Rix's standing in society would be assured. But he had to admit that it would be damned convenient if in Rix he had someone on hand to see him properly established in this most exotic of places. 'Newspapers. A consort in social calls. A friend – it seems not impossible in return for your favour in seeing me well planted in Madras, Mr Rix.' Whether he proved to be a genuine friend remained to be seen.

'Cluffer.'

'Then shall we—'

'The newspapers?'

'You shall not leave this ship without a sufficiency, Cluffer.'

'Thank you. Then tiffin tomorrow? That is, an outlandish meal we affect at one, and shall we say at Black Town, the Choultry Inn?'

42

Chapter 10

Until Kydd had received his formal orders from the commander-in-chief there was little for Dillon, his confidential secretary, to do but hold himself in readiness. When Kydd called for him, he came quickly.

'Edward. As you know we'll be here for some years, all of it based upon Madras, the seat of the reigning admiral. I find that the usual practice for captains of significance is to take residence ashore, and your Mr Rix is kind enough to take me in hand in the article of lodgings to see me well served.'

Dillon seemed relieved – either finding that his allowing Rix access had been the right move or that in the future he would have the run of the cabin while Kydd was away.

'I've been thinking that it would be to both our advantages should you join me. That is, take residence with me. On the one hand your services with hoisting in what passes for polite manners in this place and at the same time keeping a weather eye on the local scene would be appreciated. On the other, well, I have it on good authority that there are quantities of languages to be had of a most amazing complication.'

What Kydd did not say was that lonely splendour in a foreign castle was not an agreeable prospect, and a friendly face at breakfast was much to be preferred.

Dillon's dazzling smile was answer enough. 'Then the notion meets with your approbation? So – we begin at once. You shall step ashore with me to see what Mr Rix can conjure for us.'

In Black Town people of every race and colour of dress thronged the dusty roads, the markets and bazaars. With entertainers, hawkers and old women hobbling along, pots balanced on their heads, it was a swarming wonder of alien humanity.

The Choultry Inn was a welcome relief from the crowds and reek, set back from the roads. It provided shade in a wide veranda where patrons, mostly British, sat together taking their ease in the heat.

Rix, seated at a ready-spread table, gave a polite wave to catch Kydd's eye. 'Ahoy there, my good captain!' he greeted, nodding politely to Dillon.

'My confidential secretary, Edward Dillon,' Kydd said, 'as will be lodging with me.'

'Ah. Quite so. It is usual, however, to have one's man, your valet as who's to say.'

Kydd had no desire to expose the faithful Tysoe to the naked curiosity of the throng, they possibly seeing for the first time a man of quite another race. Tysoe would continue as his sea manservant and he would find another for duties in his shore residence. 'Mr Dillon is not to be troubled by matters of a domestic nature. He is by way of being my man of business.'

'I understand. Before we go further, might I introduce you to the provender on offer. Curries, meat and fish, in course . . .'

A satisfying repast followed, with not a few surprises for British tastes, served by dark-eyed men in immense turbans wearing flowing white muslin robes, large earrings and red slippers.

As tea was produced Rix stretched back. 'I have in mind a most suitable residence for your inspection and approval. It was the abode of a noted East India Company captain, whose retirement back to Britain leaves the property masterless. We will visit it shortly, but for the nonce, may I offer some insight into life here in Madras?'

Kydd gave a nod of encouragement.

'John Company has the monopoly on ocean trading east of the Cape. This is not the totality of commerce. Country trading, which is to say when the departure and arrival port remain within India and its waters, they do not care for. They maintain an army and navy to keep the peace and their trade flowing. Such is the size of the continent that they've carved it into four and called 'em presidencies – Calcutta, Madras, Bombay and Prince o' Wales Island by which they mean Pulo Penang. Calcutta is chief and where the governor general of all India holds court.

'They wisely maintain the pretence that the true rulers are the native princes, who they make treaty with to offer them protection in their tedious wars with each other, exacting taxes to pay for this but extending the priceless boon of peace and money-making throughout the land. But make no error, the Honourable East India Company is the real power in India.'

'Why, then, are the King's soldiery and ships here? Our much cried-up General Wellesley, now in Lisbon, they call the sepoy general as having won his spurs at some great battle here.'

'That's correct – some years ago at Seringapatam in which

45

he put down Tipu, Sultan of Mysore, in a grand mill to set beside anything seen in Europe. Well, the East India Company has the numbers but not the quality, and to ensure there are no perplexities should the French take the field as they did, we're provided with a stiffening of British troops.'

'To . . . assist.'

'Ah. There's the rub. When John Company marches out, they're obeying the will of India House of Leadenhall Street, not the government of the day. Their prime duty as they see it is to pacify and ease the conditions of trade, not to win territory for the Crown. That of the King's man is more narrowly in the interests of the revenue it yields for the country at large and thusly to defend against any who might challenge the Company's fief.'

'The French.'

'And rebellious princes, for the Moghul emperor is power-less and can now only sulk in Delhi. For the rest I've no doubt you'll hear from your admiral what further troubles are to be expected.'

'I'm sure of it,' Kydd murmured.

'More to the point, be aware that in professional terms a King's officer from Horse Guards has precedence over a Company man both on the field and in the barracks, and this is cause for much ill blood between them – especially when it comes to the ladies and social occasions.'

'Hmm. I shall remember that, but tell me more of life here,' Kydd said, knowing that he would get full details on such from the military he had to deal with.

'More? Then, for instance, know that the coin of choice is the Madras star-pagoda, which is equivalent to forty-two fanams, each to the value of about the ninth part of a farthing, the lower orders having resort to a coin called a "cash", of which they will need eighty to receive back a fanam. Of these—'

'Thank you, Cluffer. Um, what would this get you, say, in a common market at all?'

'I believe a prime capon would cost in the order of twenty fanams, a fed fowl but eight. A Vellore mango at a fanam for four but for a pimple nose of the first sort, ten fanams will be asked. And—'

'I see.'

'Fear not, stout sailor. Your *dubash* will relieve you of the necessity of knowing these petty details.'

'*Dubash?*'

'A species of dragoman whose sole reason for being is to walk before his master to make his way smooth. He will take your orders and compel their obedience by the lesser sort, zealously guarding your interests in the matter of transactions of any kind. You may desire him to summon a lime and guava cordial or indeed a bandy drawn by four bullocks and you will never know of the pains involved in their getting.'

Kydd was wise enough in the ways of men to see shoal waters ahead. 'I shall be paying this man for his troubles – but what is to restrain him from adding a modicum above prices or employing all his aunts and cousins at a rate much above the usual run?'

'Your *dubash* is prudent. He will ensure that he finds the best of all things for you so he may bask in your approbation and profit thereby. Besides, a poor character from you will damn him in the eyes of those who follow. You see?'

'It seems rational enough.'

'You may believe it. And here is a way you may test him. You will require to maintain your own palanquin in heat of this order. The going rate for a native to acquire a set of four bearers on field service is each to receive two pagodas a month, the head bearer two pagodas and eleven fanams. What price will you hear?'

'Your advice is gratefully received, Cluffer. I do confess I'm quite ready to see what you've conjured for my lodging. Shall we?'

It was located in an area away from the stench and crowds of the city, blessed with many shady trees and extensive grounds, and was clearly what Pellew had meant by a garden-house. The substantial mansion, circled by the now familiar veranda, had a noble porticoed entrance. The finish of the walls was a fetching white, some sort of sea-shell stucco, which had taken a fine polish.

'Not for you an abode of the vulgar sort, Sir Thomas, that which is here termed a bungalow. This, sir, is a garden-house of the first rank.'

And at the door a motionless figure was waiting.

Dressed in a white gown and embroidered cummerbund the man had on a red turban from which twinkled a substantial precious stone, and he wore upturned scarlet slippers. His ears were pierced with gold earrings, his dark eyes unreadable.

'Sri Rana Bomarjee,' said Rix, gravely. Then, indicating Kydd, he uttered some incomprehensible words, at which Bomarjee gracefully bowed very low, remaining so until Kydd could find some words of greeting.

The man straightened and regarded Kydd with something between respect and dignified reserve. 'I hope indeed I shall possess the honour of serving the worthy sea lord.' His voice was low but with an engaging musicality.

'We shall see, er, Mr Bomarjee.'

Conscious that other still figures were watching in the shadows, Kydd entered the house. The rooms were high-ceilinged and decorated in a warm and colourful Indian elegance. An Oriental fragrance lay on the air.

He was much taken with the prospect but allowed himself

to be conducted through an abundance of rooms and then the garden, with its profusion of strange trees, orange blossoms and winding paths.

Rix was waiting for him in the drawing room, taking his ease in a spacious rattan chair. 'Well, old fellow – will it do?'

If he was to spend years in Madras, then it most certainly would, Kydd decided.

A spirited three-way discussion in Indian and English followed, covering, in excruciating detail, rates and costs, posts and numbers. Mr Bomarjee, it seemed, could be trusted to regulate and supervise within these boundaries and Kydd was not to be troubled by details – until the end-of-month reckonings.

Off-handedly Kydd asked, 'My palanquin. Mr Bomarjee, what would be a good figure for bearers, do you think?'

'Ten pagodas,' was the instant reply.

It was a little less than Rix's figure – Bomarjee was playing it straight, or was it that he knew Rix would catch him out? Either way the man's manner and dignity had earned himself his place. 'I do believe this will answer, Cluffer. What do you think, Edward?' he asked Dillon, who had not spoken a word the whole time, rapt in some sort of reverie.

'Oh, er, much to be esteemed, Sir Thomas,' he stuttered, pulling himself together. 'An *arcadia in urbs*, no less!'

'Do excuse Mr Dillon,' Kydd said with a smile. 'This is his first visit to India, and he seems smitten, I do observe.'

'So?'

'Yes, I will take it.'

'Splendid,' Rix said. 'Then I'll leave you in Sri Bomarjee's hands. He'll get together a domestic staff before the end of the day and you may be assured of residence by nightfall tomorrow.'

Chapter 11

Back in *Tyger* Kydd lost no time in setting out a schedule of existence – aboard and ashore. While at moorings he had every intention of spending time in his garden-house, designed as it was for the enervating heat, unlike his cabin aboard ship, which was close and draining of energy. Bray or the officer-of-the-day could find him quickly, as could a midshipman tasked to make a regular report of proceedings aboard as life in *Tyger* continued its prescribed round.

Caught up in almost childish excitement, the following afternoon he was back at his residence accompanied by Dillon.

'Mr Bomarjee?'

The man appeared as if by magic. 'Captain Sahib?' he said, with a graceful bow.

'How do we progress, pray?'

'Much to do, sir. I'm not satisfy with the cook and his boys, and the punkah-wallahs are not yet ready at post.'

'Punkah-wallahs?'

Mutely he pointed upwards. The long hanging reed slat was motionless, no delightful cooling wafts. Someone had to operate the strings.

'Do carry on, then, Mr Bomarjee. I'll be taking a look around.'

The house was extensive, larger than a mansion in England. Was that because it was single-storeyed? Kydd wondered. There were rooms without count, regions inhabited by frightened maids and surprised housemen in a warren of cubicles and chambers. And recognisably modelled on their English equivalents – a drawing room, dining room, billiard room, each ornamented in the Indian taste, with ceramic elephants bearing ebony trays of colourfully painted baubles and massive mahogany furniture carved with writhing figures.

He stepped outside: the veranda was cool and well provided with rattan chairs and tables, the drifting scent of flowers and spices different at each side, and the garden prospect of blossoms and delicate tree fronds a sensual pleasure.

Kydd was so rapt in wonder and delight that he only heard the insistent calling from the road on a third attempt. It came from a palanquin stopped by his gate. A lace handkerchief was being fluttered by its occupant and Kydd approached.

'I say! It's awfully forward of me, sir, but I'd no idea the Eastwick garden-house had been taken.' It was a woman of his own age, comfortably attired in a cream muslin dress and parasol against the sun. 'Is this now your residence, pray?'

'It is, madam. Do meet Sir Thomas Kydd, captain of *Tyger* 32, new arrived.' He bowed politely.

She made haste to descend and returned a decorous curtsy. 'Mrs Lowther. My residence is close by in Mount Road.'

He noticed that her fashionably pale complexion was untouched by the climate and, with her slim waist and expressive features, she would be admired at any assembly in England. 'A pleasure to make your acquaintance, Mrs Lowther.'

'In like manner!' she replied, with a smile that lit her face fetchingly. 'If you're here to join Admiral Pellew's fleet, you'll be here for some time and it's so tiresome to stand on ceremony.'

Unsure of an implied invitation to further familiarity, Kydd muttered awkwardly, 'Then until we shall meet on another occasion . . .'

'Sir Thomas! You're surely not going to allow shutters to be fitted to the windows?' she said, distracted at some scene behind him.

Kydd turned to see Bomarjee supervising their fastening.

'Why ever not, Mrs Lowther?' he said stiffly.

Her face cleared. 'As is the invariable practice to those who've lived here for an appreciable time, we abandon many of our English ways to make existence here the more comfortable. In this case we hang a weaving of koosa grass, well watered, that the breeze passing through it might make the rooms both cool and delicately scented.'

'I see.'

'It's awfully rude of me, but could you allow me sight of the inside?' she asked. 'It is possible there may be advice and observations I could offer from my closer acquaintance of these parts.'

'Oh, er, if you have time, then any remarks you may have would be kindly received,' Kydd found himself saying.

She rapped an order to the palanquin head bearer and, expressionless, he had the litter taken to the cool shade of a nearby tree.

With another irresistible smile, she entered Kydd's new domain.

'Er, Mr Bomarjee, this is Mrs Lowther come to view our progress.'

Bomarjee stood back, his dark eyes missing nothing. Dillon appeared to be elsewhere.

'You intend the floors to remain uncovered?' she smiled sweetly.

Kydd had an admiration for the highly polished floor, which must have taken a full watch of the hands to bring it to such a lustrous shine.

'It is usual to spread rattan mats. While at home you will go barefoot, I dare to say,' she said, with a modest downward glance, 'and then they will be much the more comfortable. And when you are in a formal way of entertaining, they will protect your fine floor.'

For some reason she hadn't enquired after Kydd's status, probably picking up on the absence of any indications of feminine intervention, he reasoned.

They passed by the master bedroom, but social delicacy did not prevent her from peeping in. The large bed, with a carved four-poster contrivance above, was lighter in wood finish than the rest of the furniture in the house and had joyously coloured carvings. Here, too, there were suggested improvements, including a better way of draping the mosquito net.

Somewhat embarrassed, Kydd ushered her on to other rooms.

In one, Dillon hastily looked up from taking notes, glancing awkwardly at the preposterous ceiling decorations of elephant-headed gods disporting among well-proportioned ladies with a dozen arms.

'Ganesh and company,' Mrs Lowther murmured, after introductions were made. 'It is their conceiving of the beginning of the world and is immeasurably older than our own. I could tell you much of their believing one day, sir.'

The cook and his articles of cuisine apparently passed muster, but then she turned regretfully to Kydd. 'I really must go now, Sir Thomas.'

He, too, was regretful. Rix had left him to purpose his own domestic style but Kydd knew he hadn't the sure touch a woman possessed for the gracious aspects of living – and he'd been taken by her warm, almost intimate manner, which made conversation so easy. And so practical – she and Persephone would get along well together.

She stopped, then cocked her head in a teasing way. 'It does occur to me . . .'

'Oh?'

'Your cook and his boys at this moment are in sad disarray as to placing before you any kind of dinner fit for a gentleman, no doubt not having been to the morning market today. Shall I make a bargain with you, Sir Thomas?'

Before Kydd could reply, she added, 'Well, if I tell my *dubash* to prepare an Indian supper, I could have it brought to us here tonight! In return, my dear sailorman, you shall tell me all you know of the London season and the talk of the town!'

'Here? Um, do you not . . .'

Her face briefly shadowed. 'I am alone at this time, Sir Thomas. It will be no trouble, I assure you.' She brightened. 'I shall be here at seven. Till then. That is, you and your Mr Dillon, is it?'

'Quite,' Kydd answered firmly. As a married lady she had greater freedom than a spinster but there were still reputations to be hazarded in ill-considered encounters. She would almost certainly bring a friend.

She left with a gay wave and Kydd met Dillon's eye. 'A congenial class of neighbour in these parts, dear fellow, don't you think it?'

Chapter 12

Punctually at the appointed time her palanquin emerged out of the dusk, followed by a stream of bearers.

'So kind in you, Mrs Lowther,' Kydd greeted her. As he'd suspected there was another, a Mrs Milne, quiet but impish, who set to with instructions to the bearers, leaving Kydd and Mrs Lowther to take in the garden.

'We're so looking forward to hearing of the old country,' she confided. 'At times it feels a lifetime away.'

It seemed only natural to offer his arm as they walked slowly along.

'It's only a picnic I've brought – I thought it would be rather fun at night.'

A table was set up in the garden at a convenient distance from the veranda and house interior and lanterns were hung. Kydd agreed it was a delightful conceit for the warm evening.

In deference to Dillon and Kydd's untutored palates, the fare was robustly English – game pie, cold ham, a chicken with a most wondrously confected mango chutney. She had even thought to provide wine in the anticipation that Kydd had not had the opportunity to lay in his own.

The conversation was gay and, as promised, Kydd tried his utmost to satisfy the ladies' consuming curiosity in matters of fashion and London gossip, but felt he was sadly lacking in details.

'You've been in India some time, I believe,' he asked Mrs Lowther, after politely deflecting a sartorial question from Mrs Milne that he could not answer.

'Some five years,' she answered quietly.

'Oh? Then what does your husband—'

'I love India. Its mystery and allure, the infinity of its graces and menaces, fascinations and learning. I shall never return to England.'

'Does your—'

'It was India as took my husband from me two years ago.'

'I – I'm so sorry to hear this, Mrs Lowther.'

She gave him a fond look. 'You will quickly find that there is little standing between the living and the dead in this land and it were better to come to an accommodation with it. As no doubt you already have, to achieve so in your profession, Sir Thomas.'

It caught him by surprise, but she touched his arm and continued warmly, 'You are known as a fine sea warrior even here. The newspapers are full of your adventures – and I even read that you are married and live on a small estate in Devonshire. I do hope we shall get to know one another more, don't you?'

'A striking lady, sir,' Dillon said, over coffee at breakfast the following morning. 'And not without interest.'

'That she seems uncommon charmed by India? An odd taking for a woman, I'd have thought.' Kydd did not admit that he had found the lady of more than passing notice. Her warmth and intelligence, animation and inner vitality – and a quality of comeliness . . .

'Shall you see her again?'

'Possibly, but I expect daily a stern summons to duty from the admiral and—'

Bomarjee appeared noiselessly at his elbow with an unsealed note. It was from Rix and asked politely if it were convenient should he visit at eleven with a matter of some consequence.

'Of course he may,' Kydd told his butler, not enquiring as to how the reply would be returned.

When Rix bustled in, he spent little time complimenting Kydd on the rapidly transforming domestic scene and, refusing refreshments, announced, 'Dear fellow, within this day you will receive a most important invitation, one that you will no doubt treasure.'

'Why, that's so kind in you, Cluffer!'

Rix paused, frowning briefly, 'Ah, not from myself, but from the highest.'

'Who, then?'

'It's the custom of the season to welcome in the last of the monsoon fleet with a grand reception given by Neptune's closest cousin on earth, your revered Admiral Pellew, at his great house.'

'Then I will indeed treasure the invitation when it comes.'

'The reception is in your honour – that is, to all the big ships.'

'What we call "rated" vessels,' Kydd responded.

This would exclude naval officers of commander rank and below and, in fact, the honoured guests would consist only of the three newly arrived frigate captains and, of course, Pellew's second-in-command, Rear Admiral Drury. Kydd wondered if it was merely an excuse to have a grand occasion in this far outpost of the empire.

Rix continued importantly, 'Now, I should tell you the guest-list could not be more elevated. The person of the governor of the Presidency of Fort St George – that is to say, Madras – he himself no less will head it, with the commander-in-chief of the Madras Army and the chief justice of the supreme court not far below him.'

'Very well, I shall be sure to turn out in my best rig with—'

'Old fellow. My friend. There is a little matter that, if you take our acquaintance as we formerly agreed, then—'

'You desire to accompany me as my associate, my friend, in order to facilitate the introductions.'

'Nicely put, sir, and that would be the essence – unless, of course, you have another?'

'Not at all, Cluffer.'

Chapter 13

Good-natured applause met Kydd as his carriage stopped in a brilliantly torch-lit driveway. He descended to be greeted at the entrance of Admiralty House by a genial Pellew. Rear Admiral Drury was absent, apparently yet again struck down by sickness.

Avidly the onlookers stared at the handsome sea captain, arrayed in his gold-laced uniform, with the splendour of the star of a knighthood catching the light with a noble gleam as he performed his devoirs to the commander-in-chief.

Bowing to right and left and, despite the cool of the evening setting in, perspiring in his uniform, Kydd entered the high-domed hall.

Rix fell into step beside him. 'A gathering of the first rank, you'll agree,' he murmured. Then, catching sight of his mark, he urged Kydd along to a tall, spare individual with his back to them, chatting with an elderly lady. 'Henry, felicitations of the evening and do meet my good friend,' Rix called urbanely, at a pause in the conversation.

The man turned, an abstemious, flinty-eyed individual, and regarded Kydd carefully.

'Sir Henry, this is Sir Thomas Kydd of *Tyger* frigate new arrived, and therefore our guest. Sir Thomas, this is Sir Henry Gwillim, judge of the Supreme Court of Madras, and his lady.'

Kydd bowed and made reply, then shifted his gaze politely to Sir Henry's wife. 'My first visit to the East Indies,' he offered, 'and already I'm aware I've much to learn of this dominion.'

'You have, sir, you have,' she said fervently.

Rix leaned towards him as they made their way to the next. 'You must know that, despite appearances, the man's a rabid Whig, a radical of the first water. Take care in your dealings with him, m' friend.'

Wryly, Kydd reflected that the gathering was just as it would be in an English soirée of note – despite the heat and closeness the ladies were in elaborate gowns, men in tailcoats and intricately tied linen neckcloths. And there was every indication that dances were to be expected later.

This would be his social scene for some time to come so he followed Rix to be introduced to a William Hope of the East India Company, who, it seemed, was a high luminary in the thrusting mercantile heart of the Presidency, and then it was a Lieutenant General Macdowall, an acid-faced soldier, the commander-in-chief of the Presidency Army, no less.

They exchanged civilities, but Kydd thought he detected a smouldering bitterness for reasons he couldn't guess and was relieved to be extracted and brought forward to the doorway, where a crowd was thickening. With a flourish of trumpets outside, the unmistakable form of the governor of the Presidency of Madras appeared, his lady on his arm, beaming at the assembly.

A cold, unbending figure, he progressed around the room,

Pellew at his side, his features immovable as he acknowledged some, allowed introductions to others.

As he drew nearer, Rix breathed, 'That's him, Sir George Barlow, the highest in the land!' And as an afterthought, he whispered, 'Save the governor general of all India, Lord Minto in Calcutta, of course.'

Pellew caught sight of Kydd and, to the mortification of Rix, greeted him heartily, then made the presentation. Familiar with the majesty of the King of England and his court in the recent past, Kydd was rather less overawed than his new friend, but he bowed amiably. He tried to make converse with the haughty, distant scion of the East India Company but found it heavy going and was relieved when the man moved on.

The evening passed agreeably. Dancing was indeed to be had – Lady Barlow was led out by a handsome lieutenant for the first set and Kydd found himself in no want of partners. If this was how Madras society entertained itself, his time of exile would not be altogether unendurable.

At midnight the banqueting hall was opened, its French windows thrown wide to allow a night breeze to steal in, and, to a pleasant accompaniment by a regimental band, the gathering set to on the hearty English fare: sturdy soups, sirloin of beef, saddle of mutton and no end of lesser delicacies, with startling quantities of chilled champagne.

To his surprise, it seemed that this was but the halfway point. The coolest part of the night would not be wasted, and country dances would go on until four when a second supper would be announced, but quite undone, Kydd made his excuses and left a jovial crew of long-stayers to see in the dawn.

Chapter 14

Tiffin, the following day

'But what did Sir George *say* to you?' Mrs Lowther pressed. Earlier, she had apparently been passing his residence and had invited Kydd to join her table in return for a full account of the evening. For the life of him Kydd could not recall other than that the man had tried to look down his nose at him but found it not possible given Kydd's good three inches' advantage in height.

'Ah, he wished me well in my venturing upon these eastern seas and desired I should take joy in the enchantments to be had in his Presidency.'

'There! And people say he's aloof and prickly!' Her almost child-like glee dimpled her face in such a charming manner, Kydd noticed guiltily.

They were seated alone together, Dillon making his routine call on *Tyger* and Mrs Milne being otherwise engaged. Among the many busy tables there could be no question of impropriety, however, and Kydd assumed a polite attention.

At her insistence he patiently recounted what he could of

those he'd met and, in return, was rewarded with a useful summary of each's failings and attractions. No doubt Rix would later be taking him among them, and these additional insights would be to his advantage.

'So – you have made conquest of the grandest,' she concluded gaily. 'But I can offer you something much more exciting!' Before Kydd could reply, she teased, 'How would you like a ride on an elephant?'

It was soon set in motion. A hulking twelve-foot beast gave a patient rumble from deep within, and its unexpectedly soft brown eyes regarded Kydd placidly as he mounted the steps to the howdah, a lofty box for passengers. His fair companion's clutch on his arm was urgent and excited. Then, with a gentle lurch and sway, the massive creature stepped off at the command of the mahout, one foot behind each ear.

There was only room for the two of them in the giddy heights of the front compartment of the howdah. An umbrella servant perched in the rear held an enormous parasol over them. Dillon, following on another elephant, was entranced as they plodded down forest tracks into the unknown with exotic birds, a snake in a tree, half-glimpsed beasts.

Clutching his arm even tighter, Mrs Lowther confided, wide-eyed, that tigers were known to take and devour unsuspecting travellers along these very paths.

Kydd's palanquin was waiting to take him back, not unlike his boat's crew at the pier, he mused. But at his garden-house, standing coldly behind Bomarjee, was the flag-captain, Haslam. 'You have had a pleasant afternoon, Sir Thomas?' he asked flatly.

This was not a social call by Pellew's senior captain.

'Thank you, yes,' Kydd answered carefully.

'I am to acquaint you with Sir Edward's displeasure, sir. Yesterday he made visit to your ship and found her in a sad state of unreadiness. Subsequently a written order to attend on the commander-in-chief was unable to be delivered on account your whereabouts were unknown, you having neglected to inform your ship of such.'

'Ah, I do apologise for the omission, being unfamiliar with—'

'You are desired to wait upon Sir Edward tomorrow fore-noon at nine with your explanation – without fail, I am instructed to say.'

'I see, yes.'

Chapter 15

'The commander-in-chief will see you now,' Haslam said, with the barest possible courtesy. Kydd had been at Admiralty House since one bell before nine and had been waiting in the anteroom for another after it, something he'd been unaccustomed to as his seniority had advanced. But this man was the naval monarch of all he surveyed, some twelve thousand miles from any superiors, and Kydd was being brought to account.

'Captain Kydd, sir,' Haslam said, then withdrew, closing the door after him.

Pellew did not look up – he was at his desk writing, irritably dashing off the strokes in his bold scribble. At length he finished, sanded the sheet and glanced up sharply. 'You know why you're here, Kydd?'

'I understand there's some misunderstanding concerning your unannounced visit to *Tyger*, sir.' Apparently, it had been a sudden diverting after a scheduled formal call on another frigate, with a rush to man *Tyger*'s side, and the only officer left aboard, Bowden, caught in the wardroom tub. 'I can explain, sir.'

'Explain? I don't want excuses. The fact is your ship was in a lamentable state, unable to face me or the enemy, damn it!'

'I do regret this occurrence extremely, Sir Edward.'

'Then why was my written order to attend returned to me, unable to be delivered for want of intelligence of your situation? Hey?'

His broad rubicund features thrust out accusingly at Kydd. In the navy excuses were never accepted. Reasons only could be proffered. So, it had to be the truth.

'Because I . . . I was riding on an elephant, sir.'

The eyebrows shot up in incredulity and Kydd quailed.

Then Pellew spluttered and his expression dissolved in mirth. 'From anyone else,' he guffawed, 'I'd take it as an insult to the intellects. As it is, I'll accept it from you.' He blew into a large handkerchief. 'Permission to sleep out of ship is a privilege, Kydd. Don't abuse it.'

'Sir.'

'So now we'll have our little talk.'

He rose and went to the wall behind Kydd, who turned his chair to follow.

There was a large map of an area extending from the east coast of Africa to the Pacific, not far off half the planet. With a cane, Pellew drew a square on it, from the Cape at South Africa to the coast of China, and from the vast mass of Asia to the north, to the empty wastes of ocean to the south. 'The East Indies Station. My command. I'll have you in no doubt as to what keeps me awake at night and why you and what stands for my fleet are going to keep the seas until you drop.'

He stabbed the cane at Kydd, and growled, 'Thirty million square miles of trouble and woe. Every species of human threat and twice that from Boreas. And for immense stakes,

66

take it from me. If you believe the Baltic trade is at the top of the list, think again. It's important, I'll grant you, but for sheer weight of treasure, what passes through these waters knocks it into a cocked hat. The India exchange is colossal, but the China trade is set fair to fore-reach on that by a margin.'

Kydd felt his interest quicken. 'Yes, sir. It's not much spoken of, save for the fortunes to be made in these parts.'

'Ha! For my years of exile, I've naught as could be termed a fortune. Only a sea of worry.' He sighed, then looked at him directly, giving a grim smile. 'And now you're to be part of it.'

Sitting down again he continued, in crisp tones, 'The enemy. These you may accept are in their legions. The French, the native princes, privateers, pirates.' He gave a twisted smile. 'And at the bottom of most are the French. Boney has never forgiven us for the quilting we gave him at Acre when he was within a split yarn of gaining his road to India. He knows that all he has to do is establish an army in Egypt – ruled by the Ottomans who are now no friends of ourselves – and he can march across to the Red Sea. If he's the transports ready there, he can be tearing at our flanks in days, no warning.'

'There's seasons the Red Sea's not possible,' Kydd said hesitantly.

'True enough, but there's another route.'

'Sir?'

'Not by sea, which Bonaparte loathes and detests, but by land. Persia.'

Kydd looked back at the map. 'A long way, sir.'

'As never daunted the tyrant. If he cosies up to the Shah, he'll have secret safe passage an' victuals to cross to the Persian Gulf and take ship for our damn near unprotected coast in only a day or two. Or continue on afoot – nothing t' stop him – and he's at our north-west frontier without he ever gets his feet wet and with as large an army as he may. The native princelings will be up in arms all along our north to the Bengal side and I'm sanguine it will then be all finished for us.'

'But India is ours, sir, since General Wellesley returned in triumph only a year or two ago. Why do we fear—'

'India is not ours. We've a patchwork of alliances with the rulers, the nawabs and suchlike breeds, but there's colonists from half the nations of Europe still here. Pondicherry, a few leagues to our south, is a nest of French spies and traitors – and only within the twelve-month have we been able to put down Tranquebar, a Danish colony in thick with the Rajah of Tanjore. And what do we do with Goa?' he demanded, glaring at Kydd.

'I thought that was Portuguese, sir.'

'Quite!' Pellew said triumphantly, as if that answered everything. 'Our allies, but since their Royal Family fled Lisbon for the Brazils, leaving the realm in the hands o' the French, Boney is claiming the Portuguese empire as his own. And then we have the Dutch. Empire in the Malays, all the Spice Islands, Java and so forth. We steer clear around each other at the moment but rumour has it that Bonaparte is going to put another of his brothers on the Hollanders' throne so he can take up the Dutch empire. With it lying square across our passage to China, they're set fair to choke us off entirely.'

'A hard thing to think on, sir,' Kydd said.

'And with a contemptible handful of sail-o'-the-line, I'm expected to put a stop to any and all o' these adventures.'

There was little Kydd could think of that meant anything in the face of these appalling odds. 'You've asked for reinforcement, sir?'

'Ha! Denied, save you three. And if I get wind of an

invasion-fleet action, where do I send for some in a tearing hurry? The Cape at five thousand miles with two old third rates, or Gibraltar at ten thousand with a few more. A rubbish of strategy, sir!'

A turbaned servant entered with a tray of cool drinks and placed it down silently.

Pellew waited for him to leave, then said abruptly, 'As it's nothing to what I face now!'

'Sir?'

'All o' these, they're threats only, may never happen – but, by God, there's things that are taking place right now, and these damn grievous.'

'Stress of weather – hurricanoes?' Kydd ventured.

'Those, too, but, no, dear fellow, worse than that,' Pellew rumbled.

'Worse?'

'Can you conceive of the value of an Indiaman? Bigger by far than any of your usual merchantmen, stuffed with everything from specie to silks in the value of millions – each!'

'I had heard—'

'One taken is a calamity. There's been *four* lost to us in the last twenty months.'

Kydd was staggered. This was far beyond anything he'd been aware of – the East India Company must be reeling, and Lloyd's of London recasting premiums that would be nothing less than punishing.

'It can't be . . . privateers?'

Indiamen were armed like frigates and, while not disciplined in the ways of a warship, had the weight of metal to take on any privateer Kydd had heard of.

'It can and is. We've taken hard blows from Suffren in a previous war, but not so severe as Surcouf in this. A black-hearted villain of St Malo who fits out a fine big ocean

69

privateer he's had especially designed for the eastern seas and sails it here where he sets about our trade. He's returned to France with his plunder but there's another and more taking his place.'

'There must be a base.'

'Île-de-France – a parcel of islands off Madagascar sitting athwart our route to the Cape. And you'll ask it, so I'll tell you now, not to be blockaded with what ships I have – and garrisoned to prevent us taking it.'

'I see.'

'It gets worse. They've sent out frigates to be based there to add to our grief. These range far out – you'll find them anywhere as will put our commerce in peril. So, what's to do? Station my own frigates along the sea lanes or use them as convoy escorts? Send 'em out chasing last reports or in idle siege of Île-de-France?' The worry lines in his face were now marked. 'What say you, Kydd? You're one of the breed. What would you—' He broke off and gave a tired smile. 'No, that's an unfair question. Mine's the burden, not yours.'

Rising, he went to the window and gazed through it for some moments, then swung around. 'You'll sail to find and destroy *Vengeur* privateer, Pierre Rouvier, he who's taken up Surcouf's cause and the greatest menace we face. You have no other task. Clear?'

'Sir.'

'All the intelligence we have on the rogue you'll get from Haslam. I expect you to be gone within three days.'

'Aye aye, sir.'

Returning to his chair Pellew steepled his fingers. 'One last matter. Your first lieutenant has been with you some time?'

'He has, sir.'

'As a premier he's served to your satisfaction?'

'In every way.'

'Good. Then I'll have him. There's a sloop short her commander. He'll do.'

Kydd was thunderstruck. Bray, the man without whom he would never have been able to turn around the mutiny ship *Tyger*, who had—

'Your second. Ready for his step to first?'

Kydd rallied and quickly considered. Bowden. The stammering midshipman who had joined Kydd's first command, who had seen through countless adventures since and turned into the very finest kind of sea officer to be wished for. To be promoted first lieutenant – deputy captain – of a crack frigate was the greatest desire of any officer and Bowden deserved it.

But was he ready? Bray had twice the sea-time and a fierce leadership style, both of which Bowden lacked at present. Quiet, utterly loyal and more than usually intelligent, were these the qualities needed for the post? It had to be said that more to be desired was an aggressive, even merciless prosecution of discipline with an ardour in action that would have men following him without question into whatever tempest or enemy Kydd directed him towards.

He found himself hesitating. He had to do the right thing – not only for Bowden but for *Tyger* and himself as reliant on his first lieutenant. If he ignored his anxieties it could be to pitchfork the man into a situation possibly beyond him and then . . .

'Er, a first-class man but it might be a mite premature to . . .?' A stab of guilt came. Was this to be Bowden's reward for unwavering loyalty – betrayal?

'Very well. I take your word for it, Kydd. I'll find you some other.'

'Thank you, sir.'

It was done. Bowden's chance had vanished, and at his hand.

'Oh, and another thing. I have here a list . . . Where did the damn thing get to? . . . Ah, here.'

He briefly scanned a small sheet of paper. 'It's a demand on you for forty skilled and capable seamen of the qualities set down here.'

'Sir! You mean to press hands out of *Tyger*? I must protest in the strongest—'

'It's the way of things on this station, Kydd. Losses by fever, malice o' the enemy – they've got to be replaced and there's no handy merchantmen for pressing this side of the Cape, only John Company . . .'

'B-but—'

'They'll be going to where they'll do the most good, spread out among the fleet to give backbone. I thank you in advance for your co-operation.' The eyes had grown cold, calculating, and Kydd ground his teeth. A commander-in-chief was well within his rights to even up the manning of his ships, and fresh, seasoned, healthy frigate hands would be an irresistible temptation.

'I'll send them to you within twenty-four hours,' he said woodenly.

'As long as you do. Forty volunteers, turned over,' Pellew said sharply.

'Sir.'

'Well, we can't waste any more time on jawing. I'll bid you good fortune and good hunting. Goodbye, Kydd.'

Chapter 16

'Ship's under sailing orders,' Kydd snapped, as soon as he regained the deck of *Tyger*. Still smouldering with resentment at Pellew's orders, he made for his cabin and threw himself into his favourite armchair.

The list demanded a fair cross-section of valuable hands: topmen, gun-captains, sailmaker and armourer's mates, quartermaster's mate, captains of the top, fo'c'sle hands, prime able seamen. No marines or his most senior petty officers.

There would be no volunteers. He alone had the task and responsibility of choosing those to be torn from their friends and familiar sea world, banished to a random stranger. It was an agonising thing to be forced on him, and what would the chosen men think? That he'd been dissatisfied by their service in *Tyger* or that he simply didn't care for them, that he'd now see them cast out without warning?

And those left. Would they put on airs that they'd been considered superior in some way that they had been retained?

The process of choosing must look and be fair to both. He groaned at the prospect – but his own service before the mast came to the rescue. A glimmer of a way presented itself . . .

The news would get out soon enough. The quicker it was resolved, the better. And, of course, there was the matter of his first lieutenant.

The great cabin was as cool as it was possible to make it, short of anything a punkah-wallah could do. The stern windows were propped open, and cunning work with springs on each of the two anchor cables ensured that the ship was aligned with the sea breeze, which streamed in. And Kydd had graciously granted 'negative coats' for the evening – each of the officers, including himself, was in a lace-edged shirt, their usual finery absent.

The dinner went off in style, his officers knowing that Kydd's news from his visit to the commander-in-chief would be brought out in due course and their future would then be revealed. Good-natured remarks on foreign kickshaws greeted the efforts of the cook to go native, and after the brandy came out, eyes turned expectantly aft to Kydd, who made much of inspecting his glass until all talk had died.

'It's a roving commission,' he told the table.

An immediate happy babble broke out. In one, Kydd's announcement dismissed the prospect of dreary escort to a fleet that went nowhere, with the equally deadening toil of a convoy over long thousands of miles. It meant as well . . . adventure! This was *Tyger's* strongest suit, keeping the seas after some objective that—

'To put down an ocean-going privateer of size,' Kydd continued. 'We sail in three days.'

There were calls to toast the venture, the loudest from the other end of the table where a red-faced Bray was making merry at the prospect.

74

Kydd fell in with the tomfoolery, until suddenly he squinted down the table, as if in doubt of what he was seeing. By degrees the chatter fell away.

'Mr Bray,' he snapped. 'You are out of the rig for this evening. Have you an explanation?'

An icy silence fell as the table struggled with what had just happened. Their ferocious premier, brought up with a round turn in front of everyone. Had their captain been touched by the sun?

'B-but, sir,' the man spluttered, 'you distinctly ordered "negative coats" and I therefore—'

Kydd frowned deeply and rang a small handbell he had concealed.

Tysoe entered, the picture of innocence. 'The first lieutenant seems to have omitted an article of uniform necessary to his station,' Kydd told him. 'Do find one and deliver it to him.'

'Sir.'

After his manservant left, he rounded on Bray. 'Really, this is too much. I expect in my first lieutenant the closest attention to personal appearance. In fact, I believe you to be no longer suited for the post of first lieutenant, sir, and must insist you will not be accompanying *Tyger* on her forthcoming cruise!'

All about the table froze, their eyes averted from one another.

Bray goggled at Kydd.

Tysoe quickly reappeared with a silver chafing dish and cover, which, perfectly expressionless, he set before Bray, who stared at it as if it were about to explode. Then, in a flourish, the cover was whipped off.

There, in impossible glory, was the single gold-laced epaulette of a commander, Royal Navy.

There was an incredulous moment when time hung, then uproar as the implication penetrated.

Dizzy with relief, Bray's face showed first incredulity, then dawning wonder and finally whole-hearted happiness for one who had been lifted and transfigured above all others to rarefied heights.

Kydd let them go until he could make himself heard. 'Gentlemen, I believe we must wet this swab in a bumper at being so long overdue. I give you Captain Bray, as of noon tomorrow commander of *Vulture* 16, sloop-of-war!'

A hearty roar went up as every glass raised and tilted instantly.

'Captain Bray?' Kydd demanded insistently.

For the first time in his long naval career Bray got to his feet in a daze, straightened – and cracked his head on a deck beam.

Amid the laughter he ruefully rubbed it, then did his unlettered best to give vent to his surging feelings. He sat, taking congratulations tinged with envy from all sides. And then came the wondering gaze of those who had seen one snatched from the ranks of mortals to take his place among the gods.

After a decent interval Brice, the junior lieutenant, brought up the question that had been to the forefront of every officer's mind. 'Sir – any indication of, er, who the new first will be?'

It was a vital question. The character of the first lieutenant would affect every man jack aboard. A taut disciplinarian, or easy-going and soft on detail, an incompetent admiral's placeman, or a nervous fool, it would set the tone in everything from cleanliness of living quarters to the elemental pride in one's ship. And, even if he wished to, Kydd could do nothing to interfere with the man's style of leadership.

He raised his eyes, seeing all faces turned his way – and Bowden's pale features looking steadily at him. 'I'm led to understand that one will be appointed from the fleet,' he said.

That could mean anything: that no one in *Tyger* was qualified or suitable, or that Pellew had some young sprig he wanted to advance. Or even that he had obligations that could be satisfied only by an appointment to a first-class frigate over the heads of the incumbents.

Kydd saw Bowden's face set at the news and his heart wrung. His second lieutenant was endeavouring to be reconciled to his fate: in the years to come on the station it was unlikely he would see the opportunity again, short of wholesale death by fever or some such affliction.

And tomorrow he had more sorrows to inflict as he made his choice between the saved and the damned.

Chapter 17

At eight bells the hands mustered as usual but this time they were brought aft to allow Kydd to speak to them informally.

Laying out the situation on station, he told them of the commander-in-chief's demands. He had their attention but then ordered them to fall in by divisions. 'Carry on,' he told the officers in charge, and left the deck.

At each place of muster a little ceremony was performed. It was the same for all – a baize bag normally containing a cat o' nine tails was given to the first. It rattled and chinked with coins of all kinds and nations. A man put in his hand, blindly felt for a coin and gingerly pulled it out to display it. If it was a genuine King George guinea he could keep it – but he was on his way to a different future.

By the midday meal forty men had been selected, paid off and now stood at the gangway, clutching their sea-bags and chests, with no resentment, only grief in their hearts.

For Bray it was a different experience. Kydd loaned him his own barge and, in full dress and sword as befitted a captain about to lay claim to his ship, he put off for the brig-sloop anchored away to southward. When he stepped out of the boat it would be his first time to be piped aboard a man-o'-war – and it would be his own.

As Kydd turned back from a last wave, Bowden came to stand with him. 'A new age for *Tyger*,' he said.

'But still the same ship,' Kydd replied quickly. 'As needs the same attentions.'

Bowden said nothing, staring after Bray, then turned to Kydd. 'It was my lack of sea-time, wasn't it?' he asked, with a slight tremor in his voice.

'Now, old chap, you know better than to ask me what was in the commander-in-chief's mind. What you've got to hold on to is that in the naval service things can change in a brace o' shakes and you might find yourself with what you ask for a mort previous to what you'd want.'

'Yes, sir.'

The reply was low and dejected, and Kydd's heart ached for him but he couldn't show it. 'Well, we have a hill o' work to see to before we can go after this villainous privateer. Are the hands turned to, pray?'

Kydd was annoyed that the new first lieutenant had not seen fit to show his face, even with *Tyger* under sailing orders. A small confidential pack had been sent by Pellew's office early in the morning and he knew the man's name was Farrant, transferred from the post of second lieutenant in *Culloden* 74. The flagship – did this mean anything?

Irrespective, there was a grievous amount of work to do for the ship to be at sea on time, and Farrant had to get to grips with the vital watch and station bill now *Tyger* was forty men short. He would give him until—

'Captain, sir.' Brice stood at the cabin door, with an odd

79

expression. 'Er, L'tenant Farrant joining.' He gave way for another, who diffidently held back until invited in directly.

'Sir. L'tenant Farrant joining per orders.' He was older than Bray by some ten years, and greying, but his manner seemed warm and affable.

'I'd expected you earlier, sir. We sail in a couple of days.'

The man's smile was engagingly lopsided. 'I do so apologise. It was disgraceful of me, I know, but they did insist on a full hand-over.'

'If you'd been here quicker you'd have had for yourself a fine hand-over from our own previous premier.'

'My very thought, sir, but in the event I was overborne.'

Kydd bit back his reply, stood up and went around the desk to shake the man's hand. It was enthusiastically returned.

He gestured to a chair. 'Do sit down and tell me something of your service, Mr Farrant.'

It was varied, as was to be expected with a man of his evident age. '*Lyra* frigate as third in the North Sea, three hard years off Brest in *Terpsichore*, and *Medea* ship-sloop in the Caribbean before joining *Culloden* as fifth lieutenant for the East India Squadron.'

'So you were with Admiral Pellew since—'

'Since he raised his flag here in the year five, since advanced to second luff.'

'Well, *Tyger* has had her share of capers in that time. You may have heard of some.' He let it hang, expecting remarks of respect and commitment.

'Sir, you may suppose they leave me in awe. I do hope I can measure up.' It was hardly a full-hearted assurance and, with lines of care suddenly appearing on Farrant's face, it smacked of anxiety.

Kydd chose to ignore it, however. 'We'll continue our talk later, Mr Farrant. I now require you to attend on your duties

– the first of which is to present me before the forenoon watch closes up tomorrow a complete watch-bill as allows us to sail in two days. Good day to you.'

There had been no need to be short with the man, Kydd admitted, after he'd left, but there was something about his attitude that niggled. Still, it would seem he'd fit well into *Tyger*'s close-knit gunroom and that was the first vital hurdle.

Chapter 18

Admiralty House

Haslam was cynical about Kydd's privateer prey. The ship – *Vengeur*, full-rigged and eighteen guns, reputedly copper-bottomed and of fabled speed, like Surcouf's *Revenant* – had been personally designed by Rouvier, her captain, for the rich hunting of the East Indies. Well-armed, considerably bigger than the privateers infesting the English Channel, nevertheless there was no question that *Tyger* would prevail if met in a straight match at sea.

Its movements were erratic to the point of meaninglessness. Or was it that if a prize was taken off Calcutta in the Bay of Bengal, it would be sailed several thousand miles to the privateer base at Île-de-France for condemning as lawful prize? With no cause for alarm until it was reported not to have arrived at its destination – in most cases after months' delay – no pattern of captures could be established.

On three occasions it had been thwarted of its prey by the opportune arrival on the scene of a warship, but its legendary fleetness had ensured an easy escape with no clue left to betray its lurking place. Once it had apparently been seen off the entrance to the Hooghly river and again off Madras Roads some days later.

Kydd had no clue what to make of this mix of the unworkable and implausible. His orders were to find and destroy *Vengeur*. How he did it was his business, but he hadn't the first idea where to start.

Haslam saw him off with a sardonic smile that made Kydd boil – if it took for ever, he'd track down the cunning Rouvier and his phantom privateer and put paid to his marauding.

Kydd slowly paced the quarterdeck. *Tyger* was shaping up for her cruise, stores inboard and boatswain's men well exercised in fettling the rigging to perfection. With their objective now common knowledge, it would go hard for any who neglected the tiniest advantage.

Farrant was out of sight, almost certainly in his cabin and at work. Not only had he to deal with the considerable reduction in the ship's company but, when considering any redistribution, he had to find out the strengths and weaknesses he was dealing with to get a usable structure in place on time.

Kydd went below to be met by Tysoe, who quietly produced a note. It was in a woman's hand, from Mrs Lowther, but signed 'Caroline' and inviting him to an evening with friends at some temple or other. Kydd quickly penned a noncommittal 'much regret unable' and sent it ashore. There was more on his mind now, however pleasant the prospect.

Another came from Rix, promising a bracing night with some well-placed John Company functionaries and he was sent a similar note. Time for that kind of thing later, after Rouvier had been dealt his just deserts.

*   *   *

Kydd felt *Tyger* jib to her anchor and heard lines from aloft slap fretfully against masts – a squall had touched them. The heat was stifling and he was about to open the skylight, with all its unwelcome din from topside, when the monsoon rains arrived, a tropical deluge of appalling dimensions. The beating on the deck above created a booming roar, as if he was trapped in a drum.

It was impossible to work yet he had to or *Tyger* would be putting to sea with no course concluded for which to lay her bowsprit.

He held his head in his hands. Essentially, the best hunting was deep into the Bay of Bengal, covering the traffic making for the Sandheads and Calcutta, as well as the China trade heading south-west through the same waters. It was an assumption too glib for Kydd. And it was where the majority of the smaller men-o'-war were patrolling the sea lanes. But if not there, where was the prey?

He tried to shut his ears to the drumming roar. If they had any sense the merchantmen would quickly fan out into the empty ocean to hide themselves, quit the usual shipping routes and make a wide offing until they'd passed Île-de-France. Yet this was no guarantee. The privateer could select a latitude that would slice through every southward track, however scattered, then simply cruise along it until a victim crossed it near him and, with his superior speed, the ship was doomed.

So where did that leave *Tyger*? Not much further forward in the—

A tentative knock sounded, then a little louder, as if in doubt that it could have been heard against the solid roar of the monsoon.

'Come!'

It was Farrant, carrying a sheaf of well scratched-out

papers, a doleful look on his face. 'It won't fadge, Sir Thomas.'

'What are you saying, sir?' demanded Kydd, irritably.

'I've tried hard, but forty men shy is too big a hole to fill. We can have only one side of guns in use at any time, but when it comes to sail trimming in action there's too many away to allow the serving of a gun. Given I'm to estimate a one in ten casualty and sickness rate then—'

'Damn it all!' Kydd snarled, unable to contain his temper at yet another burden laid on him. 'This is your job, fair an' square! If you can't do it . . .'

The man's face set and he mutely held out the papers.

Kydd took them, ashamed at his lack of control. After a quick scan, then a sample or two to verify, he could see the problem. It took measurable time for seamen detailed to race from the guns to the upper deck, then up the shrouds and out on the yards, take in a reef, then back to the deck and to the right gun. If the gun-crew was too weakened in the meantime to run it in or out the result was a silent and defenceless ship at the height of an action.

He gave an apologetic grin. 'I take your point, Mr Farrant. Shall we see what we can do?'

There were the old tricks: gun-captains to tail on to the side-tackles instead of standing back, shot numbers to carry the ball all the way from the garlands instead of passing it from hand to hand, gun-tackle teams to serve the next gun alternately – but Farrant had put most of these into play. Kydd's respect for the man rose but it did nothing for the situation.

A frigate had no spare men at hand, her complement lean and precise to the task. Every man short left a void in her workings. It had to be faced: there was no easy solution to *Tyger*'s woes.

Except . . . something he had not had to do for years: turn out the press-gang.

It was laughable to imagine a loping press with cutlasses and ropes' ends in Madras city, for there were no taverns, dockyards or sailors' cunny burrows reliably placed to drag unwilling volunteers for His Majesty. This left a hateful resource: the raiding of merchant shipping.

Any East India Company vessel was protected from the press-gang by law but, at the same time, the John Company monopoly of trading past the Cape meant that there were no other British ships to board, so . . .

At daybreak *Tyger* readied for sea but not in the usual way. In the widening dawn of the Madras Roads boats put off from her, stretching out in all directions. In a remarkably short time they returned and, without delay, the frigate set sail, making for the open sea and leaving behind an uproar of protest.

Dejected seamen of every nationality and quality stood on her deck, looking back on the fast-receding anchorage and their recent snug berths.

Kydd had pressed what he could out of East India Company vessels. He had until *Tyger* got back to think of an excuse and for the furore to die down, while he got on with his hunt.

Kydd's plan was hazy and tentative. The richest grounds for a privateer were undoubtedly on the eastern side of India, the track taken by the Indiamen, and therefore he would not bother with the other, the western side. Sailing directly north, however, he would get there by a different route outside the usual sea lanes: more than a few merchantmen would be laying the land close by, with the idea that if they sighted Rouvier they could make a dash for the safety of the nearest harbour. Kydd suspected that Rouvier would conclude this for himself and lie in wait even closer, his full-rig at a distance resembling one of the navy's own inshore patrols.

It was a long shot, but it was something useful to do in the near thousand-mile passage to the head of the Bay of Bengal, and there was no need for haste as no one had any idea of where the privateer would strike next. And it was just what was needed to shake down *Tyger*'s new men, even now by the mainmast in the process of being rated.

Kydd left them to it and went below.

Farrant reported later that afternoon as the intense green strip of the low Coromandel Coast slipped by to larboard.

'How are we placed now?' Kydd wanted to know.

'A mite better, sir.'

'Oh? With twenty-eight good men taken off and added to our muster-roll?' Kydd said, with some heat. Such a haul was better than he'd hoped and, if Brice had chosen well, would go far in restoring their war-like standing.

'They were Company hands,' Farrant replied, injured.

'Meaning?'

'Why, in these waters they're your usual sorry crew, sir, from every nation that has a ship a-swim, doesn't have the English and can't serve a gun. And lascars – fine men at a sailmaker's needle or tailing on to a fall but run away to skulk every time action's joined.'

'Then why the devil did Brice come back with such?' Kydd said, with a rush of annoyance. 'You've been on station for years. Why didn't you warn him?'

Farrant drew a breath, then said tightly, 'As it was your notion to press out of John Company, I supposed you to know what was to be expected.'

Kydd held his temper and said, with a sigh, 'Well, do what you can with 'em. I want one side of guns at least in continuous fire.'

'I'll do my best, sir.'

Chapter 19

By the time *Tyger* had reached where the distant rumpled blue of the Eastern Ghats turned verdant, the picture had grown clearer.

There were indeed merchant masters who had chosen to take the inshore route, but sightings were very few. It seemed that a wider swing out to the east, then south, was the more favoured, and Kydd sympathised with their decision to take advantage of the vastness of the ocean to slip away.

There was nothing to be gained if he abandoned his inshore sweep now for the most direct course for Calcutta, and the head of the Bay of Bengal was the same direction – northeast. *Tyger* streamed on through monsoonal torrents and drying heat on her near-hopeless quest.

Impatiently, Kydd paced up and down, trying not to notice the ragged, slipshod figures, the surly looks and slouched airs – anything but the proud agility of a King's man, one of the legendary *Tyger*'s ship's company.

And after exercises on the gundeck Bowden told him how

the pressed men, with prime seamen away aloft, had proved themselves poor creatures, hopeless at the tight discipline of fighting a gun.

It was as well that there was time before they met the big privateer in battle.

Farrant had settled in quickly. As Kydd had suspected, his easy manner charmed the officers in the gunroom and, so far, his competence professionally was all he could expect. Yet there was something that didn't chime with his own idea of what a first lieutenant should be.

He watched the man take charge of the gun-deck for exercises – and saw what it was. With Brice at the forward guns, Bowden at the after, he was giving his orders. They were correct and well timed, but they were directed at the officers. In effect he was expecting them to carry through the required motions for him. His voice was pleasant and clear but where was the bite?

In his place Bray would be bellowing in a fury, lashing men and officers to frantically greater efforts, wringing everything from the gun-crews. Farrant was getting results, but his quiet, even gentlemanly manner was being followed by the officers and in turn by the petty officers, who likewise eased their attitude and voices to their men.

Was it his age? At a stage of life when for many a fireside and children beckoned, was he up to the job? He'd been evasive when Kydd had questioned him about how he'd been able to secure the post. Had Pellew been casting about at short notice and settled on one who would perform adequately but only under the eye of a strong figure? If that was the case he was not the kind of man needed in a frigate of the first ranking and, given the commander-in-chief's back-ground, a surprising choice.

Tyger sailed on and soon after sighted a sloop, brig-rigged, which altered course immediately to close with them.

With every curious eye on deck, the vessel was soon wallowing alongside, her blue ensign worn and ragged but nobly aloft. As her captain approached in a pinnace, Kydd took in the sight of the little warship. Compared to her sisters in the Channel, *Eaglet* was an ill-looking craft. Piebald canvas patched and mended, lines everywhere hairy with use, side timbers not bright with varnish, like *Tyger*'s, but bare and grey, streaked with tar. This was a ship that had seen long and punishing service in a climate that was exacting a brutal cost on intruders. And, with a lurch of the heart, Kydd realised that possibly *Tyger*, in the fierce sun and monsoonal cataracts, would come to look much like *Eaglet*.

Her captain, Russell, was a prematurely weathered young man and Kydd asked him how long he'd been at sea.

'Only the season, sir.'

Kydd was surprised but remembered there was no naval dockyard anywhere east of the Cape. Russell explained that Pellew was at the mercy of the Honourable East India Company, which owned the only dockyard of size, in Bombay, and his ships had to take their turn to be repaired under private contract. His funding from the Admiralty was woefully in arrears and he'd had to resort to making charge for convoy escort and patrol duties on the pretext of providing a service to the Company, refundable against the use of dockyard facilities.

Not only this but naval stores – rope, canvas, mast timber, tar, paint – were not in regular supply. In fact, the stores *Tyger* had brought from England had been eagerly snatched up and quickly distributed to the needy of the fleet, the first for some time.

It seemed that in Indian waters the navy was a resented

interloper, and if its ships were to keep the seas for extended periods, it had to be by its own efforts, frugally husbanding gear and repairing spars, ironwork and timbers with what resources the ships alone could muster in their distant stations.

'Captain,' Kydd continued, extracting a shy smile from the junior commander, 'some further questions, if I may.'

Yes, he had heard of the privateer Rouvier and his instructions were to prioritise his extermination, a hard thing for a twelve-gun brig with only six-pounders. And he had seen *Vengeur* earlier in his patrol. There had been two vessels five miles distant, one clearly in pursuit of the other. He knew that, so close to the head of the Gulf, it could have only one meaning and had clapped on every sail to close with the pair.

His action was enough to discourage the chase but, as the privateer put down her helm in retreat, it had had the impudence to pass *Eaglet* close on the opposite tack, giving Russell a close view of a be-sashed giant on its quarterdeck and a deck-line crowded with a disquieting number of jeering men.

He'd seen that the vessel's condition was remarkably good, with fresh ropery, paintwork, and canvas that was taut and new. As it heeled with the waves its copper bottom was revealed, beautifully clean and smooth to add knots to a cruiser that, very obviously, had been crafted for speed. He also noted that *Vengeur* was of a size, with rows of guns that had to be at least nine- or even twelve-pounders, the armament of a light frigate.

Russell had had his command instantly on the chase but wondered why the big privateer had not turned on his little brig and crushed it. Kydd explained that it was not the business of a private man-o'-war to take on a warship and risk damage that would cut short its cruise.

Rouvier had hauled his wind and was quickly away on a

broad reach deep into the empty ocean, leaving *Eaglet* to wallow after it, hopelessly far astern.

This was clearly a dangerous and challenging opponent.

It was a long shot but Kydd asked, 'Tell me if you can, Captain. Have we got any idea where he's seized his prizes?'

'That's what I asked the Calcutta office when I got this commission,' Russell said thoughtfully. 'And while they can't say at what point Rouvier made his captures at least they can say what course the ship was following at the time – close inshore, far out to the east and so on, because they share this with each other so they don't bunch up in going south. Rouvier likes the world to know what a fine figure of a corsair he is and freely admits to the names of the prizes he's sent in for condemning, so we know from their courses roughly at what point they were snared.'

'Any pattern?' Kydd asked hopefully.

'No, sir. Allowing he's running down a line of latitude to intercept 'em it makes no sense. Some taken in the west, others way in the east – but some quite the same time. I've a list here.'

Kydd grimaced. Even granting a wide range of times for the seizures, the man couldn't be in two places simultaneously. 'Well, I thank you for your time,' he said. 'Do crack on, sir, as shall I.'

Just where to he didn't say, for at this point he didn't know. One thing was plain. *Tyger* couldn't simply plough the seas aimlessly in the hope that she would chance on *Vengeur* somewhere in the thousands of miles of open ocean – or was that the only way left open to him?

The two vessels parted, one to continue her ceaseless watch and guard over the approaches to Calcutta and the other in a vague crossing of the waters of the Bengal coast. Past this the land changed drastically. Into the true head of the Bay of Bengal the many mouths of the Ganges issued through the tiger-haunted Sundarbans mangroves. Further on, there was nothing but the rugged, jungle-shrouded mystery of Burma.

Not the place to be looking for a hungry ocean-privateer on the prowl.

Kydd could do no more than turn around and head south again, this time along the sea-lane favoured by the China trade in its last run from the Malacca Strait before the haven of Calcutta. It would be a slow, laborious haul against the last of the monsoon, the heat in the light winds a trial.

Chapter 20

D ays passed. But then one early morning everything changed in an instant. From out of the haze that blended sea and sky at the horizon the blue-grey silhouette of a full-rigged ship firmed, crossing their bows some five miles ahead. Even as they trained their telescopes it fell off the wind and headed towards them.

Kydd hesitated only for a moment. 'Helm down hard! We're a-fly away from the beggar!'

Tyger paid off quickly, rotating until she, too, was heading downwind.

'Clear the decks! Mr Farrant, I want no more than eight men on deck at any time, the rest below out of sight.'

If this wasn't *Vengeur* no harm was done, but if it was . . .

The other ship threw out all sail possible, lunging towards them – it had to be the privateer. Kydd's gamble had paid off. From a distance, and even fairly close, a frigate resembled an Indiaman: the same size, a continuous deck fore and aft, and a line of gun-ports the whole length. And *Tyger* was as yet unknown on the coast.

'Douse the colours, and strike the commissioning pennant.'

The ensign, the long, sinuous pennant that designated *Tyger* a man-o'-war on the King's service, was whipped down from the main masthead where it had been since Kydd had read himself in, leaving a bare truck.

To the privateer a priceless catch was now in its grasp and the chase was on.

With its superior speed *Vengeur* would overhaul the frigate – but at some point *Tyger* would suddenly wheel round, deliver an annihilating broadside and end the fight before it began. Kydd began sending men to the guns in readiness.

In a show of feigned panic, the few men aloft let fly a line that had the fore topsail in a fit of sad flapping, while *Tyger*'s course was urgently shaped towards the north in a hopeless bid for the safety of the patrol line.

Kydd took out his pocket telescope and trained it on the privateer. As Russell had described, the copper at her forefoot was clean and bright, the ship's sides a deep black and, in a show to gladden the heart of any boatswain, the ratlines in the shrouds taut and straight, not curved in slackness.

'Mr Farrant reports all at quarters, sir.'

'Thank 'ee, younker,' Kydd said, with a wink to the wide-eyed midshipman. It was now entirely his call, a balance between what he knew to be *Tyger*'s tightest turn into the wind and the point where *Vengeur* would be inside the circle – the privateer was fast reaching it.

'Tell him to stand by,' he warned, eyeing it carefully. At any moment—

It caught him unawares. On board the onrushing ship there was sudden general movement about her decks and, in a spectacular swash of white at her bows, *Vengeur* slewed to starboard and off close to the wind.

'She's smoked us!' choked Kydd, in a fury. Some sharp-eyed

96

seaman in the privateer had seen a betraying feature that had given the game away and Rouvier had retreated instantly.

'All hands on deck – bring her about in chase!'

It was infuriating. They had come upon *Vengeur* at last, had been within a whisker of settling her account, only to have it cruelly snatched away.

Tyger came round smartly, but by now the privateer was a good mile off and making speed south. Light airs did not bring out the best in *Tyger* and soon all that could be seen of *Vengeur* were her topsails. It would be no use to note down her course to escape – without question, Rouvier would fall back on her true heading once out of sight.

'After him, sir?' Farrant asked.

'No!' Kydd snapped, irritated at the man's lack of under-standing and not inclined to enlighten him. In a black mood he went below again and slumped into his chair.

There was *Vengeur*, somewhere over the horizon but now on her way to who knew where. Thirty million square miles of ocean wastes made the perfect area in which to hide, and while it remained at large, every ship was under threat. If they came across Rouvier again, it was near certain that *Tyger* would triumph in a clash at arms but it would never come to pass: the canny privateer captain would again simply decline an engagement, spread sail and disappear.

An image of the trim ship came back to haunt him: the scrupulously maintained hull, fittings and rigging, as if it had just left a dockyard. After all the three thousand miles from Île-de-France? The same distance as from Plymouth Sound to Africa's Congo river? And then a flog back over the same distance to resume the marauding?

A ship in such superb condition after that length of voyage was a conundrum. But then something dawned on him. He rummaged in his pocket for Russell's list of estimated capture positions. As before they made no real sense, but he was now looking for a vital clue – and he found it.

'Ask Mr Joyce to step below,' he told the sentry, perspiring but stolidly at his post outside the cabin door.

He heard the sailing master stump laboriously down the hatchway, not yet entirely the master of his wooden leg on ladders. 'Ah, Mr Joyce,' he said. The man was red-faced with effort in the heat but nevertheless reported cheerily.

'What can I do f'r you, sir?'

Kydd passed him the list of seizure positions and waited while he took in the scatter of latitude-longitudes. 'This is roughly where we think our privateer friend took his prizes. What does it mean to you, old fellow?'

Joyce frowned in concentration, then responded, 'Why, sir, it's a-saying the villain's going main fast, that I can swear to. Near as fast as that there three-masted lugger we once ran chase on in the old *Stoat* cutter, when was it—'

'Anything else?'

'Um, they's all this side o' India?'

'There's something else.'

'Sir?'

'The first one captured early in the year, the latest only last month, and mark all the rest that lie in between. It's saying . . .?'

'I catch y'r point, sir. That's ten months in these waters. It just ain't possible, pardon m' words, sir. What ship made o' man can keep the seas for that long without it puts back for a docking and storing?'

'Quite so, Mr Joyce. Recollect how spry the creature looked when it escaped us. There's only one thing can explain all this.'

'Aye, sir. He's somewhere to go as will see him fettled and

stored without he needs to beat back to Île-de-France. A hideaway o' sorts.'

'As I thought, too. So you and I are going to ferret it out and then we'll take the beggar in his lair. Do fetch your charts and pilots and we'll work on it.'

The sailing master was apologetic when he returned. 'As best as I could find in Madras, sir, which is not saying much. Only gen'ral cover of the Eastern Seas from the Admiralty, and John Company stays with its comfortable routes, which, in any case, it's not inclined to share with others. An' I have one or two scraps from olden times as can't be relied on.'

'It'll have to do. Now let's see . . .'

Very quickly it became clear that the problem was all but impossible.

The entire length of the east of India from Ceylon to Calcutta was now in British hands. There were a few known past foreign colonial outposts but they were watched. East from Calcutta were the mangrove forests and maze of river mouths reaching to Burma, a country not in any way sympathetic to the French and very unlikely to tolerate a hostile outpost. Further south was the Malacca Strait, with its native princes and ancient colonies, not a place where it was possible to keep out of sight for long.

Islands? There were many in the Indian seas but, for Rouvier, all suffered from one crippling disadvantage: at one time or another each had been settled by Britain or her friends.

Uninhabited offshore islands? Countless numbers up and down the coast were marked on the chart as navigational hazards and it would be impossible to visit each one. They had to find one that either had a dockyard or had protected inland waters.

Kydd and the master pored over the charts, but it was hopeless. It seemed the chart makers had had no reliable knowledge or even interest in such details.

'Mr Joyce, you said you had some old Dutchy charts?'

'I have, aye, sir, but they's forty years old if they's a day.'

They were certainly of a past age: loxodrome stars liberally provided in place of the modern latitude-longitude grid but with a valuable feature – the Dutch, in their traditional rivalry with the British, had marked each island as to its national claims and, even more useful, each place worthy of a fortification or European establishment.

'So – we compare these to our current charts and see what we're missing.'

It was tedious work, but an interesting possibility began to emerge. The narrow archipelago of the Andaman and Nicobar islands was of equal distance from Calcutta and Madras. And on the old chart there were several locations with stylised forts and buildings, the word 'verlaten' under each penned in a different hand. A comparison with the more recent charts showed no trace of any remaining.

Dillon was brought in, his hair tousled – in the heat he'd taken to sleeping off his dinner for an hour in a hammock under the quarterdeck awning.

'What's this word mean?' Kydd asked.

'Um, that means "abandoned", sir.'

Kydd's interest grew. 'So these Danish, Austrian, all of 'em have given up. I wonder why.'

With a flourish Joyce produced a thick book. 'It'll be here in my Elmore, count on't sir.'

Kydd took it: *The British Mariner's Directory and Guide to the Trade and Navigation of the Indian and China Seas of the year 1802.* There was a mention of the Andamans, but only a little, warning that they should be avoided at all costs on account of the fierce savages who inhabited them and were known to massacre unwary watering parties down to the last man. An aside advised that, in the case of a westerly hurricane, shelter could sometimes be found within the enclosed waters of Port Blair – and that bearings to clear could be taken on the buildings of the abandoned British settlement that apparently still stood.

'No reasons there. And nothing on our charts of today, damn it.'

'I've my Johnson,' Dillon murmured absently, and at Kydd's look continued hastily, 'a traveller in these parts with most laudable habits of observation. His descriptions are always accompanied by explanation and—'

'Read it now and come back with an answer!' Kydd growled. While his secretary was gone, he continued to examine minutely what charts they had.

Dillon returned with a broad grin. 'All the settlements failed because of the lack of natural products to export and, with the usual tropical diseases and ferocious tribes, were not worth maintaining.' He paused significantly. 'The British were different. Their interest was to establish a penal settlement to serve India and this they built in 1789, with provision for its support.'

'Then why the devil isn't it listed in our holdings?'

'Because we abandoned it a dozen years ago. Too much mortality in the prisoners and the administration complained bitterly of its remoteness and danger from savages.'

In rising excitement, Kydd demanded, 'Any mention of a slipyard, careening, ship-working or similar?'

'Since you ask it, yes,' Dillon said, now with the somewhat smug expression of the one to bring in the answer.

'By God, I think we have it!' Kydd said. 'Rouvier has a prime lair, shunned and abandoned by all, which he keeps up with stores and privateering gear as will see him in good sea-keeping for months!' He gave a rueful smile. 'And it's all courtesy the British government as built so well, then cast it back to the jungle. Let's not lose a moment – a course to the Andamans, Mr Joyce.'

Chapter 21

The dying south-west monsoon gave no trouble in the passage south, fading to a lazy breeze and veering more northerly to provide a fair slant to the remote archipelago, five hundred miles from the nearest land.

For days they sailed on, at times the wafting winds sweltering, at others whipping squalls cooled with fractious cross winds. Occasionally, full-force monsoonal storms drummed down on the listless ship in a deafening roar, the water flooding overside through the scuppers, like a mill-race.

And then one morning they sighted the Andamans as a darker blue against a bright, hazy horizon.

The chart Kydd used was one of the master's old Dutch ones and gave enough detail to plot an approach. The settlement of Port Blair was to the southern end of the north island, within a complex of inland waters, and the little slip-yard was well inside and out of sight.

A short time later he laid it all before his officers.

'If he's not at home, we harry and raze his base, tell him he's found out. After that he's like any other privateer who can be chased down. If he's inside, we settle the cork in the bottle and put him to the finish. If he's leaving or entering, we go after him and, whatever the consequence, come back later and tear down his lair. Questions?'

The cabin was hot and stuffy, the wind on the bow bypassing the stern windows, and Kydd was not in the mood for a long discussion.

'One, sir.'

'Mr Bowden?'

'The chart shows a fine and capacious harbour. But with only one entrance – to the east and a bare half-mile across. If we enter to confront Rouvier, it doesn't take the wind to shift much to go foul and we'd be trapped. Should we not heave to clear of the entrance and instead send in the boats?'

'If Rouvier is waiting, he'll cannonade the boats out of the water,' Kydd grunted. 'Whatever the weather we go in. If the wind shifts after we destroy him in *Tyger* we stay at anchor there until the breeze is kind to us. No other possibility.'

It couldn't be a more satisfying situation – his quarry cornered in an undefended harbour with no escape and beyond a doubt only one outcome to be expected.

If he was right in his reasoning.

If Rouvier was undergoing refit.

If the wind was anywhere but in the west, which would be foul for entering.

If . . .

'Ship to quarters, Mr Farrant. We enter Port Blair as soon as it's abeam.'

His usual practice was to have a gathering of his officers before an engagement to let them know his thinking and go openly over his plans to throw up any unforeseen impediments. Both had been met, and there was no point in delaying further.

Nearer to, the island chain came into sharper view.

Set in a glittering emerald sea they were thickly covered with tropical vegetation down to the water's edge where they were fringed with long stretches of glistening white beaches. Many were jagged and volcanic-shaped, rearing out of the sea, some darkly verdant, others bare red-brown monoliths. A strange blend of unravished nature and, without a solitary lighthouse or beacon, a two-hundred-mile navigational menace to be avoided by any prudent mariner.

The islets grew ever more irregular, thrusting conical megaliths with splashes of intense red beaches and others small enough that individual palm trees could be made out along them.

'We're t' sight Ross Island as sports a fort, to larboard a mile of North Point with a similar. This is our entrance, sir.' Joyce had his Elmore out, squinting at it in the full glare of the sun now that the quarterdeck awning had been struck in anticipation of action.

Tension mounted. It was difficult to distinguish any difference in the islands, let alone spot an abandoned fort overgrown with vegetation. The thought of sailing past in ignorance, allowing *Vengeur* to be warned and slip away, was too much to contemplate.

Joyce stumped below, returning in a few minutes with a rough sketch. 'It's the pattern of 'em,' he explained. 'If you takes a line o' bearing when North Point closes on the next up the coast, why, then Ross Island bears here, in a mile is Perseverance Point, with Chatham Island a couple o' miles in deeper still.'

Kydd remembered the chart. As each headland fell astern it would eventually line up with the next. If this made the right compass heading – north-north-east – the existence and bearing of the other marks would be promptly checked, and if they fell in with Joyce's workings, they had arrived.

The breeze was hot and fitful and, while it had veered further to the north, it was still a chancy thing.

It was almost an anticlimax when just such an alignment unfolded: the outer headland, North Point, and the guardian outpost, Ross Island, framing the passage into an extensive body of water with what was presumably Chatham Island at its further reaches.

'Shorten to topsails,' Kydd ordered, then had the helm put over and they headed in. 'Take us within two cables of this Ross Island.'

Well before they made the distance several sharp eyes saw the pale-grey of stone walls nearly overgrown with hanging jungle foliage. A fort – and the same on North Point.

It was Port Blair and they were squarely across its entranceway.

'Stand to the guns, Mr Farrant.'

Tyger glided in, the well-indented jungle shore pressing in on both sides. Officers, lookouts, men at the guns peered out for any sign of human activity but other than the occasional ruin smothered in verdure there was nothing.

It was past noon and the baking sun bore down. There was no sound from the breathless, echoing stillness of the lagoon-like inlet, just the distant harsh cry of a tropical bird, punctuated by the familiar creaks and rattles of a ship ghosting under sail.

All too soon the end of the inlet was approaching. Chatham Island off the southern shoreline marked the end of the deeper water – the chart showed a sharp turn to the left where, out of sight, the navigable waters petered out in a last few hundred yards.

'Doesn't seem as if he's in this place,' Farrant said mournfully, wiping his brow.

Kydd kept his temper. It was obvious there was nothing

here, and they'd passed at least two places with shelving beaches that would have been ideal for careening. There was no need to draw attention to their failure.

The end of the inlet was coming up, a straggling mud-flat ending in mangroves but with a handy stretch of water before it, with sufficient room for their turn-about and retreat to the open sea. 'We wear about there,' he said wearily.

But as they came up to the place he indicated, Brice gave a low growl. 'Not as if we haven't company!'

As they passed a hard coral point, first a dozen, then fifty or more natives emerged from the undergrowth to stand gazing at the frigate as it slowed for the turn, hefting their spears, clubs and bows.

Nobody spoke at the sight of the barbarous savages known to slaughter any who intruded into their territory.

'Hands to go about – and look lively, or those blaggards'll be picking at your bones by sundown!'

Then two things happened simultaneously. With a gentle slowing, *Tyger* came to a stop, her sails still drawing in the light breeze. Incredulous, Kydd tried to work out what had happened and hurried to the ship's side. A brownish-grey discolouring was slowly subsiding to starboard. They had run aground on a mud-flat of sorts where the chart had shown clear water.

Joyce let out an old-fashioned curse. 'Dutchy chart – they've got the Ranger Flat shoal in the wrong place!'

'Get the sail off her!' Kydd barked, and the men leaped to obey.

Ashore a growling murmur swelled to a dangerous roar as the natives saw their plight, parting to let their deadly proas be readied for launching. These were long two-masted outriggers capable of taking dozens of warriors. If they came in on their stern in a rush, *Tyger* would be swarming in minutes with blood-lusting savages.

At the same time an urgent shout came from forward. An outstretched arm had Kydd wheeling round. Neatly alongside a crude length of pilings and a recognisable slipway up the shore was the quarry they'd been hunting, *Vengeur* – with men boiling up from below, lashed by frantic shouts and clearly preparing for sea.

It was a perfect hideaway: around the turn and quite out of sight of all except those who ventured to the end of the inlet, which any vessels sheltering from foul weather would not be inclined to do.

But it was too late: they were facing a situation turning deadlier by the minute.

Probably believing that this was a stray merchantman, the savages were gleefully working themselves up for the assault, launching more and more of the evil-looking proas, which milled about together, no doubt until their numbers were sufficient for a shrieking assault.

Kydd forgot about *Vengeur* and forced his mind to cold concentration. From their general disposition it was clear that the natives knew enough to go for the stern where most ships did not mount guns of size, including *Tyger*. However, the frigate had resources few merchantmen could match but he had to bring them to bear in a very short time. And free his ship from the treacherous mud-flat.

In many ways it was like a full-scale battle. A captain taut with strain seeing the circumstances changing in a moment to an advantage that, if taken, could lead to victory – or vicious reverses clamping in that, if not overcome, would mean all was lost. All to be decided in an instant.

'A six-pounder hauled aft. Canister.'

It was a pitiful choice, but it was the largest carriage gun that could be man-hauled along the deck and brought to train over the taffrail. And while the sleeting charge of musket balls would cause temporary carnage, the savages would renew their assault with a bloody vengeance as the gun was being reloaded.

In the heat men were dropping at the ropes and even before they were halfway along it was plain that an assault was imminent.

'Rouvier's cast off his lines,' Brice broke in urgently.

The big privateer had put off, sails quickly catching the wafting flurries of wind and making way headed straight for them.

'He's not going to . . .?' he added, in a tight voice.

But Kydd had just been handed a final predicament. A breathless messenger from the gunner informed him that there was neither canister nor grape for a six-pounder in the shot lockers. His last defence was down.

Now Rouvier was joining the fight in a long curve towards them – but was he? Either way, to make his escape to sea he had to pass within easy range of *Tyger*'s broadside, the motion-less frigate still able to lash out. If he was thinking of a gunnery duel, then as long as *Tyger* could hold off the merci-less savages he would be punished.

On the other hand, was he in mercy, with his freedom of manoeuvre, going to the rescue of fellow sailors to deliver them from a monstrous fate by fending off the natives until their ship could be refloated? And, if this was the case, what did the rules of war say about how he should respond after-wards? Let him go with his blessing and thanks, or resume the chase to a kill?

'Hold fire to larboard,' Kydd ordered, and under *Tyger*'s silent guns, the privateer drew nearer. Would it be a callous crash of guns as they passed or a holding of fire and gallant intercession across their stern?

In the event it was neither. Picking up speed, the privateer swept past – and, in a final contemptuous swash of wake, laid course to the east and away.

'T' be expected, the bastards,' Brice said bitterly. 'They're leaving us to be wiped out to keep the secret of their bolt-hole.'

It seemed the word had spread into the tropic forest. Countless figures now cavorted in anticipation, outnumbering *Tyger*'s defenders three or four to one. Eyes turned in despair on Kydd.

An image crossed his mind, of several long wooden chests lying together in the dark. What did it mean? In a sudden flash of insight, it came to him.

'The chests in the hold! Starb'd side forrard!' he roared, at a bemused Farrant.

The proas were bunching and beginning their furious charge – it might be too late but here was their chance if ever they had one.

A spreading roar went up – the savages were on their way.

Swayed out by scores of desperate hands, the heavy crates were brought on deck and torn open. Inside were four of Mr Congreve's eight-inch war rockets, still on *Tyger*'s books from their time in Spain and much cried up for their ease and celerity of setting up on the battlefield for rapid action.

'Over their heads!'

The gunner's party adjusted the big triangular firing frames over the stern and, impatiently clearing bystanders away from the rocket's rear, took aim with the first.

'Fire 'em all!' called Kydd, and, knowing what to expect, made his way hastily off the quarterdeck. The terrifying *whoosh* of the rocket's breath in reeking smoke rushed over his head. Leaning over the bulwarks, he saw the deadly projectile's trail shriek over the warriors and smash into the undergrowth, where the warhead exploded in a vivid orange blast.

The second quickly followed – it was the great advantage of the Congreve rocket that, while it lacked the accuracy of artillery, its rate of fire was unmatched. By the third, terrified savages were streaming away as fast as they could paddle and in a short time the entire stretch of water was empty.

There were well-known procedures for refloating after taking the ground on mud and the Tygers turned to with a will. A quick sounding with a lead-line gave the picture and, as a result, a kedge anchor was taken by launch well out from the larboard bow. The capstan was fully manned, guns were brought across to the opposite side of the deck and the furious heaving began. As gently as she'd run into the seabed she slid off and into deeper water.

'We go ashore to set about his works?' Brice wanted to know, as they resumed quarters.

'Remember your orders, sir,' Kydd told him. 'We go after him first, then deal with his lair. I've a notion he's still about, needing to make sure we're truly finished.'

The frigate turned her bowsprit to the open sea two or three miles ahead and, as Kydd had suspected, the tell-tale pale shapes of sail crossed their view to the right, disappearing behind Ross Island.

Before they were halfway there the sails reappeared, sheeted hard in as the privateer leaned to the wind in the opposite direction in a fast reach across the entrance to the north. They'd been sighted!

Vengeur was now in a fearful hurry to disappear into the wastes of ocean, plainly heading for the maze of islands northward where it would lose itself. Should it succeed, there was vanishingly little chance for *Tyger* to catch the speedy vessel.

The fitful wind inside the inlet was not the even stream to be relied on out to sea and Kydd cursed their faltering progress. While *Vengeur* was driving for the ocean they were leisurely taking in the sights.

Perseverance Point drew near, the last headland before they could round it and sail north.

'Lay us two cables out,' Kydd warned.

Even at this distance fangs of coral could be seen below the surface. Kydd shuddered, remembering his times in the Caribbean.

They passed it well clear and put over the helm for the run north . . . but were met by a sight that brought everything to a disbelieving climax.

The unhappy carcass of *Vengeur* was pinioned at the tip of the last foreland, North Point. In his desire to make a fast escape, Rouvier had cut it too close and had brought up on a spur of coral.

'Ha!' said Joyce, happily. 'Hoist b' his own petard.'

'How so?'

'In the open ocean like this there's no tides t' speak of, sir. But there is, should there be a blow somewheres to weather. The same drop in soundings that did for us has done for the poxy villain as well.'

Brice gave a cynical chuckle. 'To cap a perfect day, cast your peepers along the shore a mite.'

And there, gathering in large numbers, was a growing throng of natives, who were making it very plain that *Vengeur* would be made to pay for their humiliation at the hands of *Tyger*.

'A rescue, sir?'

'Not at all.'

'Sir?'

'Not until I see his damned fighting rag hauled down.'

Chapter 22

Admiralty House, Madras

'And then, sir, Rouvier having struck to me, I took possession of *Vengeur*, desiring *Tyger* in the meanwhile to deter the raging of the savages.'

'Quite so,' rumbled Pellew, clearly well satisfied. 'The prize?'

'Unhappily much mauled by the coral heads and not in a condition to refloat, so destroyed by fire. As were the slipyard and workshops ashore.'

'Nevertheless, a very fine piece of work, sir,' the admiral conceded gruffly, 'as rids me of a pestilential foe. Do take a mort of liberty ashore, old fellow – two weeks to make *Tyger* shipshape, shall we say?'

'She's in fine fettle now, sir, and—'

'I said two weeks, did I not?' Pellew said, with a fruity chuckle.

'Aye aye, sir,' Kydd replied hastily, and took his leave.

He crossed the anteroom but at the far door a figure appeared, legs a-brace and in the uniform of a post-captain, even if absurdly young. One of Pellew's sons, he surmised, brought out by his father, commander-in-chief on station, to favour him with advancement.

It was notorious how the doting father had first shamelessly made them lieutenants without the necessary sea-time, then given the youngest, Fleetwood, a sloop command at seventeen. At nineteen Pellew had contrived to promote him to post-captain and command of *San Fiorenzo*. Known as a prickly character, the young man was consumed by ambition. He had been in several minor actions but without public distinction.

Pownoll, the elder, was his exact opposite. Dreamy, sensitive and handsome, he had no aching need for the laurels of a warrior and was safely under Pellew's eye as captain of *Culloden*, his flagship.

Kydd recalled guiltily that, as senior frigate captain, he should know his captains intimately but apart from Avery of *Thalia* and Moorsom of *Hebe*, who'd come from England with him, he hadn't made acquaintance with any of the others on station. Pellew's Fighting Instructions were sparing in detail of how frigates were to be deployed in battle and most of their customary tasking had been like *Tyger*'s, individual scouting and long-distance patrols that kept them away.

'Captain Kydd?' the figure asked abruptly.

'It is.'

'Captain Fleetwood Pellew, *San Fiorenzo*.' He made no effort to move out of the way and his set face triggered a warning.

'What can I do for you, Captain?' Kydd asked carefully.

'I took sight of your dispatch. I'd be obliged if you'll tell me what you saw that made you sail direct to the Frenchy hideaway.'

'You didn't hoist it in, then. It was a matter of reasoning only, where it—'

'You had intelligence as placed Rouvier there, which you

kept to yourself, never telling my father so you could then claim all credit and distinction.'

It was ridiculous. A petulant youth without the experience to temper his impetuous nature, questioning someone of his stature.

'Not so,' Kydd replied evenly. 'As I said—'

The young officer stiffened. 'You have no need to excuse yourself, sir. Just be assured that the matter will not rest here!' He turned on his heel and stalked off.

It was almost laughable – but then again that was Pellew's son.

Chapter 23

Later, seated in his comfortable rattan armchair, a whisky by his side and the week's *Madras Courier* to peruse, Kydd was in a mellow mood. There would be gun money and head money to collect, and any reduction in risk to the Indiamen must surely put him in good odour with the John Company bigwigs.

Should he decorate the entertainment space in a more radical style? It was in his mind to make use of Cluffer and issue invitations to an evening of sorts. There must be quantities of interesting people he should be cultivating to ease the pain of exile. Dear Persephone was not on hand to arrange matters in a comely fashion but no doubt he could call on the kind Mrs Lowther to assist. In fact, she—

The ingratiating tones of Bomarjee intruded apologetically, 'Are you available to Mrs Lowther, sir?'

Kydd stood. 'Why, yes! Show her in.'

She appeared somewhat flustered. 'Oh, Captain! I'm so glad you're back from your adventuring.'

She dabbed at her brow and settled demurely in a chair.

'You see, I've a vexation new sprung on me and, well, it crossed my mind to approach you about it.' She looked up in the most charmingly feminine way, protesting, 'As it won't mean the same to a man, but to me . . .'

'Do say away, Mrs Lowther. As it happens, I'd be obliged for your kind assistance myself,' Kydd said gallantly.

'Oh? Then I believe I shall tell you. It's my cousin, Friedrich Steinberg. I'm invited to his birthday and he's German, and you know how much store they set on such occasions. My escort has let me down, a fever, poor lamb, and I should so like to attend. I know it's short notice – tomorrow night – but it would be so very kind of you should—'

'Mrs Lowther, please do meet your new escort of the night,' Kydd responded. It seemed in keeping with the mood that he took her hand and kissed it.

'Caroline, please. It seems so to distance one, the formal title, don't you think?'

'Very well, then, it's Caroline. And between us it shall be Thomas.'

She laughed delightedly. 'So what is it that I can do for you, dear Thomas?'

He'd soon laid out his feeling of inadequacy in the article of planning social diversions and she avowed herself his to consult at any time, perhaps even to act the hostess if required.

The following evening Kydd told Dillon not to wait up for his return, for in India the cool of the night was the time to disport.

Met by a gratified Steinberg and his daughters, Kydd was caught up in the happy whirl, so different from the martial discipline of *Tyger*. That he arrived accompanying Caroline was taken as a matter of nothing to comment on, and all joined in the merriment as though they'd been friends for years, the atmosphere easier on formalities than at an English gathering.

When a cake was brought in, flaming with thirty-four candles in the German fashion, it was the signal for more laughter and gaiety.

Kydd met many names of Madras society he'd heard of and understood why Caroline hadn't wanted to miss the occasion. There were Company military, Presidency officials of useful prominence, one or two of the higher merchantry, and a goodly number of guests with the conspicuous impression about them of money and position.

The most interesting, however, was one she took relish in pointing out to him. It was a naval officer, a post-captain like himself, whose identity he deduced immediately: the elder of the two Pellew sons, Pownoll. Arrayed in full-dress uniform of astonishing quality, he was nevertheless outdone by Kydd's star of knighthood, but he received his salutation with a soft respect.

On his arm was a captivating but strong-featured girl, her gaze uncomfortably direct.

'His intended,' whispered Caroline, clutching Kydd's arm to pull him closer. 'And you'd never guess who it is!'

'Who, then?'

'Why, that's Eliza, daughter of the grand panjandrum himself, governor of the Presidency of Madras.'

'Barlow.'

'He's done well for himself, the rogue,' Caroline said wistfully. 'They'll get a settlement of respectable size from the admiral, but the woman is a fine catch, with money and high connections. I'm doubtful you'll see him floating about in his boat for much longer.'

The evening finished in the early hours with a rubber or

two of whist and some of the finest cognac Kydd had ever tasted.

Returning home, Caroline sat next to him in a double palanquin and dreamily looked out over the waking city as they swayed along, the bearers in their soft, wordless chorus. Kydd felt a little uncomfortable next to such an attractive woman and kept his hands tightly in his lap. But Caroline knew he was married and, being the lady she was, would never overstep the bounds of friendship.

All too soon they reached her garden-house, a matter of a few hundred yards only from his own and Kydd handed her down.

She hesitated only a moment before firmly wishing him a good night and, with a little backward wave, vanished inside.

'I couldn't sleep, Sir Thomas,' Dillon said, rising as Kydd entered.

'A brandy posset I find a capital remedy, old chap,' Kydd said sympathetically, as Bomarjee took his uniform and prepared him for bed.

Dillon remained standing, a shadow in his face. 'You had an enjoyable evening, sir?'

'Why, yes, as it happens. A rattling fine woman, Mrs Lowther.'

'You must forgive me remarking it, but I find I must, Sir Thomas.'

'What's that?' Kydd grunted, his stockings stubborn in the removing.

'Madras is of goodly size – but at the same time a small place.'

'I don't follow you, Edward.'

'This is to say that, even as you innocently consort with her, tongues are already a-wag.'

Kydd blinked, then frowned. 'Nonsense! Caroline, er, Mrs

Lowther is a respectable widow who may choose whom she will to be seen with. There's no question of any loss of reputation, you villain!'

'I'm sorry to press you on it, Sir Thomas, but you are at prominence in this community and nothing will do other than they must discuss your . . . dalliances and—'

'Who?' Kydd snorted. 'Riff-raff with nothing better to prate about?'

'Sir, there are those who know Lady Kydd and fear for her—'

Incensed, Kydd lunged across and seized Dillon by his night-shirt. Drawing him close, he snarled, 'You hear them say anything like that, tell 'em from me that Persephone has all my heart, which leaves no room in it for any other!'

Even as he uttered the words he knew that they were spoken in the dawn of an alien world half the earth away from her, with nothing to show of it to others. He released Dillon slowly and apologised. 'I'm sorry, Edward. Not feeling myself, these all-night entertainments. I'll bear in mind what you say.'

As he lay sprawled in his bed, making out patterns in the rose-tinted ceiling, it was not Persephone's face that smiled back at him but Caroline's. He shrugged it off: surely it could only be that the woman most recently in his presence would be foremost in his thoughts.

Chapter 24

Kydd was woken gently by Bomarjee. Dillon stood behind him.

'Sir. There is a soldier-man. He has a message and will not leave until he has his answer.'

Shaking his head to clear it, Kydd sat up in bed and took the note. It was from Drury, Pellew's second-in-command. It was curt and to the point: 'You are desired to present yourself at Fort St George not later than noon this day. Your reasons for inability to attend to be notified by return.'

'The time?' he croaked.

'A whisker after ten thirty, sir,' Dillon answered softly.

'I'll be there.' There was just enough time to bathe and be shaved – but this sounded serious. It couldn't be connected to his recent dalliance . . . or could it? And why the civil and military centre of the fort, not Admiralty House?

One mystery was quickly laid to rest. Pellew and, indeed, Barlow, the governor general of the Presidency of Madras, were paying attendance on Lord Minto, the governor general of all India at his seat in Calcutta, an absence of weeks.

This explained why Drury was ordering him to report, not Pellew.

The larger puzzle remained. Received cordially by an army adjutant, he was ushered into an anteroom where a number of other officers, naval and military, were standing together. The nearest naval officer was Haslam, Pellew's flag-captain.

'Good day to you, sir,' Kydd opened. 'And we have an alarum of sorts?'

'Possibly.' Haslam sniffed loftily. 'Of a military nature, I understand.'

'Then why—'

'The army commander-in-chief is to make some motion against a defiance in the Carnatic,' he continued, in a bored tone. 'Happens all the while, but this time the knaves have rather overstepped themselves. He's required to seek counsel of the forces of the Crown before he moves Company troops against them in earnest.'

'And we?'

'For the sake of show only. A detestable creature, General Macdowall – hates the navy, hates everybody, but especially those he cannot control, like King's men but more than they, the civil power to which he's supposed to defer. Don't mistake it, however, he's the sole commander of the John Company armies over a third of India and therefore a powerful man in the land.'

'Point taken, but why me?'

'Admiral Drury making up the numbers. Flag-captain, captain of one of the sail-o'-the-line and the senior frigate captain. Don't worry, you won't be troubled for an opinion,' Haslam finished archly.

Kydd found himself placed with the other naval officers in a group far from the empty chair at the head of the table. Around him were some in plain clothes and one in what

122

could only be described as a somewhat individual naval uniform, whom he presumed must be from the Bombay Marine, the East India Company maritime force.

Further up were more of the military in full dress uniform.

Conversation ceased and there was a massed scraping of chairs as all rose at the entrance of a morose, dark-featured officer in the most ornately laced regimentals Kydd had seen outside a Horse Guards parade.

An officer stood behind him with a paper and quickly intoned, 'Gentlemen, General Macdowall. Sir, from the left I give you . . .' He rattled off the names and ranks of those present, and retired.

'This is now a council of advisement,' Macdowall growled, in a broad Scots accent. 'All views will be heard, none necessarily taken. McWhirter?'

The officer on his right stood and laid out the essentials.

It seemed that word of unrest had been received from Kotacund, a small princely state to the west. In essence, the Dalawa, or vizier, had persuaded the Maharajah Narendra to refuse to render up his subsidy due to the East India Company for their garrison guaranteeing their security against rival states and nations, including the French and others.

In a pretence at public anger, the Resident's house at Jamna had been attacked and ransacked, the Resident himself only just escaping to take refuge with the garrison, but in the process a clerk in his loyal defence of the grounds had been killed. Either the incident was to be ignored, with loss of credibility as the ruling power, or decisive action was required.

'This is not the first or the last o' these futile outrages,' Macdowall resumed. 'A show o' cold steel usually softens the temper, I've found. M' intent is without delay to set the First Battalion o' the Seventeenth Regiment o' Madras Native Infantry afoot, this for a punitive expedition into Kotacund, to teach the rajah his manners in his dealings with the Company.'

He glowered around the table. 'If any wants to dispute my rights, say now.'

Unexpectedly it was Haslam who broke the silence. 'General, I understand Kotacund is to the west some days' march away. The navy can offer transport around—'

'No! The navy will not be required in this instance or any other. I'm going overland because I want the beggars to see me, let 'em know I'm coming for them. Any other fool suggestions? No? Then the meeting concludes by concurring in m' plans, as shall be so recorded. Good day, gentlemen.'

After he'd left a desultory babble broke out and Kydd smiled wryly at Haslam. 'As you predicted, sir. At least we're free to return aboard and wait it out.'

'Not so hasty, Captain. You've your duty, sir.'

'Oh?'

'To stand with the general in review as his troops march off. Shouldn't take more than the rest of the day,' he added sourly.

Kydd generally enjoyed such military spectacles and stood on the dais at the Choultry Plains cantonment with the others as General Macdowall took the salute. Hot and dusty it might have been, but the spectacle as the Madras infantry swept by in their green facings, dark buff jodhpurs and tall shakoes above dark-complexioned faces, accompanied by the thumping of a band, was rousing.

'A brave sight, your army on the march,' Kydd said breezily, to the rather gloomy major who had been next to him as they stood down to stroll over to the officers' mess for refreshment.

'Major Richie, and I thank you for the remarking, sir,' the

younger man said, still unaccountably glum, 'but it's not to be encouraged, I believe.'

'Why so?' Kydd said. in surprise.

After a furtive look about, Richie continued, 'You've no knowledge of our John Company general, I see.'

'And you're not . . .?'

'No, old chap. A King's man, of the Thirty-third Regiment of Foot, the West Ridings. We're not to be involved in the absurdity, thank God.'

'Absurdity? To discipline your rajah?'

Richie sighed. 'The delicacy of the situation has escaped the reckless simpleton. Here we exist as effective rulers keeping the peace, which we achieve by balancing the greed and ambitions of each prince and nabob against his neighbours with tact, diplomacy and, of course, lakhs of rupees. His idea of peace is to present the India Board with the slaughter of thousands as evidence of his diligence in its pursuit.'

'He's going there to—'

'Let me put the situation to you. The Dalawa is the Maharajah of Kotacund's right-hand man but he's playing him false with the aim of toppling him and taking his place. He can do this if he stirs up a local war with the British and blames its woes on the area's rajah, and therefore garners friends who will benefit by this roguery. He wants to rule alone, unencumbered by obligations, so by an act of treachery he goes over the friends' heads and treats with the French, who promise to land a full regiment of modern artillery in order that the British are defeated.'

'Be damned to it!'

'Only if the French believe they've a chance. Now set around Kotacund there are those who will be more than interested in the outcome. The recent Travancore rebellion comes to mind and the Calicut princes will be out to go with whoever prevails, as will others in the Carnatic, such as the Mahrattas, recently humiliated by our Wellesley. Then to the north we have the Nizam of Hyderabad, who would delight in fishing in troubled waters to our embarrassment. And then—'

'So he's on his way to Kotacund to put down the commotion. With what result do you think?'

'Ah. He left with a full battalion of sepoy infantry, and the rajah is weak but listens to reason. It might well be all over before he arrives.'

'Or not.'

'Quite. We shall await developments with some interest.'

Chapter 25

With Pellew still in Calcutta and Drury taking to his sick-bed again, *Tyger* was left swinging to her anchor and Kydd at guilty leisure ashore. However, within the week news of Macdowall's progress filtered back. At first it was commendable. The force had made good time across the central plain and was closing in on Jamna, the chief town of Kotacund.

Then it all changed. The devious Dalawa had planned it well. Open rebellion broke out – and when the hapless general arrived it was to face disorderly crowds, streaming refugees and a gathering uprising.

Worse was to come, for Rajapur, the hilly state to the north, had been waiting for this moment and sent its columns down into the plains to join with Kotacund against the common foe. Quickly Macdowall found that, instead of relieving the local garrison, he must now join them in their modest fortress in preparing to be besieged. Courageous messengers pleading for relief were sent through the encircling lines to reach Madras days later.

Lieutenant General Smythe, Macdowall's elderly second-in-command in Madras, immediately called a council-of-war.

Kydd sat quietly as the situation was made known. This was quite a different kind of leader, painstaking, stolid and not inclined to haste in any wise.

Maps were hung and the beleaguered Macdowall was pointed out in the fortress before Jamna, the Kotacund forces gathering in the south and the Rajapur advance in the north to close the trap. Spies were reporting that this included war rockets and elephants and was of formidable size. It looked a grim future for the outnumbered general.

Kydd felt for the embattled men. He'd heard of massacres in India, Tipu Sultan and others wreaking terrible atrocities on their opponents, and unless something could be done, Macdowall and his sepoys would suffer similarly.

'I intend to send a strong relief expedition to their assistance,' Smythe announced, 'equipped with adequate artillery to confront the Rajapur deployment. It shall consist of—'

'Artillery will gravely slow a flying column,' Richie objected.

Smythe looked pained. 'Sir, your objections shall be heard at the proper time. As it is, I do not propose to allow any under my command to engage an enemy of the magnitude of the Rajapur force without satisfactory field equipment.'

Kydd heard a muffled snort from Richie as he subsided to hear the rest.

'Sir, you will be seeking counsel and assistance from the Crown?' Richie asked, when Smythe had finished.

'I see no reason whatsoever to do so, Major,' the general said pompously. 'The Honourable East India Company can generally be relied upon to look after its own, sir. Any other remarks or comments?'

Outside, Richie was seething. 'The stubborn ass doesn't see the bigger picture. This isn't a John Company matter now – it's far bigger than that. Should a British formation of size be destroyed in the field, the consequences will be incalculable as the news spreads. Our position will be made dire.'

'Should he not defer to the Crown at all?'

'If our blessed Colonel Snell would stand up in his corner, yes, but the old boy despises the Company and would rather they stew in juices of their own making. I rather fear that it must be me who tries to beard our General Smythe in private, Heaven help me.'

Kydd returned to his residence disturbed by what he'd heard. Jamna was well inland and this was in all respects a military matter, but the thought of a tragedy made inevitable through arrogant leadership was hard to take.

That evening, as he rose from the dinner table, he heard voices at the door and Richie was announced.

This was plainly no social call. 'Do come in, sir,' Kydd invited. 'Is there anything I can do for you?'

'There is indeed. Your advice of a professional kind at this time would be much appreciated.' The man was clearly distracted but calmed himself. 'I saw our sainted General Smythe and he's not to be moved. Therefore Macdowall and his company are doomed – they can never hold out for the time it'll take to bring up the artillery. Doomed, I say!'

Kydd murmured his sympathy and prompted, 'Professional advice? As a sailor I cannot possibly conceive how . . .'

Richie felt inside his tunic and brought out a general relief map of southern India. 'Madras – here on the eastern side. Jamna, over here, more to the west. Now mark this. Rajapur princely state in the north, its capital Bijabad there, from where they made sally southward over the hills to join the Kotacund rebellion.'

'I see,' Kydd said slowly, wondering where this was leading.

'That Rajapur crew,' Richie murmured. 'Did you know that

it's their practice to stake out prisoners taken and have them trampled to death by elephants?'

Kydd shuddered. 'I didn't – please say if there's anything that I can do.'

'In a ship, how long would it take to go from Madras to here?' He indicated a point on the coast opposite Bijabad.

'I should say days only, the monsoon holding.'

'Not weeks?'

'Days.'

Richie drew a shuddering breath and then, with a grin, relaxed. 'Then my idea is not a fantasy.'

'Do tell me,' Kydd said.

'Smythe cannot dictate Crown movements, and indeed he's refused outright their services. Thus I say we're at liberty to bundle our own troops into transports, take them to that point and make a landing.'

Kydd looked puzzled.

'Don't you see? I now have a parcel of redcoats astride the road directly towards the Rajapur capital. The rebellious dogs will be obliged to choose between having Bijabad put to the sword or continuing to assist their treacherous ally. I've a notion what it will be, and by this Macdowall will be relieved to sortie out to punish the Kotacund insurrection.'

It was a worthy conceit – and not at all what he'd have expected from a military man, the intelligent use of sea-power to leapfrog lumbering armies.

'My congratulations, dear fellow,' Kydd said warmly. 'A splendid plan. Er, thinking I'd rather suppose from a sailor!'

'It is,' Richie came back, with the ghost of a smile. 'As heard here and noted of exploits of a certain sea captain in Iberia, if you will.'

Kydd gave a grin of embarrassed acknowledgement. 'So. What do we next, Major?'

'I'm to go this instant not to Smythe but to our Colonel Snell of the King's Thirty-third of Foot. Heroes of Seringapatam they, and not inclined to look to a defeat even if it's by way of a Company affair. If you would be so good as to list down the sea requirements for our force while I'm gone, here is a hasty order of battle.'

Kydd saw he was being drawn into a military rivalry. Richie couldn't proceed without him but the stakes were worth Kydd's efforts.

He sent for Dillon. 'A distraction to our soft life ashore, Edward.' He quickly sketched out the task and, by candlelight, they set to.

With his experience in conjoint operations on three continents he knew what was wanted. This was not difficult: it was to be a flying column of basically infantry accompanied by light dragoons and the usual provisions for siege artillery. Camp followers and the like would not be wanted. Numbers therefore were a simple exercise in apportioning soldiery to sufficient transports and allowing for minimal stores and equipment.

He slept well, and when Richie returned in the morning he was ready with his figures.

'Put 'em away, m' sailor friend. They'll not be needed.'

'You're saying—'

'Yes. The colonel will not entertain any action of such a consequence that is not sanctioned by the civil power – the governor general. Who at the moment is in Calcutta.'

'He'd rather let—'

'Colonel Snell is my superior. I cannot question his judgement. The matter rests.'

Kydd could not contain his fury and contempt. 'You must leave it, but I won't,' he thundered. 'He's a colonel, I'm a post-captain and carry equal weight of rank. He's about to hear what a sailor thinks!'

At the encampment the adjutant looked in astonishment and some alarm at Kydd in his full dress. A navy fellow demanding to see the colonel that very instant was unprecedented and he was foxed as to what should be done, but he apologetically announced Sir Thomas Kydd to the colonel.

If Snell was taken aback, he hid it well. 'Do be welcome into our midst, Sir Thomas. An unexpected visit, but a pleasure for all that.' His appraising eyes assessed his visitor carefully. 'I take this to be anything but a politeness, sir.'

'Sir, I will not waste our time,' Kydd said, not taking the proffered chair. 'I'm aware of the deplorable situation General Macdowall is now facing and cannot understand why strong action is not being taken to relieve him, such as a landing by King's troops in the aggressor's rear.'

'Ah. You've been talking with young Richie – or was he talking at you?'

'What he said made a deal of sense to me, sir.'

'Just so.'

'Inasmuch as I devoted my own time to working up a scheme of transport and escort that provides for placing a substantial force ashore and under march within mere days.'

'Umm. Tell me, Sir Thomas, have you attended on conjoint operations with the army in the past?' Snell asked innocently.

'I have,' Kydd replied, in a rising voice.

'And respecting your presence, sir, I suggest that it was at the sharper, noisier end of things, never the calm of the hindmost.'

'That would be true,' Kydd growled, on his guard.

'Then it would explain why I have to lay before you elements that even a junior staff officer would find sufficiently persuasive to abandon all talk of an independent expedition.'

'Do then, sir, persuade me.'

'Very well. The first: without the civil power invites me, I am not only an interloper and species of pirate but I'm cut off from my strongest need before the first boot touches the earth.'

'Need?' Kydd asked in bafflement.

'A line of credit in the regimental ledger handed down by the duly sanctioned authority. "This expenditure against that outgoing". Leading to "This voucher against this invoice, against this expenditure, against this line of authority". Without which . . .'

'I see.' There was no counter to arguments of such magnitude.

'Your talk of ships and escorts and so forth is greatly appreciated, Sir Thomas, but without a line in the books it's as any other worthless vapouring.'

The kindly, almost cleric-like beneficence goaded Kydd. 'As I understand you, any move to relieve General Macdowall is thwarted by a lack of authority, an insufficiency of silver.'

'That is a fair commentary, Sir Thomas.'

Speechless, Kydd fell back.

'Dear fellow, do see it from my perspective. I thankfully accept your offer of full naval escort to land me somewhere on the Carnatic coast. Now, before I can move at all I must wait on transports provided by Calcutta – if they fall in with my larger wishes, which I personally doubt as by then they will be apprised of the situation and will wish to make other arrangements. Then I must victual them and prepare for the voyage.'

He gave a humourless smile. 'Here in Madras there is no harbour – how am I to load an army? I must march seventy miles south where there's a jute port of sorts. We board and put to sea . . . but sadly, by the time we arrive to begin our march, word comes that it's all in vain, the general is overcome and the victorious combined armies are forming up to face me.'

'So then—'

'At which I will be calumnied as a failure, any future decisions of mine questioned, my career at an end. If, conversely, I await legally constituted authority for a decision, it will be they who are blamed, not me.'

Kydd saw no compassion, hope or sympathy in the fastidious features. But neither was there rejection, dismissal. The man conceived his position as one dictated by logic, not controversy or debate. 'I see, sir. Yet I'm persuaded that if a way forward is found that satisfies your points, you might indeed be prompted to act.'

A wisp of a smile appeared and as quickly disappeared. 'Sir Thomas, I would not have you believe us a tribe of no feeling, especially concerning our fellow warriors. Of course I would, but this is impossible as you now must see.'

Kydd turned abruptly to stare unseeing through the window, hiding his expression of grief and fury.

There was no sound apart from the creaking rhythm of the punkah reed slat overhead but thoughts roared in his head, as they had in the despair of a battle being lost for want of a saving contrivance. And, as before, his mind produced an idea and from it blossomed a plan, a stratagem. A possibility – a chance!

He spun round. 'I shall hold you to those words, sir!'

'Er, how can this be, Sir Thomas?'

'If I can get you to the coast opposite Bijabad in a matter of days, will you release your troops?'

'Where are your transports? How will they be embarked in time? There are many—'

'Sir, be so good as to leave the sailoring to me. If I supply

134

the ships and means to load them in the next two days, will your men be ready?'

In amazement Snell leaned back and gazed at him. 'I really must believe you are in earnest, sir. But if you mean to sail within the week I shall ensure that a battalion of the Thirty-third Regiment of Foot finds that it will be going on manoeuvres at that time.'

Kydd grinned wickedly. 'We of the naval kind are accustomed to feats of initiative mainly because we so often must make shift alone. As it happens, my admiral is in Calcutta, his second is on his sick-bed and this obliges me to act on my own. You shall have your transports to take you on manoeuvres. Do please prepare and be ready to board by noon tomorrow. Good day to you, Colonel.'

Light-headed with exhilaration he returned to *Tyger* and set to work.

The ships: he knew what he would do and it was a daring stroke, but one owing nothing to gunsmoke or cutlass blades. All depended on Pellew being the man he thought he was.

Chapter 26

Kydd called for the Navy Board officer, who was responsible to the Admiralty for local contracts and disbursements. He protested that he had never heard of any action on the part of the navy in Madras connected to an army operation, let alone a line of credit in support.

Kydd affected a heavy impatience, accusing the man of impeding a vital relief effort. He demanded that in the absence of the Transport Board in Calcutta it was up to him to provide ships and that at once.

Drawing himself up, the officer pointed out that he was by no means authorised to act in their place and could not accede to Kydd's demands.

Then, like a snake, Kydd struck. Did the Navy Board officer realise that a notorious massacre was about to take place and the British government would doubtless soon need to hunt down a blameworthy victim? An individual who would not move for want of a little paperwork would do very nicely.

With an aggrieved look the man heard Kydd out. He wanted to hire eighteen vessels of seven hundred tons or more. There was that number and more in the Madras Roads. Surely they could be induced to take on a voyage of less than a week in such a cause.

Payment? He would relieve the gentleman of the responsibility. As senior officer, frigates, and officer-in-charge of the enterprise, Kydd would himself, in the absence of the commander-in-chief, undertake to sign bills of exchange drawn on the Navy Board in London, in the process thereby preserving valuable specie. The transaction would be countersigned by Pellew on his return.

While a lone captain could at times sign away a bill on London this was only in exceptional circumstances such as the purchase in a foreign port of much-needed canvas to replace storm-torn sails. Expenditure on this scale?

But Kydd knew his man. Merely as an afterthought, he pointed out that, as disbursing officer, he was entitled, of course, to a consideration on all transactions, which in this case would amount to quite a useful sum indeed.

It made its mark, and Kydd concluded with a casual request to be allowed to sign for a form of imprest, an advance in cash that would oil the wheels. This, however, was for quite a different purpose and one that Kydd kept to himself.

Every officer in *Tyger* was sent to procure charters and require the shipping to assemble about her by dawn the following day.

Going ashore for the final act, Kydd pointed out the gathering transport fleet to Snell.

'And how might we board?' the colonel asked respectfully.

'Ah. As of this moment every masula boat on the coast has been taken up, hired for the day, a rewarding thing you may believe for their crews.'

This was how the imprest fund was being deployed,

securing the masula crews' exclusive services for the entire day had taken more than a little coin.

'A battalion – a thousand men. Fifty odd per ship, eighteen ships, four trips of half an hour – they'll easily do it, the cargo-wallahs bringing out their stores in the meanwhile. Well done, sir!'

'I have to insist—'

'The troops will be paraded on the fort foreshore at first light. There will be no stragglers.'

Kydd's orders to the frigates were a matter of routine. He would employ all five available, it would not be a formal convoy, and at that strength no one but a madman would contemplate an attack. His instructions were brief and to the point. With a sense of dawning wonder, Kydd realised there was every prospect he would get away with it.

The next day, as the morning mists cleared, the regiment formed up by company at the fort with their haversacks and muskets before them.

In the crashing surf, the masula boatmen brought in their craft and, in disciplined lines, the soldiers clambered aboard, gleefully treating the whole thing as an entertainment. By mid-afternoon most of the transports had been filled and Kydd signalled to his frigates to prepare to unmoor.

With satisfaction he saw them all acknowledge, and as evening drew in with a gentle north-easterly, a promising fair wind for the south, a beaming Snell came aboard. 'As I could never have believed it.' He sighed, surveying the frigates in warlike readiness and the merchant ships, whose decks were lined with redcoats.

'Mr Brice, signal "unmoor",' Kydd ordered.

It soared up *Tyger*'s mizzen halliards and at 'execute' each frigate began to win her anchor.

Kydd left the evolution to Farrant as he was, to all intents and purposes, a full convoy commodore with all the responsibility it brought. He looked about at the orderly procedure. He'd been in convoys where putting to sea had been the signal for an unholy scramble, with more than one vessel locked in collision with another drifting helplessly downwind.

Here all seemed fine. Under the steady breeze and in Madras Roads, already in the open sea, the ships were beginning to stream out, headed by the four frigates.

Four? For some unknown reason one still lay at anchor.

'What ship's that?' Kydd demanded of Brice, who lifted his telescope, then snapped it shut.

'*San Fiorenzo*,' he replied crisply.

'Her pennants, "proceed in accordance with the last order".'

There was no response. What the devil?

From *Tyger*, Madras and the anchorage astern were fast retreating into the usual soft anonymity of distance and the disobedient frigate with it. He had to discover why he was being deprived of a fifth of his little fleet and there was no other course than to await its explanation.

'Heave to!' he snapped.

Still nothing, but when Kydd repeated the signal, this time with a gun to windward, signal flags mounted slowly up.

'Sir,' Brice said formally, '*Fiorenzo* signals "unable".'

This made no sense for she had acknowledged the 'unmoor' signal in the usual way.

'Her pennants and "query your last signal".'

The 'unable' remained close up for long minutes, then came down – only to rise obstinately again.

Kydd swore. Light was fading and the convoy was disappearing to seaward. He couldn't stay where he was for much longer or he would lose them. 'Bear away for the convoy,' he ordered, and left *Fiorenzo* at anchor. *Tyger* leaned willingly to the wind and made off in a swash of startling white wake. He would have an accounting with her captain when he returned, that much was certain.

It was Fleetwood Pellew, the commander-in-chief's son, transfigured into an ambitious and resentful rival to Kydd with little judgement or common sense. Was it too much to suppose the youth would find any excuse to avoid supporting what could well be another triumph for Kydd?

Whatever the reason, this had turned into a delicate and touchy state of affairs.

His entire squadron had been witness to what had happened and would expect Kydd to come down hard on the officer or discipline would suffer. And that couldn't come about until after the landing and their return.

But before then the governor general and navy commander-in-chief in Calcutta would have got word of the rising and would be themselves returning to Madras as speedily as possible, probably at this very time on their way. That meant Fleetwood would be in a position not only to inform his father to his advantage of Kydd's eccentric action, going as it did against every rule in the book, but as well clear his own yardarm in advance of his failure to obey orders to sail.

Whatever the outcome of Kydd's bold initiative, there would be a quantity of explaining to do when he got back.

Chapter 27

Kydd watched Snell's battalion march off into the dusty heat of the interior with more than a little misgiving, if not foreboding. India, he was discovering, was a vast and mysterious land whose workings were not readily open to a hardy English soul. What if the Rajapur rebels did not recognise a column of redcoats as a threat to their capital and finished Macdowall? Kydd had to admit Richie's talk of prisoners trampled to death by elephants had shaken him.

There was nothing more he could do for them and he contented himself with retaining one frigate and sending the others north and south to maintain guard. The arrangement was for the merchantmen to remain where they were for four days in case of a need for an early retreat, after which all would return.

On the fourth day as they shortened in on their anchors, alert telescopes picked up a sudden flurry of horsemen dashing down the hill road. Kydd was called and, with a sinking heart, sent a boat in to take the news.

It was Richie but with the best of tidings. The shock of

finding British troops in his rear astride the road to his capital had unnerved the Maharajah of Rajapur who had immediately deserted his ally to fall back. At the sight of the fleeing sepoys, the Kotacunds had revolted, demanding a retreat, which was all the provocation Macdowall had needed to break the siege.

Leaving his second to conclude terms with the maharajah, Macdowall was on his way to Kydd to demand fast passage back to Madras, no doubt to explain himself as early as possible.

There was nothing for it but to give over his cabin to the sour-faced general who, for his own reasons, kept out of the way in the few days' return voyage and on arrival quickly disappeared shorewards.

Kydd had more weighty matters to consider. The governor general's standard flapped lazily from Fort St George and, even more importantly, Pellew's pennant flew once more. He'd returned and would have heard of Kydd's highly dubious transactions. It was time to hear his fate.

Admiralty House seemed under some spell, clerks and flag-captains alike treading softly with hunted expressions. By the time he saw Haslam, Kydd was distinctly apprehensive.

'To make report to Admiral Pellew,' Kydd stated formally.

'As I'd conceive you must,' the flag-captain replied drily. 'I can give you no appointment, however.'

'This is of an importance,' Kydd said firmly, 'and I—'

'For the simple reason that he's called away, *sine die*, to the fort, where there appears to be a mort of embarrassment between our military and civil notables. If your matter is pressing, I can only advise that you go there and be at hand if and when the commander-in-chief is able to withdraw.'

Kydd wasted no time in making his appearance. He was

shown to an anteroom to wait, assured that Pellew was within the adjoining room.

There, tempers were obviously raging. Over the muffled shouts, growls and occasional thumps, Kydd could make out the high nasal tones of the governor general, Barlow, and in reply the harsh Scots of Macdowall. Every so often the moderating rumble of Pellew calmed the voices briefly but was always followed by more angry exchanges.

The door suddenly burst open and Macdowall strode out. Red-faced and fuming, he walked straight past without acknowledgement. Kydd caught a glimpse inside of a pale-faced Barlow standing rigid and Pellew bowing profusely while taking a voluble leave of the man, then stumping out angrily. He caught sight of Kydd, his flinty eyes narrow and dangerous. 'Yes?' he rasped.

'Er, to report at your convenience, sir,' Kydd managed.

'Very well. Admiralty House, now, dammit.'

Leaving in two palanquins they were unable to talk on the way – just as well, Kydd thought.

'Flags!' roared the admiral, his temper obviously not improved by the short ride. 'Whisky – *burra peg*!'

Haslam hastened to find a servant while Pellew rounded on Kydd. 'I've heard a gallows deal o' cackle concerning your antics in my absence, not any of it good. What's it all about?'

The whisky was served by a blank-faced *dubash* and Kydd could see from its generous size the meaning of '*burra peg*'.

Pellew took his fill and settled with a sigh at his desk, his eyes rolling heavenwards in relief from the madness. After a moment, Kydd launched into his explanations, including the consequences, as he saw them, of not doing something as direct.

He was interrupted before he had finished with an impatient 'So I'm to understand you funded this action by bills on me?'

'It was all I could think to do at the time, sir.'

'Hmph. As I suspected. And now you've put out of countenance every damn clerk and counting-house wallah within hailing distance and I've to square yards with their lordships for years to come – but it answered! By Jove, it did, and I honour you for it, m' boy!'

'Why, thank you, sir,' Kydd said, in a wave of relief.

Then Pellew leaned forward menacingly. 'But if you ever clap my scratch to an Admiralty scrip again, I'll see you broke, sir. Compree?'

'I do, sir.'

Pellew looked at his empty glass, then winked and loudly hailed, 'A *burra peg* for the captain – and another for me as you're at it.'

The recent experience clearly receding, he fell back in his chair and chuckled hollowly. 'A graceless and pixie-led crew, those two. One of these days there'll be a mort too many high words said, and then it'll be a meeting at dawn.'

He ruminated into the middle distance for a space, then said casually, 'My Fleetwood. A bright fellow, well calculated to a life in the Service, don't you think?' Without waiting for a reply, he went on fondly, 'Ever since he set about the Dutch in *Terpsichore* I knew he was headed for bigger things.'

Kydd kept his silence, not knowing where it was leading.

'If he's got a fault, it's only the one – he's too ardent, too forward in His Majesty's cause. Thinks after he acts as it were.'

'Still so young, as were we all?' Kydd ventured carefully.

Pellew looked up sharply but, seeing nothing in Kydd's expression, eased and continued, 'As can be misunderstood at times. Saw your signal to unmoor and thought it applied only to the transports, for instance. You didn't take it amiss?'

'Well, it was, er, unexpected, sir.'

'Um. He's been told to take station on you, a chance to learn how a frigate captain of the first sort makes his way ahead. You're senior in frigates, Kydd. I expect you to give him his turn if it comes to rough play. You know what I'm saying?'

'I do, sir.' He understood well enough – but after what he'd seen it would take much for him to trust the young man in anything like a close-run fight.

'That's the spirit, dear fellow. After your showing to pull Macdowall out of his mire I've every confidence you'll not let me down. It took moral courage to do what you did and that's more than a sea mile better than the kind you need to stand before a cannon.'

Kydd had not underestimated Pellew. The man had read him and his actions for what they were and had stood by him against the unknown shadows of detractors. In return he felt obligated to do what he could regarding his son.

Chapter 28

'I was so worried when I heard,' Caroline said, with a catch in her throat. 'Those wicked Mahrattas, never content unless they're rampaging to the cost of the ordinary folk.'

'Er, Kotacund and Rajapur,' Kydd corrected gently. 'And I wasn't on any battlefield, I have to confess.'

'But everyone is singing your praises as saving General Macdowall and his army!' she blurted, wide-eyed.

It was not unpleasant to have an attractive woman adoring him for his heroism, Kydd reflected, even if it were not exactly what had happened.

'It was the navy and army striving together that did the deed, Caroline. Never myself alone.'

'If it was, there should be due celebration to you both.'

Kydd gave a rueful smile. 'I believe that an unlikely thing in the circumstances.'

'Then I think you will make laudation yourself. Where?'

But Kydd had already come up with an idea. 'I believe the navy will honour the army for their achievement in the traditional way. A quarterdeck entertainment of sorts aboard the good ship *Tyger*.'

'Splendid!' she said, her hands clasped. 'How may I help, Thomas?'

The conceit of the navy in entertainment of the army went around the ship like wildfire. Every man knew what it meant: the success was due to the efforts of neither one nor the other but the two together and therefore the usual rivalries could be put aside. It promised to be a right gleesome occasion.

There needed to be decorations of a tasteful fashion, refreshments in keeping with the exotic character of the setting and artfully produced invitations, particular care being taken on the question of whom to invite. Kydd was firm that it was to be the military forces of the Crown alone, the Company army being only the object of their trials. And in view of the animosity between Barlow and Macdowall, this was of the nature of a private entertainment, in which case neither could expect to be invited.

It seemed that the decorations were to be left in Caroline's hands, as would be the refreshments in return for a tour of acquaint of Kydd's ship in order that her ornamentations would be in proper keeping.

Her squeals of delight at discovering *Tyger*'s secret places brought smothered grins to some.

She'd arranged to have conveyed aboard a wild profusion of flowers and vines, which she and two hands detailed for the task proceeded to intertwine among the quarterdeck bulwarks and lower rigging. A further contribution came from the signal master's mate, who roused out ensigns and signal flags to be displayed at Caroline's bidding.

Kydd's invitation to Snell was answered by the man himself, who diffidently enquired if there was any contribution the regiment could make to the honours of the evening.

*　　*　　*

At eight precisely, as the last of the dusk was turning into a warm velvet night, the guests arrived, thrillingly by torchlight, through the breakers in the masula boats. At the ship's side they were greeted, the ladies and the officers swayed aboard by boatswain's chair in the charge of a man in a huge red turban and silk pantaloons with an enormous sash. He wielded a silver call with suspicious ease.

A small military band played soft airs as they boarded and all were suitably enthralled at the scene from on deck: the startling dash of white waves in the night and then, stretching up and down the coast, the friendly dense twinkling of the lights of Madras, leaving themselves a little island of gaiety in the blackness.

Just abaft the mainmast a small table was set up and the youngest midshipman was given the assignment of dispensing Indian punch from the rather splendid gold-chased and naval-ornamented bowl. Illustrated by vivid scenes on the side, this had been presented by *Tyger*'s crew to the ship in commemoration of her famous three-frigate engagement.

'Cluffer, ahoy!' Kydd called to his friend. 'Who's that you have alongside?' The man next to him was fair-haired and stooped, his brow prominent, with a changeless pensive expression. Was he some form of scholar? An odd sort to be tagging along with Cluffer.

'Why, this is the assistant colonial secretary from the Presidency of Prince o' Wales Island, wants to make your acquaintance. Name of Raffles, Thomas Stamford Raffles.'

The man bowed absently. 'Sir Thomas Kydd? As I've heard something of your intrepid exploits in Iberia. A dashing spirit that is so sadly needed in these times.'

Kydd returned the bow. 'Prince of Wales Island – which we knew before as Pulo Penang when last I sailed past.' He didn't add that he had been but a humble able seaman at the time. 'Would it be impertinent to enquire what finds you in these parts, sir?'

'Of course you may. It's on account of a friend I remembered in Ceylon that I much desired to see again. Would you like to meet him?'

'Er, yes, that would be polite in you.'

A hand went to a voluminous pocket in the old-fashioned frock coat and, after feeling about, came out to reveal a black object in the palm. Not sure what it was, Kydd leaned over to get a better view.

It moved. To his horror, Kydd realised that, in the subdued light of the lanthorns, he was looking at an enormous beetle, the horns adorning its massive head slowly turning this way and that, its carapace gleaming like gun blacking.

He jerked back, seeing Raffles gently stroking its back and murmuring, 'Yes, I agree, a magnificent specimen worthy of our utmost admiration.'

Cluffer snorted with amusement. 'Singular pleasures my friend indulges in. Insects, tigers, reptiles – collects 'em as others do old paintings.'

'Um, then I give you joy of your creatures, sir,' Kydd said, taking his leave.

As all the guests had now arrived, an army trumpeter sounded the parade assembly. First Kydd, then Colonel Snell mounted the makeshift dais to address the gathering. The respectful applause was tinged with not a little awe.

Kydd stepped forward and stood tall. 'Mr Pipe-bosun ahoy!' he thundered.

The same odd figure as had swayed the ladies aboard strode to the front, his arms folded and a scowl on his tawny-stained face.

'Pipe – hands to entertainment!'

An ancient boatswain's call was whipped out and flourished theatrically. A masterful cascade of silvery flourishes split the air, the most ornate and accomplished trills and warbles imaginable but in truth having not the slightest meaning for any of His Majesty's tars.

From the darkness stepped a figure dressed in a seaman's rig of a different era with petticoat trousers and a tarpaulin hat. He stood, striking a thoughtful pose, while two ship's boys scurried up and knelt each side, holding up a lanthorn that illuminated him in a beguiling, romantic way.

Out of sight a violinist bowed a delicate chord, long drawn-out, then fading into nothing. There was not a single movement among the audience but Kydd found that in some way Caroline had taken his arm in hers. It would have been boorish to disengage her so they stood together in thrall to the enchantment.

Into the night air came the sentimental strains of the 'William and Mary' of another age:

> *The topsails shiver in the wind*
> *The ship she's bound to sea;*
> *But yet my heart, my soul, my mind,*
> *Are, Mary, moored with thee.*
> *And after toil and danger past,*
> *How sweet to tread our native soil;*
> *With conquest to come home at last,*
> *And deck our sweethearts with the spoil.*

The carefree seaman Doud, whom Kydd had first known as a shipmate, had matured into a fine singer, whose broad, manly tone and near theatrical presence would have earned him a place in any playhouse.

The piece ended with a general appreciation, acknowledged with a grave and dignified bow. Then the violin struck up a sturdier note and Doud stood square and uncompromising, launching into the complexities of a true man-o'-war ballad, a raw account of meeting a blow at sea.

> *So hard-a-weather goes the helm,*
> *Let fly your main-sheet now with speed,*
> *The furious squall will soon be o'er,*
> *It breaks apace as you may see.*
> *The down-haul tackles must be manned,*
> *Clew-garnets, bowlines, leech-lines too,*
> *Loose off the sheet, let rise the tack;*
> *Come now, my boys, and lift her clew;*
> *Belay of all, secure the yards,*
> *And up aloft and furl him snug,*
> *Coil up your ropes and then lay aft;*
> *All hands to tipple the nut-brown jug!*

At the end it brought a roar from the sailors and polite incomprehension from the army but then, with a sprightly embellishment, the violin introduced a piece that had Doud drowned out in a familiar full-throated chorus from every seaman, including Kydd, and had the singer stumping about in well-feigned dudgeon.

> *When we sail with a fresh'ning breeze,*
> *And landmen all grow sick, sir;*
> *The sailor lolls with his mind at ease,*
> *And the song and the can go quick, sir.*
>   *Laughing here,*
>   *Quaffing there,*
>   *Steadily, readily,*
>   *Cheerily, merrily,*
> *Still from care and thinking free,*
> *It's a sailor's life at sea!*

The audience dissolved into laughter and merriment, and as Doud left to claim his reward, Colonel Snell clapped his hands smartly. From somewhere below two soldiers stiffly mounted the ladders to the quarterdeck and marched together to the exact centre where they stood rigidly to attention, muskets at their sides and a soldierly blank stare ahead.

They were old soldiers, the lacing and chevrons of a sergeant major prominent on one, and by their bearing the proudest the regiment possessed. A drummer appeared on each side, their accoutrements a blaze of scarlet and white, their snare drums burnished to a lanthorn-lit glitter.

They snapped their drumsticks to the horizontal, then, in a practised tattoo of sound, played a stirring ruffle. It ceased abruptly, the signal for the soldiers to present arms in an elaborate 'general salute'. The colonel removed his hat in response, Kydd following his example.

Snapping back to attention, the drummers paused for a moment then began a brisk volleying. In a bewildering and eye-catching display, the pair, in perfect time with each other, went through every fire-lock exercise known to the infantry manual, throwing their heavy Brown Bess muskets about as if they were toys.

They were much applauded, and at the conclusion Kydd ensured a due libation was sent to them.

And then all eyes turned to the two 'ladies' assisted up the ladder from the main-deck. In the pink of fashion, with outrageously large hats and dresses of a distinctly individual cut, they were helped to a small table by two burly seamen, who were dismissed with a sniff.

'Well, my dear, and here we are at tiffin.' The contrived falsetto fooled no one; the eldest midshipman glared about her at the burst of helpless laughter while her diminutive companion looked in astonishment through a lorgnette at the ill-behaved throng.

'And so we are,' she said, in wonderment. 'And what must we do now, cousin?'

Midshipmen Gilpin and Rowan proceeded to delight the audience with a racy account of what might be expected of any who thought to exchange the civilisation of Oxford Street for the deceiving exotics of Madras. Unrestrained and extravagant advice was liberally given to the gullible cousin that had the audience, newcomers and old hands alike, in stitches.

Caroline's eyes shone. 'So the play-halls have Jack Tar to a nicety.' She laughed. 'How I envy your life on the briny deep, Thomas!' Her grip on his arm tightened.

A diffident young army subaltern took the stand and, in a most creditable tenor, delivered songs more usually to be heard at a picnic on the banks of a dreamy river in the English summer countryside, an unaccountably moving experience so very far away.

She listened in rapt attention and Kydd, turning to make a remark, saw the glistening of tears begin, but she ignored him and, pulling herself together, clapped vigorously as two sailors leaped on to the quarterdeck.

One of them could not be mistaken. With his powerful build, dark features and piratical looks, Tobias Stirk padded to the centre of the deck and stood impassive, his arms folded. He had no need to dress the part for, with his gleaming brass earrings and his red kerchief worn as a bandanna, and his striped shirt, duck trousers and bare feet, there could be no failing to recognise the very essence of a deep-sea mariner.

The violin began a brisk and lively melody and Stirk, with a thump of feet, burst into action. A hornpipe – performed with a perfectly controlled expression and from the waist up a fierce rigidity, interrupted only by the tune's demands for gestures of 'looking out to sea' and realistic rolls to ocean swells.

From out behind him leaped the other, a spry youngster who danced in fast measure to Stirk's deliberate movements, the thump of their feet intertwining in a complex rhythm that gripped the senses. Insistently the violin urged and drove, faster and faster, bringing gasps of admiration from all.

Kydd had never seen Stirk at a hornpipe and was fascinated that his gunner's mate and long-ago gun-captain was capable of such mastery. So taken was he that at first he didn't feel the polite tap on his arm.

'Sir? Sir Thomas?' Dillon repeated.

'What is it, Edward? Are you not enjoying our entertainments?'

'It's word from shore. We're vexed to know what to make of it, but it's grave news. It seems the army is in some sort of defiance against the civil administration of Madras, as it were, and no one knows what's to do.'

Chapter 29

The army barracks, Choultry Plain, twelve miles outside Madras

Officers in their mess-kit in every stage of intoxication were laughing, quarrelling and belching in the close warmth as the long evening progressed. A drunken roar sounded over the din: 'That soldier at the end o' the table!'

Ensign Lawson snapped upright. 'Sir!'

'I see your glass is yet a-swill, sir. Is it that ye're not in harmony with yer fellow officers? Won't drink to the ruination of that verminous crew in the Presidency? Tip us a right good toast as will show us all where ye stands!'

'S-sir!' Lawson stuttered. Demanding the declaration was not the adjutant, or even the colonel of the regiment, but the commander-in-chief of the Madras Army himself. Not that it meant much – anything said within the mess by long tradition stayed there.

He stood and cleared his throat, a few dull eyes swivelling to notice him, the rest continuing noisily with their carousing. 'Er, gentlemen,' he called, as loudly as he could manage. 'I give you General Macdowall as a safe pair of hands on the reins and be damned to all others who dispute his right to take them!'

It brought a rumble of careless agreement and a flourishing of upended glasses but it seemed to answer. The scowling features of Macdowall eased as he turned away to resume a hectoring conversation with a major to his left.

Lawson let out his breath and gave a weak smile. He was new to India and hadn't known what to expect – certainly not this hard drinking, endlessly boring life in the heat and dust when anything that broke the tedium was to be fervently welcomed. The Kotacund rebellion had seemed just such until they'd found themselves trapped – and then to be rescued by the navy of all things. Morale had slumped as the endless lethargy of the cantonment had taken hold once more.

He'd heard of the feud between their commander-in-chief, Hay Macdowall, and the governor general of the Madras Presidency, Sir George Barlow.

Macdowall was a bitter man. Others of his generation coming to India, like the elder and younger Wellesleys, had done brilliantly, making a fortune while achieving spectacular victories over the forces arrayed against them. Macdowall had been left to a steady and mediocre rise through the ranks. Lawson had heard why it was: the personal rancour and opposition of the civil administration of the East India Company was at work against him, as personified by Barlow. The man, by his very character, was to Macdowall as a red rag to a bull. Starting as a lowly clerk in the Company, by unstinting hard work and the currying of favour in India House, he'd passed through the hierarchy to the highest office in the land – the governor general of all India. But then interests had been brought to bear in London and, extraordinarily, he'd been relieved of the post and demoted to the

Presidency of Madras. In sour isolation he'd been diligently starting to make a name for himself as standing against corruption and venality, in the process trampling on hallowed army practices that made existence in the field less contrasting to that of well-paid district officers.

The army despised Barlow for it and voiced even more contempt when his spirited and attractive wife took up with a young officer, the affair known to all Madras except himself apparently.

Lawson was too junior to have strong views on the matter but the poisonous atmosphere emanating from the top was having a corrosive effect on loyalty and commitment, and he was unsure how to act. Better to keep his doubts to himself and fall in with whatever his seniors saw fit to do in the circumstances.

The following day Lawson awoke to a general pandemonium. 'Well, get 'em fell in, then!' the cantankerous major growled at him. It was incredible to the point of disbelief that the entire barracks were being turned out on parade, not just without notice but so early in the day. The rumour was that something of great significance was about to be announced – and by the commander-in-chief himself to the common soldiery in grand assembly.

Drawn up in ranks and then ceremoniously closed up, the parade ground resounded to the shouts of officers and sergeants until the mass of men was ready for inspection.

General Macdowall appeared at last, dressed in full military regalia and accompanied by the adjutant general, Colonel Capper. There was no inspection. The two mounted the saluting dais and faced out over the parade.

So it *was* to be some form of announcement, Lawson realised, with a quickening of interest.

The sun was not yet high but on the open expanse of the parade ground the heat was making itself felt as Capper brought them all to attention and reported them to Macdowall.

The general acknowledged, then advanced to the edge of the dais and, in a bull-like bellow, he began. It didn't matter that only the first half-dozen ranks would hear him, what he had to say would most certainly be passed on to the rest as soon as the parade was dismissed.

But Lawson was standing close and what he heard staggered him. Macdowall started by praising the soldiers. He told them he well understood the hardships of army life at their level, the poor food, inadequate uniforms, worn weapons and equipment. Their pay was pitiful and chances of a spree in town near hopeless. And all blame could be fairly and squarely put in one quarter: the government of Madras. With growing incredulity, Lawson heard bitter taunts against Barlow and his administration, condemnation and bitter accusations, all in a public diatribe no longer confined to the privacy of a regimental mess. What was he about that he was addressing his own men so?

It got worse. In sorrowful tones he sympathised with the men, that if they found the rank betrayal by Barlow and his authority too much and desired to take matters further he could not find it in him to condemn them, for his addressing them like this was as an expression of army brotherhood, commander-in-chief to private soldier.

The parade was dismissed. The men returned to their barracks to try to make sense of what they'd heard, the officers crowding around a red-faced Macdowall in their mess.

'Ye want to know why I spoke out, do ye?' he hissed, the venom in his voice chilling. 'So I'll tell ye! I took delivery this morning of an order – an order, mark you, from a civilian commoner to the commander-in-chief! In it he tells me we can no longer lay claim to Tent Contract, would ye believe?'

There was an instant growl of dissatisfaction. This long-standing allowance had been brought in to offset the costs of an officer on campaign living under canvas at a time when armies took the field for many months. These days, almost the entire year was spent in a permanent military camp, but the stipend was still jealously guarded.

'It's a disgrace! Against our honour and standing as officers of an old and noble regiment. And I've given my response, never fear o' that. I've sent back to Mr Clerk-As-Was Barlow that I don't recognise his authority to cut off our due pay without so much as a by-your-leave – and in the future he's to keep his damn nose out of the army's private business.'

The discontent became whole-hearted, with growing cursing and shouts of damnation.

'And don't think I have no thought of where he's getting his demented ideas!'

The hoots and calls died away.

'Munro.'

This was the army quartermaster general. Cerebral and quiet, hero of Seringapatam, he was known to be in thick with the Company at a high level.

'How so?' came a cry.

'So simple, so contemptible,' Macdowall spat. 'Fills Barlow's ear with stories of depravity and degradation in the ranks as sets the man into a flat spin and a right raging tantrum.'

'Our Mr Munro?'

'Yes. Wants to advance over our heads to make *burra* nabob. And there I have him!'

'Sir?'

'He's still army and under discipline. And I think ye'll agree that all this amounts to conduct unbecoming an officer and gentleman from whatever perspective ye looks at it.' Macdowall looked about impressively. 'Therefore without further ado I'm going to court-martial the rogue.'

There were gasps of disbelief. It would mean the end for Munro after a lifetime in the regiment but, more than that, going well beyond personal animosity, it would signal open warfare with the civil administration.

'Where is he now, the traitor?'

'In his office, working,' came a call.

'Very well,' Macdowall boomed. 'Inform the provost marshal that by my order Colonel Munro is to be placed under arrest pending court-martial.'

Within two days there was a response from the hand of the governor general himself. It stated that by his conduct Macdowall had shown himself unfit for a place at the governor's ruling council and henceforth would be excluded from its assemblies.

The officers erupted with indignation, not so much that Macdowall had been slighted but at the banishing of the army from deliberations at the highest.

The commander-in-chief shut himself away for two days, sending only for food and whisky. On the third he emerged, red-eyed and determined. 'There's only one answer and I'm the man to do it.'

The mess held its breath.

'Barlow has lost his mind. He's no longer fit to govern. Tomorrow I'm to move on Madras and put an end to the business – charge that he steps down, yields up power to another.'

'Or?'

'Or? I'm at the head of an army of thirty thousands. Not even a fool like he would dare oppose the demand!'

Chapter 30

Madras Roads

K ydd and Snell headed ashore together. At the moment, with Pellew transferring to winter anchorage at Bombay, Kydd was once more the senior naval figure on station and it was imperative that he discovered what was brewing.

Colonel Snell was tight-mouthed and tense as they hurried to the fort. It was clear that something grave was afoot. Even in those early hours the city was in a ferment of fear and excitement.

'Wait here, old fellow, and I'll find out,' Snell said, disappearing inside his headquarters. He reappeared after only a few minutes. 'We've something like a civil war broken out,' he muttered, distracted. 'The commander-in-chief has taken leave of his senses and rumour has it he's on the march here as we speak. Come to depose the governor general no less.'

Kydd could hardly believe his ears. 'So as King's men and true you'll be called out to defend Madras against the East India Company. It's . . . it's . . .'

Snell managed a wan smile. 'Be careful what you say, dear

chap. I'm to take steps as you say – but only if requested. Aid to the civil power, as we term it. My men stay in barracks, I believe, until I hear from Barlow.'

From as far separated as Istanbul to Cape Town, Kydd had seen for himself what happened if order on the streets was lost under a looming threat from the outside, and here was Snell keeping his troops battened down when they should be visible to quell panic and disorder.

'If you think it best,' Kydd answered guardedly. 'I've to decide if the navy can do anything to assist.'

Snell brightened. 'Of course you can. If things take a bad turn it'll mean an encounter of a more or less bloody nature. Take it from me that then there'll be every sort of wretched castaway wailing to be taken off. Have you your ships ready?'

It was an appalling prospect. And it was only by sheer chance that *Tyger* was in Madras Roads, for the other frigate Pellew had left him was out on patrol across the shipping lanes until it was her turn for time in port.

Morning light was beginning to steal in, a lovely display of soft rose-grey out to sea, but it did little for Kydd's mood. The city could be in flames and ruin by midday. There was one thing that was his duty to do – go to his garden-house and retrieve all naval documents and papers. After that he should return on board and begin the business of negotiating or requisitioning shipping to meet any sudden flood of souls fleeing the carnage.

Bomarjee was imperturbable and helped with the packing, occasionally making comment about the Vellore mutiny, which had taken place only thirty-odd miles to the west a bare handful of years previously. There had been a quick but sanguinary end to it and for weeks afterwards executions daily, the usual conclusion to these affairs, it seemed.

But this was different. It was not a native insurrection but supposedly disciplined British men set one against another, here, where the only law was primacy of gun and bayonet.

Just as he prepared to leave he was struck by guilt. The least he could do was to check on Caroline, that she had made suitable arrangements to flee when the marching columns came into sight. There would be no English lady left to face the calamity alone. He would see to that.

It was not far to her residence but before he'd descended from his palanquin she ran out to meet him. 'Oh, thank God you're safe, Thomas!' she exclaimed, clutching her hands nervously. 'What's happening, do you know?'

He ushered her back into the house and told her gravely, 'A serious matter, Caroline. Listen, the commander-in-chief of the army is marching on Madras to unseat the governor and—'

'Macdowall? Marching on Barlow?' she said faintly, eyes wide. 'I know they loathe each other but to . . .'

'He is. Not in sight yet, but he's on his way. Now I want you to throw your valuables into a single chest and go with it to the fort. I'm arranging ships to take off any who want to flee so you'll be safe there. Do you need help? Where's your *dubash*?'

'He ran away with the others. I'm on my own now.' She spoke calmly, without any indication of panic.

Kydd bit his lip. He couldn't delay taking charge of the shipping: too many were depending on him. 'I shall send my *dubash*, Bomarjee – he's a stout fellow and will see you safely on your way.'

'And you, Thomas?' she said in a small voice. 'Where will you go?'

He didn't answer immediately. Looking into his eyes she leaned forward and very gently kissed his cheek. 'I understand. Take care, my dear man, do take care.'

Chapter 31

Aboard *Tyger*, Kydd was met by a distraught first lieutenant, to whom he'd sent a message to begin the process of approaching the merchantmen with a view to their requisition. 'Sir, it's not possible!'

'What is not possible, Mr Farrant?' Kydd replied irritably.

'They're all putting to sea, don't want to be in the vicinity when . . . when . . .'

Kydd could see that he was right. There were many fewer ships at anchor than he recalled and some of those were hauling in as he watched. The navy had no authority over the fleeing vessels, out of convoy and within port limits. Short of firing on them, he would not be able to stop them.

This was now a deadly serious matter. There was nothing for it: he had to get ashore again. The authorities must be told that a mass evacuation was not possible and some other move had to be considered.

Cursing roundly, he took boat for the fort and headed straight for Snell, whose headquarters was now guarded by armed sentries. Inside, the area was rapidly filling with people.

'Any word from Government House?'

'He's not to be moved. Insists he's staying and declares that the government of Madras will not bow to military coercion and will continue to function where it is at present.'

'Then the outcome is inevitable.'

Snell paused. 'I regret it exceedingly, but I can see no other course. I will turn out the Thirty-third and others to form a line of defence to the north-west.' He reflected soberly, 'My greatest lack is artillery, and for cavalry I have only a paltry force of dragoons.'

So the battlefield would be where the road from the interior led into Madras from the west. In the whirling insanity about to fall on the oldest city in Britain's Indian empire there would be nothing the navy could do. It wasn't their fight and their role would be held to picking up the pieces afterwards.

Kydd clutched at a shaft of hope as it took hold. 'Colonel. There has to be a way to stop the madness and I think I've an idea how to do it.'

'Do tell, Mr Sailorman – but I'm sore pressed for time.'

'The whole business is on us because of a personal affair between Barlow and Macdowall. The army we can do nothing about, but we can with the governor general.'

'What do you mean?' Snell snapped, plainly wanting to be away and preparing for the assault.

'Should Barlow be in *Tyger* frigate when the hordes arrive, he'll be completely out of reach and your forces can retire, no one left to defend. Macdowall must halt his troops and, with no one to fight, there can be no battle. He'll be at a stand and must parlay.'

'A good notion – but with one flaw,' Snell said, though obviously struck by the possibility. 'Barlow is a proud, angry man and he's already stated he has no intention whatsoever of fleeing.'

'I heard you. He knows by his actions he's condemning men to their death for appearance's sake. I find that despicable in a man, however high placed.'

'So, you'd have him meekly give up his sword and sceptre when asked and depart his kingdom for ever?'

'I'd have him . . . Damn it, you know what I mean!'

'I do, but he's not about to take his leave at your saying. So?'

Kydd fumed in frustration, then said boldly, 'So we take things into our hands. We persuade him forcibly as we must say. We – we kidnap him.'

'What?' spluttered Snell. 'We're talking about—'

'Either spill the blood of hundreds and bring odium on us all or solve the crisis in one.'

'Er, you may be right. But we'll both be complicit.'

Kydd could sense it went against the dignified officer's every instinct but continued, 'When the first ranks show over the hill, send your officers to conduct the governor general down to the foreshore. The rest is my business.'

For now the plan must remain discreet. But Snell was right: it would later, without doubt, see both of them explaining themselves in court.

Kydd returned to *Tyger*. The ship was aflame with rumour, which was whipped to fever pitch when he ordered his cabin spaces cleared.

At about four in the afternoon the signals team Kydd had posted on the roof of Fort St George hoisted 'enemy in sight', the nearest the signal book could come to reporting the sighting of a hostile commander-in-chief.

With at least four telescopes trained ashore through the heat shimmer, *Tyger* waited for Fate to make its move.

By five there had been no sign of firing or opposition but

166

on the other hand no indication that thirty thousand soldiers were flooding into the city. Neither was there a party of officials escorted down to the foreshore ready to be taken off. Surely this didn't mean it was all over without a shot being fired.

As the evening drew in and the light was failing fast, the signallers threw out 'the van of the enemy is now engaged'. What could that mean?

Kydd could bear it no longer and went ashore, leaving strict instructions with Farrant what to do with *Tyger* if things turned out for the worse.

To his astonishment Madras seemed to be going about its business as if nothing had happened, no military presence beyond the usual, no tension in the air.

Snell was in his office, lounging behind his desk, looking decidedly bored. 'Hello, old fellow. If you've come for excitement, I fear you'll find none here.'

'Macdowall, did he—'

'He's here, but not at all as we'd expected. Our information was wrong in the particulars – he's come to unseat the governor general right enough but not at the head of an army, just his own over-mighty vanity and a clutch of staff officers to exhort Barlow to step down.'

'No thousands?'

'None other than they, and all are at this moment in Government House locked head to head in violent difference of opinion. How it'll end I've no better idea than you, but we must each of us stay our hand until it all be known.' He stretched and went to a cupboard, found glasses and returned with a restorative.

'My money's on Barlow. A cold fish but can cross blades with the best. On the other hand—'

'Colonel Snell, sir!' A breathless major poked his head

around the door. 'Sorry to interrupt but you're wanted at Government House this instant.'

'We have a verdict? You'd better come along, old fellow. Who knows what's in waiting for us?'

The governor general rose from his desk and advanced on Snell, acknowledging Kydd with a nod. Macdowall was nowhere to be seen. 'Colonel Snell. As ranking officer of the Crown, I desire you will carry out my instructions in the matter of General Macdowall.'

Kydd held his breath. If this was formally pitting Snell and his regiment against Macdowall it could hardly be more disastrous.

'Sir, I have been informed by that officer that he wishes to resign his command and proceed forthwith for England. Kindly see that he departs this Presidency with full military honours on the first available vessel.'

Snell glanced sideways at Kydd with a raised eyebrow.

'There is an Indiaman in the offing,' Kydd remembered. 'If we can tempt him inshore once more.'

'The first available.'

'Sir.'

They stiffly withdrew.

Outside, Snell let out a long breath. 'Don't believe Barlow has won this little *rencontre*. No, sir, not at all.'

Kydd looked at him quizzically. 'He's banished his opponent from the field, sent the rascal packing. Why do you not account this a victory?'

'You don't see? While Macdowall's here it's all contained. Now he's on his way to London to raise a wind with the Honourable Court at East India House, who'll listen to him, while Barlow cannot be heard. My money's now on the general.'

'But here . . .'

'Barlow hasn't won here either. He's notional head of the army until they appoint a new commander-in-chief and won't hesitate to meddle further in their affairs. I can tell you the officers in Choultry Plain will be boiling with rage at what they see as the dismissal of their leader without recourse. God help us, we haven't heard the last of this miserable episode.'

Chapter 32

The officers' mess, Choultry Plains

Sitting in a rattan chair, Ensign Lawson tried in vain to concentrate on his newspaper. Besides the dreary creaking of the punkah-wallahs and the subadar major's hoarse shouts of command on the parade ground outside, there was the constant drone and occasional raised voices of the clique of officers in the corner.

As usual at its centre was Capper, the adjutant general and one-time intimate of Macdowall. There was no doubting his view – that the governor general of Madras had seen fit to be effectively rid of the supreme head of the Presidency Army on a civil pretext was monstrous, unjust and unprecedented.

Others agreed that it signalled the taking over of army affairs by civilians, which was intolerable: something had to be done before it was set in stone. Would the navy have stood for the dismissal by his juniors of Pellew, their naval commander-in-chief at Madras?

The continual ill-tempered murmurs irritated the ensign. He slapped down the newspaper and stood to go.

'Where are you off to, Lawson?' the raised voice of Capper called across unexpectedly.

'I've evening parade, sir,' he replied carefully, 'as requires my appearance before the men to be beyond reproach.'

It brought a sarcastic snort and Capper turned back to the murmuring group.

Lawson felt unsettled. What did the man have to hide that he didn't want broadcast? Something was in the wind and he didn't like it.

That evening Capper called his senior officers into the inner guest room of the mess and pointedly closed the door. Whatever was brewing was coming to the boil.

Lawson had finished his dinner and was lingering over a glass before going on duty. He looked up as Bailey, a fellow ensign, came over, agog with excitement. 'They're at it again, William,' he said gleefully.

'I've eyes of my own, thank you, Ralph.'

'It's going to be a settler, I'll wager.'

'How will you know?' Lawson replied cynically.

'We can listen.' Without waiting for a reply, Bailey carefully positioned a table as close to the door as he dared and took a chair to it. 'Come on!'

Lawson had no intention of deliberately eavesdropping on a conversation between gentlemen and shook his head. Bailey gave a twisted smile and, sitting down, pulled out a pack of cards and began a game of patience.

Lawson left for duty. Darkness was falling quickly and it was quiet, with nothing reported out of the ordinary. Then, at a little before ten, Bailey came up, flustered, clearly with something on his mind. 'Have I got a tasty morsel for your ears, William!'

'So tell me, you wicked spy.'

171

Bailey looked around nervously, then said that Capper had brought out a proposal that stood fair to achieve what Macdowall had failed to secure. It was to be a protest, nothing less than a petition to the governor general of all India, Lord Minto in Calcutta, to have Barlow removed for demonstrably failing to retain the loyalty of both the army and citizenry.

'Will he go through with it?'

'All those in the room with him have sworn to put their names to it and it'll go out in tomorrow's dispatches to Calcutta.'

This was open revolt and could very well succeed, given the dislike of Barlow and what he stood for in Madras. If the army took the lead in this, a united front would face the Madras government. Lawson would not be among them. It was not why he'd joined the colours. The poison that Macdowall had left in his wake was plainly still doing its work, subverting the loyalties of an army he had sworn to lead in the East India Company's service. There was no denying the situation put at risk the stability and security of British India at a time when Bonaparte was turning his attention to his empire beyond the seas.

The response was immediate and dramatic.

Even before the morning had passed, a fast messenger galloped into the barracks. He bore an order signed by Barlow himself to Colonel Capper, requiring him to appear before the ruling council to explain himself.

'Barlow?' snarled Capper, holding the order theatrically at arm's length. 'And I don't think I recognise the authority of this paper over an acting head of the army. I refuse to sign for its receipt.'

The messenger swung himself up into the saddle and headed back to Madras.

The defiance was now so explicit it would be impossible for Barlow to ignore it.

'This is our answer,' muttered Bailey, as the messenger arrived once more, leaping down from his horse and producing a sealed pack.

'Duty officer to sign,' he demanded.

This time Capper accepted it and disappeared into his office. A few minutes later his fellow signatories were called to him. They conferred together into the night behind closed doors.

At daybreak they emerged – to the astonishment of all, in civilian plain clothes.

Without a word they marched together into the mess and waited patiently for all officers to gather.

Capper then stepped forward, his face grim. 'I have to tell you that, as of the receipt of this order,' he flourished it for all to see, 'I and the officers named are herewith suspended from duty, by order of the office of the Presidency of Madras.'

There were gasps. As of that moment the Madras Army had lost most of its senior officers and was leaderless.

'This is, as I trust you'll perceive, a calumny and travesty of authority. I'll be brief – it's past the point where talking will remedy our grievances. Only direct and forceful action will secure our cause, of a degree that should have been employed from the first. Are you with us, gentlemen?'

The cheers were weak and uncertain, and Capper frowned. 'We're in mufti for a reason. If we're suspended, we're free to go abroad as we wish. And we will – to every garrison in the Carnatic to tell them of our underhanded treatment at the hands of the civil power. And to invite them to join with us in a just resistance to these acts against our honour.'

Lawson was chilled. It had gone beyond defiance now. It was nothing short of incitement to disaffection, sedition – mutiny. The Honourable East India Company was at war with itself. And where did he stand in it all?

Chapter 33

The residence of Colonel Snell

'Sir, I know it's late but it would be of the greatest service to me should you grant me a few minutes of your time.'

Colonel Snell was in his evening attire, plainly curious at the appearance of a Company subaltern at his house at that hour. 'Very well, Ensign . . .?'

'Lawson, sir, of the Ninth Madras. I – I have a problem in connection with the late unpleasantness between the governor general and the Madras Army, and I'm vexed to know how to act in the matter.'

'I see. Well, do come in and perhaps we'll discuss this over a brandy.'

Once they'd both taken armchairs, Snell opened, 'You've come for advice. May I ask why myself?'

'Sir, my own colonel – the other officers – these are my difficulty. I thought that as a King's officer you would—'

'The same loyalties motivate both, but I understand your position. Your dilemma, if such is your asking?'

'Circumstances have taken a wry turn. My officers are of

175

a view that is not mine and in fact could mean their allegiance is no longer firm. They have now gone on to take actions that are . . . questionable and I ask whether I should tell of them and thereby betray my brother officer.'

'I quite see your difficulty, Mr Lawson. And I have a ready answer to it.'

'Sir?'

'You will tell me. I swear to you if I judge that what you inform me is not of a consequential nature I shall forget it directly. Otherwise I shall take action and thank you for doing your duty. Will that satisfy?'

'Perfectly, sir.'

Four days later news was passed into the Company barracks. Three garrisons had sworn to rise as one, a formidable horde of over thirty-five thousands, to concentrate at the northern fastness of Secunderabad, then march south to Madras, gathering other cantonments to their cause as they progressed.

Lawson heard the news with horror. This was the reality of all the posturing and wild talk – an army on the march with mutiny in its heart.

That night a devoted bearer slipped out of Choultry Plain with a folded slip of paper concealed in his shoe.

The result of his race became known later when an extraordinary account of what had happened came through. From Madras a single officer was sent to confront the advancing army. In an act of astonishing courage, the officer, a longtime colonel of native infantry, rode his charger among the sepoys and, speaking to them in their own tongue, declared the iniquity of their officers and promised forgiveness if they stayed faithful to their salt and ceased their march.

The officers in rebellion, with no comprehension of what

176

was going on, couldn't stop the man and, having no enthusiasm for firing on him, let the day slip away from them, and the rising faded.

But before relief could set in the situation changed for the worse.

A galloper arrived in a lather at the main gate, demanding all officers. This was an emissary from the west, Mysore, where scenes of great bravery had been seen some years before against the fearsome Tipu Sultan.

A far more serious insurrection had risen and spread among the veteran officers there, with reports of the Madras government dismissals. An advance on the legendary fortress at Seringapatam was put in motion as a prelude to a wholesale descent on Madras by the combined might of the Company army in which they were invited to join.

This was a far more dangerous situation and that night Lawson took horse for Fort St George.

Snell thanked him gravely and, without wasting a minute, turned out his men.

'This will be the end and finality of it all,' he threw to Lawson from atop his snorting horse, dressed in full war array. 'It must be finished – one way or another.'

It was pitiful: less than two battalions of foot, two squadrons of dragoons and no artillery to face whole sepoy regiments.

Lawson watched helplessly as Snell's little force marched out of sight.

Chapter 34

Fort St George

'Thought you'd want to know, sir. *Tyger* frigate has just been sighted inbound.'

'Thank you, Sergeant.'

Lawson remembered this was Colonel Snell's navy friend. Having been relieved by the other frigate to revictual and water she would be putting out before long to continue the ceaseless guarding of India's sea-lanes. But in the weeks away she'd missed the bloody climax of the army revolt and, most of all, its grievous toll on the colonel.

A little later in the afternoon an orderly knocked on the office door. 'Cap'n Kydd to see the colonel.'

'Do come in, sir,' Lawson said politely.

The naval officer was every inch a sailor, deep-chested and with easy, sea-capable limbs, his features in some nautical way managing to be hard but at the same time good-natured and assured. 'The colonel?' he asked respectfully, removing his cocked hat to reveal rebellious dark locks.

'I'm grieved to have to tell you that he is at present indis-posed.'

Kydd hesitated.

Lawson was torn, but Snell had been most insistent that he be left alone as he mended after the disastrous final confrontation.

'It's no matter,' the captain responded. 'I came only to pay a friendly visit. Do mention that I called and perhaps I'll return later.'

He left quietly and Lawson came to a decision. He hurried across the parade ground to the officers' quarters, to the larger one at the end. He was let inside and stood outside the darkened bedroom. 'Colonel Snell, sir?'

There was a muffled reply.

'Captain Kydd has returned to port and desires me to tell you he called. Shall I—'

'No!' The voice was weak. But after a pause it firmed. 'If he's still about . . . do say I'd be happy to see him.'

A runner down to the foreshore passed the message and Kydd returned immediately.

'The colonel is recovering of his hurts, Sir Thomas, but the hardest wounds he bears are those of the spirit, to his honour,' whispered Lawson outside Snell's room. 'It was a singularly . . . unfortunate engagement. Pray do not linger on the details.'

The bedroom was hot and close, and in the dimness Kydd found a chair and sat in it gingerly.

'I do thank you, Mr Sailorman, for your kindness,' Snell said huskily, levering himself out of the bed. It had been four days since he'd talked to any but the faithful Lawson, and six days since he'd been carried into Madras on a litter to make his formal report to the governor general and then to his sick-bed.

'Not at all, dear fellow,' Kydd responded warmly. 'But a mite dismaying to see you low in the water, as it were, drifting with the tide. You were wounded, I hear.'

Snell sat unmoving for a space, the scenes of unyielding savagery at close quarters still before him. With an effort he asked, 'It seems a sad neglect of a guest, my friend, this sepulchral gloom. Do open the window, let in a little of God's sunlight – and hail that lazy punkah-wallah to put in a bit more effort.'

While Kydd did as he was bade, Snell made himself more presentable, swinging his bandaged leg down and ringing for tea. After nearly thirty years in army service he'd never had the need to be open with his feelings, but if there was any in Madras to whom he felt he could unburden himself it was this uncomplicated, intelligent and intrepid mariner, his equal in rank.

'You'll want to know what happened.' In the silence the tea gurgled noisily into the cups.

'*Tyger*'s anchor kissed the seabed only hours since and the first news I hear is that there's been a cruel contest in the Mysore uplands. I know nothing more – no one will speak of it.'

'Quite so,' Snell said harshly. How history would treat his actions and their consequences, he suspected, would not be with anything like understanding and forgiveness.

'If you'd rather . . .' began Kydd, uncomfortably.

'No, let me get it off my chest – but don't, I beg, judge me before you've heard it all.'

For Kydd's sake he mentioned events leading to the fatal confrontation, adding that it was as well he'd been informed in time by one Ensign Lawson, who'd defied his fellow mutinous Company officers to alert him of this worst of the uprisings. As a matter of fact and practicality he'd since been granted a transfer into the King's service, Snell's own regiment, as a staff officer.

'We took the road in a forced march directly for the rebel forces, needing to throw ourselves across their path to prevent their flooding on to the Madras coastal plain. I ask you, dear fellow, to conceive of the fatigue and hurry of spirits we experienced when scouts brought word of their movements.

'Three garrisons, twenty-seven thousands, with elephants and artillery.' He paused, recalling with a chilling clarity the far-off glitter of war impedimenta through the dust clouds of their advance, the frightful spread of troops in four snaking columns marching inexorably towards them.

'I knew we couldn't survive for long on open ground so I made for the hills, trailing our coats before them as it were. They followed, but I set our infantry in defensive echelon once we'd reached the high ground among the ridges.'

Again the heart-chilling waiting and endless review of his deploying. And as well the grotesque need for out-thinking the enemy – when this was none other than officers he knew.

'The men held staunch. I sent one battalion beyond the ridges, out of sight, the other in retreat up a broad defile. It wouldn't delude a seasoned commander but it would put me in a good position to harry his flanks. Think, then, how confounded I was when the first companies of sepoys marched on without a pause after the "retreating" men. What did it mean? Were they, with their numbers, playing a deep game?'

With thumping heart he'd looked down from among the rocks to see the steady stepping forward of the Indian native infantry on command from their mutinous officers, ready to obey their orders whatever they were.

'Then I saw my chance. I turned about my "retreaters" to face them and at the same time used my dragoons – all of them, on horseback, to cut the advance in their rear.' He paused, watching for Kydd's reaction, and, on seeing incomprehension, went on, 'I expected a halt to form squares or some such. They didn't. And in the rear there was confusion of a lamentable scale, which I was scarce able to credit in a disciplined body.'

A sudden flash of inspiration, of desperate hope – and his orders went out. His last remaining infantry were to pierce the vulnerable confusion to isolate the forward foot-soldiers; his dragoons would then be free to do their business. If they succeeded, the carnage they could accomplish would seriously deter the remainder and he'd achieve at the very least a pause in the descent on Madras.

'I set loose the dragoons. On the sepoy infantry rank and file.'

It was as if they were leaderless. No attempt at organised defence, no flying cavalry sent to their aid, just a stolid, pitiful and doomed resistance to the hacking being inflicted on them, falling in their dozens while attempting to keep faith with their last order to advance.

'I – I could not call off the dragoons. They were maddened by blood lust and battle fever, and when they left the field it was strewn with the corpses of those – those brave sepoys, who lay there, lives ended, duty done . . .'

Snell's hand bunched in anguish. It began pounding on his thigh in a wretched distress. 'All at my order, my word.'

'In war one has to give orders that—' Kydd tried to say.

'I didn't know. It wasn't given to me to understand what had happened.' The voice had turned thick with misery.

'What was that, sir?'

'I didn't know – I swear I didn't know – that their officers, sworn to loyalty, had discovered they were facing forces of the Crown sent against them. And the wretches abandoned their men to face the wrath of the King quite alone, leaving the havildars and subadars of the regiment to lead the sepoys on in obedience to the last order.'

The harrowing remembrances returned: the dragoons charging the valiantly trudging foot-soldiers, who hardly turned to meet the death-blows that cut them to pieces. The inconceivable lack of orders to take defensive formation, the realisation that they were now entirely at his mercy and he could do nothing about it.

'It was only then, when the whole field was a vast, crowded rout, that it became clear what had happened. To the eternal shame of their regiments, these mutinous scoundrels who had begun the insurrection had in the end fled the field of battle.'

Kydd now knew what had pierced his soul and lay so heavily on his honour. 'I can understand your grief, Colonel. Yet in all this there's one thing you can take to your heart.'

Snell's head was down but he eventually looked up at Kydd. 'Do tell me, sir. If there's anything of substance or honour to take away from this calamitous event I would like to know it.'

'Sir – would it not be right to declare that the whole sorry affair is now over? By your actions, however clouded in treachery and deceit, all this misguided revolt by the army is now ended.'

'You are right, of course. It is ended – but history will record the shame and dishonour for ever. They will call it "The White Mutiny" or similar, and my name will be there recorded for all of time.'

Chapter 35

At sea

With the steady monsoon wind in her teeth *Tyger* stood out to sea and Kydd was more than content. This was what it was to be a sailor, free of the shackles of the land and its complications, once more in the comforting embrace of sea routine and straightforward purpose.

Unconsciously he took his usual eleven paces forward on the weather side of the quarterdeck, turned and went eleven paces back. His eyes flicked up to the mastheads, taking in the pure curves of the edge of the sails as they drew to full satisfaction, the result of a conscientious trimming by the officer-of-the-watch, Brice. He was now standing at the conn by the wheel, not too near to irk the quartermaster and helmsman but close enough to catch the compass heading in the binnacle.

Men were at work part-of-ship and Kydd had the good grace to step around them as they spliced, swabbed and polished. Their eyes were not on him but on the first lieutenant, whose duty it was to bring the ship up to a suitable level of perfection for her captain. As far as he could tell, Farrant was succeeding, but the man's leadership had yet to be tried in the crucible of battle.

On the main-deck below he surreptitiously watched the gunner's party as, in accordance with *Tyger*'s standing orders, her armament was tried and tested in the first hours at sea after weeks in harbour. There would be no time to be about this job should they fall in with an enemy soon after leaving harbour.

And there were the midshipmen, doing what midshipmen always did – one on the weather side shrouds racing the other on the lee shrouds aloft, the first to touch the main truck the winner. Absently, he wondered what the wager was.

Reluctantly he decided it was time to go below. Victualling was done in an odd way in the East Indies and the result was more work for the purser and an increase of signatures due from himself. Signing off on the upcoming voyage storing was the first thing to be settled before the weekly account of expenditure was—

The hail came pure and clean from on high in a practised cadence. '*Deck hoooo!* Sail eight points t' loo'ard.'

All the excuse needed to stay – until this stray sail was resolved. Kydd resumed his pacing, patiently waiting for more information. The sighting placed the distant ship out on the starboard beam, almost exactly downwind from their position, so no preparatory manoeuvring would be necessary if he deemed an intercept was needed. It would be some time before sail could be made out from the deck so everything depended on the lookout.

'On deck there! I see two sail – no, belay that, three standing towards.'

It had to be a fleet. But the northbound East India convoy

destined for China had passed this way some weeks before and certainly Pellew was by now comfortably quartered in Bombay.

His thoughts raced. If it was French, knowing of the naval presence, why were they passing so close to Madras? Dutch? Not possible in these days of decline. Then . . .

'Course to head them off,' he ordered.

'You have the ship, sir,' Brice corrected formally.

'I do,' Kydd snapped. 'Hands to the braces. Down helm.'

In a broad swash of white, *Tyger* came around before the wind and, gathering speed, bore down on the unknown fleet.

Before long, things became clearer. This was nothing less than a battle fleet: four ships-of-the-line, frigates and accompanied by no transports or other encumbrances, a fearfully dangerous threat in these waters. His duty was clear: to take its measure and track it until its destination was known.

Closer still.

'Clear for action, Mr Farrant.' But there would be no fighting in the near term. His responsibility was to keep from crippling close action to be able to break off and report.

Such a sized fleet at sea here. What did it mean?

'They're English!' sang out a sharp-eyed signalman.

'I knew it,' rumbled Joyce, the sailing master. 'Reinforcements, is all.'

The challenge of the day was returned correctly, the escorting frigates not deigning to vary their course on the wings of the fleet. These were friends.

'I'd swear that the two-decker in the van was *Culloden*,' Bowden said, peering through his pocket telescope.

'Can't be,' Brice retorted, his own glass on the big ship. 'She's wearing a vice admiral's flag on the fore, and it's blue, dammit!'

Kydd knew *Culloden* was Pellew's flagship but his flag was of the red, not this blue, and he was only a rear admiral.

'Our pennants, and "assume the rear".'

To know the coded pennant assigned to *Tyger* implied a closer acquaintance than usual and—

'It's Pellew,' Kydd said, with satisfaction at his realisation. 'As has been promoted.'

But what was Pellew doing back at Madras when he'd transferred his main fleet to Bombay?

In ceremonial line, Pellew's ships came to anchor, Fort St George thumping out the seventeen-gun salute due an admiral.

Without delay Pellew was ashore and summoning all captains. Bluff and jovial he made his announcement. 'For those who haven't heard it, I give you news that their lordships have seen fit to give me my step to vice admiral before relieving me as commander in this station.'

Pellew – leaving the East Indies? Here since those inconceivably far-off days before Trafalgar? Who'd held the line to keep the India and China trade routes secure no matter what Bonaparte hurled at him – and as stout-hearted and congenial a commander as it had been Kydd's pleasure to serve?

And, he recognised, no longer in a position to advance Kydd's interests where it counted. 'Sir, we give you joy of your flag,' he said impulsively, 'but are grieved you're leaving us. If you were—'

'I thank you for your words, Kydd, but advise you'll have a wider audience for same shortly. I shall be throwing a grand ball for all Madras in gratitude for their support over my years here. I'm sanguine you'll find a trim-rigged barky to escort, hey?'

A grand ball – and held by one whose good-humoured liberality and gregarious charm was well known. It was to be the occasion of the age and the recent unpleasantness was entirely forgotten in the surge of excitement and goodwill of the upcoming event.

The notice wasn't long for Pellew had the intention of escorting the homeward-bound East Indiamen and had the hand-over to his relief to complete – to Rear Admiral Drury, his present second-in-command. The act would take place at Prince of Wales Island, Penang, where Drury was lying with his squadron, awaiting the China fleet to escort, unaware of Pellew's elevation.

For now Kydd made his way quickly to the one who would most appreciate the bright, lavish event. His knock on the door was answered by her *dubash*, who solemnly informed him that Mrs Lowther was unavailable, being up-country on a visit to a relation and unaware of the occasion.

To his surprise Kydd experienced a pang of something approaching loneliness.

The ball was as grand as expected. From the driveway to Admiralty House, illuminated by burning torches, to the arms of England fresh-painted on the ballroom floor, it was an impressive affair.

Prominent among the guests were the sea officers in their restrained but splendid blue and gold and standing out even from them was Captain Sir Thomas Kydd in his star and sash, the object of many admiring feminine glances.

The ladies in turn outdid each other in their silks, richly worked brocades and pearls without number, whirling across the floor in gay dances as if this was yet another fine English estate in the country. In the first set Pellew's elder son,

Pownoll, led out the senior matron at the ball, Lady Barlow, in a triumphant swirl of colour but everyone knew that his eyes were on Eliza, her daughter who played with her fan to one side.

Chilled champagne was flowing in abundance, and Kydd felt its heady influence as he made gallant conversation to this one, then that, before going to the lavish supper table. There, he came upon Fleetwood Pellew, his face in a scowl of sulkiness. It wasn't difficult to make out why – his brother was standing centre of attention with his radiant betrothed, his father hidden in a covey of the great and good of Madras and, compared to the more mature sea captains, his marked youth ensured that he wasn't much burdened with female attention.

'A notable evening,' Kydd ventured, 'our esteemed commander-in-chief being in the first rank of hosts.'

Fleetwood looked at him sharply as if suspecting mockery. 'There are those who'd call this a fine time,' he spat. 'I do not!'

'Others would take joy in the evening as one so splendid seldom comes our way,' Kydd responded mildly, offering him a vol-au-vent.

'Be damned to it – and your peacocking, Kydd. Don't think I haven't seen how you're putting yourself about with that grand star on your breast, trying to catch women's eyes.'

Kydd went to move away, to leave the youth to his moods, but the voice followed him, raised and querulous. 'And don't think I'm ignorant how you earned it – all the world's heard of your toadying after the Prince o' Wales and his cronies!'

Several nearby looked up in surprise and Kydd stopped in his tracks, turning back to confront him.

'You're an ill-natured ninny if that's what you believe,' Kydd

said softly. 'Have a care, Mr Jackanapes, or I'll . . . I'll . . .'
He paused, for he'd just been confronted by the appalling
image of a meeting on the duelling heath with the son of
the commander-in-chief he greatly respected.

'You'll what, Kydd? I've a notion you're not half the man
they say you are,' he sneered. 'Lucky in battle, touched by the
gods, and the world thinks it's all your doing.'

Several passing guests stopped to listen.

'This is not the place for talk like this,' Kydd said, through
his teeth. 'Brace up, sir!' he hissed.

'The subject's not to your liking, then?'

Kydd took a deep breath and catching the youth by his
elbow urged him through the open French windows into the
warm darkness of the garden outside. 'Now hear me, you
whippersnapper. If for one minute I thought you meant what
you said there'd be a mort of trouble a'tween us. I'm taking
it that the champagne's doing the raving, for any who has
the facts knows as well that Curaçao was a near-run thing
and the honour was for my ship as well.'

Fleetwood stared at him sullenly, as he continued, 'I don't
know what it is that's riding you but isn't it about time you
faced up to the fact that being a leader of men means you're
first a man, one who knows what it is to be the other creature, to take understanding instead of thinking all to be a
contending rival. You've a lot to learn and—'

'I was right. You're full of talk, not action!'

Kydd could only stare at him in disbelief.

'No? Then put up your fists, sir!'

'You – you're offering fisticuffs to a fellow officer?' Kydd
blurted, stupefied by the gesture. Fortunately, the garden was
in darkness, lit only by the light spilling out from the ballroom.

'Now, sir!'

'You're an imbecile if you think—'

The left fist flew out and caught Kydd a ringing blow in the side of the head, sending him a step backwards.

'Kydd the Frog-slayer, they call you – I've seen better men in Ma Ridley's circus!'

Clearing his head with a shake, Kydd was able to dodge the accompanying right punch but knew he had to keep his temper. He'd been formed in the lower deck, where rough justice was so often handed out at the end of a fist, and he knew all the low tricks. If he needed to, he could in seconds send the whelp down in a mewling heap, but the downstream consequences didn't bear thinking about.

Another left-right came, which he avoided by simply ducking low.

'Ha! Can't stand the heat, then. Take this!'

An upper-cut that started much too high was easily countered by Kydd with a sideways chop, following through with a hard slap to the youth's face.

With a snarl of disbelief, Fleetwood reeled back, then flung a high-fisted blow at Kydd, his judgement now drowned in rage.

It had to be stopped.

Parrying with his left, Kydd straight-armed a right to take the youth's nose squarely, jolting his head back and sending him to his knees.

'You bastard!' he gasped, and hurled himself at Kydd, who side-stepped neatly, tripping him as he blundered past.

He rose slowly, hatred flaring in his eyes and launched himself bodily at Kydd, both hands extended.

If that was the way it was going to be . . . Keeping his head down, Kydd avoided the onslaught and, getting inside his reach, planted another blow fairly on the bleeding nose.

It halted the rush, ending with the youth on hands and knees, panting.

Kydd waited a step away, his arms folded.

The head came up, eyes bloodshot and nose dripping while Kydd waited patiently.

Fleetwood got to his feet, dishevelled and wary, his hands loosely to his side. 'So, I didn't know you could sling your mauley like a ripe 'un,' he muttered obstinately. 'Doesn't change what I said.'

'No, it wouldn't,' Kydd said acidly. 'Because you've a lot to learn still. Like don't take a set against a man until you know him inside and out, both. You've been hearing a heap of cat-blash about me because there's a lot who're green envious and resentful, and you've believed it, the more fool you. What you didn't know is that I came aft through the hawse – and on the way I met a lot of gentlemen as would put you to the blush and, at the same time, hoisted aboard a gallows deal more than if I'd been bound in, always aft.

'So, listen to me. You'll be on your way back to England. Take back this lesson if ever you want to be an honoured leader of men. Make measure of your man always, and whether he's a friend or your enemy, give full respect in accordance with what you find. Or you're like to miss stays in your manoeuvring.'

Seeing the sullen expression, he impulsively took the young man's hand and said simply, 'God be with you – and always steer a course that's straight and true.'

He left the youth still standing – and it could have ended so differently.

Chapter 36

It felt like an age ago, the last time Kydd had sailed *Tyger* as part of a fleet, an obedient attendant on an armada, interceptor of strange sail for the admiral and guardian of the van. This one, however, was no majestic battle fleet covering miles of sea, only two ships-of-the-line, transports and a handful of frigates, but the flagship wore the colours of a commander-in-chief and was on an undeniably important mission.

Pellew had wasted little time in dispensing with the trappings of power: he was a successful commander who had held the line against all that Bonaparte had arrayed against the British Empire in the east and was in a hurry to return to England with his fortune. There was the little matter of handing over the sovereignty and responsibility of commander-in-chief of the East Indies station to Drury, waiting at Prince of Wales Island, then comfortably returning home as escort to the immensely rich China fleet.

Kydd had missed the high-society wedding of Pellew's son Pownoll to the daughter of the governor general of Madras, but was not sorry, for although he had not heard of any consequences following his confrontation with the younger son he hadn't wanted to see him again.

The army insurrection had largely been dismissed and the ringleaders hunted down with a view to a mass court-martial, but with Macdowall and his canker removed from the scene, order had been restored to general satisfaction.

Yet Kydd felt discontent and it centred on *Tyger*. Perhaps it was unfair – but he missed his old first lieutenant, Bray, his massive presence, the towering, battle-hardened figure always at the back of whatever difficult situation he and *Tyger* faced. His utter reliability and strength were token that the rest of his ship's company would follow him without question into the fires of Hell.

Farrant was not in the same class: older, giving the impression that his years in the East Indies had desiccated his soul, taken the joy and ambition from him and were grinding him down. In a way Kydd could sympathise, for this station was one of security and defence, not war-winning deep-sea actions. Not his fault, of course, but it was the little things, like Bray's habit of bursting out on deck in the cold of night to catch out a sheltering lookout, his prowling the gun-deck to check the priming hole under the apron of this gun or that, and woe betide the laggardly gun-captain who had not reamed it lately.

Farrant's work was competent. He'd dealt with complications, such as ensuring the bitter and sullen pressed men from the Indiamen were integrated into *Tyger*'s far more willing and professional company by intelligently isolating them from each other to absorb the spirit of those around them.

What was increasingly sad to Kydd was that Farrant seemed not to take pleasure in the company of the gunroom. By all accounts he'd sit quietly through the meal and, as soon as he could, would retire to the loneliness of his cabin. He was always courteous, did not take advantage of his station and was well liked, but had no particular friend or confidant. Was it because all aboard had tales of derring-do that could easily overtop anything he could show?

He shouldn't need to make excuses for his first lieutenant, and neither would he, but life in a frigate could turn severe in minutes, and he needed a deputy at his back he could entirely rely on. Was Farrant the one?

Still, there was time in hand to measure up. In a fleet in this part of the world there was very little prospect of combat of the kind *Tyger* had seen in the past. With the possibility of such an event slim, there was plenty of opportunity to learn the ropes.

And Pellew was taking things easy on his last official passage with a fleet under his flag, nursing the three Indiamen that were acting as transports for some hundreds of sepoys and their officers on passage to Pulo Penang and Drury for some purpose or other.

Kydd wondered at how Pownoll Pellew's bride was taking the voyage. As a young lady out of school she'd come to India with the 'fishing fleet' to find a husband, and only months later had caught the eye of the handsome, dreamy sea captain and now they were wed and on their way back to England. But her honeymoon would be spent kept out of sight below decks in borrowed cabins of a man-o'-war for the many months it would take. It would not do for the sight of a pretty woman to distract a seaman from his work, but it was a hard start to married life.

The passage to Prince of Wales Island was in the teeth of the north-easterly monsoon, now well set in. In deference to the lumbering sailing qualities of the transports, sail was kept scant in the frigates, and the long reaches on alternating tacks became increasingly tedious for a greyhound of the seas.

Chapter 37

Eventually, under leaden grey skies, they raised the broad entrance to the Malacca Strait and offshore, on its far side, their destination, Prince of Wales Island. Then it was past its northern uplands and the inner plains to see Georgetown, the island capital, opening up.

For minutes on end the thumping of guns sounded from Fort Cornwallis ashore in respect to Pellew. *Culloden*'s return salute was followed by a thinner sound from the single sail-of-the-line inshore, Drury's flagship *Russell*, and then the return due her.

As the smoke drifted away, each of Pellew's ships anchored, the small bay appearing suddenly filled with vessels – but nowhere was there the distinct huddle of the China Fleet. They were too early.

Kydd stood down sea watches and went below. This was now the meeting of admirals and no business for a frigate captain. And in the absence of the ships from China no one was going anywhere.

The climate was pleasant, the north-easterly breeze over so many miles of sea cooling and refreshing. The usual bum-boats made their appearance, and before long Tysoe appeared proudly bearing a plate of fresh fruit – pineapple, mango and a small white-fleshed delicacy called rambutan.

It was too much to face his paperwork now, and Kydd wandered up on deck again, absently finishing a piece of fruit. Approvingly, he saw that *Tyger's* hands were giving her a fine scrub down, and the boatswain was out with his note-book listing his defects. Who knew how long it would be before they were in such idleness again?

Brice had the deck and amiably shared his knowledge of what was going on with Kydd. It seemed that Drury had made his duty call on Pellew, presumably to hear of his own promotion, and afterwards had returned to his ship. No colours had been struck or thrown out in *Russell* so it would seem their old commander-in-chief was still in command. And several boats had put out from *Culloden* in which the gay sight of ladies and parasols had been observed. It was not hard to guess who was fleeing the martial confines of a ship of war for the exotic sights and sounds of the island.

On the third day with no China Fleet on the horizon, Kydd put *Tyger* in 'river discipline', a form of relaxed work and increased liberty, and the men flooded ashore watch by watch. Georgetown might have been one of the most beautiful and airy ports in the east but it quickly palled as a rendezvous for joyous sailors with little in the way of coin in the pocket. The age-old fine-weather pursuits were soon to be seen on the hatches and fore-deck – scrimshaw, yarning, intricate ropework. There were also 'jewing firms', who would perform fine tailoring for sailors on a promise ticket, and more than a few sleeping forms.

Then in the late afternoon, as invariably happened in these latitudes, it rained, heavy and relentless, easing off after an hour or so, and all activity that had transferred itself rapidly to the mess-deck reappeared.

After five days with no end in sight, *Culloden* hung out a signal in the evening requiring *Tyger*'s captain to report aboard.

Kydd was curious but obeyed quickly. *Tyger* was in good shape and he had nothing to fear, even when Pellew himself welcomed him at the ship's side. 'Good to see you, Kydd, dear fellow!' he boomed, shepherding him below. 'As I suspect, you're as jaded as I at this lying to our moorings all the hours God gives. No chance to smite the heathen, let a little powder fly.'

He offered Kydd one of the armchairs in the palatial surroundings of the 74's great cabin.

'Your ship ready for sea?' he asked abruptly.

'Stored and watered, yes, sir.'

'Then I've a quick job for you, keep you from grounding on your own beef bones, heh heh,' he chuckled.

Kydd smiled dutifully at the old joke.

'I'm weary of this waiting about. I've a yen after all these years to set foot on England's green and fair, and don't fancy waiting for much longer. Do make a cast south, see if the China Fleet have not mistaken the new rondy. They could be sitting preening 'emselves at the old assembly anchorage wasting everyone's time.'

'Which is at?'

'Pulo Singapura Strait.'

Right at the tip of the Malay peninsula, at least three or four days of active cruising there and back. Kydd grinned. Just what he needed! 'I'll sail at daybreak, sir,' he responded quickly, noticing Pellew brighten at once. 'I'll bid you good evening, if I may, and see to the barky.'

He stood up but saw something like dismay. 'Sir?'

'Kydd, m' friend. The ship can take care of itself, surely. I'd look upon it kindly if you'd stay for my little entertainment tonight. I rather sorrow that we shall not be seeing anything of each other after the fleet gets in at last and I'd like to say my goodbyes in a mite more sociable surroundings. Besides, I want you to meet some particular gentlemen who'll be figuring in your next adventuring.'

'That's most obliging of you, sir, and I'm happy to accept. If you'll excuse me just for a brace of shakes, I need to write something for my premier.'

Paper and pen were quickly mustered and Kydd dashed off a quick note for his first lieutenant, requiring him to proceed to lay along lines, rig anchor fish tackle and make other preparations to allow a smart departure precisely at dawn. He folded it and handed it over to be taken back to *Tyger* by his barge, knowing it would be received by the Tygers with excitement and satisfaction that their boredom was now at an end.

The dinner was served with its usual lavish elegance and Kydd enjoyed its cunning mix of Oriental and English cuisine, along with superb wines.

A number of East India Company gentlemen were present, the chief of whom was seated next to him.

'These are John Company supercargoes,' explained Pellew, and proceeded to name them. The one by his side was apparently a Mr Roberts, a rather portly and, to Kydd's sensibility, a somewhat self-important individual. 'They are well practised in the China trade and will form a select committee to advise Admiral Drury on his mission. Mr Roberts is its president.'

'Mission, sir?' Kydd said, mystified.

'Have you not been told?' The close-mouthed Drury was apparently not going to say anything about it to his subordinates until he had the full weight of command.

199

'Not yet, sir.'

'Then I'll let Mr Roberts inform you of what's afoot.'

The table quietened.

'You'll recollect the business with Goa, Sir Thomas?'

'Only briefly, sir.' It was the chief Portuguese settlement in India, and before Kydd's arrival there had been a flurry of disaffection that had apparently since been settled.

'Well, sir, it was decided by London that, since the unfortunate departure of the Portuguese Royal Family from Lisbon and the country's subsequent invasion by the French, it could well be construed by Bonaparte that, with his brother on the throne, all Portuguese overseas territories had by this happenstance fallen into his hands. Should Goa thus revert to the French our situation in India would be rendered intolerable. Therefore we landed a strong force of redcoats and their support to aid the Portuguese in resisting any French descent. They were not overly amused but, after persuasion by Lord Minto, were brought to an understanding.'

'I see.' Remembering the proud Portuguese he had known, Kydd realised this forced invasion had to be a considerable understating of what must have occurred.

'Since this success, His Excellency is minded to move to protect the China trade in like manner.'

'Not . . .?'

'A similar landing to pre-emptively occupy Macao before the French strangle our vital trade interests at source.'

'This is Admiral Drury's mission?'

'It is. We, the select committee, are here to smooth his path with both the Chinese and Portuguese.'

A memory came to Kydd of the last time he'd been in Macao, a humble seaman in the 32-gun *Artemis*, talking with a dignified and scholarly priest, who had told of his fears that the turbulent and thrusting English would some day

200

take the ancient colony for their own. He'd laughed at the time but now here he was, commanding forces with just that object.

'A mission from Lord Minto in Calcutta,' Pellew intoned impressively, 'as I believe we should raise our glasses in a bumper to its success. Gentlemen?'

The evening progressed in a warm and amiable atmosphere, leisurely and courteous, and when Kydd was ready to leave it was with the glow of a superb cognac suffusing his being.

'So, it's farewell, then, old fellow,' Pellew mused, as they watched Kydd's barge make its way in the darkness to the side-steps. 'I really wish there was more I could do for you, but it's been unconscionably quiet these few months, nothing to tag a distinction on of any sort. You'll go with my full approbation of conduct, my commending to Admiral Drury and so forth, but there we are – you'll be making your own way on this station for the future.'

It was a wrench, the parting. The bluff old frigate captain and the new generation of the breed recognising in each other the qualities that had placed them both at the top of their profession, the older man with the generous spirit of one without the driving need to prove himself before the world.

Kydd boarded his barge and growled the order to return, the men at the oars leaning into it obediently for the distant silhouette of *Tyger*, which lay still and somnolent. Odd that there were not more lights abroad on deck but Farrant had probably completed the readying for sea and considerately sent the men to their last all-night-in, a humane act that did much to restore Kydd's faith in him.

'Oars.' Halgren's order was soft, in thoughtfulness to the men below sleeping at this late hour.

The boat was hooked on and Kydd went up the side,

looking forward to getting his own head down with an early start in the morning.

In accordance with his standing orders there was no piping aboard or side party in the silent hours, and only the duty quartermaster was there to greet him. Kydd felt uneasy but there was nothing outwardly wrong. The officer-of-the-day was not there because he would be comfortably on call in the gunroom. The wheel was deserted, and the watch-on-deck hunkered down around the fore-hatch with the solitary lookout disconsolately forward, peering out over the rails.

Then it came to him. Where were the lines laid along the deck, the beckets thrown off under the hatch coaming, the jigger tackles ready for those awkward moments in setting sail? Why wasn't the cable ready buoyed, the anchor fish tackle rigged? . . . There'd been nothing done in preparation for sea at all.

'The officer-of-the-day – on deck, now!' he snapped at the quartermaster.

He waited impatiently for the officer to appear and when he did he rounded on him. 'Mr Bowden. What's the meaning of this?'

'Sir?' He was sleepy and rubbed his eyes in astonishment, trying to make out what the captain meant.

'Don't play the ignoramus with me, sir! I distinctly gave orders – written orders – that the ship be put in a state to proceed to sea at break o' day. Why hasn't she been readied so?'

Bowden blinked helplessly. 'Um, my night order-book gave no such—'

'Damn it, man. You've been officer-of-the-day this evening. Did not the ship receive an order by hand of my coxswain sometime in the dog-watches? Addressed to the first lieutenant? There's your order, sir!'

He felt himself get distinctly angry and glared at Bowden as he reached for a reply. 'Um, yes, sir, we did.'

'Well? Why didn't the first lieutenant take action, pray?'

'Er, I'm not sure, sir.'

'Is it me or just the world that's gone mad? Who took the note to the first lieutenant?'

'I'd hazard his servant.'

'Rouse him out and ask him when it was delivered into Mr Farrant's hands,' Kydd fumed. If he found he'd forgotten to hand it over or some such stupidity he'd be a very sorry individual before the next day was out.

Bowden came back but with an odd, defensive expression. 'He swears he gave it to the first lieutenant as he was leaving the gunroom after his dinner.'

'Fetch Mr Farrant to me this instant, if you please.' Kydd was now icily angry.

A little later Bowden came back. 'Sir. The ship's corporal reports he is unable to wake the first lieutenant,' he said, in a stilted, formal tone.

It was naval custom that a member of the ship's crew could not physically shake an officer to rouse him from sleep as this could be interpreted as striking a superior officer.

'Then wake him yourself,' snarled Kydd. 'This has gone far enough, damn it!'

To his surprise, Bowden did not hurry off but said desperately, 'I doubt he will come, sir.'

'Pray why not?' Kydd said dangerously, crowding him.

'Er, because, sir, I believe that he, um, might be flustered from drink . . . sir.'

'What?' Kydd recoiled, incredulous. As far as he knew there hadn't been any uproarious gunroom revels while he'd been gone.

And then it began to dawn on him. 'How long has he been,

as who should say, a friend to the bottle? Speak up, sir, I'll have my answer!'

The sorry tale came out in fits and starts, a sadly not uncommon one in a navy stretched in its commitments and keeping the seas for years at a time: a first lieutenant without watchkeeping duties and able to retire to the privacy of his cabin taking to drink to lay his demons to rest, whatever they were. The man hid the habit with excuses and deceptions but was unable to keep it from his messmates, who, if he was popular, would loyally cover for him, as even would the lower deck.

On a quiet station there was little chance of being caught out by a sudden call to action out of the night, or complex evolutions sprung on him as the ship settled to its nocturnal stillness. It had simply been his unfortunate luck to have Kydd make demands on him during his accustomed fuddlement.

'Did the first lieutenant receive my order into his hands?' he demanded coldly. If he had, it was dereliction of duty of the first rank with the severest consequences.

'Um, it was not marked "urgent" on the outside, sir,' Bowden offered miserably.

It was now after midnight. He'd promised Pellew he would be on his way at dawn and it would be mortifying to a degree to end his last service under Pellew's flag in a broken assurance and shower of excuses.

'Mr Bowden,' he grated, 'for now, you are acting first lieutenant. You will turn up the hands – yes, all of them, including the idlers – and set them to readying *Tyger* for sea.'

'Er, sir, it would—'

'By lanthorn-light if need be. Well – what are you waiting for?'

'If Mr Farrant wakes and—'

204

'He's confined to his cabin until I send for him. You'll have a clear run, Mr Bowden.'

It was grimly amusing to see the entire ship's company stumbling confused, unable to credit why they'd been turned out, then seeing Kydd on the quarterdeck, in full dress uniform and decorations straight from the flagship, standing akimbo with a ferocious glare, daring them to whine.

A despairing Bowden was everywhere, the darkness making every faking out, seizing and bending on by feel, a trial. Petty officers reporting their lists hurried down the deck, looking vainly for him in the chaos. Shouts and angry hails set parties of men in the gloom to tailing on the wrong rope and more than a few wandered dazed and leaderless.

It was costing Kydd a lot to remain on deck after his fine evening, slowly pacing and throwing a caustic remark here and there.

At length an exhausted Bowden had all in hand, but in the immutable way of the navy, it was not considered a fact until reported.

'Sea watches at eight bells,' Kydd grunted. Four in the morning. 'You have one hour to get your head down.'

Kydd didn't let what he had to do in the near future interfere with his sleep. By his actions in getting to sea promptly he'd gained for himself time in the next week or two to think what to do before it was passed to higher authority and out of his hands. He drifted into a dreamless slumber.

Chapter 38

'Come.' Kydd leaned back in his chair, his expression granite.

'Reporting as ordered, sir,' Farrant said quietly.

The joyous early-morning sunlight dappling the deck-head from the sea outside was of unfair brightness, catching his face full on, unhealthily pallid and set.

'You were taken in drink, sir, and unfit for duty. Have you anything to say?'

'Nothing that might be calculated to take your sympathy, sir.'

After some moments Kydd continued, 'I cannot conceive of a more reprehensible charge against a naval officer, let alone the first lieutenant of a front-rank man-o'-war.'

Farrant remained silent, his gaze elsewhere.

'You know what I have to do,' Kydd said heavily. 'And I have no alternative.'

The gaze focused back. 'Yes. Do feel free to do your duty, sir.'

Kydd felt a backwash of guilt and a degree of sympathy. He'd known officers who, in the cant of the wardroom, were 'in the grip of the grape' but all of them had had their reasons. Who was anyone to judge?

He picked up a pencil and fiddled with it. 'Sit down, Mr Farrant. You don't have to answer but could you share with me why you . . . you needed this comfort? Nothing for me to write down, of course.'

His first lieutenant looked at him closely, then eased. 'I do believe I will tell you,' he said, almost inaudibly.

'I was third of the *Iphigenia* 74, a fat and languid member of Admiral Pellew's squadron, then to *Culloden* and for some reason – I'd offended least or some other – I was plucked from there to this ship, and as first lieutenant. The plum appointment in this fleet!'

'Thank you,' Kydd said, without thinking.

'Then I took it up. And discovered what it was to be premier of a crack frigate – no, the most famous frigate of the age.'

'Go on.'

'Let me be truthful. Your officers were welcoming and loyal to me – but there was no hiding the fact that they could bring to mind capers and escapades that left in the shade anything I could show. How could I put myself forward as their leader in battle?'

'That's up to you,' Kydd harrumphed, a little ashamed of his glib reply.

'Quite,' Farrant agreed. 'But it misses the essence.'

'Oh?'

'Am I up to the job?'

It slammed in with all the subtlety of a back-winded fore topsail. 'You're concerned you can't stand with the Tygers in the article of fighting the enemy?'

'I heard tales in the gunroom about your engagements as would petrify the devil himself, and putting myself in Mr

207

Bray's shoes, I knew I couldn't match his example,' replied Farrant, quietly, staring down at his hands.

'A man finds himself when he's stiffly challenged, I've discovered, and—'

'There is a final matter that makes it all a rubbish of logic,' Farrant said flatly. 'I came on board with high expectations – being premier in one of *Tyger*'s famous actions and thereby eventually achieving my step to command. Now I find it to be a threat, not a promise. Where are my hopes now? That we soon find ourselves yardarm to yardarm with a Frenchy battler – or that I'm lucky enough to avoid same, sparing me from being seen to fail on the day?'

Kydd could find nothing to say. If this was what had grappled his first lieutenant by the throat it was a reason to find refuge from it. But it was the business of every naval officer to make himself fit for the human demands of the position, whatever it took. He'd long ago come to an accommodation, but Farrant seemed to have spent his formative years in the profession quietly, most recently as ranking lieutenant in a ship-of-the-line where individual initiative and courage were not encouraged. Unable to test himself in action or develop means of coping with the fierce life-and-death demands combat generated, was it so surprising that he'd gone the way he had? The proper course for Kydd to take was open arrest and referral to the admiral, the dour and pitiless Drury. Farrant would at best be cashiered, dismissed from the navy and disappear into the larger world, no doubt to misery and family contempt. It would destroy him.

On the other hand, there was no excuse for the offence in an officer. The revealing of his failing had now brought him low, robbed him of his moral authority, his standing before the men he must lead. The sooner he was out of *Tyger* and a new first lieutenant appointed the better.

'I thank you for telling me, Mr Farrant, but I can give you no hope that it can be overlooked,' Kydd said. 'You are no longer confined to your cabin but at the same time you are stood down from duty, sir. Mr Bowden will be acting as first lieutenant and will attend on you shortly to receive your ship's papers.'

Farrant was mute and rigid during the pronouncement, and Kydd's heart wrung at what he was doing to the man. 'I don't believe *Tyger* will be facing the enemy in the near future and therefore your departure from this ship will be made final at Madras on our return.' Kydd paused before continuing in a kindlier tone, 'Up until now you've discharged your duties aboard my ship to my satisfaction, sir. Um, if there's anything I can do to . . .' A foolish question that he wished hadn't escaped him.

With a touching dignity Farrant drew himself up and said, 'Sir, my course is run. There's nothing any might do to stay my fate – but I thank you for the kindness in asking.'

To see one with such an inner decency being martyred by the demon drink was pitiful, but in all charity Kydd could do nothing about it. 'Carry on, please, Mr Farrant.'

There was a brief hesitation, a flicker of emotion across the pale, set face. 'Sir Thomas. I will not beg. Neither will I waste your time in foolish repine. I ask only for due consideration to my plea. Sir, it's this: should I give my solemn, sworn pledge never to allow a single drop of alcohol to pass my lips ever again, would this allow you to reconsider?'

Kydd sighed. Wasn't this just a remorseful toper struggling to avert the consequences of his weakness? And how believable was his oath?

'Mr Farrant. We both know that—'

'Sir. I've looked into the abyss. I mean what I say!'

There was something about the intensity of his words that

gave Kydd pause. He'd already determined to land Farrant at Madras after they'd got back. Whether that was after a soul-destroying non-existence of ghost-like wandering the decks, or after a useful period as a working lieutenant, was not material, for in both instances he was going out of the ship. It made sense therefore to keep him administratively in post until the new one was appointed.

But there were more than a few problems with that. The man had lost all authority. How could he be expected to lead, to retain the confidence and trust of the other officers? Would the seamen look aft and see him for what he was?

However, if Farrant kept his word and arrived back at Madras without incident and dry, he'd possibly look at the whole thing again. If he lapsed, as was probable, at that instant Farrant would be finished as a naval officer as if it were this hour again. But how could he manage to salvage his authority and standing?

'I take it you are asking me to reinstate you as my first lieutenant in return for this, er, pledge?'

'I am, Sir Thomas.'

'It is a monstrous difficult thing you ask, sir, but I'll think on it.'

'Where's Mr Joyce?' Kydd demanded. The officers in the gunroom looked about but then there was a jolly hail from the doorway, and in clumped the sailing master, breathless. They were all here – except one.

Kydd did not sit at the head of the table. He didn't intend this as a formal address and, in any case, this was their own mess and he was a guest. 'Thank you for your attendance, gentlemen,' he said, with due gravity. He could see by their expressions that they were expecting a pronouncement on Farrant.

Kydd had formally asked Bowden that he might be allowed to be present at their next gathering, which it seemed co-incidentally would be in the next half-hour. 'I'll be brief. This concerns one of your number, who has asked me to bear a hand with a problem he has.'

Kydd saw both understanding and feeling in their expressions and, encouraged, went on: 'You don't need me to tell you of the magnitude of the burden he faces. He desires to tackle it nevertheless and I'm minded to allow him his chance.'

There was a rustle of surprise and one or two exchanged glances.

'He pledges that he will abstain heart and soul in return for his post. In all other respects a good first lieutenant and, knowing what a hardship on you officers it would be to carry his work upon yourselves, I'm inclined to grant it. Yet I cannot and will not do so over your objections. I now ask you to consider whether or no you will allow Mr Farrant to resume his dominion over you in the full post and title of first lieutenant.'

In the shocked silence he added, 'I leave this with you, and Mr Bowden will convey your thoughts to me privily in my cabin.'

There was apparently little discussion, and Bowden soon let it be known that the quarterdeck agreed that Farrant be given his chance. Kydd took the opportunity of extracting a promise that there would be no concealing a fall from grace and no mention of their discussions to Farrant.

'Desire the first lieutenant to see me, if you please.'

Farrant was pale but controlled when he stepped in. 'Sir?'

'I've given consideration to your request, sir. And will accede to it with the understanding that, should you ever be found with a glass in your hand or a bottle in your cabin, it is over, finished. Until that happens you shall be as you were before, first lieutenant of this ship. The log will show that you were taken ill for that night but are now recovered.'

'I thank you, Sir Thomas, from the bottom of my heart and shall not break your trust.' His voice had a betraying tremor, which Kydd chose not to notice.

'Then you meet the hardest part of all – face the Tygers and assert yourself.'

'I'll do that, sir, and . . . and . . .'

'Carry on, Mr Farrant.'

For the sake of tact Kydd allowed an hour to pass before he ventured on deck.

Farrant was on the quarterdeck, to windward of the others, who had yielded his prerogative to him, but he was alone, with a faraway gaze directed forward. As soon as he saw Kydd he in turn yielded up the weather side. 'Good morning, Mr Farrant,' Kydd said neutrally. 'Anything to remark?'

'No, sir.' The first lieutenant came back immediately, which he could not have done without earlier having checked with the watch-on-deck.

'Very good,' said Kydd.

The men had completed their morning deck-scrub and were hanking down gear. One of them, a quarrelsome Irishman, contemptuously flung down his coil on to the belaying pin without the customary through bight.

Kydd glanced sideways. Farrant had seen it and was taking action.

'You – O'Dwyer!' he hailed strongly down the deck. 'And I'll see that line properly belayed.'

The man looked skywards, his hand shading his eyes, as though he'd heard a mystical voice from aloft, then elaborately turned his back on Farrant and padded away forward.

Kydd saw his chance. 'O'Dwyer!' he bellowed. 'Lay aft this instant!'

The Irishman stopped as though lassoed and guiltily retraced his steps.

Kydd waited for him with a thunderous expression. 'It's been some time since you've had your back scratched. Are you asking for it now?'

'Ah, and I don't know what y'r worship means, sure I don't.'

'An old haulbowlings like yourself, you don't know the meaning of "silent contempt", then?'

From time immemorial the charge had been known as 'the captain's cloak': it could be made to cover any one of the many ways in which a seaman could express mutinous feeling without uttering a word.

The man stood sullenly, shuffling his feet.

'You deliberately turned your back on Mr Farrant, the first lieutenant of *Tyger*. I'll have you know that, as a duly appointed officer over you, he is deserving of respect and, be damned to it, if you fail to render such you'll be making your acquaintance with the cat again. Do you hear me?'

It was as unambiguous a declaration of his support for the first lieutenant as if he'd cleared the lower deck and made it an order. The word would spread fast that, whatever else had occurred out of sight, Farrant was now back in his post and had better be obeyed.

Kydd kept his smile of satisfaction to himself and leisurely paced back aft.

Chapter 39

Out of the soft morning mists to the south the grey silhouettes firmed of a half-dozen or so ships. The China Fleet under small sail was beginning its final run to Prince of Wales Island, having anchored for each night in the Malacca Strait in deference to its sprawling, shifting mud-banks.

They were welcomed with relief and, within the day, had fallen in with Pellew's escorting warships heading out for the long voyage to England.

Rear Admiral Drury's small squadron was left at its moorings: three transports guarded by *Russell* 74 and two frigates, *Tyger* and the light frigate *Dedaigneuse*, a French prize that appeared so like his old *L'Aurore* that Kydd had to look again with a catch in his throat. The odd unrated cutter flitted between them and other small fry were about their occasions, but it was a puny enough expedition to set against the vast Chinese empire.

The punctilious Drury struck his blue ensign when Pellew's sails were barely below the horizon, slowly raising his own to mark his elevation to command.

Dutifully *Tyger* and *Dedaigneuse* noted this by exchanging Pellew's blue for the red with an accompanying seventeen-gun salute.

Within minutes the 'all captains' was hoisted in the flagship and the three captains of rated vessels assembled in Drury's austere but well-appointed great cabin.

Drury was a pompous individual, a stickler for the formalities, and took his seat at the table with exaggerated dignity. There were many vacant places but the East India Company representatives were distributed in open chairs against the bulkhead. Kydd noticed Mr Roberts with a guarded inclination of the head and was returned a dry smile.

'Gentlemen,' began Cox, captain of *Russell* and now presumably flag-captain of the station, 'it is my duty to have to present you to your new-sworn commander-in-chief, Rear Admiral Drury.'

So, Drury was playing it by the book. The blank expressions on the other captains' faces showed they were as unimpressed as Kydd was. They already knew Drury from his post of second to Pellew.

'I will now lay before you the nature of the mission entrusted to us,' Drury opened ponderously, managing to avoid looking at any one captain.

What was said was not news to Kydd but he knew better than to say so and sat with a look of polite interest.

At the conclusion Drury introduced Roberts and the Honourable East India Company Select Committee of Supercargoes, who looked back warily. 'With the guidance of these gentlemen I have no doubt that we shall be enabled to make our landing and occupation without hindrance and, this being an action employing Company troops for a Company objective, their counsel and direction will be regarded by Lord Minto as binding.'

Kydd continued to hold his tongue. A commander shackled by the orders – even if disguised as advice – of one not bound by military discipline had to be a recipe for confusion and disaster. And where the commander had such lofty disdain for all non-naval breeds as Drury exhibited, calamity lurked.

'Admiral. If you'll permit me to explain . . .' began Roberts.

Drury frowned. 'Mr Roberts, this is a military planning council and your observations have no place here. They might more properly be put before me later, at the appropriate time, sir.'

In the frigid silence that followed, Drury outlined the strategics. There would be no objections from either the Chinese or Portuguese because the chief aim of the mission was simply the preservation of trade, which all devoutly wished for and was colossal, probably amounting to more than that won from all of India. The consequences to the interests of all sides if open warfare broke out with the French were all too evident.

At the earliest possible time it would be made clear that Company men would be landed and discreetly quartered in various parts of Macao, only to be called out in the event the French made a descent. No territorial claim of any kind was being made.

Kydd caught Drury's eye. 'Sir, may we know if we are expected? That is to say, has the governor of Macao been asked to grant his permission for our occupation?'

'No, Sir Thomas, he has not,' Drury replied frostily. 'It has been advised to me that it would not be in the best interests of retaining discretion in the matter of our presence to give advance notice.'

So, the British would appear offshore in warlike array without any warning, demanding to take over the island of

Macao in that hour. Honour undoubtedly demanded that the governor make resistance with what forces he had at hand.

'The Chinese?'

'Do allow that the committee know their business, sir. As Macao reverts to our control, it is intended to communicate directly with the viceroy at Canton in order to facilitate matters, never fear.'

Kydd said nothing more. The Chinese would be confronted by a *fait accompli* with no recourse. They would never accept the insult and the result would be slaughter – one way or the other. It was lunacy.

'We frigates, sir?' the eager Rigby of *Dedaigneuse* asked.

'The Pearl river is too hazardous to risk a vessel of the draught of *Russell*. When we reach Macao Roads I will shift flag into *Tyger* and both frigates will move inshore to cover the landings. Now, if there are no more questions . . .'

Next morning the squadron slipped south through the strait, leaving the city of Malacca, white-hued and in sleepy colonial decay, close to larboard. Dillon was eager to point out that what they were seeing had been continuously inhabited by Europeans since the Portuguese freebooters had arrived in 1511.

Kydd's mind drifted back to the last time he'd been that way, a seaman in the legendary *Artemis* involved in transporting an ambassador to the Chinese emperor's court. Aboard there had been noble ladies and haughty gentlemen from whom he'd been kept well apart as they made their stately way southwards.

At that time he had known little of the hazards of the passage, the turgid swelling of currents, the contrary breezes after a monsoonal downpour, the lack of seamarks to denote their passing. In happy ignorance he'd marvelled at the wild profusion of jungle down to the water's edge and the surly gathering of the afternoon rain clouds. Now, in place of the exciting mystery of making landfall in fabled China, he was more than a little apprehensive of what they would be met with. Certainly not a passionate woman in a pagoda, as he had then. Would he see more gruesome decapitations in Canton . . .?

'Fish traps, sir,' Brice, the officer-of-the-watch, sighed.

More of the pestilential artifices lay ahead, nets strung across the current between poles with no indication of where they were. *Tyger*, now lead frigate, had to pick her way around them with a flag over her taffrail to the next astern as warning where to steer if they were to avoid an unholy scrimmage.

And then the Malacca Strait narrowed to starboard from a coastline a good thirty miles off to a constriction barely ten miles from side to side.

Joyce, the master, was satisfied. It was going to be easy sailing now – as long as the transit was made in daylight.

The fleet duly anchored for the night in the open waters, and in the morning formed up for the passage. Islands loomed one by one, Joyce noting them. Then courses were laid to thread through, past the low, jungle-smothered island of Pulo Singapura to larboard, quiet and somnolent in the enveloping heat of its position, a single degree off the line of the equator.

And then they were into the South China Sea on a direct course for China.

Chapter 40

The immeasurably ancient land lifted above the horizon, at first in the form of offshore islands, steep and rocky, with clusters of rickety grey bamboo erections on stilts, fishing harbours of a kind. On one island, above a temple, a solitary statue, white and distant, stood near fifty feet high.

Kydd saw myriad junks, their three ribbed sails and energetic rolling only to be found in that part of the world. Whole families were on board, the children effortlessly moving about briskly heaving decks.

The characteristic whiff of the Orient greeted them, a somehow homely odour of wood fires, noodles and humanity.

Offshore, the sea was a clear jade green, but nearer to the estuary of the great Pearl river it discoloured to a dispiriting drab grey as soundings decreased.

No officious customs or harbour authorities came out to investigate them, most likely because all merchant shipping would make for Macao itself. It gave Drury's flag-captain adequate time to decide on moorings, and the little fleet came to its rest some fifteen miles south of Macao, sheltered and out of sight among the Ladrones islands.

Drury wasted no time on his transfer. Kydd yielded his great cabin and living spaces to the admiral and took up the first lieutenant's quarters in the gunroom, a considerable step down in comfort and with a feeling of trespass on another's private domain. And irritation that his personal gear was not within reach at all times.

An immediate conference was called; as ship's captain Kydd was asked to make himself available.

Cox, the flag-captain, was to remain with *Russell*. The three transport captains were Company men and therefore Drury had only Kydd and the youthful Rigby as his colleagues to stand with him.

'Mr Roberts, I do welcome the committee to our first council-of-war, as it were.'

'Thank you, Admiral. We're ready to serve each in our way, ha-hmm.'

The other four sat mute.

'Very well. I believe as the first item for—'

Roberts, however, had fumbled a cigar from his waistcoat and now began preparing it. 'You'll not mind if I indulge, Admiral?' he asked genially.

'Yes – I do! Filthy habit, sir.'

The Company man paused, his eyes flinty. 'Then I shall not.' He made much play of putting it away and looked up stonily. 'Please to continue, sir.'

'My orders state that—'

'I rather think that to be "my advice has been", wouldn't you, Admiral?'

'The orders that I received from London concerning co-operation with the Lord Minto on this expedition,' he said heavily, 'lay emphasis on an early occupation of Macao.'

'Indeed. They must!'

'I rather think that a precipitate course to take, given we

220

have at this time no knowledge of the military or other resources awaiting us.'

'I contradict the gallant admiral. Information from our own mercantile sources gives a more than adequate picture upon which we will base our advice.'

Drury took a breath. 'It's less the numbers and more how they are used, sir. Is the governor of a mind to resist fiercely? Has he military acumen, artillery, the support of the populace? These are matters you are ill-placed to consider.'

A cold silence followed, which Drury broke, now speaking in a more placating tone. 'There is no doubt that our presence has been reported, and I have every reason to believe that I will be received amicably by the Portuguese governor. After all, we are allies,' he finished uncomfortably.

'To what end, pray?'

'With the object of persuading the governor to allow a peaceable occupation.'

'A poor notion. I know Lemos Faria. He will play for time to call for reinforcements.'

'Nonsense!' Drury snapped. 'The nearest he can conjure any is Formosa, which, in the teeth of the nor'-easterly monsoon, is weeks away. We will have concluded our business well before these can possibly intervene.'

'And then—'

'And then this governor will see it as his duty to his country to safeguard trade by conciliating the Chinese in respect of our presence.'

Roberts leaned back in his chair, his features unreadable. Then he snapped upright. 'Very well, Admiral,' he said haughtily. 'You go – and with our best wishes for your success.'

Taken aback, Drury mumbled an acknowledgement and ended the conference.

If he had been fooled, Kydd had not. It was plain that

they were setting the admiral up so that if he failed on any count it would be his fault and not theirs.

'Captain Kydd,' Drury said, after the committee had left the room.

'Sir?'

'I will take your barge and will be obliged for a boat's crew of trusties and your company.'

'Aye aye, sir.'

Time was passing and the mission was urgent, but things had to be done correctly. Full dress, swords and decorations for both, boat's crew in *Tyger* stripes, a Union flag at the fore, a red ensign at the staff. A marine escort of four, unarmed.

Sitting bolt upright opposite the admiral, Kydd cast his eyes over the unfolding scene, letting his mind go back to the last time he'd been there. The experience had created a deep impression on his unworldly young self for it was there he'd had his first real encounter with a woman. That it had later come back to haunt him added to the poignancy of this return.

Ahead were the same time-worn, seaweed-slimed steps to the Macao wharf area, and atop the stone pier the familiar motley guard drawn up in their faded red and tasselled uniforms, along with an anxious, corpulent guard commander.

Chapter 41

The governor was in the Fortaleza do Monte, an impressive colonial fortress in the centre of the island, not far from the noble façade of what had once been São Paulo Cathedral. Admiral Drury and Kydd were ushered into the presence room, almost quaint in its great age, that of Drake and the dawning era of heroic exploration.

A neatly dressed, courteous and canny individual, his manners and address those of another century, rose to greet them. Several others, equally of an age, remained sitting to one side, their features rigid and unyielding.

'*Sua excelência Bernardo Aleixo de Lemos Faria, sob Deus, Governador de Macao,*' intoned a bewigged equerry.

Drury rose from his elaborate bow and, in laboured French, began his entreaty, but Lemos Faria cut him short. 'The British are the greatest traders here, so your language is well understood, sir.'

'Then, sir, I will tell you of the purpose of our visit. Our two countries are allies and His Majesty views the late exile of Dom João as a necessary evil in the face of the overwhelming French aggression against Iberia and desires to do all he can to preserve the Portuguese nation's ancient lands and rights.'

It brought only a thoughtful nod of acknowledgement.

'We are desirous that such belligerence shall not extend to this part of the Portuguese empire, with all its vital trade, and have brought to you some valuable reinforcements in the three transports you see offshore. It would be of service should you allow us to land them directly, they having been kept in confinement aboard for some weeks.'

'That is kind in you, Admiral. Yet I am able to assure you that we have no need for such in Macao. I'm confident we retain sufficient force to oppose any assault by the French.'

Drury, put out, tried again. 'Bonaparte's troops are veterans of many years of conquest and may well deploy artillery and irregular forces in addition. I strongly advise you to accept our offer in case of sudden incursion from the sea by the same soldiers who took Lisbon.'

'Sir, where are these French coming from that could give us cause to fear? We've heard of none closer than some thousands of miles.'

'This is my point, Your Excellency. You will have no warning of their coming and so it's most prudent to strengthen the defences of your territory.' The note of warning in Drury's voice had a definite edge to it.

'I understand you, sir, but this is a matter for ourselves, not you, and my decision is not to take advantage of your kind offer.'

'Sir. My orders are from London, not my own, and they require me to press you to allow our reinforcements to enter Macao. You see how overborne I am with decrees imposed on me from above.'

The calm and composed expression did not alter. 'Admiral, I do sympathise with your situation. I, too, am burdened by mandates from on high and they enjoin me most strictly not to allow foreign troops on the soil of Macao under any circumstances.'

A chill silence descended.

The affair had developed into the very confrontation that Drury needed to avoid and as such implied a landing by force, which must inevitably end in tragedy.

'Your Excellency,' Kydd found himself saying. It brought a glare of reproof from Drury but he went on as though he hadn't seen it. 'There is one means as will allow you to accept our offer.'

'Oh? Do say on, Captain.'

'Should our soldiers be named as auxiliaries of the Portuguese, brought in as relief for your garrison, there is none who could object to this simple device as we are allies.'

The silence reasserted itself, but this time with an air of expectancy as Lemos Faria gave it concentrated thought.

'This course has its merits,' he said quietly, stroking his chin, 'and, as you say, deals with the chief objection. I can barrack them out of the way, with victuals and drink and so forth . . . Yes, it could be possible.'

'Er . . .' Drury began but did not continue.

'Admiral? Do I take it that you are able to agree to proceed in this way?'

'Provisionally.' It was as if the word had been extracted from him by force.

'Excellent. I do believe I will move forward on this.'

'Then—'

'Your troops will be admitted into Macao under these terms, sir. I will see to it immediately.'

'Sir, your understanding and amiability is a credit to your country. I shall tell the transports to prepare for disembarkation.'

'Perhaps not at this hour, sir.'

'I beg your pardon?'

'Do allow I have *my* authorities to satisfy. When I said "immediately", that is what I meant. This very day an aviso will be sent to my captain general in Goa requesting his compliance. When that is received you shall not be delayed a minute longer.'

'Goa!' Even for a fast cutter, the voyage there and back would take many weeks.

'That is where the Portuguese colonial headquarters are situated, Admiral. I can hardly bring it nearer, sir.'

'The delay I find very difficult to accept, sir.'

'I will put in hand this day a system of supply to each ship of fresh victuals and water. You have no need to concern yourself with their health, sir.'

Kydd knew Drury was in a difficult situation indeed. He could not bring more pressure to bear, and if he was to violate the territory of Portugal while routine formalities were still in train, it would at the very least reflect badly on Britain as a bullying power no better than the French.

'Thank you, Your Excellency. Your attentions in this regard are most obliging.'

'We are allies, Admiral.'

'Yes. Which is why I know you will see that, if events turn against us in the nearer term, I shall be obliged to land in any case to occupy Macao by way of a deterrent. This, of course, will not mean to imply an act of territorial acquisition.'

The courteous expression did not change. Neither did the soft tone of voice. 'That may be so, sir. But should you attempt to land men before I receive my orders, I will resist your invasion with as much force as is within my power to put against you.'

Chapter 42

'We rather wondered how the beggar would do it,' Roberts said smoothly, contentedly drawing on his cigar, in *Tyger*'s great cabin with Drury and Kydd.

'He has a point, I'm persuaded,' Drury said, eyeing the cigar with loathing, 'for no immediate reason, being asked to allow an occupation by foreign troops against his explicit orders.'

'But Goa? Surely he has the authority to make decisions relating to Macao alone.'

'Concerning an international incident liable to cause impediment to the most valuable trade in the world? His actions are mild, sir, I believe.'

'Then you think it right and proper to delay the landings?'
'I do.'

Roberts didn't reply at first, puffing luxuriously. Then he raised a languid eyebrow and conceded, 'Perhaps you're right. The devil is quite correct in saying there are no Frenchmen he knows of in the offing. We can afford to wait.'

Kydd's humour wilted. To be trapped for weeks in idleness was a wretched existence for a man-o'-war.

'Unless, of course, you stand firm against the villain and go by your original orders.'

'To occupy by force if need be, the delay being our *casus belli*?' Drury snorted. 'With the Chinese looking on?'

'Admiral,' sighed Roberts, 'far be it from me to tell you your job but those ridiculous war-junks would not last five minutes under the guns of your famous *Tyger*. They'll see the fate of the first and scuttle away to hide, leaving us masters of the Pearl river even to Canton.'

'Nevertheless, Mr President, my orders do not include an invasion of Macao, still less a war with the Chinese emperor.'

'Invasion? The first thing we did after the Portuguese royal family went into exile was "invade" and take their territory of Madeira. I've heard nothing about consequences and neither any demands for us to return it. How different is Macao?'

'Mr Roberts, you can be sure I shall give it much thought and will let you know my decision. Good day to you.'

The abrupt dismissal clearly annoyed the East India Company notable, who rose slowly, fixing Drury with an expression close to despising.

Kydd also got up, believing the meeting over, but Drury motioned him back wearily. 'No, Sir Thomas, I'll have your views before you leave, understanding that I am not bound to agree with them.'

'Sir.'

Drury was in a quandary and wanted to take in all sides, but the stiff-faced senior officer would not want to hear any 'if I were you' opinions. Kydd's belief – that if there was no immediate French threat they had no business to send in their military unasked upon an ally – would not be heeded.

'Sir, should we not await the reply from Goa? If positive, we stand to achieve our goals with no ill feeling while if—'

'I don't trust them.'

'Er, who, sir?'

'Roberts and his crew of supercargoes. Can we really believe what they're telling me? Or have they some hidden plan of sorts to further their situation? Remember that they're merchants, damned traders and storekeepers only.'

'We cannot know, sir. In this land we are the strangers and can never be privy to local concerns.'

'I'd give a year's pay to learn the truth of what's to weather ashore,' Drury muttered.

Kydd realised it was a measure of how distracted he was that he had let this slip out. 'Sir, there may be a way to win intelligence of such a sort.'

Weary eyes rose to meet his. 'Oh?'

'I have on board a confidential secretary who has been of much value to me in the past in the seeking out of information ashore. He is a young man of initiative and enterprise and blessed with an ear for languages,' he added lightly. 'I dare to say if we let him loose he'll come back with more than a little of your truth.'

'No. He'll be caught, taken up as a spy. And what can he discover in days, let alone hours?'

'Sir. He's a resourceful young man and no stranger to disguise and dissembling,' Kydd answered firmly. 'Might we leave it to him to decide the issue?'

Chapter 43

'It would be an honour – and my pleasure, too, Sir Thomas. I believe it was mentioned that the Lord Farndon himself was once here, accompanying the Elmhurst diplomatic mission,' Dillon added.

Kydd choked back a laugh at the remembrance. He was in the same ship as the distinguished delegation, but at that time his friend would have been unrecognisable as a thin and rangy seaman spending his time as Kydd did, chipping paint and scrubbing decks. 'Ah, I believe he was, but not necessarily as a member of the mission. I doubt he'll be remembered.'

'Oh. Well, nevertheless, I will do my best to honour his name with my conduct, sir.'

'I'm sure you will, Edward. Now, you are aware of what would be prime information?'

'Sir, you may trust that I have a grasp of the essentials,' Dillon said, wounded.

'And how will you proceed?' Kydd asked, with concern. 'To be seized as a spy would be a hard thing.'

'I will desert, sir, in the character of a foremast hand.

Bribe passage in one of the bum-boats plying with the shore.' A man-o'-war would normally be guarding against this, but *Tyger* with her volunteer crew would not be taking precautions.

'A good plan, dear fellow. And then you'll . . . ?'

'I have a course of action at hand, you must believe, but there is a difficulty.'

'How's this?'

'It requires I visit a tavern of the lower sort, and I have no knowledge of same, of course.'

Kydd replied, without hesitation, 'The Solmar on Praia Grande will answer, I believe.'

Dillon blinked in surprise. 'Why, thank you, Sir Thomas. How do you . . .?'

'I have heard it mentioned,' Kydd said airily. 'Now, time is pressing. Is there anything further you need?'

That evening during supper, with most hands below, Kydd took a turn about the decks, glancing surreptitiously towards the bow. He knew eyes would be on their captain, a distraction for what was going on around the cathead. Noting with satisfaction an indistinct figure scuttling from the fore-hatchway to lower himself clumsily over the side, he sauntered below and prepared for a lengthy wait.

It was not something he would have asked Dillon to do in normal circumstances but he knew him to be ardent, unattached, and with more than a hint of the mature sagacity to balance it that Renzi had always possessed. Yet this was not a place where the elements, political or social, were going to reveal themselves easily.

Why he was so confident Dillon would come back with a good and truthful picture was not easy to say.

He would give it seventy-two hours, and if he had not

returned by then he'd have to . . . Well, he couldn't send out to find him. It would have to be some sort of rescue mission.

Dillon returned within less than a day.

He didn't waste words. 'I have what we need,' he said, gratefully taking the hot port and lemon he was handed. 'And a pretty tale it is, too.'

Kydd raised an eyebrow. 'Leaving aside how you could possibly come by it in hours, my dear fellow.'

'Why, this is easily told, Sir Thomas. I merely followed your wise words – from our venturing in the Baltic. "Should you want the true story of what is afoot in a seaport, find a merchant whose business depends on it." And I did. In China the species of man who is a merchant is the lowliest of all, but because of this he needs the liveliest understanding of the sinews of commerce and government.'

'Go on.'

'There is one kind of especial interest: he who stands between the native Chinese trader, who is ignorant of the outside world, and the foreign devils who know nothing of the Chinese. He is called a compradore and understands much.'

'And he told you . . .?'

'The overriding imperative is to keep the realm unsullied by the practices of the foreign devils, who are in effect confined to Macao to live and to Canton to trade – under penalty of death. This raises the strategic value of Macao for us to a shocking level.'

'Clearly.'

'The Chia Ch'ing emperor in Peking cares not a jot about this distant part of his empire so long as it is kept up as a place of isolation of the foreigner. His representative in

Canton is the viceroy, one Na Yan Ch'eng. The emperor –
the Son of Heaven – is not to be approached by anyone save
through this viceroy.

'There is now a matter of delicacy concerning that of trade
with the foreign devils, which is great at this time, all in favour
of China. The English have taken to the imbibing of tea in
colossal quantities, it having to be paid for primarily in silver
specie, which is the only payment accepted by the Chinese.
Should you add a punishing rate of customs, then the value
of Canton to China is very great indeed.

'The viceroy does not defile himself by dealing with foreign
devils, still less merchants, so he appoints one who does. This
is the *hoppo*, whose sole duty is to make sure that a river of
silver flows to the imperial court at all times.

'Then we have the guild of Chinese merchants, the
Co-hong, who are the opposite principals to the European
and American traders, but in all this we have to understand
that it is entirely corrupt with cumshaw – squeeze – being
demanded at all points.'

Kydd tried to take it all in. 'Then how does our China trade
work – make a profit?'

'Inbound ships must go upriver to one place: Whampoa
Roads. This is the only landing place tolerated and is where
cargo is unloaded and spread out for the *hoppo* to inspect and
levy his dues, however disguised. The Co-hong have a
monopoly in dealing with foreigners and will buy cargo at a
rate they think we will accept, knowing that if it is too low
the ship will not return.

'Outbound vessels fare the same, except the ship is as well
minutely examined to detect smuggling and vast sums are
extracted to ensure timely departure. Profit on all sides is still
great as it is in the interest of everyone involved to make it
work so.'

'And how about your compradore? Where does he do his work?'

'A minor individual indeed. At the low level of tally-books, go-between, factotum. The value of his position depends on knowing intimately what is hatching out of sight, and his word may be relied upon, I believe.'

Kydd gave a tight smile. 'I see how it is now. Then I have to ask, what is his reckoning of the position of our Mr Roberts and his committee?'

'My man is to be trusted in these matters, sir,' Kydd replied, hiding his irritation.

Drury was finding it hard to credit that one of his captains had access to intelligence that he did not and had to be appeased.

Phrasing his summary carefully, Kydd came to the nub. 'Sir, the compradore points out that this entire expedition is nonsense, based on a false foundation, and therefore is bound to fail.'

'He dares to—'

'Sir. It is a fact. Macao is not Portuguese. They administer on sufferance from the emperor of the Chinese in the form of a lease of some kind, a condition of which is that they do not allow foreign troops to enter. It's not theirs to vary these conditions without petitioning the emperor himself.'

'I see. Roberts and the others must have known this – why do they insist on an occupation?'

'Our source says the answer to that is as plain to him as it is simple-minded.'

'Well?'

'They wish to precipitate a confrontation with the Chinese that sees you and your men-o'-war overwhelm the viceroy's war-junks, leaving the way open for an advance on Canton.'

'Good God above! This would destroy the very trade they hold so precious.'

Kydd tried not to sound cynical but the point had to be made. 'He believes their thinking is that, with the *hoppo* and Co-hong both put to fright, the ruinous exactions that are now imposed will be relieved. That is all.'

'War with the Chinese? They're demented – I won't do it!'

'They will—'

But Drury was incensed. 'Desire Mr Roberts to attend on me – at once!'

'Admiral?' Roberts said, as soon as he'd taken his chair.

'Answer me this, sir. Why do you so vehemently demand I occupy Macao?'

'Why, is this not the wish of Lord Minto?'

'Your advice is at the root of it, sir.'

'It is sound advice, too. And – may I remind you, Admiral – by the terms of your orders, that which you are bound to observe, sir.'

'Unless the Portugee orders from Goa arrive in support of it, I will not do it!'

Roberts stirred lazily. 'Events may well dictate you must, and that very soon, sir.'

'What do you mean by that?'

'It will not be long before the inbound China Fleet arrives. This whole business must be settled before then, or they risk being frustrated in their dealings.'

'We still await the Goa orders.'

'I think not, Admiral.'

Speechless, Drury could only stare at him.

'The committee is unanimous in its view that an occupation be mounted immediately before the China Fleet is here. Furthermore—'

235

'Dammit! Did you not hear what I said, sir?'

'I did. And I'm desolated to have to point out that the soldiery in the transports are entirely Company men under my orders. They will land on my request.'

'I will not allow—'

'Admiral, you can and will. This expedition is under the final command of Lord Minto, who is the senior East India Company official in this part of the world and may not be overborne by any agent of the Crown without due reason.'

'Then you will land these forces in—'

'No, sir. *You* will.'

'I will not be party to—'

'As in accordance with your orders, Admiral.'

Chapter 44

Almost in a sense of unreality plans were agreed for the taking of Macao by force of arms, an act of aggression against the oldest ally Britain had in a world almost entirely arrayed against her. Kydd's memories of the ancient Oriental outpost of years before were now buried under the urgency of immediate action.

'Mr Bowden, you will lead in the boats of the naval division, your object to secure the landing place.'

'Sir – I protest,' Farrant blurted. 'As first lieutenant that honour belongs to me!'

'It does, but in this instance Admiral Drury may very well have recourse to step ashore with me. *Tyger* must be left in safe hands, sir.'

It was all very hurried, sketchily planned in contrast to the shore landings Kydd had taken part in before – such as those at Cape Town and Copenhagen. No previous inshore bombardment of the landing area, no offshore guardships or colour parties to plant their banners to guide in the regiments. In fact, after consulting the pompous Lieutenant

Colonel Wickes, in command of the occupation, Kydd was not sure there were any orders he could conjure specific to the invading of Macao.

Where were the main strongpoints to be reduced and in what order? Would the advance be by column or line and, without accompanying field artillery, how were the landing places to be cleared of their lines of waiting defenders?

And, most ambiguously, what did they do once established ashore?

Lieutenant Bowden looked down on the launch and cutter being boarded by their boat's crew, then taking on their apportioning of Royal Marines. His was the most responsible task in the whole campaign but it was not something he would have chosen to lead. There was no distinction to be had in an offensive against a loyal ally, and whoever fell in the engagement would be forgotten by history.

It was straightforward enough. He would be in the van leading boats from the navy carrying armed marines and seamen, who would be put ashore to secure a toehold while the boats from the transports came in behind with the main body of troops.

He'd seen how it went in other times and had no illusions. Their objective was the Praia Grande, a sweeping waterfront boulevard stretching along the whole width of the bay, overlooked by imposing colonial edifices closely packed together. Beyond was hidden the heart of the city of Macao, with all its ancient grandeur and mystery – its military fortresses and barracks.

Putting ashore on the well-sheltered, accessible roadway should be trivially easy and setting up a pair of outward-facing lines of marines to cover the landings the work of minutes – but it wouldn't be like that. He'd heard that Lemos Faria, the governor, had sworn to resist any attempt at arms with as much force as he had at his command.

Simply a brace of twelve-pounder artillery concealed in the alleyways between the buildings could blow any boat out of the water well before they were in musket range. And if, by some miracle, they got close, even a small detachment of infantry deployed among the buildings could, in the broad spaciousness of the boulevard, easily pick them off as they struggled on shore.

For him there would be only one decision: when to call off the landing and retreat – if he was still alive to give the order.

It was a long pull from the ships, the oars rising and dipping in the Pearl river estuary so turbid with mud that the blades disappeared from sight within an inch or two. Bowden glanced behind: the boats from the transport were in a straggling line across his field of vision, so few compared to what must lie ahead.

He concentrated on his mark, the centre of the broad sweep of the boulevard. Figures moved about the roadway as if they were part of a carefully prepared defence, some with knapsacks, others with carts, probably of ammunition.

It seemed they were expected. 'Stretch out!' he growled hoarsely, his pulse beginning to race. 'Stretch out for your lives!'

The whites of their eyes showing, the seamen pulled hard and deep, the marines between the thwarts keeping their heads down and fingering their muskets convulsively.

It would not be long now, and the heavy guns would open up.

First there would be ball: iron shot plunging and skittering with shocking violence, then, closer in, a merciless blast of canister and grapeshot, which would leave the grey seas running crimson with blood.

It would not take long.

They came nearer but so far there was no sudden angry roar of guns. The scene was changing fast – the figures were running, and in different directions. Did this mean guns were being pushed into position?

The oarsmen panted and strained, willing on their craft into the jaws of death. Bowden, with a stab of frenzied pride at their naked bravery, took courage from it. Standing at the tiller he yelled a warlike cry and, looking back, beckoned on the boats following with his sword.

Still no guns.

They were very close now. The running figures had disappeared and the boulevard was completely clear.

The launch headed for a small jetty and came in quickly. The bowman leaped off with the painter and secured it. Then the marines scrambled out.

But where were the defenders? It was past belief that they hadn't made their move yet and Bowden breathlessly looked about. 'Into position!' he roared to the marines, gesturing down the road. The other side would be taken by the second boat, Maynard's.

A short time later East India Company soldiers were pouring ashore and forming up in loose groups, if anything looking bewildered and frightened, their sergeants not much better, uncertain and glancing around furtively.

Lieutenant Colonel Wickes finally landed, his eyes bloodshot – the result of some Dutch courage before the assault? 'Where's the enemy?' he puffed.

'None in sight, sir,' Bowden said coldly.

'Ha! Run away, then?'

'Sir.'

Wickes turned to his men and drew his sword. 'Wa-hey! Forward, the Thirty-second!'

The troops looked at him, baffled.

'Follow me, y' useless blaggards!' he bawled, and reeled off towards an alleyway. A few soldiers trotted after him, then more, until they'd all vanished between the buildings, heading vaguely into the centre of Macao. The boulevard was empty once again.

Bowden was dumbfounded. What the devil was going on?

Then he heard shouts and cries. Beyond the building façades there was an encounter – not a clash of arms for there were no shots or clang of blades but a disordered uproar, like a frightened mob.

The boats' crews looked at each other helplessly while Bowden thought furiously.

If he put back to the ship, duty done, it might be that the landing party met the defenders further in and, after being repulsed, needed to be taken off, rescued. On the other hand, if, improbably, the troops were winning their way through to the heart of Macao, they would need reinforcing and support.

Unsure, he waited, the crew in the boat ready for anything.

The sounds of disorder rose and fell, and much further in, a coil of smoke rose until frayed by the wind. If the city was taking fire this was a catastrophe of the first order for the expedition.

'Stannard!' Bowden called to the petty officer at the stroke oar. 'Take three men and find out what the devil's going on in there.'

They departed quickly and Bowden was left to fret.

They were gone nearly an hour and returned panting. 'Sir, it's all ahoo in town. Folk runnin' here an' there, no one knows what's abroad a-tall, and without the lingo we can't ask, sir.'

'Any, who's to say, dead bodies about?'

'None as I saw, sir.'

Chapter 45

Aboard Tyger

'Thank you, Mr Bowden,' Kydd said heavily. 'You did what you could.'

Drury was in his cabin, prostrated by the sickness that seized him from time to time. Kydd could not have been described as his designated second-in-command yet something had to be done to sort out the confusion ashore.

'Mr Dillon, I need you to find your compradore friend again. Ask him what's happening.'

It didn't take long – and the news was not good.

'The whole of Macao is of a fright for no one believed the British would actually invade and can't understand what it means. The governor is hiding in the biggest fortress, the Fortaleza do Monte, and won't come out. As a result, there's panic and fear on all sides. The Portuguese are barricading themselves in while the Chinese, traders and workers both, are fleeing the city for Canton and begging for protection of the viceroy. It has to be said that the presence of quantities of redcoats roaming free on the streets is causing much fear and dread and by now Macao is out of control – of anyone.'

It had not gone as the select committee had said it would. In fact, it was a shambles that had no foreseeable ending and Kydd could do nothing about it. To land more men on his own responsibility, seamen and marines, would only make things worse. To take off the soldiers already landed would reverse any advantage there was in the sorry situation and only antagonise the select committee. Ultimately this was Drury's affair and he was on his sick-bed.

Kydd went below to see the man. He was lying senseless, a deathly pallor on him. The surgeon sitting by his bed shook his head mutely and continued his vigil. Kydd hesitated, then left.

In the morning, as a wan sun cast its growing light over the scene, a boat was sent in to make investigation but came back with more of the same tale. A now nearly deserted town, wreckage and ruins on either hand, no markets or signs of life whatsoever.

Kydd had to get Drury to make over some form of authority to him, even if he had no idea what he could do.

The admiral was awake but his face was pallid and drawn and his hands trembled. 'What is it, Captain?' he enquired, his voice faint but firm.

Kydd unburdened himself.

Drury spoke with a fragile determination. 'Captain, I'm going ashore to see what's to be done in this lamentable situation. I shall need the assistance of you and your man. Do, I beg, keep that villainous committee away from me.' He called weakly for his manservant and doctor.

He was bowed and exhausted on the journey to the jetty but as soon as he stepped ashore he straightened, stood every

243

inch the admiral, and strode forward into the deserted streets, no vice-regal carriage this time but accompanied by stolidly marching marines.

Kydd could only admire his tenacity and willpower. Who knew what pain and suffering he was fighting in order to do his duty? Fortunately the fortress was not far, and its ancient grey stone battlements loomed quickly.

At the double-arched entrance gate there was an immediate commotion, and after some delay, a Portuguese guardsman with feathers in his helmet appeared and demanded their business. Dillon stepped forward and explained.

Centuries-old iron screeched, and while the marines were ushered to the guardhouse, a flanking escort took the trio into the inner fastness.

Governor Lemos Faria stood as they entered and were introduced. He was in some disarray of dress, neither statesman-like nor war-like but with a gorget and sword over his finery and a hunted expression. 'What have you done, Admiral? Are we then at war?' he demanded, his voice tight with emotion.

'Certainly not, Your Excellency,' Drury answered pleasantly. 'Is any visit of an ally an act of war?'

'Do not bandy words with me, sir! Macao has been violated and the rule of law no longer endures in my dominion.'

'I am truly sorry to hear of this,' Drury replied smoothly, 'particularly as such disorder appears to be the result of a common enough military precaution.'

'Sir, know that my captain general in Goa has been informed of this act and will take the sternest measures, I assure you.'

Drury swayed slightly and continued in a voice suddenly husky. 'It would be most obliging should we sit. I am somewhat indisposed, I regret.'

Lemos Faria was transformed – at once caring and sympathetic, coming out from behind his desk to assist Drury to the largest armchair. 'My dear admiral, do sit. Guards! A restorative for our guest.'

Kydd fell back from the pair. It was quite out of his control and all he could do was keep his silence.

It was a knife-edge situation: not only had Drury to find some way to restore the governor's authority but at the same time win his compliance so that, together, they could put up a bold front to the Chinese. A wrong decision could turn every player against him.

'Thank you, Your Excellency. Your kindness does remind me of the essential amiability of our two countries as will be good assurance we shall find a desirable course acceptable to us both.'

The governor stiffened, but then smiled. 'Do you have any notion of what this can be? I vow I cannot see such a way forward myself, sir.'

Drury sat forward and began earnestly: 'As I understand it, Excellency, the late disorder has been caused by the unexpected appearance of our soldiers on the streets of Macao.'

'In flagrant breach of the convention.'

'As it may be – the actuality is that this is as a result of my orders, which originate from the highest and which I cannot defy.'

'And therefore—'

'Your Excellency, I have a proposal which I'm sanguine will meet the essence of the situation.'

'I'd be interested to hear it, sir.'

'All British forces in uniform, the redcoats, the officers and so forth, all are taken off the streets and kept out of sight. In their place are restored all the accustomed soldiers and officials of the Portuguese administration, who resume their duties of governance and surety to all citizens quite as before.'

'How can this be? Our barracks are too small and—'

'Excellency, I was not thinking of barracks. Something altogether more secure and with high walls to discourage peeping eyes. Sir, should you emerge and resume your residency at your palace on the Praia Grande it would leave this very edifice as a place of confinement of our troops.'

'Admiral! How can you—'

'For you, the world will understand that you have rounded up the troublesome British and have them all under lock and key. For me, I have fulfilled my orders by landing at Macao and have billeted my soldiers safely in a fortress. A temporary solution, true, but it will serve to restore the serenity of old Macao.'

Kydd saw how much this was costing Drury. He was impressed with the admiral's practical suggestion and care to preserve appearances.

The governor held silent for a space, then gave a slow smile. 'It seems you have a commendable solution to which I will probably agree. And now you must go on to face a far bigger predicament – to persuade the shrewd Chinese that in order to prevent another foreign-devil people from taking arms against Macao, you have done just this yourself, and without permission of any sort.'

Chapter 46

Aboard Tyger

Under leaden skies Captain Kydd took position at his lectern, the master-at-arms to one side, divisional officers to the other and, behind, a Royal Marines guard.

'Able Seaman Salter did set at defiance the first lieutenant an' when remonstrated with did swear against his honour and dignity . . .'

'Ord'nary Seaman Lowkes was taken fighting in 'tween decks with cook's mate Brown, no defence given . . .'

'Petty Officer Mawes was apprehended in the silent hours smuggling liquor through the hawse . . .'

Kydd could feel it happening exactly as it had in *Artemis* those years ago when long days at idleness in this same port had rotted the spirit of the ship's company. Senseless bickering and violence had broken out.

In a way this was worse. There had been no shore leave, the sweets of the land so tantalisingly close with the old town under their lee. They were neither one thing nor the other, in action or at peace.

Now, for the first time in an age, the cat would see daylight and something in Kydd shrivelled in despair.

When it was all over, Roberts was waiting for him, wiping his face after a fine dinner with his fellow supercargoes.

'Ah, Captain Kydd. You'll know the admiral has been called to his bed again?'

'I am aware.'

'We've an important resolution to put to him. Or is it to be to your own good self?'

'Sir, as I've said before, I'm captain of this ship, not a member of his staff. I have no powers to act upon any matter you put forward.'

'Hmph. Should Admiral Drury prove unfit for the post of carrying through his orders then someone must be found who can. And that is likely to be you, Sir Thomas.'

He didn't argue. If Drury was truly incapable, replacement of a commander-in-chief was out of their hands.

'The admiral will be recovered shortly, I'm persuaded.'

The next day Drury could be seen taking the air on deck although he appeared frail and slow. He was quickly surrounded by Roberts and members of his committee, then hustled below. Kydd followed hastily.

'Admiral. In view of the unsatisfactory state of affairs, we have determined that a firm course of action is required.'

'Oh?' Drury said wearily.

'Indeed. The Chinese must be convinced that their interests lie in complying with our dispositions in Macao. The best way of achieving this, we feel, is to make a determined thrust up the Pearl river past the Boca Tigris and on to Canton. You have two first-class fighting frigates, yes?'

'That if the Chinese resist you will expect to open fire and destroy them?'

248

'Quite. That will serve as an exemplar to our intentions.'

'No.'

'I beg your pardon?' The astonishment in Roberts's expression was almost comical.

'I said no. I will not perform this action. It is repugnant to my nature and not one to be contemplated by any civilised nation. Recollect, sir, this is their sovereign territory and we are the trespassers.'

'Admiral, if you do not carry out our wishes you may be sure the Lord Minto will hear of it!'

Kydd warmed to the sick man. He was standing by his beliefs and humanitarian principles of conduct in a way that Nelson himself would have understood, and in spite of his affliction, he was not going to abandon them.

'I have spoken. Be so good as to leave me now.' Drury turned and painfully paced away forward.

A little later that day circumstances took a fateful turn. Roberts and his entire committee crowded into Drury's cabin, all babbling at once.

'Silence! Do be silent, I beg,' the admiral said, with a weary gesture. 'Mr Roberts, pray what is the reason for this disrespectful intrusion?'

'A development,' he replied with theatrical gravity, 'of the most urgent nature, sir.'

'Oh?'

'The working of cargo at Whampoa and Canton strand are ceased indefinitely.'

'I see.'

'Do you, Admiral? The actions of the *hoppo* and Co-hong in withdrawing their coolies can only be termed calamitous. The China Fleet is here and its cargo remains under hatches. I speak only for myself . . .' he looked at the nodding heads

249

signalling their agreement and continued importantly '. . . but this represents an adversity in trade I own I cannot easily withstand.'

'And you are saying that—'

'Admiral, I'm saying that if you do not move upon Canton this hour,' he spoke with the heaviest significance, 'you will be responsible for the ruination of many of our country's finest merchant houses.'

Drury gave a slow smile, delaying his reply, which made the president smoulder. Then he spoke. 'Sir. Be aware that I have discharged my orders from the governor general to the full. I have appeared before Macao and subsequently occupied same. The French are thereby denied the territory. You are now demanding I take it further. This, Mr President, I am not authorised to do.'

'Be damned to your orders! That is, of course, to your extreme interpretation of them, I mean. Can you sit there at leisure while we are brought down by those villainous Chinamen or will you not do something?'

Easing himself in his chair Drury regarded him steadily. 'Mr Roberts. There are some who would believe this expedition to be entirely unconnected to the French threat, driven more by your desire to wrest commercial advantage from the Chinese. Very well, we have occupied Macao – if there are unfortunate consequences these must be accounted entirely your doing.'

'How dare you?' exploded Roberts, red-faced. 'This is a one-sided act by the *hoppo* and has nothing to do with us!'

'Nothing to do with the fees and exactions that would be much lightened should Canton lie under our guns?'

'Not at all, dammit. This is our defence and safeguarding from foreign powers – French, Dutch, all those lying in wait for us for oceans around.'

Drury's slow smile returned. 'Then I have a proposition that meets both our positions.

'We are already in Macao. Why do we not fall back to here, bring with us the factories of Canton and the wharves of Whampoa. Here we will demand to trade and in no other place.'

'Wh-what?'

'This will dish your *hoppo* and Co-hong quite radically, they having no trade to squeeze. A good plan, I believe.'

He ended with a dry coughing fit while the committee looked at each other in horror.

'Er, not so, Admiral – not so.' Roberts was clearly in distress for words.

'Pray, why not? If the defence of Macao has been achieved, then what better?'

'To be quite open with you and to save time in evasion, I have to allow that the *hoppo* is heavily in our debt. He's accepted cumshaw, and without our cargoes are landed and progressed, we cannot recover our return.'

'I see,' Drury said cynically.

Roberts bridled but went on, 'Besides which, advances for this season's tea have been placed with the Co-hong, which in this event will be forfeit altogether.'

'A sad loss.'

'A desperate one – the court of the East India Company will then be well exercised to explain to the public of England why their accustomed tea is of a sudden not in their pots. Their shares will swoon, the Company will face ruin. And they will look to the cause, sir,' he added, with pointed gravity.

'Your remedy is to make a flourish with my frigates.'

'It is.'

'Even if it results in wholesale despoliation of the Chinese?'

'If need be.'

'I won't do it.'

Visibly frustrated, Roberts pushed past Kydd and stormed out of the cabin, followed by the other jostling supercargoes. When Kydd looked back, Drury had slumped in his chair, his head in his hands with despair.

Chapter 47

After two days of tedium, tense with the inactivity of stalemate, Drury sent for Kydd.

'This can't go on. It's intolerable. Never has a commander-in-chief been so sorely tested, and on his own station. I won't have it.' His voice was firmer – he appeared to be recovering.

'Sir.'

Kydd wondered why he'd been sent for. Two of Drury's staff had arrived from the flagship and had set up in the coach. There was now precious little room for Kydd and *Tyger*'s own people.

'Captain, I've a mind to cut through all this damned nonsense in one.'

'How's that, sir?'

'I'm going to make visit to the viceroy himself and knock something out between us. What do you think?'

It mattered little what Kydd thought but he knew the reason for the question. Drury wanted to see if there were any hidden objections that Kydd had spotted. He hadn't.

'A good idea, sir.'

'In boats.'

'So as not to alarm them.'

'Yes. Sir Thomas, I desire you have your barge ready for passage under sail to Boca Tigris and thence Canton. Three launches and cutters to follow at a cable's distance armed with muskets and cutlasses. You will accompany, given that it may prove hazardous at any time.'

'Sir.' For his commander-in-chief to go to a crucial meeting alone in these circumstances was unthinkable.

'Then shall we say ten tomorrow?'

The word got around *Tyger* like wildfire and caused strong misgivings.

'Sir, why should it be you? We have Admiral Drury's flag-lieutenant on board. He should go with him – and the Chinese are angry and not to be trusted in any wight,' Bowden finished helplessly.

'The admiral is visiting the viceroy of a province of a hundred millions,' Kydd said, in a tone somewhere between awe and trepidation. 'He needs as much appearance as he can manage.' His was the only knighthood in the immediate vicinity and his star and sash would add to their dignity.

'Union flag at the gaff, red ensign aft. Crew in *Tyger* colours.'

Halgren, the captain's coxswain, was in the barge and an all-volunteer crew – petty officers Stirk, Doud and Pinto, and others.

In the muddy grey of the Pearl there were few watercraft: some fishing vessels under their bamboo battened sails, a single Western barque putting out to sea, and a sprinkling of sampans. When the naval boats got purposefully under way for the narrows of the Boca Tigris, there was a general flight. Uneasily, Kydd noted that most turned about and headed upriver towards the presumed protection of the Chinese imperial forces.

254

Beside him Drury sat in full admiral's dress uniform with a grim expression that did not invite conversation. The barge heeled sharply at a monsoonal squall but Stirk's handy easing of the sheets kept the boat dry and on course without drama.

They headed further and further from the offshore islands of the Macao Roads into the estuary, which would contract to no more than a mile or so wide at what the Portuguese called the Boca Tigris, the mouth of the tiger. This was where the war-junks kept their guard on the approaches to Canton.

Several hours passed and the rocky bluffs at either side began narrowing, quite suddenly to no more than three miles or so. This was not the Boca Tigris, which lay a further ten miles upstream but, ominously, a quantity of war-junks were now massing, the gaudy banners and staring eyes at their bows unmistakable even at distance.

'Keep on, sir?' Kydd asked quietly.

'Certainly,' Drury snapped, rigid at the sight. He glanced astern: the other boats were closing on them as if moving in protectively, but Drury ordered Kydd to tell them to fall back.

Nearer to, figures crowding the decks of the junks resolved into imperial bannermen, dressed in ostentatious Oriental regalia, shouting and screeching at the impudent foreign devils.

Drury had brought along a Chinese interpreter but he cowered below the gunwales as the uproar grew nearer. There was no mistaking the malice in the shrieks and cries, and Kydd saw that many were moving to the guns, swivels and low dragon-headed pieces, some with what appeared to be old-fashioned blunderbusses.

'You, Mr Chung Lee or whoever,' Drury hissed. 'Hail them, say I'm the Lord High Admiral of the Foreign Devils and to let me through as I'm to make my obeisance to the viceroy, whatever his name.'

The little Chinese stood fearfully in the bows, his long pigtail carried to one side by the stiff breeze, and called across, his voice thin and apprehensive.

There was no change in the barbarous din and he tried again, this time bringing mocking laughter from the nearer war-junks.

'Press on,' Drury growled.

Halgren glanced about: there were no passages through the bucketing junks so he headed in the general direction of the centre, where criss-crossing vessels passed each other closely, thinking to take advantage of the junks masking each other if it came to play with the guns.

But as they drew nearer it grew uglier. Shouts coalesced into war-cries and there was a concerted move by the war-junks to trap the boats. 'Stay clear of 'em,' Kydd snapped at Halgren, who wisely swept about to go under the stern of the nearest and out of the bearing of its guns.

'Try once more, Mr Lee,' Drury ordered, as the barge came round.

It was no use: the frightened man could never be heard against the din and he fell back in the boat with a cry.

At the line of one junk's lofty stern-quarters a crowd of angry faces looked down. Then a rain of missiles and filth pitched into the sea near them.

Minutes later first one and then another dragon-mouthed swivel gun puffed their anger.

A line had been crossed.

'Pull back!' Drury rapped.

As they did, other guns – alien matchlocks and bizarre rocket tubes – took up and the air was ripped apart with a whirring and tearing. The crude projectiles, shot, stone and jagged iron fragments, splashed around them. A gasping cry came from forward and the starboard bowman let fly his fore-sheet, clutching at his arm, which was now spouting blood.

Kydd pointed astern. 'The boats, sir!' The three navy craft were closing fast, their sails sheeted taut in a frenzy to come to their rescue.

Along the centre line marines readied their muskets, but Drury waved angrily. 'Hold your fire! Put down your guns, do you hear me?'

They hesitated, plainly outraged by this assault on their admiral, but Drury was adamant. 'Retire! All boats – retire!'

Tyger's barge wallowed around in a full circle and, with the others, fell back crestfallen to return whence they'd come.

Chapter 48

Roberts was incandescent with rage. 'To go off like that, against our considered advice – and in *boats*, can we believe!'

The admiral said nothing, glowering at the president of the select committee of supercargoes.

'Why the devil didn't you take your frigates and—'

'I've said why I won't above a dozen times, Mr Damned Roberts!' Drury exploded. 'And you still don't seem to have a clue what you're risking!'

'An afternoon's sport to put down a parcel of junks?'

'No, sir, not at all,' Drury ground out. 'Consider this. The Chinese have just shown us that they're not in the slightest cowed by the threat of our frigates or any other. Sir, they're not to be bullied. Therefore, it follows that if I make a punitive strike, they will resist and—'

'Be damned to that. If they want a fight we can give 'em one. What you should do—'

'What I should do? This is what I should do. If we suffer even one seaman killed in an engagement with them, I'm obliged in honour to retaliate and burn down Canton. This,

Mr President of the Select Committee, will be the final end to your trading here, sir!'

Roberts breathed hard and his nostrils flared but he could find no response to make.

'So, we're locked into an intolerable situation,' Drury continued. 'We occupy Macao to the distress of our allies and the fury of the Chinese, and for what? At this moment our trading fleet lies in Whampoa unable to discharge, the season's tea out of reach. This expedition, sir, has amounted to little more than a comedy of blunders. And, what is worse, we cannot even retreat without we lose countenance and reputation.'

Kydd felt for him. This last was an unanswerable outcome with little to expect of it other than his removal from post for failure, even as it was the result of his moral principles being held higher than the commercial.

Frustration spread into every part of the ship, its nonsensical cause and bungled resolution bad enough, but to be scorned and driven off by a crew of Orientals was insupportable. Opinions on the mess-deck were dark and brooding. Yet none, high or low, had any idea how to extricate themselves with honour from this predicament.

The admiral kept to his cabin, mercifully not this time in his sick-bed, apparently spending his time rewording his dispatches. As he always took his meals alone, there was no chance for light conversation and his thoughts on their state of affairs remained unknown.

Kydd was driven near demented by vexation. Captain of his own ship and exiled to a small cabin, even the coach denied him by the tight-lipped staff of the reclusive commander-in-chief. He had taken to the open air, pacing the decks to the despair of the officer-of-the-day. In all his experience in frigates – from the lightsome *L'Aurore* to his present splendid command – he had never had to spend so much time in idleness and frustration.

When would it all end?

There were no lookouts at harbour stations, only the officer-of-the-day's telescope at the ready. Kydd, at forced leisure, spotted the curious sight first. From upriver, lordly driving between fleeing sampans and fisher-craft, came an oddly shaped vessel, not large but richly decorated and under two sails.

It shaped course directly for *Tyger*, no doubt with a river pilot aboard who could point her out, but why? Interested at this interruption to the day, Kydd took out his pocket telescope.

Apparently not armed, only a few figures were on deck but they wore sumptuous robes. And with no less than three immense triangular banners aloft, elaborately trimmed and with Chinese characters in proud view, this was an official visit of some kind.

'Rouse up Admiral Drury,' he advised the first lieutenant. 'I've an idea this is not a chance call.'

The craft came to and an imposing figure in a yellow gown raised a hailing trumpet and bellowed an incomprehensible demand.

'Get the admiral's interpreter – what's his name? Mr Lee.'

Drury and Lee appeared on deck at the same time, the admiral in some irritation. When Lee saw the craft he fell to his knees. '*Kwang Chou, cheung tu!*' he babbled, unable to take his eyes from the sight.

'Say again?' Kydd demanded.

'This is the boat of Na Yan Ch'eng – you say the viceroy of Canton,' he said, in tones of utmost awe.

There was another hail from the boat and Lee managed a reply.

'He tell you his master the viceroy bids you must follow him to Hu Mun, there to hear the word of His Celestial Majesty under Heaven, Emperor Chia Ch'ing.'

Kydd heard the quavering little man with some sympathy. Probably of humble local folk, picking up his English who knew where for business purposes, he now found himself in the forefront of a clash of civilisations.

Drury came up, annoyed that Kydd was using his man. 'I'll make the hails, Sir Thomas. You, Lee, ask them why I should go.'

The interpreter could hardly speak for reverence, although for who was not immediately clear. He didn't bother with a hail and said simply, 'Ah, sir, the viceroy has ordered it.'

'Sir, I rather think we should fall in with the desire, if there's any chance of parlay.'

'Of course I shall,' barked Drury. 'Hu Mun – where's that?'

'The Bogue, sir. Where the narrows of the Pearl river are scattered with islands.'

'Then ready *Tyger* for sea. She shall be my conveyor.'

Kydd nodded. She'd not only be a surety against what they'd so recently come up against, but in making parlay with the viceroy would provide an impressive show of war-like might.

It was easier said than done. As routine in harbour, all sails had been struck from their yards and sent below to prevent their weathering in wind and rain. These now had to be brought up from the sail lockers and bent on, lines reeved and running rigging clapped on and run out, a strenuous exercise of several hours, but it gave the admiral more time to prepare his speech.

No doubt the viceroy would make a gesture of reconciliation, recognising the one-sided situation for what it was, and graciously allowing residence for the British in Macao. In that event he could at long last be rid of the lunacy that had dogged the expedition and sail away.

At last *Tyger* was declared ready for sea and, with a remarkable excess of flags and bunting, she fell into line astern of the imperial craft.

It was more than thirty miles to the Bogue and it didn't surprise Kydd to be told to anchor for the night some hour's sail short of their destination.

In the morning, as dawn stole in, tipping the hills to larboard with a soft rose-flushed light, they set off once more and fairly soon made out their objective, an island that was one of several but set in the exact centre of the channel and resembling a crouching lion.

The imperial craft rounded some hundreds of yards offshore and demanded they anchor there.

Then the spectacle began. On the highest point of the island there was an elaborate gateway arch, noble and tall. A single rank of bannermen in blue and white gowns stood motionless facing them, their hands concealed in voluminous sleeves. Silhouetted against the early-morning light, they ran the entire length of the island down to the sea on each side. It was a simple, deeply impressive sight.

'We go to hear,' Lee said nervously, indicating the richly decorated and impossibly curved watercraft alongside. Kydd made to board first, navy fashion, but was pulled back by a horrified Lee. 'Honourable lord admiral only!' he stuttered.

Kydd had to be content to watch the commander-in-chief being sculled away to a position immediately before the gateway where they stopped and waited.

And then in the centre archway a single figure in a gold and yellow robe appeared.

Something like a sigh ascended, and on every side, men

dropped to their knees and bent in kow-tow, holding their position for long minutes.

It had to be Viceroy Na Yan Ch'eng himself.

A rectangular casket was brought, the messenger carefully paying obeisance to it a full three times before retiring. From it a vermilion scroll was carefully extracted.

The viceroy held it aloft while another three-times-three kow-tow was performed. Then, in a voice too far away for Kydd to hear, he began a chanting recitation, several times shaking the scroll for emphasis. At the end the scroll was returned to the casket and the viceroy bowed low to it.

An honour guard conveyed it to the water's edge where it was solemnly handed into the admiral's boat, which put about and sculled back to *Tyger*.

Expressionless, Drury mounted the side and, piped aboard, immediately went below.

Torn between wanting to see the remainder of the exotic Oriental procedure and attending on the commander-in-chief, Kydd hesitated, then chose the admiral.

The cabin was crowded and noisy, Roberts and the select committee in full flow, but Drury, sitting in the centre of the storm, was unmoved, his expression one that Kydd had never seen on the dour admiral. He was smiling, a serene, satisfied smile. He noticed Kydd and greeted him light-heartedly. 'Come in, old fellow, hear the news with the others.'

At last the babble subsided and Drury held aloft the vermilion scroll. 'Gentlemen. This has solved all our problems. Every one.' At the sudden outcry he motioned for quiet and went on, 'I can tell you now that it's from the hand of the Emperor of China, Chia Ch'ing himself, Son of Heaven and so forth, and is addressed to me, leader of the, er, barbarians.'

A sober quiet spread to hear the word of the emperor in Peking.

'A translated copy of his address is included, courtesy of those useful fellows the Jesuit missionaries attending on his court. I shall read from that, I believe.'

He picked up a closely written single sheet. 'He does not notice you gentlemen, of course, and begins by noting that the British offer to protect Macao from the French offends him for he is quite capable of defending his own dominions. He does not believe a word of it and considers this an excuse for seizing Macao for ourselves and will not tolerate it.

'He is inclined to show mercy and understanding to the barbarian British, however, and declares that if they quit Macao without delay he will allow them to leave, but if they fail to do so, not only will their entire trade with China be lost to them but an army of a size to be counted as infinite will be sent against them.

'He ends by reminding us that the Middle Kingdom has a sufficiency of all it desires and any trading that takes place is only for the convenience of the barbarians and may be forbidden by him at any time.'

Roberts was the first to recover. 'Why, that's nothing but bluster! We should—'

'Mr President, I received intelligence this day to the effect that an army of eighty thousand Imperial Bannermen lies in encampment about Canton. Do you think our hundreds will dismay them?' He smiled wickedly. 'No, sir. By this noble letter we have achieved our expedition goals. No Frenchman will threaten Macao because the emperor will see to it that British and French will be like treated – expelled in quite the same way without fear or favour.

'So, gentlemen, what is it to be? Have your trade restored to you in full flow and under imperial guarantee, or shall I stay, incur the emperor's wrath, and you see it swept away?'

Chapter 49

With the north-east monsoon in their favour, the East India Squadron stood out into the Indian Ocean bound for Madras, duty done and bearing back every one of the occupying soldiery. With the admiral restored to his flagship and *Tyger* his once more, Kydd felt contentment ease back.

His morning pace around the decks now had purpose, but even these few months in the heat and wet of the tropics was having an effect. Paint was shrivelling and peeling, cordage was fraying and strained, and their valuable canvas was baggy and greying, turning his ship into one of the drab workhorses he'd seen when first on station.

There was little that could be done, with no royal dockyards in this part of the world, but there was no excuse for sloth. Lee shrouds were industriously bowsed in to a becoming tautness: there was nothing worse for smart work going aloft than having the ratlines slack and flogging in the breeze underfoot. And while their fair-weather suit of sails was now sadly out of countenance, the sailmaker and his mates were doing their best to retain their curves with a little more at the gore or a judicious taking in of the roaching.

Day after day the small gaggle of ships led by Drury's venerable flagship, *Russell*, headed south-west across the miles of ocean. Kydd could only imagine what life must be like for the soldiers, packed in their hundreds into the transports in the heat with ruthlessly rationed water and bare preserved rations. But it was the same as always – after ships sailed, each became a world of its own until the next port, with laughter, strife, amusements and differences that were as individual to the ship as it was impossible to conceive of from another sailing only a hundred yards away.

On the fifth day out the little world that was *Tyger*'s own was shaken to its core.

'Yes, Mr Bowden?' Kydd said mildly, putting down his well-thumbed book. It was one of his pleasures now to sit by the stern windows, dappled by the sun, and take in a worthy tome at his ease.

'Sir, a . . . an unfortunate thing has occurred as I believe you'd want to know.' His face was drawn and serious, and Kydd sat up quickly.

'Yes?'

'Sir, I'm grieved to say it, but the gunroom has to report that a bottle of the second-best brandy must be accounted missing.'

It could have been anything, but Kydd's heart fell. The most likely explanation cynically thrust itself forward and he found himself saying heavily, 'Thank you, Mr Bowden. Do remain for a moment.'

Kydd knew there could be no other course – it had to be done. 'Mr Brice has the deck?'

'Sir.'

'Desire him to show the first lieutenant the condition of the larboard fish tackle.'

266

'Er, aye aye, sir.'

'Then come back here directly,' he said, in a low voice.

The business with the fish tackle was, of course, an excuse. On his turn about the decks that morning he'd noticed the stropping on the upper block was worn through. It would be enough to occupy Farrant for a sufficient time to do the job.

Bowden returned quickly, having guessed Kydd's next action.

The two slipped down to the gunroom, which at this hour of the morning was deserted but for servants squaring away in the various cabins.

'Leave us,' Kydd ordered. 'Not you,' he added, pointing to the first lieutenant's man, a rumple-faced ex-marine, Williams.

'Sir?'

'I intend to make search of Mr Farrant's cabin,' Kydd said sharply.

'S-sir? You can't—'

'I can and I will,' Kydd snapped. The man had been Farrant's servant for several years, coming aboard with him when he joined *Tyger*, and would know intimately the man's habits.

'Now, answer me. Where does the first lieutenant hide his bottles?'

'H-hide . . . his b-bottles?'

'That's what I said.'

'I don't know what you—'

'Yes, you do. You've been his servant long enough that he hasn't any secrets from you,' Kydd said brutally.

Wide-eyed, Williams hesitated.

'Come along, man, we haven't all forenoon.'

Without a word he reached up and, from behind a neat bookshelf under the deckhead, extracted the bottle of brandy and shamefacedly held it out.

Grimly Kydd took it and went to his cabin. He put it into a drawer and waited.

In a few minutes there was a knock on the door and Farrant entered, his face white as chalk, and stood stiffly before him.

Before he could say a word, Kydd took out the bottle and stood it on the table between them, looking up accusingly.

The man's countenance sagged and he averted his face with a look of the utmost misery. 'I tried – God is my witness, I tried. And . . . and . . .'

'Yes, you tried,' Kydd said sadly. 'But it was not enough.'

'Sir, I . . . I . . .'

'Mr Farrant, I'm obliged to put you in remembrance of what I said before. That you would remain *Tyger*'s premier while your pledge was kept that not a drop would pass your lips. I have kept my word. You have not. As a consequence, you will be relieved of your post and landed the day we reach Madras.'

His features crumpled. 'I understand, sir.' He gulped.

'I grant you'll remain in post until then under the same conditions, providing you steer clear of liquor, else you'll be made to suffer confinement.' Kydd sighed and finished, 'I'm grieved that your service to this ship has to end in this manner, but the needs of the Service must take precedence always, as you must know.'

Kydd felt pity and remorse but knew there was nothing else he could have done. Life would go on in *Tyger* after Madras but with a new first lieutenant.

Chapter 50

Kydd's thoughts turned to Persephone, as they had done more frequently of late. By now, months into the commission, there should be letters waiting for him in Madras. Precious letters that had crossed the thousands of miles of ocean from her hand into his, her thoughts and love made real.

But just now she was a frozen memory – those last frantic minutes in Plymouth Sound before putting to sea and then . . . nothing more. In a way it was like a death: the living, breathing loved one gazing and responding, then snatched from the present existence to recede, perfectly unchanged in every detail, further and further into the far reaches of time, last images often brought out and lovingly burnished, but becoming ever more unreal.

He sighed and got on with the tedium of checking and signing the ship's accounts, to be rendered on arrival at Madras.

In a few days the East India Squadron raised the latitude of Madras, and the next day saw the distant blue-grey hills of

India, well before the plains, and at last the crowded anchorage of Madras Roads.

There was no point in putting off the matter of his first lieutenant any longer and, in full-dress, Kydd took the masula boat ashore to go to Admiralty House and the commander-in-chief.

'What is it, Kydd?' Drury greeted him. 'I'm damnably busy, I'll have you know.' His desk was piled with dockets and threaded reports and he had three staff officers in attendance.

'Sir, a matter of some discretion,' Kydd said pointedly.

The officers left at a look from Drury. 'So?'

'I'm sorry to say that one of my officers has been taken in drink at sea.' Ashore was another matter but being incapable at sea was unforgivable.

'Oh? Can't you—'

'My first lieutenant.' The next most important figure after the captain. It had to be acted upon and not by that captain.

'I see. Well, he's to lose his post, of course. Leave it with me – I'll find another for you,' he said irritably. 'Stays where he is until the new one comes aboard.'

'Aye aye, sir.'

Farrant took it well. 'I see, Sir Thomas. Then you'll not be vexed with me again,' he replied distantly, when told to get his gear together as he was under notice to quit the ship.

The ship's mail was expected. In the early afternoon it finally arrived, the mailbag spilling out its contents in the coach to be distributed to the gunroom and messes by Dillon in lordly dispensation. An unnatural quiet would soon descend as tidings from home were eagerly digested, the captain able to savour his in the privacy of the great cabin.

But shortly Kydd, with a lurch of the heart, found there was none for him. It was hard to take. Reasons could easily be found but Persephone would not be unaware of the opportunities those in the know had in getting their missives away by accelerated means. Post-office letters were sent in bulk at irregular intervals on lumbering, if safe, merchant vessels but for a fee could be consigned as a 'ship's letter' personally to the captain of a smaller but faster ship, gaining weeks but at the price of risking its loss by storm or enemy action.

She would as well have the sympathy and favour of any naval vessel outward bound to station, but these would be at the mercy of the service, delays from any one of a dozen causes having the same effect. There were faster methods for the privileged – for an admiral in Bombay, dispatches were sent expensively overland from the Mediterranean and through the Red Sea, reducing the time, but that was out of the question for private mail.

As it was, any ship taken by a marauding privateer could expect its mail to be ransacked and then, valueless, thrown over the side. At the very least a ship captured by a man-o'-war would in all honour have its mail sent on but with a grievous delay.

Truly, the blessing and wonder of mail was in many ways a very chancy thing and perhaps he should not expect it by right.

He took up his book again and settled by the stern-windows but almost at once Dillon entered, carrying a small parcel. 'I found this at the bottom of the sack,' he said, with a mysterious air.

It was addressed to Kydd in impeccably polite formality in a hand he didn't recognise.

He opened it carefully and nearly dropped it in surprise. It was a small but elaborate carving in jade-stone of what appeared to be a grotesquely dancing half-human elephant.

'What the devil . . .?'

But there was a small note with it in the same tiny but immaculate handwriting with just the words, 'You were right.'

It was signed 'Fleetwood P'.

'An Indian icon,' Dillon suggested.

'I can see that. What does it mean?'

'I really can't say. There's so many of 'em, each with their own cryptic meaning.'

Fleetwood Pellew – and he was saying something that could be either a mortal insult or . . .? He slipped the artefact into his pocket. 'Ah, well. I'll find out soon enough. I'm for stepping ashore to pass a spell in the garden-house. Are you coming, Edward?'

'Alas, my work is not yet done, Sir Thomas.'

The heat and closeness of a ship not designed for the tropics was tediously enervating and Kydd had no compunction about spending time in his residence. It had been a stressful, frustrating recent experience that had ended less than gloriously, but once in its agreeable surroundings he eased quickly.

Even more pleasantly, Bomarjee had conjured up a masseur and he now relaxed naked under the oily blows.

His mind drifted, taking pleasure in the singular experience of luxuriating in his own habitation in this exotic land, half-focused images of India forming and dissolving – but then his thoughts returned to the letters not arriving.

He'd gone over the reasons in depressing detail but there was one that he'd been unwilling to confront, that was all too possible, one he'd seen happen before to others.

His eyes flicked open as he unwillingly visualised it. A ship, gone foreign for months, years. A beautiful but bored wife surrounded by persistent admirers knowing of her loneliness and laying siege to her affections. The inevitable happens and—

'That'll do, damn it!' Kydd snarled at the astonished masseur, snatching up his towel. The man hurriedly left.

It would explain a fall-off in the numbers and tone of letters, but he'd had none. Had she so quickly . . .?

No! Never! She had been so warm and intimate in her love for him.

But did that in itself mean . . .?

He got dressed quickly, trying to put aside the turmoil he was feeling.

He knew virile young men overseas often chose the easiest route. 'Every man is a bachelor who passes the Strait of Gibraltar' was a famous saying of Nelson before he had taken up with Emma Hamilton in Naples. Some installed a discreet paramour, but here in India it was more open, the sultry climate blamed for a rise in animal spirits that required a suitable *bibi* as a matter of course for many.

Others took ready advantage of the moment, particularly in a distant colony where a fresh young man in the prime of life was greatly prized. And—

Dammit! He would never do anything like that!

Kydd settled back in his armchair. '*Chota peg*, Mr Bomarjee,' he called. '*Jowlah jowlah*, now!' As the *dubash* returned with the whisky he remembered the strange fetish sent by Fleetwood Pellew.

'So you're back, you dear man!' Caroline laughed when she saw who it was. 'I heard those cannon banging away at the fort in salute and I did so hope it would be you returning.'

Kydd swept down in a bow. 'M' lady. New returned from the Middle Kingdom – and damned glad to be home,' he said, with hearty sincerity.

'Pray do come in, sir,' she said, with a curtsy. When she rose, her cheeks had a fetching glow and her eyes locked with his for a moment.

'I didn't wish to intrude,' Kydd lied, 'it's just that I have a queer sort of mystery I'm trusting you'll solve for me.'

'Oh, a puzzler! Of course I shall try to help, Thomas.'

There was nothing for it but to accept tea and dainty cakes and hear the latest gossip before Caroline asked, 'Well, what is your mystery, my dear?'

Kydd gave an enigmatic smile and brought out the little figurine.

She took it curiously, holding it out to arm's length the better to catch it in the evening light. 'Then what is your perplexity, Thomas?' she asked.

He told its story without mentioning names while she listened attentively.

'Well, now. I can tell you that this is Ganesha, offspring of the dread Shiva and the beautiful Parvati, mother of the universe,' she said seriously.

'Oh, I see. Then what in Hades can it mean, the fellow giving it to me?'

She gave a teasing smile. 'I think it's plain enough.'

'Damn it, Caroline, tell me!'

'If you'll temper your language in front of a lady, sir.' She pouted prettily.

Kydd felt colour rise. 'I beg your pardon, Caroline, but—'

'Ganesha is revered as the deva of wisdom, the getting of learning. And a remover of obstacles,' she added archly. 'By this I believe you are being told that a lesson has been learned that has made the way clear, where before it was hindered.'

'Ah. Thank you. I believe my mystery is solved.' It seemed the young man had taken note of his last words to him and, in circumstances Kydd would never know, their value had been proved.

Chapter 51

'A gentleman to see you, Sir Thomas,' Dillon announced, with a tinge of curiosity.

'Mr Raffles, I believe?'

'Just so, Sir Thomas,' the scholarly-looking man said, with a pleased smile.

'Then is there anything I might do for you, sir – providing it does not include aught to do with beetles?'

'Not at all, sir. They may be my pride and joy but do not in any way constitute my duty. No, sir, my desire is much more mundane, as it were. Sir Thomas, it would greatly oblige if you were to share with me the details of your late incursion into China. You see, my position as assistant colonial secretary to a presidency impels me to discover what I may of events involving the Company and therefore myself in any way.'

'Surely you have word of your own,' Kydd said guardedly.

'There have been contradictory accounts and your observations as a gentleman of reputation in the navy are greatly to be welcomed.'

Was this a spat between John Company factions that he was being drawn into? If so, he wanted no part of it. On the other hand, this mild-mannered gentleman did not seem the politicking sort.

'Very well. Refreshment?'

Raffles listened politely as Kydd described the shambles of the expedition, asking acute but scrupulously polite questions at several points. At the end he sighed and looked up with a twisted smile. 'Much as I feared. Little men with smaller minds avid for anything that smells of profit. My thanks for your frank account, sir, and I'll be on my way.'

'Do stay a little longer, Mr Raffles. I'd like to know why you cast them down so readily.'

'A simple enough reason. If in every corner of our scattered empire in these parts men acted in their own interests and to a local object, where then is the strength and cohesion of the whole? How will it be possible to spread our gospel of peace and trade?'

Kydd looked at him intently: an assistant secretary speaking like a visionary. 'The pursuit of profit surely is a well-founded engine of trade.'

'Undoubtedly. But within a framework, sir. The Honourable Company does afford such, but if its agents act to their own interest only, never will there be a true empire.'

'An empire of trade.'

'Indeed.'

'So, what can be done?'

'Of my own self, very little. No one is inclined to pay me heed, you'll understand. Yet a shining goal awaits if only resolution and unity are shown.'

'What is that, Mr Raffles?'

'From our defence against to the very conquest of the entire Dutch East Indies – their empire of the east that has existed since King Charles's day.'

'This is not possible, sir,' Kydd said immediately. Dutch

rule was no longer direct but from the earliest times massive fortresses had been built on all the major islands, which would require a long and systematic reduction over years and covering of vast distances to support any long-term engagement.

'I understand your hesitation, Sir Thomas. But the prize is unarguable. Besides possession of all the ancient Spice Islands and control of their product, it must occur to the least observant that this empire sits squarely at the intersection of all sea routes to the China Seas from the west and the south. And even the east, given the prevailing winds.

'And now there is a new spectre come to affright us: Napoleon Bonaparte. Having so recently taken the Netherlands for himself and claiming its empire for his own, there is little preventing him sending a fleet from Europe to be stationed there, effectively cutting us off from our most vital China trade.'

'That must be so,' Kydd replied. 'Yet I'm sure their lordships have considered the matter.'

'They have, several times, but at each have decided that the reduction of strongholds one by one is beyond their means at the time and have delayed from action.'

'In which case there is nothing more to be said,' Kydd agreed sorrowfully. 'For want of resources we cannot proceed.'

Raffles gave a small, secret smile. 'Not altogether lost,' he replied softly. 'You are much more in the military line than I and can be relied on to make sound judgement on the strategicals. I have an idea that I'm sanguine you'd be interested to hear.'

'Please do tell, sir.'

'Very well. The value to the Hollanders of their empire lies in the extraordinary prices they can levy on the spices produced only in this part of the world, those that were much striven over in times past by half the nations of Christendom. My observation is simple enough. If those islands – a select few only in the region known as the Moluccas – were taken, the value of their empire in all would be reduced to such a level that it would not be worth the zealous defending and the entirety would readily fall to us.'

He watched Kydd narrowly.

'A reasonable enough deducing I would believe,' Kydd said shortly. 'But if they are so valuable then for a certainty they will be well fortified against this.'

'I know it to be so,' Raffles replied, unperturbed. 'There are those Malays on my staff who have fled the islands and have told me of it.'

'And if I remember rightly, the Moluccas are in the remote centre of a great sea surrounded at a distance by concentric rings of archipelagos ruled by native princes and pirates to be shunned by all right-thinking mariners.'

'Again you are correct in the essentials. But if I place before you a modus of assailing, as it were, you will listen?'

'Go on, sir.'

'Then it is this. We turn what you have said to advantage. The Moluccas are remote – but this implies that if we make our descent stealthily they will have no time to send for reinforcements. That they are far from the sea lanes means that this can be assured. The excess of fortresses is in our favour, too. If we are rapid in our conquering, these are ready-made defences, stoutly manned, for any attempt to seize back the islands.'

'This would be true. It must depend on the quality and quantity of the forces thrown against the objective, of course. And surprise, without question,' Kydd agreed.

'Yes, surprise. I have an opinion on that which I'd be gratified should it be thought practical.'

Kydd listened with grave concentration. It was well thought out, as he would expect from this gifted individual.

The great interior sea, the Sea of Java, extended from the tip of Malaya unbroken eastwards until it ended in the unknowable darkness of the island of New Guinea. To the south it was enclosed by the long islands of Java, Sumatra and Timor and, to the north, Borneo, the Celebes and a maze of lesser islands. The Moluccas were at the far eastwards of this sea.

'There is a regular tangle of islands here, Mr Raffles. Which do you think should be first?'

'Would you believe that the entire world's consuming of nutmeg is supplied from one and only one islet in the Moluccas?'

'I'd find it difficult, sir.'

'The Dutch uprooted trees on all other islands to concentrate on one without it had competition.'

'Ah.'

'Yes, it is called Banda Neira. So, conveniently, if this were taken, we have the tender heart of the Spice Islands and in one stroke the greater portion of their value to the Dutch.'

'And how will we—'

'This is my scheme to achieve a surprising. Do stop me if I'm adrift in my nauticals, as it were.'

'Do clap on sail and stand on, Mr Raffles.'

'Very well. The interior sea leads all the way from Java to the Moluccas in a straight line and is for the most part sheltered from hurricanoes and similar. Any descent on the Moluccas would therefore be expected by the Dutch along this path and their defences will thus be laid.

'Instead I propose another route. Sailing from Penang, your swift-flying fleet follows the route of the China argosies away from the East Indies – but then leaves to sail north-about the mass of Borneo into the seas between it and the Philippine islands. Then on into the Pacific while it tracks along outside the upper fringe of the East Indies until it meets with New Guinea island.

'There the fleet drops down through the boundary islands into the interior sea and is then miraculously in a position to close with Banda Neira – but in a hooking movement from the opposite direction, where we may apprehend that no defensive preparations lie. A possibility, can you say?'

Kydd shook his head slowly in admiration. 'Sir, I'm held in nothing but awe by your sea invention. Yet I'm in the obligation to ask, have you considered why ships do not follow your example?'

'You will say they have no need.'

'No, sir. It is because in a sea territory infested with myriad islands, we can be sure that with them will come quantities of the most deplorable and wretched hazards – coral reefs hungering to tear out the bowels of trespassing ships, tiny islands lying athwart the bow that in night-time may only be seen in the minutes before a vessel ends its life on them. Not to mention that this is the natural abode of pirates and head-hunting savages.'

Raffles gave a pained smile. 'Do believe me when I say that this is not unknown to me. Yet could I bring to your attention that Magellan and Drake both sailed these waters, uncharted for them and with impunity. I'm given to affirm that the Royal Navy of King George will not in any wise quail at the adventure, Sir Thomas.'

There was no counter to that and Kydd graciously conceded.

'Not that there is any prospect the enterprise will be taken up, of course.' Raffles sighed, slumping back in sudden dejection.

'How can you say that, sir?' Kydd spoke with heat. 'A

rattling good stratagem as is sorely needed while the French sharpen their blades. A lance into the heart and the body dies. It stands to reason!'

Raffles, clearly flattered but cautious, said carefully, 'If you knew the sainted hierarchy of the Honourable Company you would be aware that even should they be persuaded it will be not in this age that a decision is taken and then longer for the resources to be found.'

'Ha! There is another way, dear fellow.'

'How's that?'

'You look at this as a Company affair, the freeing and extending of trade far into the eastern seas only. I see this as a master blow against the French as will deny them a princely rival empire in these waters. In other words, a matter for the Crown.

'Sir, you and I will finish your scheme and take it to one who can do something about it. To the commander-in-chief himself, whose word can in a day launch scores of ships in a conquering fleet. We will place it before him together!'

Chapter 52

The Admiral's House

'Captain Sir Thomas Kydd, sir.'

Kydd entered the sanctum respectfully. Drury was at his desk, his flag-captain standing behind him. He looked up, and Kydd was startled by the fatigue and sickness he saw in the drawn face. The voice, however, was firm and careful. 'Ah, Kydd. I was about to summon you.'

'Sir?'

'Your first lieutenant. I'm pleased to say I've found a replacement. Young fellow like yourself and happy to serve under you.'

So, this was the end for Farrant.

'Thank you, sir. When might I expect him aboard?'

'Um, quite soon. He is in fact in command of *Rupert* cutter but she's still out on a cruise, expected back within the week. You can keep the old one until he makes port.'

'Sir.'

The lieutenant-in-command, but only of an unrated cutter, much like the old *Seaflower*. To move up to be premier of a crack frigate would be a gratifying coup. No wonder he was happy to make the move. For the time being Farrant would have to revert to a twenty-four-hour warning to land.

'Anything more, Captain?'

'Er, yes, sir, there is. Have you a few minutes to spare that I can outline to you a possible stroke against the enemy?'

Drury frowned. 'This is a trifle irregular, Kydd. Any suggestion or appreciation should be tendered in writing in the usual way. Why the haste, may I ask?'

'The imminence of the arrival of French forces in the East Indies compels me to speak now, sir.'

'Very well, then. But be brief.'

'May I bring in the original mind behind the scheme, sir?'

'This is not of your conceiving?'

'My contribution has been to verify its military practicality, sir.'

'Carry on, then.'

Raffles was called and entered softly, bowing to Drury.

'Why, isn't this Mr Raffles? A colonial secretary to the Prince of Wales Presidency lately taken to butterflies and beetles, I've heard.'

'A natural philosopher of note, sir,' Kydd hastened to intervene. 'With singular devotion to the advancement of the English tribe in these parts.'

'With a notion of strategicals, he claims.'

'It is a conception worth hearing, sir.'

'You have ten minutes, Kydd.'

'Sir.'

It took less than that to outline the project, and a single chart of the East Indies was sufficient to bring alive the central concept.

At the end Drury spoke. 'Have you anything to add, Mr Raffles?'

'No, sir. Sir Thomas's maritime eloquence does the matter more than justice.'

'Then be so kind as to step outside as we make conference together.'

When Raffles had departed, Drury regarded Kydd with a caustic expression. 'I find it most peculiar, if not curious, that you should be gulled so comprehensively, Kydd.'

'Sir?'

'This entire farrago has no basis in military logic at all. Not at all. That is true, is it not, Flags?'

The flag-captain made haste to agree and added his frown to Drury's.

'But, sir, the—'

'You can't be expected to understand at your station in the Service, so I'll be brief. It is an axiom much venerated by our brethren ashore that it is an error of unforgivable proportion to advance with an unreduced fortification in one's rear. You're asking to advance over some thirty-five degrees of longitude into wholly enemy territory, leaving an uncountable quantity of fortresses quite untouched in your wake. This is not to be borne, sir.'

'If we—'

'No. I will hear no more. I commend your spirit, sir, and that of Mr Raffles, of course, but that is an end to it.'

'May I say—'

'You may not. I will confide to you that a much more important feat-at-arms is being planned at this moment and I have no time to spare for trifles. I do not want to hear of this again. Do you understand me?'

'Aye aye, sir.'

Drury seemed to have second thoughts for he laid down

his pen and said gruffly, 'Do not take it amiss, Kydd. Your devotion to duty is noted, but there is much you will need to learn before you hoist your own flag. Carry on, please.'

Outside, Raffles gave a sad smile. 'My thanks for your attempt, Sir Thomas, but I was never sanguine of a hearing.'

Kydd burned. 'The navy is different from the army,' he fumed, 'and goes by different rules. Fortresses that squat unmoving on islands can never be compared in any wise to the same on land where a soldier can march from one to another and none may oppose him but with another army. Never fear, Mr Raffles, your scheme is sound in all particulars and I honour you for its creating.'

'But never will I see it in truth.'

'Damn it all!' Kydd exploded. 'Such a stroke within our means and we're thwarted by our own side. I'm grieved to say it, Mr Raffles, but I can see no way ahead for us.'

Raffles walked on without a word, then straightened with a boyish grin. 'My friend, have you ever seen a *Rhombocephalus smaragdinus* at all?'

'Not as if I would know it,' Kydd snorted, still smouldering.

'A most delightful creature. A species of carnivorous centipede from Borneo capable of devouring a complete forest scorpion. Of quite formidable size – I've seen one a foot long hurrying after its prey and have a live specimen just this day sent to me by my collectors.'

Kydd gave a tight grin. 'Ah, perhaps another time, old chap.'

'From Flag, sir,' Midshipman Rowan panted, his eyes wide at the sight of his captain naked under the hands of a masseur.

'Thank you, younker. Wait there, will you?'

Reluctantly Kydd heaved himself up, slipping on a luridly emblazoned gown, and padded into the drawing room.

It was a personal letter from Drury. It seemed he'd received a request from Calcutta that an officer of rank be made available to the governor general to detail and clarify the recent events at Macao.

Kydd knew immediately what it was: Drury and his actions were not in question but the Presidency needed all high-level particulars in hand should consequences follow, a summons to the actual commander-in-chief to explain himself carrying undue significance.

Kydd was best placed to describe events, having been present in the deliberations with the standing committee. He was enjoined, ponderously, to be perfectly frank and open about what he had heard and not to hesitate from a misplaced sense of delicacy. It was obvious what Drury wanted him to say and he saw no reason why he should not tell it as he had seen with his own eyes.

His orders were simply to proceed to Calcutta to make witness, then return without delay. *Tyger* would take him there. *Rupert* had not yet returned so Farrant would have to wait a little longer to be quit of his post.

An inconvenience, though. Cluffer had invited him to a party that he'd promised would be one of the highlights of the season. And his new friend Raffles had let it be known that, with his business concluded, he would soon be on his way back to his post on Prince of Wales Island.

'Mr Rowan, return to *Tyger* and desire them to make ready for sea. I shall be with you presently.'

At least he could bid Raffles Godspeed.

A swift note was sent, which had the man hurrying to him. 'You're going to Calcutta, then?' he demanded, his eyes sharp and alert.

'Why, yes. To speak with the governor general concerning the China expedition.'

'Ah! That we have such a chance!'

'I beg your—'

'I'm known to the noble Lord Minto, who trusts me,' he said urgently, seizing Kydd's arm. 'My friend, if you will be so good as to be at my side as I make my case to the governor general it would add so much weight to my plea. Will you in all charity give me passage and support both?'

Chapter 53

Calcutta

Kydd was seated in the cool of a spacious reception room in the splendour of the Government House and attended by an amiable equerry.

'Sir Thomas?'

He rose and followed the aide into the council room, taking in the rich gold ornamentation, pale alabaster and ornate dark-wood carvings. At the centre of a massive table sat Gilbert Elliot-Murray-Kynynmound, Lord Minto, the governor general of India. Thin-faced, with a forbiddingly distant patrician presence, he regarded Kydd for a moment, then gave a polite smile and invited him to sit opposite. Four others were also gathered around the table.

After introductions had been made, Kydd's initial summary was heard attentively and ended with a respectful acknowledgement. Questions were few but pointed: what was his understanding of Drury's decision to approach the viceroy of Canton by boat only? Was there an animus evident between the select committee and the commander-in-chief? In his estimation did this affect subsequent decisions or proceedings?

Appearing pleased with Kydd's presentation, Minto progressed from a courteous but wordless presiding to a more active questioning.

At the completion of the testimony he made much of *Tyger*'s captain's service to him.

This gave Kydd confidence to put forward their plan. 'Sir, I have a matter of unusual moment that I'm persuaded is of particular merit to our interests here. If I might be granted some small time to disclose it to Your Lordship I would be infinitely obliged.'

It was readily granted, and he laid out the essentials, emphasising the key element – the bypassing of all strongholds in favour of a deadly thrust to the heart of the Dutch empire.

Minto was plainly taken with the concept and his interest quickened. How might this be attained with the forces the British commanded in India? Could surprise be guaranteed? In his opinion, how could the progression to full conquest proceed?

An adjournment was declared while senior officers of the Presidency were summoned to hear the proposal, and in the meantime Kydd asked to introduce Raffles, who was greeted with the warmth of mutual respect.

Now equipped with charts and sailing directions he went through the presentation once more, this time with Raffles contributing. Kydd heard him crisply and concisely detailing at the highest level the advantages that would accrue should the British conquer this rich corner of the globe, and realised there was much more to his friend than he'd known.

At the conclusion Minto glanced at the others in turn, then addressed them both. 'I'm minded to give this project the serious deliberation it deserves.'

Kydd's pulse quickened.

'But I cannot.'

'Sir, if you—'

'Because time is too short. Sir Thomas, if you would indulge me for a space to consult further with Mr Raffles you shall receive my decision shortly.'

The aide appeared noiselessly and he was conducted from the presence.

As they walked the officer stroked his chin and chuckled. 'I've not seen His Nibs so exercised for some time. You seem to have made an impression of some significance for a naval officer.'

It had been a suspiciously easy conquest – was Minto going to take Raffles's idea and make it his own?

The afternoon wore on and Raffles made his appearance, weary but with a look of satisfaction. 'He's going to take up the venture,' he said, with feeling. 'Banda Neira first and, after a decent interval to allow Dutch resolution to decay, a move against Java itself.'

'Can he do this? He may be a governor general but that requires fleets and armies.'

'Certainly he may. East of the Cape is the Honourable Company's remit and the forces of the Crown are here only to render assistance when called upon. I believe to this end a requisition in aid is being drawn up at this very moment.'

'You're not suspecting, he agreeing so quickly?'

'Not at all. I've known the noble lord from a long time past. He will retire from post in the next several years and desires nothing better than to do so covered with laurels in some daring act of empire, to the marked advantage of his fortune. We have fortuitously given him the chance for a speedy exploit employing comparatively small local resources, thereby ensuring there will be no sharing of the glory, all provided he acts fast before others hear of the adventure.'

'Who will be in command?' Kydd wanted to know. Drury was utterly opposed to it in principle and would be at best half-hearted in an expedition that would, if successful, directly contradict his stand. His nominee would follow the commander-in-chief's lead and not necessarily be of the bold and fearless character necessary for a defiant thrust deep into enemy waters.

Raffles gave an odd smile. 'As I mentioned, were I to make recommendation then only one name would I suffer put forward – Sir Thomas Kydd. The governor general's requisition will make explicit that you shall be in seaborne command of the entire project.'

Kydd's heart leaped. A proper fleet – this was a commodore's command! He would, for the first time, hoist his flag, and even if he had to strike it after the event it would be on record at the Admiralty. And, as with Duckworth, made commodore for the Minorca success, perhaps it could lead on eventually to his admiral's flag.

Chapter 54

The vice-regal dictate safely under hatches, *Tyger* had joyously spread sail and headed south to Madras. In the mysterious way of the foremast jack, it became known that their ship was marked for great things in a venture of consequence, and that soon enough.

Kydd was happily torn between decisions – if he was to be commander of the expedition, he should hoist his flag not in *Tyger* but in a ship-of-the-line. And, in a final irony, if *Rupert* did not show herself before they left, it would be Farrant who would command his ship in every action with the enemy.

It gave him pause but there was much else that needed his attention first. The voyage had given him the chance to sit down with Raffles and cover the detailed planning. The requisition demanded that Kydd be given all resources that could be spared, but he knew he would have to justify numbers to Drury. A minimum order of battle had to be drawn up.

Their information was that on Banda Neira there were two major fortresses and many batteries. The Dutch had cannily sited one inland, well back from the other to cover it, and even the heavy guns of a battleship would be hard pressed to make an impression. The island was defended by some several thousands, requiring at least two regiments of British troops to match this and therefore at least half a dozen transports.

And four frigates would be needed to patrol at the four points of the compass to delay any attempt at relieving, with the usual complement of minor vessels, on an ocean voyage at the least brig-sloops rather than cutters and inshore craft.

The charts were adequate, if dated, and sufficient to make a preliminary sketch of proceedings. It was a heady experience, knowing there would be none in sway above him to interfere or deflect his purpose. Once at sea with his fleet, he would be in command. What he was preparing now were *his* orders that would be obeyed to the letter under all the dread penalties of the Articles of War.

By the time Madras Roads was sighted he had a workable plan and the whole thing was looking very possible.

Tyger's anchor plunged down and, in rising excitement, Kydd gathered together his papers and marked charts and ordered a masula boat.

'Sir?'

It was Farrant, one with whom in the normal run he would be sharing his intentions. It caught him aback, but he replied, as kindly as he could, 'I'll find if the new man is ready ashore but you are entitled to one-day notice.'

'Thank you, sir.' The soft voice was pathetic but there was no hostility.

'I shall see you before you go, in course.'

'Sir.'

The seas were up and the trip inshore a wet one, but this

did not dampen Kydd's spirits: he had what every naval officer dreamed of, an independent command of nothing less than a fleet.

A short time later he was standing outside Admiralty House baffled and frustrated. Admiral Drury had gone to his sick-bed once more and left strict instructions he was not to be disturbed. His staff could only suggest Kydd enquire each morning until he was well enough to receive him.

There was nothing for it but to retire. Raffles had hurried off on some business connected to the project, and in the absence of permissions and direction, Kydd could do nothing, except take his ease in his residence.

This time his *dubash* had conjured something new for him: a vast bath, cunningly portable and erected on a ring of ceramic elephants. A powerful fragrance of rose-water arose from the depths and pink petals were liberally strewn about. On an extravagantly carved small dark-wood table a whisky glass and decanter waited discreetly.

'Why, well done, Mr Bomarjee.' He laughed, stripping to get in. It was as well that his Tygers could not see him now, he reflected guiltily.

The morning did not bring any news from Admiralty House but an invitation to tiffin arrived from Cluffer.

Why not? He was at leisure and Dillon was off all day on some sort of expedition to a temple reputed to be of immeasurable age.

'What ho, the sailorman!' called Cluffer, from the shady outer tables of the Choultry Inn.

Kydd grinned at the eccentric figure the man cast and took a cane chair opposite. 'You've only invited me as you want to hear of my adventures among the heathen Chinee.'

'Not as if it were so important,' Cluffer grunted, raising his glass to Kydd.

'Why so?' he answered curiously.

'All the world knows your Chinaman will never be moved. Stands to lose too much squeeze if things change and, besides, he's a mile more terrified of his emperor than he is of us.'

Kydd leaned back. 'As is the whole story, Cluffer. We went there—'

'Good day, gentlemen!' came a familiar female voice.

'Caroline – how pleasant to see you!' Kydd said warmly, rising quickly to his feet. 'Won't you join us?'

Her face dimpled with pleasure as she daintily took a seat. 'I didn't know you were back in Madras, Thomas.'

Kydd was happy to answer her many questions about China, a land she had never visited, the meal continued on well into the late afternoon.

'Well, I suppose I must be on my way,' Caroline said, collecting her reticule.

'I was thinking more of a promenade of sorts among the bazaars,' Kydd responded, a little too casually, 'as the best of the day lies ahead.'

It was not as if he had designs on the woman, he told himself. It was only that he was missing female company of the superior kind.

Her face clouded. 'Cluffer, if you could . . .?'

'Of course, dear lady,' he said immediately. 'Tongues shall not be set to wagging if I can help it.'

The threesome began their stroll, Caroline taking Kydd's arm, as if it were the most natural thing in the world, while Cluffer politely fell behind.

With the sun approaching its evening glory, it was a most pleasant time to be abroad. Enticed by exotic sights and smells, they marvelled at monkeys, fakirs, magicians and numerous stalls of mysterious produce.

Thinking perhaps Caroline might be growing weary, Kydd asked, 'A little rest and refreshment, my dear?'

'That would be welcome indeed,' she said, and turned to Cluffer – but he was nowhere to be seen.

'Oh, the villain!' she said in vexation, her hand dropping away from Kydd's arm. 'He's probably got bored and wandered away.'

She bit her lip, then said brightly, 'So I shall take you home and . . . No, I can't do that. I gave my *dubash* the day off for some festival or other.'

'If you can abide being an unaccompanied lady in a gentleman's home you are welcome to take refreshment with me,' he came back gallantly.

'Why, thank you, sir,' she said, with just the hint of a blush.

'Mr Bomarjee, ahoy!' Kydd called, when they arrived. 'Can you conjure us a cooling drink? Mrs Lowther has had a tiring afternoon.'

She settled in a rattan armchair with a comfortable sigh and looked about her with interest. 'My, but you've done well in the article of decoration.'

'Under your advice,' Kydd said generously.

'I do adore those wall hangings,' she said, gazing at the gloriously coloured tapestries.

'You would like to see my hibiscus?' Kydd dared. 'New planted and well tended, they've grown so well in this climate.'

'Oh, yes. Flowers carry such a spirit of brightness and hope in this difficult world.'

Outside, evening had advanced into that particular time of magic peculiar to India – a warm dusk suffused with a violet charge that lay on the senses with all the excitement of the east.

He felt her take his arm and, despite himself, was aware of a mounting flush of arousal.

'You know, I really don't know what to do about you, dear man,' she said softly, with a squeeze of his arm. 'You undo all a woman's best intentions.'

They walked on slowly, Kydd unsure of himself and fearful of breaking the spell.

They stopped by the side of the house, still out of sight of the road. She looked at him, her eyes large and round, and reached out to take his hands. 'Thomas. We have to—'

A figure, startling in the dimness and the suddenness of its appearing, came from around the side of the house and stopped, unmoving.

Kydd recovered first, freeing his hands awkwardly. 'Mr Dillon. Are you, um, looking for something?'

There was no answer and Kydd was aware of his gaze on them both.

'I said—'

'I thought I heard someone out at this unseasonable hour,' Dillon said quietly.

The spell had been broken.

'I do thank you, Sir Thomas, for showing me those delightful blooms. An entrancing sight, sir,' Caroline said unsteadily. With a glance at Dillon she walked slowly back to the house.

'Tell Bomarjee we shall be with him in a trice,' Kydd said tightly, and followed.

The morning brought both manly exulting and guilt. Caroline Lowther was attracted to him, of that there was no doubting. But was it because he'd led her along? Had he gone too far? She was a mature woman and would know where she stood, surely.

What should he do? It would be unmannerly, boorish, even, to cast her aside in some way, but if he did not, where would it all end? And what of Persephone?

News arrived to interrupt his thoughts. The admiral was up and attending to his duties from his home. If Kydd was going to make his play it must be soon, he knew, before the admiral woke up to the fact *Tyger* was due another working cruise.

Drury found time for him that afternoon. The man was stooped and slow, whatever his illness still holding sway.

'Ah, Kydd. Your ardent devotion to duty is a lesson to all the lazy vagabonds in my fleet. Do not concern yourself. Your orders for a cruise about Ceylon are being drawn up directly. How did you fare with the governor general, pray?'

'A good meeting, sir, and he quite sees the propriety of your actions before Canton.'

'Admirable. You'll go far in the Service, Kydd, you mark my words. Is there anything else before you go?'

'Er, yes, sir. Lord Minto showed interest in the scheme I described to you the last time—'

'Showed interest? You mean you took it upon yourself to broach the subject with him?' Incredulity was quickly transformed to anger. 'I distinctly said I didn't want to hear any more of that contemptible nonsense!'

'Sir, this was Lord Minto, not yourself.'

'Even worse. If he laughed in your face it's no less than you deserved. I'm surprised at you, Kydd, surprised – do you hear me?'

'Sir, he approves of the plan,' Kydd said quietly, 'and desires me to convey to you his requisition for same.' He took out the papers and handed them across.

Drury exploded. 'I'm appalled – scandalised! You've gone over my head to the highest in the land to peddle your inanity, an unpardonable arrogance!'

299

'Sir, you would not hear any—'

'In some way you weaselled your way into a position of trust and confidence, then laid out your pathetic views to one who is not in a position to understand. Damn your blood, Kydd – I'm commander-in-chief and the strategical authority on this station, not you, for God's sake! You've gone too far and I'm to see you'll not hear the last of it. Get out!'

'Er, the venture, sir. It requires dispatch and—'

'I don't care what it requires!'

'Sir. If the governor general hears you are delaying the project . . .'

Drury hesitated, drawing a deep breath. 'Very well. It shall receive my attention, but you shall rue this, Kydd! That I vow!'

'Then, sir, if—'

'Return tomorrow, God help you.'

'Aye aye, sir.'

Shaken, Kydd made his way out, nearly colliding with Raffles, who must have heard of his visit to Drury.

'A hard beat to windward,' Kydd muttered, telling him of the stormy meeting.

'Unfortunate, but recollect, he must comply. However much it goes against the grain, our expedition with its fleet will be made to go on its way.'

It was past noon the next day before Kydd faced the admiral again.

The man had changed. Ill and bent he might have been, but the eyes held a feverish gleam as he fixed Kydd with a savage glare. 'I have this requisition,' he said, waving it in front of Kydd, 'and I have the rest of your demands.' He flourished a sheaf of papers in his other hand.

'Sir.'

'It reserves the command to yourself, Kydd, and thus now I understand,' he went on with a rising snarl. 'That an officer on my station should stoop so low in the pursuit of promotion by any means is hard for me to accept, harder still to tolerate.'

'That is not what I—'

'Save your words, sir. Your command is safe.' An odd smile played as he regarded Kydd. 'I'm bidden to furnish you with as great a fleet and its support as is within my power to grant.'

'Thank you, sir.'

'But what you and your friend failed to take into account was the greater strategical situation. Yes, sir! The grander and bigger picture, which you are in no position at all to appreciate.'

'Sir?'

'I can confide to you that nothing less than a descent in force on the Île-de-France is being put in train. That chief nest of privateers will be wiped from the map at long last and thus our trade within the Indian Ocean made safe.'

'A worthy advancement,' Kydd murmured.

'Quite. And by orders from London I'm enjoined to make every effort to provide forces of a strength commensurate with the importance of the objective.'

'Sir.'

'Orders from the Admiralty, their lordships!'

'Yes, sir.'

'Who rate a damn sight higher than a John Company panjandrum!'

Kydd was wearying of the farce and wanted to get started on his considerable list of tasks. 'Sir, there's much I must do. If I can be given details of my fleet and military?'

'Ah, your fleet.' A cynical smile briefly appeared as the

commander-in-chief found a paper, which, with exaggerated politeness, he handed to Kydd. 'Here you are, sir.'

The headings, with careful tablature of guns, manning and commands, held just three names: *Tyger*, *Piedmontaise* and *Barracouta*. His own ship, another frigate and a brig-sloop. No ships-of-the-line, military transports, support craft, regiments of troops.

Kydd looked up in bewilderment. 'Sir. What does this mean at all? I set out requirements for an assault and capture of the most valuable islands in the Dutch empire. Where are my ships-of-the-line and—'

The smile turned angelic. 'I only follow the very letter of your requisition, Kydd. A fleet as great as is within my power to release to you. And, in view of the urgency of the Île-de-France objective, I very much regret that this is all I can spare.'

Kydd reddened. 'I find this monstrous! I'm charged by the governor general to take and hold the Spice Islands and all you can give me in support is two ships of inferior weight of metal and no troops?'

Drury gave a saintly sigh. 'Look at it thus. If, as a consequence of being so far in advance of the enemy, you are surrounded and overcome, His Majesty will thereby be deprived of only a paltry number of sail, just you three.'

'Sir – where are my soldiers? Capture of the islands is one thing, holding them another. Without military to man the—'

'I find the Crown has need of its professional army. Perhaps you could practise your charms on the sepoys.'

It was all he could do to hold in his fury, and Kydd left in a raging mood, seeking out Raffles without delay. 'We're beaten, m' friend,' he fumed. 'No fleet, no soldiers – we're scuppered before ever we begin.'

Raffles, grave and studious, did not speak for some time,

then said, with quiet resolve, 'Not necessarily. Stealth, dispatch and cunning at arms may well prevail over brute numbers, I'm persuaded.'

'What are you saying?'

'You will meet my Malay friends. They will tell you more about Banda Neira and then you shall decide how to act.'

Chapter 55

Kydd returned on board and it gave him no satisfaction to see officers and men scatter in front of him at the sight of his grim expression. On the way another thought had occurred to him. It was now without question that he'd lost his 'interest', his patron, who could be relied upon to put his name forward where it counted, to place him in the way of a plum cruise that would result in them sharing prizes, distinction, even. In fact, he'd managed to achieve the worst prize of all for a naval officer. He'd made a mortal enemy of his own commander-in-chief.

Only one thing could in any way compensate: that by some miracle and against extreme odds he could bring off a coup of sorts in the Spice Islands. He would know fairly quickly if he had any chance after speaking to Raffles's islanders.

They came aboard with him to not a little comment among the Tygers and were quickly bundled below.

'You speak English?' Kydd asked loudly of the older of the two, a constantly smiling individual wearing an earth-coloured sarong and patterned shirt.

'Hasan does not. He has no need for it. I shall translate,' Raffles said.

It was strange to hear the gentlemanly secretary effortlessly discussing matters in a musical but totally incomprehensible tongue.

Hasan confirmed much of what Kydd already knew. Banda Neira was one of three closely spaced islands, each volcanically precipitous and with a single harbour and settlement situated on the only level plain between them. It was well defended by not one but two fortresses. His estimate of the size of the defending garrison was in the thousands, concentrated in the strongholds and with field artillery on hand to deploy.

The younger Malay, Ali, had useful insights. A fisherman, he brought the perspectives of a sea-goer to his descriptions. All three islands were so mountainous it was impossible to see from one any activity behind the other. Not only that but a complex of currents swirling around would, if foul at that time of day, make it very difficult for the enemy to send out their boats. Further, the harbour was cramped and set about with coral and could never be thought of as a haven for ships of war, the nearest big enough being hundreds of miles to the north.

The lad had fished all about the Banda group and swore that the distant lookouts and forts were to be found in the scatter of islands to the west, just as Raffles had indicated. A hooking advance from the opposite direction was seeming more than feasible, if a secretive approach was needed – and, with the chief settlement and harbour concentrated in one place, it made sense.

Raffles was right. Good seamanship and practical use of the conditions would go far in righting the imbalance – but for the great odds. Thousands against a couple of hundreds.

The battle-hardened men of *Tyger* could be relied on to give a good account of themselves but would it be anywhere near enough?

The Dutch captain general of the East Indies, Daendels, would have spies everywhere and would eventually hear of the planned assault. If Kydd was going to make a move on the Spice Islands, it would have to be very soon or not at all.

Once again Kydd reviewed his forces. Two frigates and a brig-sloop. Even assuming he could lay hands on some army volunteers, there was little room in a frigate, and the most he could hope to land, including seamen and marines from all three ships, was five hundred men. Four or five to one. Was it morally right to throw men at such odds?

He made his decision. 'I believe we shall make our descent on the Spice Islands, Mr Raffles,' he announced, noting the gleam in Raffles's eyes at his words.

'Then I shall do all in my power to assist you, Sir Thomas.'

'Thank you, but I do not think it proper for a colonial secretary to be implicated in an act of war – you understand me?'

'I do,' said Raffles, softly. 'Although I pray matters do not reach that point for your own good self.'

Unsaid was an acknowledgement of Kydd's motive that, in the event of complete destruction or capture in the affair, the enemy would be deprived of the satisfaction of laying hands on one at such an eminence.

Energised, Kydd set about the preparations but the stores, powder, provisions and all that was needed for an extended voyage were within the purview of the commander-in-chief who, it seemed, was in no hurry to sign away on them.

However, the next morning Madras Roads showed only empty spaces where *Tyger*, *Piedmontaise* and *Barracouta* had been moored. The expedition had sailed without the stores but Kydd knew where he was going to get them.

Chapter 56

It was a cunning move. Raffles was aboard *Tyger* to be taken back to Prince of Wales Island, as he had every right to be, and the real stepping-off point would be that Presidency, a much more obliging administration – and it was the nearest sphere of authority to the Moluccas.

The little squadron swept into the northern end of the Malacca Strait and anchored together opposite Fort Cornwallis. With Raffles to smooth the way, the ships were stored and watered for the long passage and, more importantly, several hundred of the 102nd Regiment of Foot embarked, delighted to take part in an action of note.

It was Kydd's first chance to take proper measure of his force – the ships and the men.

He invited the two captains aboard to join him in the great cabin.

'Charles Foote, *Piedmontaise*.' A cautious, somewhat deliberate and careful individual, he was nevertheless a long-experienced frigate captain. He'd been given the ship when it had been repaired after a heroic three-day battle at which *San Fiorenzo* had captured it in the year previous.

The brig-sloop commander was much the opposite. 'Richard Kenna, *Barracouta*, Sir Thomas.' Young and exuberant, he radiated confidence and boldness.

Kydd leaned back in his chair. 'Gentlemen, I can now tell you the object of our cruise.'

He nearly broke into laughter at the sight of the curiosity on their features for he knew what he had to say next would rock them beyond anything they might have thought.

'It is . . . to sail into the heart of the Dutch empire to seize and hold the Spice Islands. This to render their continued presence in these waters valueless as a precursor to our detaching the whole.'

Foote shook his head as if to clear it. 'Do I understand you to mean that we're to undertake a seaborne assault on a well-defended island deep in enemy territory with this? When do you expect the main invasion convoy, sir?'

'Besides a single transport for the redcoats, this is all our force, Captain Foote.'

'But how . . .' Kenna trailed off, as the scale of the challenge penetrated, his young face puzzled and not a little apprehensive.

'By stealth and cunning,' Kydd said, as positively as he could manage. 'The Dutch have no idea we're coming, and when we do, it'll not be from the direction they think.'

The charts came out and he traced their route outside the islands before their lunge south through them and then the hooking final curve.

'Have we an indication of the enemy's force?' Foote asked carefully, his feelings not well disguised.

'We have first-class intelligence of same, sir.'

'And these are?'

'Not only do we have numbers, but where they will be found.' It wasn't answering the question but would do in the circumstances.

'Are your orders to us made final, Sir Thomas?' Foote tried.

'The essence of this affair is speed – this is a flying squadron as must get under way with the least possible delay in order to preserve surprise. You shall have them before the final meeting prior to our assault.'

'If I be permitted to speak, Sir Thomas?'

'Do.'

'To an outside observer this entire business must appear hasty, not to say premature. It might be supposed that our descent will be successfully resisted, in which case the Dutch will be brought to a realisation of the vulnerability of these islands and doubly reinforce them – an outcome worse than the defeat.'

'Sir. You're entitled to your concerns. I've no doubt that if you wished to withdraw then I'm certain Lord Minto, who personally gave orders for this venture, will quite understand.'

'Not at all, sir!' Foote protested. 'I merely give an opinion. My loyalty to the expedition is unquestioned.'

Kenna was wise enough to let his seniors make the running, and when Kydd glanced at him questioningly, he hastened to agree. 'Myself also,' he said, with something like conviction.

There was little more to discuss. Passage charts were being obtained and copied, wood and watering places identified, and routine matters, such as foul-weather rendezvous points, decided. When the two captains left, it was with marked seriousness and none of the usual joking confidence. Kydd wondered, not for the first time, whether he'd made the right decision.

The squadron put to sea in another of the rain squalls that came and went at this time of the year, standing south in the strait as Kydd had done not so long ago en route to Macao.

In a way it was madness: *Tyger* in the van followed by

Piedmontaise, then the faded old transport *Mandarin* with the lowly *Barracouta* coming on behind. Just these few to fall on the most valuable prize in the Dutch empire.

Rounding the Malay peninsula, course was shaped through the Singapura Strait, then northward in the wake of the China Fleet until, at the passing through of the sprawl of the Rhio archipelago, the helm went over and the little squadron was on its way to the east and its destiny.

Days later, far to leeward, the lush jungle forest of Borneo lazily emerged from the mists, a place of the utmost wildness to be avoided by all sane mariners. Kydd's charts were none too trustworthy and the only certainty to reach the furthest northern tip of the giant island was to stay in with the land.

For the best part of a week they headed up the coast, the rich stink of the soil wafting out in the steaming heat until, abruptly, the wind-sculpted sandy tip of Borneo hove into view. At last they could lay course east and on towards the finality of their voyage.

This was now the Sulu Sea, separating Borneo from the Philippine Islands.

And a quite different kind of sailing. The waters were rife with coral, reefs, islands and isolated heads, any one of which could gouge the soft bottom of a ship, tearing the life out of her to leave her bones for others to take heed.

Given his experience of such menaces in the past, Kydd could deal with it, but now a deadly new factor was added.

Sailing day after day to the east, every morning they would be greeted with a fat and bloated tropic sun that blazed directly into their eyes. As it rose it turned the sea ahead into a rippling sheen from which the sun's rays beat up, changing the clear depths instead into a silvered mirror, effectively concealing every hazard and danger lurking there.

The elements were yet another trial. The equatorial heat affected everything. Despite the rigging of windsails, life in the mess-decks without the bigger ship's gun-ports to bring in a breeze was an ordeal. The torrid humidity made it impossible to sleep, and meals had to be taken to the upper deck to eat.

Deck seams worked open, the tar soft and limp. Several spars developed long drying splits and canvas took rot where it was furled over the yard; the metal of guns radiated a dull heat, like a red-hot poker.

And, as regular as clockwork, rain showers came, some in a blissful cool mizzle, others in spiteful roars of tropical intensity. From a cloud-darkened sky a cataract would thunder down, huge drops in a continuing deluge that mercilessly hammered any caught in the open, forcing them to lower their heads in order to breathe.

Occasionally the sight of a waterspout stilled all chatter, its pale stalk rearing up to the darker clouds and maintaining a steady progression across the sea, a white fury at its base. It was sometimes close enough to hear – a sullen thunder, like a waterfall underlying the shrill whipping of its own circling winds and disappearing as quickly as it had arisen.

Most unpleasant were the electrical storms, with their ceaseless ear-splitting pealing of thunder and the savagery of the bolts forking out of the torn, driven tar-black clouds, some copper and green-tinged, in all a primeval show of grandeur and spite. It was soberly recalled that, only two months previously, *Piedmontaise* had lost her entire mainmast to lightning.

The days mostly passed with oppressive, fluky winds over a glaring silver sea until they reached the arc of islands marking the end of their passage across the north of Borneo and into the Celebes Sea between the Philippines Mindanao and the true East Indies.

First one, then another island rose above the horizon and, soon, many. As advised in their sailing directions, they stood on close to the largest, Jolo, and were through, but beyond the last island there was a surprise.

A ship came into view – not a large one, a two-masted vessel canted over and unmoving, hard aground on a reef. All about it were a dozen or more proas, small outrigger craft with a single inverted triangular sail. They scattered as soon as they sighted Kydd's ships.

'Pirates!' spat Brice, contemptuously.

Almost certainly they'd been disturbed while plundering the merchantman that they had forced to its doom on the reef. It was not worth a chase – the flock would disperse, like starlings, before the bow of a frigate slowed by light winds.

'Do take away the cutter, Mr Brice, and let us pray we're not too late.'

Kydd kept the squadron hove to while the third lieutenant made for the sorry wreck. He watched Brice board but he soon returned. 'Quantities of fresh blood,' he said, in an odd voice, 'And this.' He held out part of a human scalp, still with an ear attached.

The squadron got under way and as they crossed the Celebes Sea the first languorously long swells announced the Pacific, and then they were in the open ocean. It was years ago that, as an able seaman, Kydd had last been in those parts but he'd never forgotten the lazy heave of the immense waters, the sense of the limitlessness of this, the largest ocean on earth.

Somewhere to the south was the rim of the Dutch empire but no one there could have any idea that passing by far to the north was a squadron of the Royal Navy intent on their destruction. Kydd's spirits rose. When they had reached 130 degrees of east longitude it would be time to make his lunge into its heart.

It was invigorating, the cool deep-sea breeze constant and true, and it was with something like regret that at the right meridian the squadron left its eastward tracking and struck south.

In less than a day the masthead lookout sang out that land was sighted.

It was a fine landfall – on the far tip of the unthinkably remote fastness of New Guinea, a massive island that extended out a full twenty degrees of longitude of rugged, trackless jungle forest.

Yet, paradoxically, this was among the best-known and charted parts of their voyage: it was here that both Magellan and Drake had left the Pacific to enter the great inland seas and, in the process, thrown open the secret of the Arab spice traders. In the centuries since, many nations had competed for the islands until the Dutch had achieved supremacy and driven all others out.

Their passage was nearly over, and they had not been sighted. And in a day or two they would be within striking distance of their objective: Banda Neira.

The tropical heat returned and, with it, the sultry weather of rains and bluster, but the squadron sailed on until it raised the big island of Ceram and with it the Moluccas. After a hard and wearying voyage, they were about to erupt on the enemy.

Chapter 57

'Thank you, gentlemen. Do find in front of you your orders,' Kydd said, as his captains took their places in his great cabin. Each had been relieved of his coat on entering and they sat in shirts and breeches, grateful for the open windows across the sweep of *Tyger*'s stern.

The transport captain had no role in this and had not been invited, leaving just Foote to Kydd's right and Kenna on his left, a ludicrous number of commanders claiming to be an assault force.

The orders were not extensive, consisting of little more than that each vessel was to be alert for signals from the 'flagship' specifying the action expected of them in accordance with developments. Their entire ship's company, less a skeleton crew, was to be armed as boarders, and boats at all times be made ready to put off for the shore as required.

'There's nothing here about the redcoats,' Foote said accusingly, holding the sweat-smudged page of orders. 'I'd believe that the entire object of this expedition is to get them ashore to march on the enemy fortifications.'

'This is because it's not yet been decided where they should be landed,' Kydd said patiently. 'Shall we proceed?'

Charts were laid out, the most important being the neat book-sized production of some twenty years previously by a trader captain. In beautifully hatched fine lines, the islands' topography was built up, with tiny notations – coral bottom, a three-knot northerly current before high-water springs, no anchoring in south-easterlies. A labour to occupy an active mind while awaiting a cargo but priceless to them now.

Kydd had taken the information from the Malays and placed the fortifications on the main chart where they had told him they were, adding assumed firing arcs and any other useful points.

Foote and Kenna regarded the chart dubiously. What it showed was an odd mix of islands indeed. Banda Neira was the easternmost of a pair, itself mountainous and rough but with a relatively flat area at its south. Directly opposite there was a much bigger island in the shape of a perfect cone – a volcano? The third island, labelled Great Banda, was the biggest of all and its spiny heights swung protectively around the first two, as the Malay Hasan had said, effectively concealing them.

The sole settlement was on the only flat area on Banda Neira, which meant they had to land on that island and no other. It was where the harbour was located – and where the fortresses were placed to command the approaches. The Dutch had sited well, for they were faced with a choice between landing on the undefended but almost impassably rugged upper region or on the much easier levels, but under the guns of the two fortresses.

'Further to the east?' asked Kenna, indicating a small beach at the other side of the level area from the settlement.

316

'Possible,' murmured Kydd, noting that there were precious few other places without either an offshore coral reef or impossible going once ashore. And where would the Dutch put their outer defences against any landings such as they were planning? There was no knowing.

So, the best choice seemed to be Kenna's beach. 'The squadron approaches from the east. Not only is this a direction they are not expecting but we will be hidden from them by the length of Great Banda. We'll have *Piedmontaise* in first, entertaining the defenders at the settlement, and shortly after *Tyger* will oversee the landings at Commander Kenna's beach. The troops, once formed up, will march at best speed into the settlement from the interior, trusting to reach and quickly subdue the lower and smaller stronghold, Fort Nassau.'

'Can we expect the larger one on the hill to tolerate this behaviour without it takes action against us?' Foote asked peevishly.

'If they open up on us with guns, they will be destroying their own fort and people.'

'They will sally with their superior numbers. Some thousands you said earlier, Sir Thomas.'

'Our men are superior and battle-hardened. Theirs have probably never left the island. Enough of this wry talk, Mr Foote. We know what we have to do and will do it. The fighting will be close and hard-going but our cause is of the greatest importance. The Tygers will acquit themselves nobly. Will your ship's company do the same, sir?'

After they'd left Kydd felt a pang of dread. Foote was right – the whole thing sounded so ramshackle and amateur, and the odds were ridiculous.

He had surprise on his side, the only thing he could count on. Would it be enough? If only he had more men, more

317

troops. He could then throw a division into the enemy rear and . . . But he hadn't. If only there were something else, an advantage or coup he could bring to bear at the last minute that would offset those wretched odds . . . But there wasn't and there was no use wishing it.

He was committed. He had to make the attempt: he couldn't simply retire for fear of odds. It had to go ahead and without delay.

They were in the last part of their hooking curve that would take them from the east into the seaward side of Great Banda. There, out of sight, they would prepare for a landing at dawn the following morning, emerging at speed from behind the sheltering island to make straight for the little beach, which was on the nearest point of Banda Neira, while *Piedmontaise* made play with her guns on the opposite side. After that, who knew what the day would bring?

The elements were on their side, a fine haze at the horizon helping to conceal them as they made their approach. To the west there were half a dozen or more islands, like sentinels, but on this side of Great Banda there was just the one, well offshore but handy as a point of rendezvous and preparation.

Kydd's squadron under easy sail slipped into its lee – but then from the northerly headland, almost invisible in the undergrowth came first one, then a second heavy concussion. Guns! Eighteen-pounders at least and firing on them, but what was worse, their unmistakable roar would easily carry to distant watchers and could mean only one thing to the defenders.

Even before they'd started, they'd lost their surprise.

Cast down, Kydd was not going to show it. 'Rig the boats for landing, if you please, Mr Farrant,' he said, in a business-like way. He'd thought about whether he wanted his broken reed of a first lieutenant to be part of the landing but knew that, with so few officers, he had no alternative. Every boat would be used, the seamen equipped as in a boarding, relatively lightly armed in the usual way, the soldiers with their musketry and several pairs carrying scaling ladders, others with grapnels.

They would set out in the early hours, a bright moon promising to see them safely navigated to the right place to scramble ashore as dawn broke.

Would there be any enemy waiting for them? They would have to see, but Kydd was relying on their impatience – if fire was opened on them as they came in, he was prepared to haul off and try elsewhere, but if they held their fire until his men were ashore it would lead to a surrender or bloody massacre.

The hours passed. Every man knew what was in store for him but there was no despair in their words, no accusing glances flashed aft, only the usual pre-battle banter and quietness.

'Coming on to blow, I would say, sir.' The master, Joyce, was shaking his head gloomily as dusk began to settle and the occasional white flash of a wave showed vividly out to seaward as the breeze got up. Overhead the stars were disappearing as cloud wrack spread across the sky.

A drift of fine rain briefly touched them, leaving the decks glistening. Minutes later a harder fall swept down, and men scurried for shelter while Kydd called for his oilskins.

'For pity's sake!' groaned Brice. 'And now we're to have our powder wet as well?'

To storm ashore with every gun a useless weight – nothing much more could happen to them, Kydd thought miserably.

A sudden flash and thunderous blast away to the east made him spin round in consternation – but it was only an approaching storm of the kind they knew all too well. Preceding squalls blustered and bullied, the taste of salt from spray flung up by hard-driven waves bursting on *Tyger*'s side, now reaching considerably higher than before.

He stood there, stupefied by the change of events, staring out into the rapidly advancing darkness now charged with chaos.

'Stand down the men, sir?' Bowden asked apologetically, the water streaming from his foul-weather gear.

To give up? Sail away claiming insufficient forces given him for the task?

'Sir, I said, shall we stand down . . .' Bowden trailed off in bafflement for Kydd had unexpectedly broken off and hastened to the ship's side to stare down into the depths.

It was not impossible . . . In fact, it made every bit of sense! A rising tide of elation seized him. Sunk in despair he hadn't noticed that he'd been granted what he most craved: a stroke of events that made nonsense of the odds, putting common valour and resolution back in the equation. The tropical storm.

To a land-dweller, these were elemental beasts to take shelter from, to hide away until they'd passed. To look out to sea was to pity the ships and sailors caught up in the blackness and fury – or assume they had been forced away to ride it out.

The very last thing they would believe was that their British foes would take to their boats and strike for the shore in this.

'Mr Farrant!' Kydd bawled, above the wind's roar. 'Pass the word – we're going to give the Hollanders the fright of their lives and make the landings directly!'

The man's face turned pale but, without a word, he went to the boatswain and started the process in train.

Bowden loomed in the dimness. 'A spanking good notion, sir!' he said happily. 'As the Dutch guns will be made silent in these conditions.' The same wet that had rendered their own muskets useless would work against the defenders as well.

Farrant returned. Kydd ordered him to tell the seamen to leave their muskets, their pistols and take up cutlasses, pikes, tomahawks, anything as long as it was bladed.

He looked again over the side. And what he'd noticed before was still the case: in these confined inland seas the intense squally blows had little fetch, that long surface of sometimes hundreds of miles over which a gale could stream to build up massive waves of the kind that made the Atlantic so dangerous. Instead the waves were short and fretful, and until the storm increased its strength to produce a respectable fetch, this would not be a threat.

'Mr Brice. Take away my gig and inform *Piedmontaise* and *Barracouta* to prepare for the assault after dark on my order.' The soldiers in their transport would be called on after the dawn made clear their way ashore.

The officer did not question the order, taking one look at the seas and mustering his crew. Brice was a natural seaman, born and bred in the wild north of England and no fool. Kydd would see by his handling of the boat how the rest would fare.

The craft bobbed and jerked, but as the waves slapped and jostled it there was no indication of water being taken in. As it stroked and bucketed into the white-streaked waters Kydd could see that he was right: the larger cutters and pinnaces would have little trouble cresting these seas.

Something inside him burst into joyous song. The Fates had swung a full compass card about in his favour and they had a chance!

Meanwhile the light had faded. The weather had grown more boisterous, the storm-clouds low and murky, with visibility in the hissing rain-squalls to be measured only in boat-lengths.

As darkness was added to the wild scene, Kydd knew it was time.

Boats were manned and, as they did, were made to lay off in *Tyger*'s lee until all were primed and in readiness, as many as could be mustered for the assault. A rough count gave about two hundred men, which with the later reinforcing by soldiers would be no more than four hundred.

He shrugged it off and, screaming into the wind his last-minute instruction to keep together, he headed out.

The wind, spray and rain hit them like a wall as they passed out of the lee of the frigate but thankfully the wave direction was from ahead, the gig taking the seas on the bow. He peered down at the compass wedged into the bottom of the boat and shaped course to round Great Banda.

He snatched a glance astern: the other boats were barely perceptible in the murk but were faithfully following, the closest being Farrant's. Kydd had noticed with a twinge of pity that Stirk had made it his business to be in Farrant's cutter. If the first lieutenant failed him, Stirk would take action on the spot.

Sometime in the early hours they had advanced up the coast to the end of Great Banda and the last lap was now ahead. A three-mile thrust over to the south-west – and Banda Neira.

As soon as they came around the point Kydd knew they had problems. Before, the succession of storm waves had come from ahead but now they were nearly on their beam, causing the boats to roll wickedly. And the spite of the gale had increased, the spray and spindrift obscuring completely the land ahead. Not only that but the wind and seas coming in abeam were making holding course a chancy thing: with each boat blown to leeward at a different rate, they could soon fall out of sight of each other.

It would be daybreak shortly, and if the assault was to consist of isolated boats landing at random points along the shore, it would be a hopeless disaster.

Kydd glanced astern and saw Farrant's cutter hanging grimly in his wake, several others close behind him, but nothing else in sight. Was his precious advantage going to be snatched away before he could do anything with it?

Out of the welter of seas he noticed a pattern. The wave-fronts had altered their direction. Instead of coming in on the beam they were now imperceptibly becoming aligned more with the course Kydd was taking with the compass, surging the boats forward. He knew at once this meant the waves were feeling the ground under them, which was shallowing fast. They were about to land on Banda Neira.

He peered into the fretful blackness ahead but saw nothing. One of the oarsmen caught a crab, his oar slewing the gig madly.

'Out of the boat! Take her in,' Kydd yelled, understanding what had happened.

The first one out stood unsteadily on dead coral, buffeted by the wind, his face lowered to avoid the rain and spray. Others shipped their oars and took the gunwale, and the gig bumped over the wind-torn shallows to a shingle and sand beach, the indistinct darker shadow of the interior behind.

A short distance further down, Farrant did the same and others beyond him.

They all closed on Kydd, huddling in the shelter of the cutter.

He thought furiously. They had got away with it so far but

to move forward without knowing what was there was begging for trouble.

'Mr Maynard,' he called, to the master's mate of his boat. 'I need to know what's before us. See if you can find anything of the enemy before we move off, if you please.'

It was unfair – the young man was a sailor, not an experienced light infantryman, but probably the nimblest of those he had with him.

'Aye aye, sir,' he said imperturbably and, leaving his cutlass, he wriggled through the fringing grasses and was immediately lost to sight.

Kydd lay there, listening impatiently to the appalling crash and bang of the thunder, and was thankful that the ceaselessly lashing rain was tropical, almost warm.

It seemed an age before Maynard returned. 'Sir. Grave news,' he panted. 'Seems we've chosen to come ashore just where the Dutch have sited one of their gun batteries. Can't be sure but there's about ten long eighteens, all trained seawards . . . and every one manned.'

Of all possible ill luck! Cannon – with grape they could wipe them from the face of the earth with one volley. And without a formal reconnaissance there was no way to know which way to turn to escape the murderous fire.

The shocking revelation spread among the men, who needed no telling what lay in the future when the grey dawn broke.

Should he order them back into the boats, to flee before they were spotted? He looked back out to sea and saw that heading into the white-streaked breakers would be an atrocious fight against the elements, but if they didn't . . .

Distracted by thought, Kydd didn't notice Bowden wriggle up to him. 'Sir, I have to tell you, Lieutenant Farrant has departed the field and a quantity of men have followed him.'

An uncontrollable fury shook Kydd. To desert in the face of the enemy, yet more contemptible in an officer, to make a craven example of himself to the weaker-hearted men, was in the extreme unforgivable. He should never have given the coward a second chance.

He cudgelled his mind as they lay under the storm's careless roar, trying to think of a way out of their situation, but it was difficult to throw off the rage caused by Farrant's act. The best he could think of was to wait until they could peer through the storm fret to find some direction to flee to.

It was a pitiful course, but any other . . .

He became aware of movement to his left and swung around to see.

'Mr Stirk! What the devil?'

'Went at 'em like a demon, he did!' the big man said, standing upright with an inane grin on his face. 'Like a reg'lar-built farm bull. See, we goes at 'em from behind, they're not expecting it. They has match alight t' fire their cannon well enough, but can't figure on using muskets in this. Sees us coming wi' pikes and blades only an' they breaks an' runs! Sir.'

'You're saying . . .'

'I am, sir. Mr Farrant took us all in on th' run and the battery's ours.'

In a haze of unbelief Kydd got to his feet and walked towards the hidden guns. And there was Farrant among them, briskly detailing men to secure prisoners and pile weapons.

'Er, Mr Farrant. Am I to understand you led an unsupported charge at the guns and were successful?'

'I did, Sir Thomas. I trust you approve?'

There was something ethereal in his features as he stood calmly, almost as if seeing a plane of existence denied to others.

325

'I cannot be otherwise, sir. You saved us all.'

Farrant gave a slow smile. 'As I felt it my duty, sir.'

Gathering his wits, Kydd reviewed their situation. The darkness was giving way by degrees to a grey, wan light, which was beginning to reveal details through gusts of rain. And the bluster and vigour of the storm was ebbing as well.

A daring idea thrust itself at him. The tropical storm had secured for him a victory of sorts. Why not take it further, chance his luck right to the gates of the enemy?

Chapter 58

The upper fortress, Belgica, which stood arrogantly above the settlement, was a little under a mile away. While the storm still raged, they had a chance of closing with it and, who knew, wreaking some damage.

'All hands – muster all hands!' Kydd ordered, the wind whipping at his words.

The men came loping up from all directions, falling in by divisions as if they were aboard ship, revealing that he could count on no more than a hundred and forty seamen and marines, armed with nothing more than edged weapons. But these were Tygers! For valour and fearlessness there were no better anywhere, and if the odds were extreme then so was the courage.

They stood before him, whipped and buffeted by the gale but ready to follow him into Hell itself. He knew he could go anywhere with men like these and drew his sword, stepping forward, with his head held high. 'Tygers!' he bawled. The wind-blast shredded his words, so he raised his voice to a bellow, as if to the fore-yard in the teeth of the worst of an Atlantic blow. 'The storm and us – we have the enemy on the run and I mean to finish the job. Fall upon Fort Belgica, while they're still cowering in the cellars! Raid and destroy, fight and win! We'll do a famous day's work, as will be talked of for ever wherever sailors meet for a brimmer of grog! Those who are with me – forward!'

He didn't look behind him as he stepped grimly away up the track behind the battery, which led to the heights ahead, now invisible behind curtains of rain.

It was hard going, the path lashed by waving fronds and sharp foliage. And, too, there was mud underfoot and water-filled ruts, but they carried no heavy weapons or ammunition and loped forward swiftly.

The track grew steeper and then above them, seen once through a passing break in the driving squalls of rain, was a vision, made all the more dramatic by the concussive bangs and echoing rumbles of thunder all about it.

High on the crags, louring down, was a castle. In pale stone, complete with battlements and lofty round towers, it looked like something from a fairy-tale – and then the curtains of rain hid it once more.

But Kydd had seen what Fort Belgica held for them. Far from being a medieval relic, this was a relatively modern pentagonal fortress, a tower on each corner and with a low outer wall commanded by a much higher inner, a total of no less than fifty-two heavy guns behind their casemates waiting for any foolish enough to trouble them.

And his information was that there were between one and two thousand men inside – odds against them now some-where between ten and eleven to one.

But Kydd was suffused by a surging exaltation and pressed on hard.

As the steepness fell away, they came to the edge of the rain forest. The undergrowth levelled to give the lower wall guns a flat field of fire, and directly ahead through the driving rain was the castle.

Kydd peered forward. A limp, sodden flag of some sort hung at the staff but beyond that there was no sign of life. No sentries pacing the battlements, no sentinels at the embrasures.

And then he realised: there had been no firing anywhere since the two shots from the island, and the bang and thunder of the storm had lulled them into ignoring it. Besides which it was ridiculous to imagine any attempt on the island in these hurricane conditions: better to keep out of the elements while they raged on.

'Half to storm this side, the remainder the other,' he ordered. He would command on this side. Who best out of sight on the far side?

'Mr Farrant, would you . . .?'

But the officer was already on his way, his sword out, his men close behind. There was a deadly menace in the bright steel carried by every man. Glistening with fine raindrops, it was a fearsome sight.

They would soon be spotted – Kydd had to move, now.

He didn't bother with noble battle-cries. It was a matter of desperate speed and determination.

Beckoning his men forward, he ran at the inner wall. Heart in his mouth, he watched the black gun embrasures. They did not fill with the deadly muzzles of cannon but from one or two pale faces showed and then they were at the wall.

Scaling ladders went up and, with the litheness of topmen, seamen swarmed up, Kydd with them, his heart pounding. They spread out, then dropped down inside to confront a shocked few who came out from the casemates, unable to credit what they were seeing.

Some had snatched up muskets, but in the tempestuous

rain they were useless and were thrown down under the threat of cutlass and sword. Others made a run for the inner wall but were cut down before they reached it, the blood of their corpses swiftly diluted by the deluging rain.

'Get 'em secured!' Kydd roared, gesturing back at the casemates with his sword, his cocked hat lost, his hair plastered to his face.

From somewhere in the citadel the thin sound of a trumpet quavered an alarm, but it was drowned in the crash and roar of the storm.

Then in a fierce run they covered the ground to the inner wall – but the scaling ladders were too short for the mighty main citadel.

Panting, Kydd pressed up to the wall, gathering his thoughts.

They were trapped. Safe while they pressed up against the wall beneath the muzzles of the guns but eventually they would be fired on from above and slaughtered.

If they retreated, they'd be leaving the security of the wall and—

The second miracle of the day announced itself without fanfare. Halfway along the wall there was a sudden loud creak and the massive gates of the fortress swung outwards. Through it spilled a rush of men. In the open they slowed, confused, peering around, shielding their faces from the stinging rain. An officer raged at them, his sword shaking.

With a shout of jubilation, the seamen raced forward with their cutlasses, swords, pikes and tomahawks, all well-known and familiar tools of boarding, and set about them with barely restrained savagery. The hapless enemy, armed only with useless muskets and bayonets, small-swords and even jungle machetes, could not face them. Nothing in their training or experience could have prepared them for a fight with sailors, one man swinging a cutlass, another flinging a tomahawk.

It was the pike-men that turned the tide. A hulking seaman coming at them, jabbing a ten-foot pike, was never met on the general run of battlefields, and was more than most could take. They turned tail to run.

With a yell that even a storm could not smother, the Tygers leaped after them and into the fort.

The officer, red-faced with fury, slashed about randomly as they fled and Kydd hurried over to put a stop to it.

'Yield, sir!' he rapped, his sword at point.

The man went berserk, flinging about his heavy Dutch sword like a madman, forcing Kydd to defend himself. With an anvil-like clash of steel their blades met and slithered, and the man's face, distorted by hatred, was briefly thrust into Kydd's own.

This had to be the fortress commandant, roused out of a comfortable breakfast by a report of an attack from nowhere in the middle of a tropical storm, which he had shrugged off. When it had turned out to be true, he'd looked out and seen a few men only, then had made the disastrous mistake of opening the gate to deal with them.

Now he was paying the price – and he'd chosen to go down fighting.

He made another bullying rush, but this was not a killing lunge: it was the clumsy onslaught of one who'd not tasted war, let alone the lethal ballet that was a combat to the death.

The Dutchman's sword swung like a pickaxe, the *whoosh* of his breath betraying the effort. Kydd's simple side-step avoided it completely, leaving the man's body stooped and bowed, waiting for the pitiless plunging sword thrust that would end it all for him.

Kydd couldn't do it. He stepped back and called again, 'Give up, sir – you've done enough!'

Without warning, there was a crazed upward stab with the

big blade, aimed at Kydd's jugular. His parry was only just in time, but the move made him stagger back and his feet lost their grip in the mud. He fell.

With a screech of triumph, the man lifted his sword for the killing blow – but it never came. Through eyes near-blinded by rain and sweat, Kydd saw the bloodied head of a pike erupt from his opponent's chest and the body brutally levered to one side.

'Bastard,' a voice growled, an indistinct figure stepping on the corpse to extract the weapon.

Kydd pulled himself up, now mud-streaked and bloody, to see Farrant approach with the same other-worldly look about him. 'Sir, I hand you the keys to the magazine. The castle is yours!'

'How did you . . .?'

'The enemy broke and ran for the town on seeing us within the castle. Only a trifle remain.'

So that was why they hadn't been set on by the thousands – in irony, the Dutch had no idea how many British were attacking: that they'd breached the inner citadel so rapidly must have been because their force had been very great. They'd simply fled.

As was the way of it in these regions, the storm was blowing itself out, sulky squalls between calmer periods, the rain no longer in violent downbursts.

Through the gate he could see his men herding small groups of prisoners. Then Stirk appeared, sheathing his cutlass – bloodied, Kydd noted. 'Mr Stirk, I give you joy of your victory!'

'Thank 'ee, sir,' the big man rumbled, touching his forehead. 'An' it was Mr Farrant who was in front, an' all.'

Kydd shook his head in wonder, speechless.

'Sir, and the gunner is asking when he should start spiking the guns.'

332

He turned to the midshipman. 'Why, Mr Rowan – you've been wounded.' His head was roughly bandaged, a bright patch of blood on one side.

'Yes, sir,' the youngster said proudly. ''Twas nothing,' he added, like a seasoned old tar. 'I've seen worse.'

Kydd warmed, imagining the lad's yarns to his old schoolmates in Guildford with all about him enraptured and envious at his tale. 'I'm sure you have, squeaker, but the battle's not over yet.'

He forced his mind back to the present. Through the euphoria he saw danger looming to destroy everything they'd gained. Their prodigious triumph over the odds could all be reversed. In the light of day, cooler heads in the fortress below, realising the actual situation, and with fire-locks now effective, could send a formidable column against them.

Kydd had to stop them. 'Go down to our landing and tell 'em to send every redcoat they have up to us here,' he told his messenger. 'And tell the gunner on no account to spike the guns. He's to wait on orders.'

Another order went out to *Tyger*, and then it was the last act.

As the sunshine broke through on a glittering, rain-washed island, quantities of red-coated soldiers were seen serenely pacing the battlements under the Union flag of Great Britain. To the governor in his mansion below, it was a dire sight for he held in his hand a demand from the British commander that, unless all hostility ceased, signalled by the lowering of the Dutch flag in Fort Nassau, the heavy guns of the upper fortress would be turned to the destruction of the lower, while the frigate now to be seen entering the bay would begin a systematic bombardment of the town.

Banda Neira had fallen.

Chapter 59

'I can't promise it, Mr Farrant,' Kydd said, after they'd regained the sanity of *Tyger*'s quarterdeck, 'but I'll do what I can to see you reinstated as first lieutenant of this vessel.'

Farrant bowed politely but did not reply. His experiences in the action had changed him, of that there was no doubt. Calm, assured, dignified, his future now lay before him.

'As you have my full approbation of your conduct, but I cannot answer for the commander-in-chief, whose actions in the matter may be too far advanced.'

'I understand, Sir Thomas.'

But whatever Drury's reactions to their achievement he would endeavour to see justice served for his premier.

Kydd went ahead in *Tyger* as herald of victory, leaving *Piedmontaise* and *Barracouta* to escort the transport back. He would see that Raffles was first to know and, under a press of sail, before long *Tyger* raised Prince of Wales Island.

'Dear fellow, and I've been quite worn out with anxiety since you sailed against the foe,' Raffles greeted Kydd, when they met in the grounds of Government House. 'At times quite a-flutter when I heard that Governor Daendels was casting about for ships of force to send to the Spice Islands, even as he failed to find them. And now you have the most golden prize of all, Sir Thomas!'

He held out both his hands in sincere homage, and Kydd felt a wash of pleasure that he'd been the instrument of fulfilling this gifted man's vision.

'Yes, and I'm to sail this hour to acquaint Admiral Drury of the success of his arms.'

'I'd rather you didn't, sir.'

'Er, why so?' Kydd had entertained himself for hours on passage in conjuring various ways in which he'd modestly allow that, despite every obstacle put in his way, he'd brought off the central requirement of their vision.

'The reason? Quite simply that news of this magnitude is for the ears not of mere naval commanders-in-chief but those of the highest, the governor general of India and its territories, which must now include a certain valuable acquisition. Not only that but events must pass quickly if we are to realise on our opportunities, and where else but the *fons et origo* of all puissance in these lands?'

'I see.'

'Consequently, I shall beg you will give me a berth in your good ship and accompany me to Calcutta.'

Their reception was quite different from before. A delighted Lord Minto went out of his way to make sure they were comfortable in the richly appointed drawing room as Kydd told his tale. Afterwards he gave sincere congratulations. 'A blow worthy of Nelson himself, I swear,' he said in admiration. 'A strike into the very heart of the Dutch empire as turns to ashes Bonaparte's seizing of the Hollanders' homeland.'

335

Raffles inclined his head, and added, 'Were we not to delay our follow-through, my lord.'

'Yes, yes. The path ahead is clear. We should now contemplate the laying hold of the greater reward – the East Indies itself. From the shores of Arabia to the Pacific Ocean in unbroken succession, these lands shall acknowledge the suzerainty of the Crown of His Majesty King George in peace and amity to the undoubted prosperity of all.

'Gentlemen, as of this hour my staff and I begin planning the final reduction of Dutch dominion. The invasion of Java and the taking of its capital, Batavia.'

To these words, Kydd could think of nothing to add. They were imperial, conquering, the stuff of history.

Minto seemed struck by his own flights of declamation, pacing dreamily until he stopped abruptly. 'Whisky, gentlemen?' he asked, quite as if they were guests at his house. 'I'd wish to be in the Dutch captain general's palace when he gets tidings of Banda Neira.' Minto chuckled light-heartedly. 'He now knows that we can take any of his possessions, but he can do nothing about it, his naval reinforcements so paltry. Without the nutmeg revenue of Banda and cloves from the rest of the Moluccas, there's no income to speak of for him to spend on defences. Bonaparte won't send him any – in the absence of a stream of revenue from these parts they're not worth the defending.'

'We will move with celerity, then?' Raffles asked.

'Certainly,' Minto said sharply. 'I'd give it time for word of Banda Neira to get out into the larger realm, so to speak. Let the rot set in, the spirits sink, the hopeless prospects loom. After all, why fight to the end when it's only for the cause of the Corsican tyrant? And it gives me time to work up the plans for invasion. A devil of a lot of sweat and trouble for the commander is your common invasion, is it not, Sir Thomas?'

'I would think so, sir. I believe I will sail directly to alert Admiral Drury of these developments.'

'More than that, Sir Thomas. I desire you will take my orders for an invasion convoy of the proper sort to be made available to me without delay, his business with the French now over.'

'Sir?'

'Of course, you couldn't know.' Minto harrumphed. 'The nest of privateers that was Île-de-France is no more. Taken after a mort of pother this last month while you were otherwise engaged.'

This was the action that Drury had used as an excuse to deny him resources. Now it was over, there could be no reasonable basis for refusing him. With a lurch of excitement, Kydd wondered if this at last would bring him his commodore's pennant.

'Then, sir, we stand free to sail against the Dutch. The hour I receive your orders, my lord, is the hour I depart for Madras.'

Chapter 60

In the last of the north-east monsoon, *Tyger* stood south, her progress now not what it had been: the weed was thickening along her hull, rigging stretched by continuous use and canvas greying with exposure.

It was an uneventful passage. Without a base anywhere in the Indian Ocean, no enemy privateer could sustain the predatory cruises of before and the seas were now thick with friendly merchant shipping, a wonderful sight.

Madras Roads, however, was crowded with country traders but bare of naval vessels. It was puzzling, for Kydd had not heard of any move by the enemy that would justify an entire fleet putting to sea. And, besides, after an action of apparently some severity surely Drury would want to rest and refit his fleet.

His dispatches and the precious orders he carried were of the first importance, however, and it was his duty to inform the office of the commander-in-chief of their existence.

'You'll just have to exercise patience, dear fellow,' the flag-captain told him. 'I haven't a date for Admiral Drury's return, you see.'

'May I be told the nature of the alarum?'

He gave a brief smile. 'I don't see why not. In short, the admiral was taken ill again and formed a desire for the fresh sea air to give him relief, he so much afflicted. That is all.'

It was a let-down, but Kydd would get his satisfaction in the end. He left the papers with the flag-captain for Drury's urgent attention on his return and retired to his residence, thinking to host a dinner that night.

'A delightful evening, Sir T,' Cluffer burbled, geniality itself. 'Quite up to the highest standards an' so forth. Much enjoyed.' He leaned over and offered gallantly, 'Shall I summon you a palanquin, my dear?'

Caroline Lowther smiled sweetly. 'Thank you, but I have my own waiting.'

'Then I'll take my leave, dear lady. And farewell, Mr Empire-builder.'

'I hope you enjoyed the dinner, Caroline,' Kydd said, having seen Cluffer to the door.

She looked at him fondly. 'Of course I did.'

There was no sign that she intended to leave soon and Kydd was glad. A woman's company was a sovereign cure for the tedium of waiting for a commander-in-chief's return.

'Tell me, Thomas, what will you do now that the excitement of conquest is over?'

She seemed genuinely interested but Kydd had no ready answer. 'Oh, well, I'd take it as a blessing should I be allowed some quiet hours in my garden with a book. You've no idea how clamorous a ship-of-war at anchor is for those seeking surcease.'

She brightened. 'Then I've just the article. The *Mahabharata* – a Hindu poem. It's long, mind.'

'How long, pray?'

'Verses? Not above two hundred thousands.'

'Ha! Well, I shall stay with my library. I have one, you know. The last tenant had one built, small but useful.'

'A library! How exciting. Do show me, Thomas.'

She followed him to the rear of the house where he opened a diminutive double door. Inside there was a musty blackness.

The oil lamp, it seemed, had not been filled recently. 'A moment, I'll get a light.'

A candle flickered and steadied to a strong illumination, bringing out her soft features and adding a halo of wispy golden hair.

'How delightful!' she said, clapping her hands. 'A treasure of books!'

She reached up and pulled one down, bringing it nearer the candle to read its title. 'Oh, dear me, and I didn't know you read novels, Thomas,' she said in mock-horror.

She showed it to him: *Sin in the Sun, or, The Parsee's Daughter Untimely Sacrificed.*

'Ah. These are not mine, Caroline. They belonged to . . .'

He tailed off, for something had happened in that moment that had left her rigid, watching him intently. Her hand had not released the book and he felt its shake as she drew him closer.

Her voice was low and urgent, 'Thomas. This, answer me true – do you have feelings for me?'

'Caroline . . .' She was very close now – her eyes would not leave his.

'Of course I have feelings,' he stuttered. 'Many feelings. You must believe me when I say that! You're the kindest creature I've ever met here and . . . and, I declare, the prettiest!'

For a moment longer the intensity remained, then her eyes dulled and the book fell to the floor.

Stepping back, her head fell, and when she raised it again Kydd caught the glitter of tears.

'You've answered me, Thomas,' she said huskily. 'I understand.'

He reached out but she pulled away, a single sob escaping.

'Do think of me sometimes, dear man, won't you?'

'Caroline, I . . . I . . .'

'I really have to go now, Thomas. Goodbye.'

Without a backward glance, her head held high, she left.

Chapter 61

Kydd had taken to staying aboard his ship, unsure of how he would react should Caroline call at his residence again. It had shaken him, what had passed between them in the library.

He looked up from his work at a sudden confusion of voices on deck, and soon after the officer-of-the-watch popped his head around the door. 'To tell you, sir – the fleet's in, Admiral Drury's back. I thought you'd like to know.'

'Thank you, Mr Brice. Usual marks of respect and I'll be on deck shortly.'

It was not beyond the bounds of credibility that, his ships anchored, Drury could signal an 'all captains' and Kydd was not going to be last to report. The only question was whether to lay open his success before the others or to wait until he'd had the inevitable confrontation with the admiral. Either way, he needed to be in his finest uniform, a plaguesome bother in this climate.

He hadn't been long under Tysoe's ministrations, the thud of the saluting guns above now stilled, when a midshipman messenger came down. 'Sir, respects from Mr Brice, to say that Flag has taken boat for the shore.'

Odd, but perhaps Drury had already read Minto's order and wanted to be back in his administrative headquarters quickly to attend to the Java invasion preparations. Then he realised that in the face of these larger events his news and dispatches might well be considered of little significance – only one island taken? That it had been the means of destroying the enemy's will to fight Drury simply wouldn't admit, so it was as well he hadn't loudly claimed a victory.

Feeling more than a little deflated, he changed back into sea rig and, with a sigh, pulled across his work but as he did so he heard what sounded suspiciously like a cheer. It quickly died to silence, leaving Kydd intrigued. He was about to go and investigate when Dillon entered, bearing a battered parcel.

He smiled wickedly and dropped it on Kydd's desk. 'For your immediate attention, Sir Thomas,' he said, and hurried out.

The package was obviously well-travelled, for it was not only frayed and sea-stained but had seals and scrawled offi-cialese from half the world – Halifax in Canada, the Caribbean Leeward Islands, the Cape of Good Hope, others.

He sawed at the string and it fell open. In a flash the mystery was resolved. The parcel was a bundle of letters – from Persephone.

He guessed immediately what had happened. Taking the first he ripped it open in a fever of anticipation, scanning the first few lines – and found he was right.

> . . . *and I remembered Father sending his mail to Mother by 'ship's letter' so she got them weeks earlier. So I had a clever idea and asked that nice Captain Strawbridge of* Bucephalus *to take them as he'd been ordered out to India with the next China convoy. I do hope he remembered to give them to you, and . . .*

Bless her adorable heart! *Bucephalus* must have been reassigned at the last minute to the North America station and Strawbridge had handed them in there to be forwarded on. In ignorance they'd been taken to the summer station in Bermuda and there a puzzled clerk had sent them on to the Cape, on the sea lanes of so many of the world's ports. Unfortunately, being outside the post-office system there they'd stayed, for the navy of the Cape Station never intruded on that of the East India Station, and only the recent Mauritius campaign had brought Drury's fleet in contact with the Cape squadron.

It was only the inspired act of some unknown clerk at Cape Town that had seen the mail embarked for India and to its final grateful recipient.

Sorting the rest quickly by date he went to his armchair and settled to devour them.

What was immediately clear to him was her love and devotion – would he ever forgive himself for doubting her?

Chapter 62

It was irritating that Drury was still seeing no one for Kydd needed to make his report known, if only to ensure that the garrison he'd left at Banda Neira was supported. And there was the matter of Farrant. Kydd wanted him back: he'd proved himself in more ways than one, and to see him quietly refuse every offer of wine was telling. Even for the loyal toast a blank-faced mess servant would solemnly pour a teaspoonful and that would but touch his lips. Kydd was prepared to beg for his reinstatement, if necessary.

Five days passed and then the shocking announcement broke that Rear Admiral of the Red, William O'Bryen Drury, commander-in-chief on the East Indies Station, had died in post and would later be buried with full honours in St Mary's Church, Madras.

Kydd hastened ashore, to pay his respects, where he met the other captains in mutual shock. Various fevers had taken off officers in the past, but this was the first time in these parts that a commander-in-chief had died in the line of duty.

What in decency was not raised was who would succeed, particularly in view of the upcoming operation. The level of command involved was a decision not only for the Admiralty but had high political complexities. The news had already been sent by the fastest means, to the Red Sea and overland to the Mediterranean Station, thence on to London, but a reply would be months away.

Eventually Kydd was able to corner a harried flag-captain. It seemed that, for the immediate future, the squadron would be commanded direct from Calcutta. The whole thing was an unfortunate inconvenience, particularly as the planning and completing for the imminent Java invasion was now well advanced. As it stood, Admiral Stopford at the Cape had been asked to take command of the operation but had not yet arrived, and Kydd should expect orders from Calcutta at an early date.

About to leave, Kydd thought to ask after the state of his request for a replacement first lieutenant. After an age of rummaging it was found that Lieutenant Farrant had indeed been removed from post, but while an entry had been made of the intention to appoint the commander of *Rupert*, the paperwork was by no means complete. Perhaps Farrant could stay with Kydd – given that nothing could be settled until the new commander-in-chief had taken up his appointment, it would be the least inconvenient solution.

And it appeared that the unfortunate captain of *Rupert* would soon be on hand with the others and could be told directly of the situation.

Back aboard, Kydd lost no time in summoning his first lieutenant. 'Mr Farrant, I have to tell you that I've been successful in making plea for your retention in *Tyger*.'

'Why, thank you, sir.' Curiously there was no sudden delight or other show of emotion, just the serene contentment of before.

346

'Do you not feel it a relief, if not an honour?'

Farrant gave a slow smile. 'Sir Thomas, may I speak freely?'

'Certainly.'

'I admit most heartily to the relief, sir. But not in the way you might suppose. You were right to act as you did towards me – in fact you've been more than generous in your actions. But I was far gone in my degradation and to be elevated to be premier of a crack frigate was too much for me. I've never faced the enemy or taken command of fighting men in battle, and the thought of how I might behave in such preyed on my mind most pitiably. Sir, there in the field I found my answer – and more than that, I found myself!

'On that day I knew, in my own way, how it was to stand and face the enemy, to take the war to him with fine fighting seamen at my back and risk every sacrifice. I realised, as well, that no longer did I have to prove my valour to myself or to anyone else. In fine, sir, I was free of the fear that rode on my back for so long.'

Kydd murmured something, not sure how to react to this outpouring of feeling in his senior officer aboard. 'Um, then I take it, Mr Farrant, you are able to resume the post of first lieutenant in a permanent capacity?'

The man gave another saintly smile, this time tinged with sadness. 'It is with many regrets I have to decline your offer, Sir Thomas.'

Stunned, Kydd heard him through.

'You see, I have come to another understanding of myself, which is to say that, although I can now hold my head high for having proved myself in battle, I do recognise that this is not my nature. To be premier of a capital frigate such as *Tyger* requires fire and drive at all hours and this is not in my constitution, as it were.

'Instead I believe I will retire from the sea, in the knowledge that I shall be returning to my homeland having served it faithfully, and there enter in upon a more reflective existence.'

'I wish you well of it,' Kydd said sincerely. 'What shall you do, pray?'

Again the saintly smile. 'I will assist my father at his stationer's profession in the publishing of fine works.'

'You will remember your time in *Tyger*, I trust.'

'With all my heart, sir.'

Watching his old first lieutenant take boat for the shore, Kydd had mixed feelings. That an honourable man had won his dignity and chosen future in *Tyger* was a fine thing but at the same time he had to furnish his ship with a replacement without delay.

'Make to *Rupert* "captain to repair aboard", if you please.' There would be at least one who would be more than passing content before the day was out.

'Er, can't do that, sir.'

'Oh? Why not?'

'She sailed this morning.'

This was more than an annoyance: *Tyger* could not sail and certainly could not face the enemy without her second most important officer. And, with the Java offensive very close, she had to be ready.

There was no flag-officer to provide a new one and in the time remaining it was out of the question to send a despairing dispatch to Calcutta.

Only an initiative by Kydd for approval later gave any hope of a resolution. And one came to mind – Bowden. Second lieutenant and long aboard *Tyger*, he knew her ways and, more importantly, her men. Kydd had always seen him to be utterly reliable, and loyal to a fault – but he'd not put his name forward to Pellew essentially because of his quiet nature, the lack of drive and fiery ardour in leadership that

Kydd saw as so necessary in the first lieutenant of a crack frigate.

Had he changed since then enough to justify Kydd's decision? In a moment of insight, he knew that Bowden hadn't, but his own perceptions had.

He now had the example of Farrant, who had basically been wished on him and had turned out to lack those very qualities as well, yet when they were most needed the man had found them within himself. Who was Kydd to say that Bowden would not, given similar circumstances?

'Sit down, Mr Bowden. I have something to ask of you.'

He couldn't help noticing the youth still in the officer, the deference that had been there since their earlier days, even before Kydd's professional success, the intelligent wariness. Was he right to think there was a Bray somewhere beneath that would come roaring through when the time came? He nearly weakened, but if it had happened with Farrant he owed it to Bowden to give him a chance, too.

'I'm minded to appoint you the first lieutenant of HMS *Tyger*. Can you do it?'

It plainly came as a shock, but Bowden controlled himself. 'Should you not request one from the commander-in-chief, Sir Thomas?'

'Not enough time, I'm persuaded.'

'Sir. On the last occasion, Admiral Pellew saw fit to appoint another as premier,' he said carefully. 'Does this not imply that shortcomings in my experience, sea-time or some other, is an impediment?'

With a twinge of conscience, Kydd went on briskly, 'I wouldn't have thought so. Nevertheless, it's within my powers to make you up to acting first lieutenant on the spot. What you make of the position is your affair, but I can tell you

349

that, should you satisfy myself and the admiral both, it will be made permanent. What say you to that?'

There was an awkward pause while Bowden looked away. Kydd waited patiently.

In a voice not much above a whisper he answered, 'I can never be a Mr Bray. It isn't in me.'

'Nonsense!' Kydd said, as heartily as he could. 'I wouldn't expect you to be a fire-eater like him. Perhaps be a little sharper with the laggardly, a mort louder with your orders. And you're free to stand as tall as you like, being the first lieutenant of the finest ship of the age!'

'But—'

'You don't need me to tell you, Charles, that this is an opportunity like no other you will come across. How can you say you want to turn it down?'

Pausing only for a moment, Bowden answered, 'Then . . . then I do accept your offer in all gratitude, Sir Thomas.' It was delivered in a shy, affected way, and again Kydd nearly had second thoughts but rose to take his new first lieutenant's hand.

'Splendid! But if we're to work together, I have to demand you belay that "Sir Thomas" tally. Stout sea cant will do.'

'But—'

'I insist.'

'Aye aye, sir.' There was now a firmer smile.

'Shift your gear into the first lieutenant's berth. I believe Mr Farrant has left the books shipshape enough for the next man to take up the reins directly. I shall make the announcement in due course.'

After Bowden had taken his leave, Kydd leaned back, pondering his action. Right or wrong, a surge of feeling quickly overcame any regrets – like any other officer in his position, Bowden would have to measure up by his own efforts or fall by the wayside. That was the way of the Service and that was how it would be with his new first lieutenant.

For the next elevation it was not so difficult.

Brice, with his early acquaintance of sea life at its most brutish, had all the seaman-like attributes he could desire and, while not yet truly tested in battle, he had few doubts about the man. Here was his second lieutenant. Which left empty the post of third lieutenant, with no officer to appoint to the position. But he had an acting lieutenant waiting in the wings, Maynard, master's mate and something of a hard man. Another long-time *Tyger* mariner, he knew the ship and the men – and was respected by them.

Lieutenant Maynard. It fitted.

All in all, a satisfying morning's work. He'd clear lower deck and make pronouncement, and this evening the gunroom would resound to huzzahs as promotions were consecrated and Maynard was taken into the fellowship of the quarterdeck.

Tyger was now whole again.

Chapter 63

The Calcutta orders came through and they were plain and to the point. The Java expedition would proceed in three divisions: one originating in Madras, the second from Calcutta, both to come together at Prince of Wales Island. A third – bearing the commodore and military leader – would rendezvous with the first two at Malacca.

This was a major operation, far above the scale of the Spice Islands adventure. Broughton was to be commodore, flying his flag in the big 74, *Illustrious*. There would be five battleships in all, a number not much below the major squadrons off the coast of France and not seen in these waters this age.

The station had been stripped of almost any ship that swam to bring this to a successful conclusion.

Kydd leafed through the rest of the orders. Twelve thousand redcoats from the British Army and more still from the Bengal Native Infantry. This was a momentous effort, but he was experienced in landings on a hostile shore and it didn't take much imagination to know that the numbers would pale into nothing compared with the native battalions the Dutch could command from a country of millions.

Only the spread of the demoralising news of the Dutch empire crumbling about them was working in favour of the British. Would it be enough?

More pleasing were the terse lines specifying that the first Madras division would be commanded by Captain Sir Thomas Kydd in *Tyger*. That the division was little more than transports for the army contingents and escorting frigates did not lessen its importance.

The day of sailing saw *Tyger* importantly hoist her signal to assemble the convoy to seaward and herself proceed to sea. The three other frigates had the tiresome duty of whipping the stragglers along and into their rightful place, leaving Kydd to stand off at a lordly distance and throw out encouraging signals.

'The ship is yours, Mr Bowden,' he said casually, stepping down from the conn.

'Aye aye, sir.'

Striking a convincing quarterdeck brace, the first lieutenant gave a thunderous frown and bawled, 'Flat in those headsails, there! You want the fleet to think we're manned by a parcel o' wharf rats?'

Tyger fell into line in the rear of the convoy, a frigate on either beam and one out ahead, and the expedition's first division was under way.

It was an uneventful passage and Prince of Wales Island was raised on time, the second division already there at anchor. Stopping only to water and take aboard provisions, the two sailed together for the palm-tree-overhung walls of Malacca where, as instructed, they awaited the third division.

Some days later Commodore Broughton's broad pennant was sighted in *Illustrious* at the van of the main fleet and the Java expedition was complete.

*   *   *

'Sir Thomas, happy to make your acquaintance,' the commodore said gracelessly, not bothering to look up from his desk in his great cabin. 'You've brought your division to rendezvous without loss, I see.'

It would be very strange if he had not, Kydd thought, offended. It was well-known, though, that this was a very ambitious officer who must have worked hard to achieve his pennant for this expedition.

'Sir.'

'Then you are released.' Broughton fixed Kydd with a supercilious gaze. 'And ready for my orders.'

'Sir.'

'Which are that as senior officer, frigates, you do take a squadron of the lesser sort to the coast of Java and there rake and harry the enemy by way of distraction as to our main objective. You do understand me?' he drawled.

'Understood, sir,' Kydd ground out. What kind of officer did he think he was that he couldn't grasp elementary strategy?

'Conditional on your success or otherwise in drawing off the enemy, we will be making a landing to take Batavia at the first. You'll have six days of distractions. Then I want you at the landings.'

This was boldness indeed. Expecting right at the outset to capture the capital of the whole Dutch East Indies and end the war in one! Kydd's role had suddenly become a crucial part of the operation.

'When shall—'

'I expect you to lose not a moment, Kydd. Here is an order detailing your squadron and tasks. That is all.'

In the sanctity of *Tyger*'s cabin he studied the papers carefully. There were six frigates and four sloops in his command, which could never be considered an excess of force in a descent on the six hundred miles of coastline on both sides of Java.

The tasking was sketchy at best, merely mentioning some of the ports along the coast with the implication that these should be his first concern. The actuality would be much different, for every kind of hazard could be met in pressing home an attack on what was essentially an unknown seaboard. Not only the usual perils of the sea but whether the Dutch had forts protecting the harbour or substantial garrisons of native troops able to pour out and overwhelm whatever landing parties had gone ashore.

As to the distractions . . .

He could sail up and down the coast, firing randomly at fortifications or settlements but such would not meet the chief objective: to draw the enemy away. It would have to look like a determined assault, a credible threat aimed at a valued target, or it would be seen for what it was: a lure.

The Dutch chart could hopefully provide the answer.

It did. At a handy position halfway along the north coast of Java, Semarang was a substantial township of the same order of size as Batavia itself. If an invader was looking for a location that gave access equally to either end of Java to the bafflement of the enemy, this was it.

He looked closer. There were two forts: an impressive city fortress and a smaller located on a peninsula overlooking the harbour. That was it!

The squadron sailed the next day, passing the low, densely forested shore of Sumatra into the Java Sea, a glaring expanse that lay supine under a giant blue bowl of sky. With Semarang somewhere not far ahead, they hove to.

Kydd laid out his plans: to land and take the outlying fort with as much noise and fuss as possible, to destroy it in sight of the watching town and at nightfall, with dark hiding them, re-embark and depart.

It sounded simple enough but so much could go wrong, and Kydd's particular nightmare was that the landing parties would be left to an ignominious surrender should the Dutch appear with unknown superior naval forces.

Kydd's squadron loomed out of the morning. The Dutch would have sighted the ten warships heading for them as a fearful portent of doom when the most they would have seen before was a single curious sloop or cutter.

The town was located on the edge of the coastal flatlands and low-lying, the little peninsula alone having a slight rocky spine, the fort at its end squat and ugly. With battle ensigns aloft, the squadron fell into line ahead and shaped course to sail past the fort, which, at this hour of the morning, had not yet hoisted its colours.

The ripple of gunfire slammed out from each ship, one by one, iron balls skipping and battering at the stronghold in an endless succession until the squadron had passed and put about to allow the guns of the other side to resume the cannonade.

It was too much for the defenders, who began streaming out, fleeing for their lives along the peninsula and into the town.

'Make the signal to assault,' Kydd growled.

Heaving to, every ship in the squadron launched boats, and the sea became alive with craft all swarming in the same direction – the deserted fort. To watchers ashore, a British invasion was under way. No doubt after the fort was secured, soldier transports waiting over the horizon would come to discharge their cargo of thousands to begin the conquest of Java.

It was all so easy – or was it? The men manning the fort should have stood fast, opened fire on their aggressors as was their duty, but they had not. Their spirit had been broken – they could not find it in them to defend their flag and honour. They were defeated before they started.

'Away my barge,' Kydd ordered impulsively. He had a yearning to set foot on the enemy soil he had won – a childish notion, but hadn't it been he and *Tyger* who had brought this about?

'You have the ship, Mr Bowden,' he said crisply, and boarded his boat.

He found Brice on the parapets directing seamen and marines in the preparing of the fortification for destruction.

'I do believe we can improve the shining hour,' he said.

'Sir?'

'Shall we not turn these guns on their owners? Fire on the town, if you please, Mr Brice.'

Tyger was lying offshore, a vision of war-like grace and lethal beauty with, closer in, some of the sloops. It had been a good start and—

'Sir!' The cry was urgent, demanding.

Wheeling round, Kydd's heart went cold. Issuing out from the inner harbour were gun-vessels, not one or two but a tight flotilla of close to a dozen, each mounting a major piece of artillery on its fore-deck. Together, it amounted to the equivalent of a full broadside from a frigate.

From each flew a single ensign, not Dutch but French. It seemed some of Bonaparte's promised reinforcements had already reached the East Indies, and who knew what further ugly surprises were lying in wait?

To be caught out of his ship in an enemy attack was the stuff of nightmares for Kydd.

He pounded down to the sandy cove where his barge was

pulled clear and bawled for it to be launched. But if he put out now, he'd end up in the middle of the charging gun-vessels. All he could do was stand and watch how it would play out.

Intelligently, the gun-boats kept together. They carefully selected a victim and made a concerted lunge towards it, no doubt with the intent of disabling it and going on to the next in quick order. These were professional and experienced, probably trained by the Danes who had perfected the art.

In helpless anguish, Kydd saw that they were circling around to take on one of his brig-sloops. There was another of his vessels in position for them beyond and he tensed for the finish. One gun fired in the leading gun-vessel but it was a trifling puff. Their next move, however, was astonishing: like a covey of frightened grouse, they wheeled as one and headed back at speed into the harbour.

It was Brice who first saw why. 'Sir – *Tyger*.'

Further out to sea the frigate had braced around and, under what sail she could, was making not for the gun-boats but heading directly for the harbour entrance. The commander of the gun-boats had seen the danger of being cut off and had promptly retreated to the safety of the town fortress.

This was quick thinking by Bowden and, in a jet of warmth, Kydd acknowledged it to himself.

The afternoon was spent exhausting the fort's magazines with firing at the town, and by evening Kydd was preparing for their withdrawal under cover of darkness.

And then there was a shout. Close to the shoreline, a fore-and-aft-rigged aviso, a fast dispatch vessel with all the sail it could carry, was making a wild break for the open sea.

They weren't the only ones to see it and several of the sloops loosed sail to go in chase. The nearest was in a good position to head it off and took brazen risks in the shallows to prevent word of their raid getting out.

'Be damned to the lunatic!' Kydd spluttered. 'His pennants and "abandon the chase"!'

It needed a gun from *Tyger* to bring its attention to the signal, for it was vital to allow the aviso to escape. A sudden panic-stricken report of a landing in force by the British was precisely what he wanted to be received in Batavia. It would provide all the distraction needed. Columns would march out from the Dutch capital to confront the landing, hollowing out the opposition the actual landing would face.

Would it do? Kydd thought so. With every evidence of a hostile landing, and in a credible location, any more gestures would confuse and delay the response. It was time to join the main act.

Chapter 64

Off Batavia it was apparent that the landings had already begun. With the unanswerable might of four ships-of-the-line in a protective shield, more frigates and transports – near a hundred ships in all – this was a serious and fearful act of war.

Kydd lost no time in taking boat for the flagship, *Illustrious*, but saw that her commodore's pennant no longer flew. Instead an admiral's pennant was aloft in another of the battleships, the massive 74 *Scipion*, and course was duly altered.

Admiral Stopford glanced up at his flag-captain's introduction. 'Ah, Captain Kydd, or should it be Captain Sir Thomas Kydd?'

After a hurried explanation at the side-steps from Johnson, *Scipion*'s captain, Kydd understood that Stopford had been brought from the Cape Station to take command of the expedition and had only just made his appearance. Broughton had been superseded on the spot and, bitterly striking his flag, promised much argument on being robbed of his rightful command. But this was not Kydd's concern, only that his past record and causes would have to be repeated for yet another flag-officer, the third after Pellew.

'I should tell you, Sir Thomas, that we have been most successful in our endeavours.' His manner was like that of a country prelate at harvest home, Kydd couldn't help thinking.

'We chose this point to land, twelve miles from Batavia and out of sight. It answered admirably,' he went on, fixing Kydd benignly from behind his spectacles, 'the French being decoyed from their designs by distractions elsewhere. Before they came up to dispute with us, we were able to get ashore six regiments, which is to say eight thousands.'

'French, sir?'

'It better describes what confronts us. There are four of Bonaparte's generals here who, in accordance with his orders, have removed the command from the Hollander Daendels and placed it in the hands of one Janssens, who not only commands all forces but is made governor general of the Dutch East Indies *in toto*.'

The name struck a chord in Kydd. Then he remembered. 'Janssens? I've faced the gentleman before, sir. He it was in the year six we fought to a finish before Cape Town. Then he led us a merry dance into the mountains.'

'In which case I devoutly hope we do not have to repeat the exercise,' Stopford grunted. 'As it is, we have a pretty problem. Our soldiery marched off in fine style for Batavia and found it undefended, an open city.'

'Undefended?'

'Just so. Janssens and his legions had quitted the place. But there's the rub – he retreated in good order to Fort Cornelis.'

'Which, in course, we have invested?'

'This fort is of prodigious size, more than a mile across, and on its present resources can maintain a siege indefinitely. Within, he has men who more than outnumber us and therefore I'm advised we cannot take it by storm.'

'Starve them out?'

Stopford took off his spectacles and made a performance of cleaning them before resuming. 'As would be expected by any reasonable field commander, but here we have a quandary. General Auchmuty is of the opinion that this is a considered ploy to remain in being while native regulars are summoned from all over the country. If this is so it will not be long before we find arrayed against us a host that is capable of crushing us utterly.'

'Then we're trapped, unable to move.'

'In a word, yes.'

The fort could not be left alone while British troops moved out to secure Java for they were tied down by the siege – while at the same time great numbers were massing to close in.

'The navy can't assist in any way?'

'I cannot think it.'

On his way back to *Tyger* Kydd took in the powerful squadron – the battleships, frigates, others – an armada that could stand against anything afloat that the enemy could produce and prevail handsomely.

Yet it was helpless.

Chapter 65

'I have the deck,' Maynard said formally, accepting Brice's officer-of-the-day's token, the big signal telescope. 'Nothing?' he added, in a more conversational tone.

'Nothing.' It had been some days since the siege was begun and boredom was setting in.

Brice was showing no great inclination to go below and it suited Maynard to have a talking companion. 'As I'm not grieved we don't go ashore,' he said lightly. 'The ladies are reputed dark and heathen.'

'I'm never to step off in Batavia on anyone's account unless ordered,' Brice retorted. 'The fever here's the worst of any, even Bengal. The sainted Bligh, after his open-boat voyage, only lost men when he made Batavia.'

It cooled the talk and Brice looked moodily ashore. After a moment or two he asked for the telescope, swinging it up and training it along the palm-tree-fringed shore. 'There – see what's happening?'

He handed over the glass and indicated what looked like a long caterpillar of slowly moving figures. 'That's another village gone down with the bloody flux and they're moving 'em to somewhere different. Always having to do it.'

'I don't think so, Peter,' Maynard said evenly, keeping it trained and watching carefully.

''O' course it is,' Brice said impatiently. 'Give me that.' He focused it slightly and snorted. 'There – even got out the beadles to move 'em on. I've seen this sort o' thing before, a lot of times.'

'No, that's not—'

'There's a bottle of good claret in my cabin that's saying it's a fever camp on the march.'

Maynard gave a half-smile. 'I've seen like it more'n a few times, too. I take your wager and say it's not.'

'What is it, then?'

'You're looking at prisoners. Prisoners of war.'

Brice looked again. 'Can't possibly be. Where would they get all those from?'

Maynard went aft to the stern rail and hailed down to the duty boat. 'Younker! Take your cutter in and find out what the devil that lot are doing. Sharpish, now.'

When the boat returned, the midshipman was wide-eyed. 'Have t' see the captain,' he blurted, as he clambered aboard and hared off for Kydd's quarters.

'Sir! Sir! Have t' report, the siege is broken!'

Kydd rocked back in amazement. 'Slow down, ease away there! Now, what are you saying?'

With great courage the 69th Foot had secured a redoubt and stormed another. It was the key to victory – the fort had been rushed and taken, most of the Dutch throwing over their hated French allegiance and the native militia deserting in large numbers.

The siege was indeed over.

'So General Janssens is captured?'

'No, sir. He escaped, got out with some others, but we've quantities of prisoners, sir, you've no idea!'

'And we . . .?'

'Colonel Gillespie has sent a flying column in pursuit. They know where he's going – a deserter told the colonel. To Boyten-zog away in the hills, his summer palace.'

It had to be the closing scene.

Cornered, secured and in chains, the unfortunate Janssens would formally surrender his fief and the Dutch East Indies would be British.

'Sir?'

Stopford looked weary, downcast. 'You're expecting words of triumph, elation, perhaps. I haven't any, Kydd.'

Was it because Lord Minto had made it his business to be transported to the scene, conceivably to have his name at the head of the victors of Batavia?

'The army reached Buitenzorg, and at the sight Janssens did everything other than strike his colours to us.'

'Sir?'

'He disappeared. Think what this means for us! Without he claps his scratch to an instrument of capitulation, he can carry on as the focus of every uprising and rebellion conceivable. He's somewhere out there and, until we can lay hands on the villain, we're at his mercy.'

'Sir, may I ask why I am called?' It was not part of his duty to listen to the woes of a commander-in-chief.

'You are senior captain, frigates.'

'I am, sir.'

'You had a squadron, frigates and sloops.'

'I did, sir.'

'Then form them up. I've work for them.'

'Sir.'

'There will be regiments of redcoats on the march up and down the coast. They're looking for the accursed Janssens. One of them will find him and then there'll be a fight. What I want you to do is set your squadron to make themselves available, first, to let me know of developments and to be of any assistance they can.'

Six frigates and four sloops – he could easily quarter the coast, but what could they do?

'Sir – a suggestion. The army are looking for Janssens on the coast where they can move the fastest. My ships will be offshore, pacing them. While they're on the march I'll send parties from each ship to penetrate inland to hear if any have word of our friend.'

'Do so, if that's what you want,' Stopford said heavily.

Kydd sympathised with his frustration. This was precisely what Janssens had done once before, at the Cape – he had disappeared to be found months later in distant mountains. To keep a sizeable army and an entire fleet at idleness while he was tracked down was intolerable. And to have Lord Minto present while the situation deteriorated would be galling indeed.

The squadron put to sea that very afternoon, Kydd's orders clear. Spacing his ships equally along the coastline he landed signal rockets to the nearest marching column with instructions to fire them should they make contact with Janssens. If the landing parties heard anything, they were to alert the nearest army formation and leave it to them.

He himself would take the mid-position between Batavia and Semarang, the furthest point credible for Janssens to have reached and he would send his own party ashore.

The long search had begun.

*   *   *

366

'Stir y'selves along, then,' Sergeant Nunn called behind him. All four marines were well out in front, but the three seamen were straggling and snorting along. Although they'd made a good few miles along the jungle track into the interior it was not at all to the sergeant's satisfaction.

'Stow it!' was all that gunner's mate Stirk could manage, as he plodded on. It was hot and foetid. Sharp fronds of tropical vegetation whipped at him, and alien creatures scuttled across his path. What had impelled him to volunteer for the shore party he couldn't imagine, for this torrid land had lost any allure it once had.

The track had taken a distinct upward incline, winding around the side of a steep ridge towards the mountains that Nunn seemed bent on reaching. Behind him Doud was toiling, with Pinto further back. It was then that the heavens decided on a deluge.

Stirk swore bitterly, bringing a reproving look from Nunn. 'Stap this!' he spluttered. 'I'm away t' find somewhere out of this'n.'

His feet slipped in the rapidly forming mud and he howled and cursed as concealed thorns took their pleasure on his body, but he'd glimpsed a native hut at the edge of the undergrowth. It was in ruins but had sufficient palm leaves still spread to hold off the worst of the downpour.

'Over here, y' shabs,' he shouted and, not waiting for them, plunged for the shelter.

None seemed inclined to press on and he was joined by the whole party where they hunkered down as best they could.

'How much further?' Doud sourly wanted to know.

'We touches the mountains an' returns,' the weathered sergeant grunted. 'Them's m' orders.'

'What say we sits it out here, starts back later, like?' Doud growled. 'No one t' know and we ain't seen a soul the whole time.'

He felt around in his haversack and found a squat, dark bottle. 'We's the doings, won't go thirsty.'

The bottle went around. It was arrack, the native palm-sap liquor, but it found an appreciative reception and no one felt inclined to shout down his earlier suggestion.

An hour passed, then another. The rain slowed and petered out, leaving the ground gently steaming with a rich, reeking forest odour on the air.

'We'll give it another hour, then be on our way back,' Stirk said, at his ease. 'Don't envy them lobsterbacks down there on the flat, caught out like this. What does ye, then, Paddy?' he threw at the sergeant, lying full-length with his eyes closed.

'Marches on, never pays mind to it,' Nunn answered, his eyes still closed.

'Well, an' if I was a—' Stirk broke off, for the marine had tensed, his eyes wide open.

'Did y' hear that?'

'What?'

Nunn sat up suddenly, his head cocked and straining to listen. 'Again – bugger it, out there!'

The men froze at the crash of hidden vegetation. Something big was the other side of the track.

'Don't worry, it'll only be a tiger,' Doud said weakly.

No one laughed. They had only a pair of cutlasses and unloaded marine muskets between them.

Leaves shook and they leaped to their feet.

Out from the greenery staggered a figure, gaunt, sun-reddened and in the rags of a uniform. He lurched towards them.

'I give! I give!' the man gasped, falling to his knees in front of Stirk.

'What's this?' Stirk answered gently, helping him up. 'Easy, we're y' friends, mate.'

The seaman looked at him with staring, red-rimmed eyes, took a juddering breath and said, 'Pliss – I give, I surrender! Now, I surrender – to you! I'm finish, cannot run more!'

'Poor bastard,' Doud said softly. 'Wonder who he is.'

As if overhearing the man swung on him. 'I – I am Janssens. Gouverneur-generaal Janssens van de Nederlandse Oost-Indië. I will surrender, I will give up – to you, here, now, Mijnheer!'

Chapter 66

Aboard Tyger

'What in blazes . . .? Dillon, go and find out what all that din is about, if you would.' Kydd was in his armchair, trying to make sense of a turgid but improving volume of philosophy, which the evening's heat did not make any easier for him.

'Sir. It's Mr Stirk and he insists to show you his prisoner.'

'He knows the regulations,' Kydd said irritably. 'To the fore-deck until the master-at-arms can deal with him, in chains if he shows fight.'

'Um, I really think you should see him.'

Kydd knew Stirk must have a good reason. He trusted him above almost all others aboard. 'Very well. Ask him to step in.'

The shocking sight of the figure who stumbled in made him scramble to his feet. 'Sit him down, then,' he said, noting the remnants of elegance in the bow the wretched man gave.

Stirk stood behind, a twisted smile on his face. 'Did give himself up t' me, he did. Insisted I take his surrender so the

370

poor bastard could rest at last. So I did.' He paused for effect before adding, 'Name o' Janssens, gov'nor o' Java.'

Kydd stared in shock. 'You are . . .?'

'Jonkheer Jan Willem Janssens, Gouverneur-generaal van de Nederlandse Oost-Indië.'

'Says he's our Mr Janssens.'

'Thank you, Mr Dillon. I'd gathered that.'

It was beyond belief that the man hunted by half the world had apparently laid down his arms to a humble seaman – and if he went to the commander-in-chief claiming so, and this was a fraud, he'd not be thanked for it.

He racked his brains and came up with a test, one that only the Janssens defeated at Cape Town back in 1806 could know.

'Ask him – in Cape Colony when the British took Bloubergsvlei, where did he go next?'

The answer came back promptly. 'The Tygerberg mountains, as being impregnable to the British strangers. He says why do you ask this?'

It was Janssens well enough.

Setting his squadron the agreeable task of finding the marching army and informing them, Kydd set sail for Batavia.

Scipion's captain was not helpful. 'Admiral Stopford is ashore. If you wished to see him it would have been proper to send ahead for an appointment.' He eyed Kydd's disreputable but now clean friend with frosty disapproval.

'It was not Admiral Stopford I came to see.'

'Oh?'

'The Lord Minto, who, I believe, will be interested to meet this gentleman.'

'Impossible! Sir, how you can have the gall to—'

'Captain, if you do not allow us the interview, I do make

prediction that you will be summarily laughed out of the fleet.'

Minto was in the great cabin in conference with Raffles and looked up in annoyance at the interruption. 'I gave orders not to be disturbed. Why are you . . . Oh, Captain Kydd, I see. Is this a matter of urgency, sir?'

'You shall be the judge of that, my lord. May I present Jonkheer Janssens, governor general of the Dutch East Indies?'

Raffles's head jerked up and Minto slowly stood. 'Are you sure?'

'I have positive proof that he is your man, sir. And this is Mr Dillon, whom you may trust to act the interpreter as you no doubt wish to offer Mr Janssens terms for the capitulation of his realm.'

'Good God!'

It was Raffles who came to his senses first. 'I shall leave you for a space to avoid embarrassment, my lord. I've no doubt you will wish to discuss many things with Mr Janssens in which I might figure.'

Kydd and Raffles went on deck together and, grateful for the evening breeze, paced the quarterdeck companionably.

'Embarrassed?' Kydd asked curiously.

'Ah. You see I'm to be given the governor-generalship of what must now be described as the late Dutch East Indies in succession to that same gentleman.'

'Are you, my dear friend? Most hearty congratulations are due!'

'In large measure it must be said as being your doing, and I pray the world does note it.'

'As it was your foresight, sir,' Kydd said sincerely, and added, 'So now it has been realised, you will take your rest?'

'Not at all. My vision remains but is now so much the larger, to have our empire of India and the west linked to the emerging powers of China, even Japan, in a seamless sea road to which we hold the key. I believe that for the future of the trade of the world we can no longer ignore this great and populous region and the British are the fittest nation to lead forward in this enterprise. Therefore I make it my life's work to see this made true.'

Kydd felt the intensity of the man's convictions and was humbled. 'It would be my honour to be with you and at your service in this great undertaking, my friend.'

Raffles stopped pacing and looked at him with something like fondness. 'I'm sure you would, Sir Thomas, but it can never be.'

'I don't understand.'

'Your navy has prevailed once again and another corner of empire is secured, our enemies cast down and swept from the seas. Why then should a mighty fleet like the one we see around us be kept in idleness here when it is so sorely needed by England?

'No, sir, you will be gathered back, recalled – Sir Thomas, you'll be going home!'

Glossary

a-cock-bill	when alternate yards are tipped to an angle across the deck instead of squarely horizontal. The sign of mourning in a vessel
arcadia in urbs	peaceful bucolic setting in the middle of a bustling town
bandy	a common cart used for trivial moving
bibi	native mistress
Blue Peter	blue signal flag with white square within; indicates ship will sail within the day
Bombay Marine	naval force maintained by the East India Company for the protection of its local country trade
bunting	flags in general
burra peg	a large whisky; *chota peg* a smaller
careening	to heave the ship down on one side to scrape the bottom clean of weed and barnacles
cat-blash	what a cat brings up with a fur-ball; derisory substance
chevron	V-shaped badge worn on the upper arm by soldiers to indicate rank
Co-hong	cartel of Chinese merchants with monopoly of dealing with foreign cargoes
compradore	native Chinese trader's intermediary
Congreve rocket	a war-rocket invented by William Congreve as powerful as a cannon but far less weight, even as it proved in the main unreliable as a weapon
Dalawa	first minister of a small princely state
devoirs	duties of politeness
dragoman	the word for an interpreter more used in Europe; Greek *dragomanos*

375

dragoon	horse-mounted soldier able to dismount and fight on foot
dubash	an interpreter, literally 'two languages' in Hindi; usually has additional supervisory duties and deals with cultural disharmonies
factor	an agent empowered to buy or sell goods for a third party
fanam	an Indian coin of little value not normally carried by the well-off
fret	unsettled, grey weather
Ganesh	an elephant-headed Indian god known for removing obstacles, son of Shiva and Parvati
gore	the widening of a sail from its yard downwards
haulbowlings	old shellback sailor
hoppo	imperial official appointed to safeguard the emperor's interests in dealings with foreigners
howdah	seat or platform with canopy for people to be able to ride atop an elephant
jackanapes	impertinent, presumptive youth; from Duke of Suffolk arms showing an ape in chains
Knowle Manor	the Kydds' new-bought home in Devonshire
lakh	the number denoting 100,000, usually associated with currency
lascar	sailor native to India
lorgnette	pair of spectacles mounted on a handle
Mahrattas	caste of peasant-warriors in unrest at this time in Maharashtra region
masula boat	found only in Madras, built with planks sewn with coir yarns to give flexibility when thrown ashore by the huge surf. Used to take passengers to land from anchored ships
mill-race	the water shooting over a mill-wheel
mizzle	rain so light as to be hardly distinguishable from heavy mist
mobility	euphemism for quantities of the lower sort of people – hence the mob
mufti	the wearing of civilian clothes by a normally uniformed officer
nabob	a wealthy and influential person having made his fortune in India; from nawab, viceroy under the Moguls
Navy Board	the professional wing of the Admiralty for adminis-tration and regulation
palanquin	a litter in the form of a covered box with poles for men to carry it and its passenger
panjandrum	self-important or pretentious official

376

pier-head jump	joining a ship at the very last minute by leaping from the quay as it puts to sea
pimplenose	slang for pamplemousse fruit, a type of pomelo
privateer	a vessel outfitted for taking prizes as a private business authorised by the state
punkah-wallah	the servant who operates a swinging screen to raise a cooling draught
roystering	making merry ashore
ruffle	low continuous roll of drum in respect to a senior officer
rutter	old-fashioned term for bound sailing directions contributed by previous voyagers
scuppers	apertures in the bulwarks to allow water on deck to go overside
sepoy	native Indian soldier in service of the Crown
snaffle	to purloin
supercargo	those charged with the commercial affairs of a vessel
taffrail	the upper part of a ship's stern, usually with carved work
tiffin	light meal taken at midday
toper	habitual drinker
two cables	one cable is a length of a hundred fathoms
viceroy	provincial official who acts for and rules in the name of his sovereign
ways	the actual slip upon which the ship is built and then launched

Author's Note

As I live in Devon, many's the occasion that has taken me to Plymouth, that maritime icon of England's rugged south-west that's so resonant of the sea history it's seen down the ages. And to me there's nowhere this is more evident than Plymouth Hoe. From the time of Francis Drake onwards, this broad green sward has been the gallery in the theatre of global striving, where ships could be seen in all their reality and immediacy putting to sea to wrest supremacy in the race to empire.

Probably no destination caught the imagination more than India. Fortunes of a staggering magnitude were gained, making the East Indian nabob a stock character of the times. But existence in this sometimes violently exotic land was often not easy.

By Kydd's day the high tide of fabulous riches to be won was ebbing in the face of the increasing importance of the China trade but, on the other hand, life for the well-placed expatriate in India was becoming increasingly comfortable.

As a keen collector of word fossils I'm delighted to note that, to this day, the ventilation ducts that convey fresh air to compartments below decks in Royal Navy warships are called 'punkah-louvres', even if few sailors know the origin of the term.

Besides a 'punkah-wallah', the well-found expatriate might have recourse to a 'sleeping dictionary'. Nelson's aphorism that no man is a bachelor once he passes the Rock of Gibraltar is topped only by the future Duke of Wellington who, in the sultry evenings of India, with staggering insensitivity once wrote to his wife in England, 'As for sex, one must have it in this climate.'

Many naval careers were shaped and developed by the East Indies, among them that of Charles Austen, the younger brother of Jane, who went on after Pellew to be commander-in-chief of the East India Station before being carried off by Bengal fever and buried in Ceylon. Pellew himself retired with his fortune to Devon, to be famously roused out to command in the bombardment of Algiers in 1819. The shameless nepotism of his sons on station didn't survive their return to England. Pownoll had married well and left the sea while Fleetwood had a mediocre career, failing to get further promotion until 1846. His main claim to history is as the captain of *Phaeton*, near half a century before Commodore Perry opened up Japan to the West, entering Nagasaki in pursuit of the Dutch reeling from their loss of the Indies. In the face of eight thousand samurai, he demanded supplies and water or his guns would level the town. The shocked Japanese were forced to comply, resulting in the high magistrate being afterwards obliged to commit *seppuku*, and at the same time a recognition in Edo that a new race of barbarians had arrived on the scene.

To me, the most bizarre aspect of India was that well into the Victorian age it was controlled entirely by a private company licensed to rule. In the main they managed the task with remarkable success. A handful of directors and some dozens of clerks in India House in London's Leadenhall Street conducted their business at six months' remove from a continent of millions, but were often hindered by the politics of the day.

In one instance the East India Company traded the island of Run, an outlier of the fabulous Spice Islands, but in a practical sense indefensible against the conquering Dutch, for the cold, windswept and decidedly non-exotic island of Manhattan. Despite a grovel to the future king, then the Duke of York, by renaming the main Dutch town of New Amsterdam to New York, they suffered humiliation, finding later that they were stuck with the deal.

They learned a lesson, and in the matter of the 'White Mutiny' depicted in this book, they moved fast and decisively to oil the waters as news of the insurrection reached Britain. In a strange twist of fate, the savage mauling of the homeward-bound convoy by one of the greatest hurricanes of any century removed most of the principals, lost to the sea, including Macdowall, who hoped his version of the mutiny would sway the court of the East India Company, and Capper, whose intemperate ravings did much to provoke it. Of those left to face justice in India for the last slaughter of sepoys by their own side none met their just deserts: the matter was dealt with quickly and quietly for fear of awaking an adverse reaction on the financial markets.

The remote Andaman and Nicobar Islands have seen little of civilisation in the years since. Their very isolation has preserved the privacy and independence of the indigenous peoples who, as portrayed in this work, have always fiercely resisted the outside world. In fact, the most recent killing took place as recently as 2018 when fishermen, despite warnings, landed a devout missionary on one of the Andaman

Islands only to see him go down instantly under vicious clubs and a hail of arrows. The body has not so far been recovered, the authorities considering it too dangerous to land.

Incidentally I was delighted to discover on my charts, just twenty miles north of Port Blair, a Kydd Island, named after a certain Captain Alexander Kydd of the East India Company not so very long before.

To find relics of the only British invasion of Macao is near impossible. On my location research to Hong Kong, neither the staff of the truly excellent Maritime Museum near the Star Ferry terminal nor their opposite numbers in Macao could bring it to mind, although a large war memorial in Canton celebrates the plucky resistance of the Chinese people to the incursions of the Royal Navy into the Pearl river at that time. Drury's plan to remove the European and American trading depots from the control of the Chinese in Canton by relocating them to Macao was in fact acted upon as soon as practical, albeit to an uninhabited rock called Hong Kong on the other side of the estuary, where firms such as Jardine Matheson still conduct business.

The most unlucky wight to be mentioned in this book is undoubtedly Jan Willem Janssens. As a servant of Napoleon Bonaparte, he was dispatched to be governor of Cape Colony just in time to be defeated by the British in a stroke of empire and sent back to the Netherlands. He was then appointed governor general of the Dutch East Indies only to be again comprehensively routed by the same British, his exhausted surrender of his dominions to a file of marines the stuff of legend. At the hundred days when Bonaparte attempted a return, he chose the wrong side, and after the war and restitution of the Dutch holdings in the east, he was denied his old job for political reasons and retired to a faded grandeur.

As for the empire the Dutch lost in the East Indies, it was

ruled wisely and well by Stamford Raffles but was traded back after the Napoleonic war by the British for a consolidation of their holdings in Malaya and India. At least one remembrance of his time as ruler is maintained by Indonesia to this day: all traffic still drives on the left as he decreed. His vision was completed, of course, with the foundation of Singapore where he is still revered.

After the climactic fleet actions that locked Bonaparte into a European prison, Britain's energies turned outward into creating an empire, one that still ranks as the greatest the world has ever seen, that when this author was a small boy still held sway over a quarter of mankind. It was put together by innumerable small but fiercely fought actions that have never received the attention they should – the insane odds mentioned in Kydd's seizing of the most valuable of the Spice Islands are in no way exaggerated. The actual incident on which it was based had the real Captain Cole modestly putting down his resolution, courage and seamanship mainly to luck. On his return he received due admiration from his professional colleagues, but for the world at large, the taking of yet another small island was not to be noticed. In a pleasing twist I noticed that Cole has the distinction of being the very last to capture a Spanish treasure ship – even if it was in 1814 and under French control, an incident I shamelessly stole for the conclusion of *A Sea of Gold*.

This is all to say that our watchers on Plymouth Hoe could never be sure that the humble man-o'-war beating out into the autumn bluster was not bound for some breathless adventure on the other side of the world or to some humdrum naval duty. It is a source of some satisfaction for me to bring the former to life for the modern reader.

To all those who have contributed to the research for this book, I am deeply grateful. In particular I thank Roy and

Lesley Adkins for generously sharing their knowledge of the history of Banda Neira. My appreciation goes also to my agent, Isobel Dixon, my editor, Oliver Johnson, designer Larry Rostant, for his inspired cover, and copy editor, Hazel Orme.

And, as always, a shout-out to the other half of Team Stockwin, my wife and literary partner, Kathy.

So, it's all a-taunto as I set forth for Kydd's next adventure.